OUTVIEW

OUTVIEW

BRANDT LEGG

THE SAGER GROUP

Artifex Te Adiuva

OUTVIEW

Published in the United States of America by The Sager Group
Copyright © 2013 by Brandt Legg
All rights reserved.

Original poems attributed to Linh written by Roanne Lewis

Cataloging-in-Publication data for this book is available from the Library
of Congress.
ISBN-13: 978-0-9881785-3-3
ISBN-10: 0-9881785-3-2

Cover designed by: Caitlin Legere
Formatting by: Siori Kitajima and Ovidiu Vlad for SF AppWorks LLC
Title page illustration by: Siori Kitajima

www.TheSagerGroup.net
www.BrandtLegg.com

PUBLISHER'S NOTE
This book is a work of fiction. Names, characters, places and incidents
are products of the author's imagination or are used fictitiously. Any
resemblance to actual persons, living or dead, businesses, events or
locales is entirely coincidental.

For Teakki and Ro

I kept running. Nine of us had sworn our lives to protect the precious artifact sewn inside my belt. Six were already dead, maybe more. Struggling for breath, I pushed through the tangled jungle toward the majestic pyramid. That's when I heard the horses. Scanning wildly, I knew my life meant nothing unless the treasure was protected. A conquistador's maniacal cry ripped the air. The glint of a sword flashed; my chest sliced open. I crawled a few feet toward a deep, sacred pool. Soldiers laughed as one pushed my gutted body with his heavy blade. He teased me to the edge of the limestone cliff, then shoved its point through. Smiling, I fell ninety feet before plunging into the water.

A car horn startled me. The taste of blood still filled my mouth, my body screamed in pain. I was losing my mind. What the hell was going on? "My name is Nathan Ryder. I'm sixteen. I'm in eleventh grade. This is Ashland Oregon. It's Friday, September 12th... " I repeated the mantra until the tragic scene in that ancient Mayan pool receded and I was fully back in the present. I had lived through at least a hundred deaths since the "Outviews" began a year ago.

I strained to get up off my bedroom floor, a burning ache in my chest. I was surprised to be already dressed for school. Outviews weren't mere dreams, as their torment and physical impact could last for days. The car horn blared again.

Kyle, my best friend, was waiting in the driveway. I dashed out of the house.

"Man, you look like hell. What happened?" He greeted me with a concerned look as I climbed into his old Subaru Outback. Kyle was almost two years older than me, but we'd been in the same grade since he'd arrived from Vietnam. Back then, his English was pretty bad. When the other kids were either ignoring or making fun of him, I asked if I could take a picture of the incredibly elaborate ancient city he was sketching. The drawing was so realistic you'd swear it was a photograph. He wanted me to wait until it was finished, which took another couple of days. We'd been friends ever since.

"Rough night." I riffled through the CDs he kept in a shoebox. "Thich Nhat Hanh, Einstein's Theories, Stephen Hawking… come on Kyle, don't you have any music in here?"

"Too much to learn, no time for music, except maybe Mozart."

"Kyle's the only teenager I know without any music on his iPod," his cousin, Linh, my other best friend, said from the backseat. "Why was it another rough night?"

I turned around and looked at her. She was a grade behind us and didn't look as Asian as Kyle because her father was Irish, but there was an exotic beauty that disarmed me. Her name meant "gentle spirit" in Vietnamese, which was fitting. Her presence made me feel grounded, and during these tumultuous times, being with her was addicting.

"Just couldn't sleep." Normally, I told them everything, but the Outviews were too hard to explain, especially after what had happened to my brother, Dustin.

I struggled through the school day, but at least it was Friday. Linh and Kyle convinced me to come home with them.

"Nate, you really do look awful."

"Thanks, Linh, you look great." Her long black hair in a ponytail, a few strands dangled around her high cheekbones.

"I'm sorry." She put her hand on my shoulder as we were getting in Kyle's car. "Oh, I just realized it's your dad's birthday." She closed her eyes and hugged me.

"It's not that, really."

"How old would he have been?" Kyle asked as he got in the driver's seat and slid a cigarette in his mouth. He never lit it, but whenever he drove or worked on his computer, he usually held one in his lips; he said it reminded him of his dad. We had that in common, losing our fathers. It was part of our bond.

"Forty-seven today but— "

"It wasn't your fault," Linh said.

"I killed him Linh. Whatever you say or think doesn't change it."

"Nate, you're the only one who believes that."

"Really? Ask my mom why she can hardly look at me, why she works around the clock so she doesn't have to be around me."

"Your mom and dad built that restaurant together. She's just trying to keep it going."

"Linh, I know you like my mom, but let's get real. The Station is one of the most successful restaurants in town."

"How would you know? You never even let us go," Kyle said. "Have you even been back in the four years since the funeral?" He shot me one of his stern looks, peering over his mirrored shades. His mop of coal-black hair, shaggy and unkempt, combined with the cigarette to give him a tough guy image.

"What is this, gang up on Nate when he's down day? Let's go."

Kyle began the short drive to his house.

"It wasn't like I lost just my dad. The whole family was obliterated that day." My voice cracked. "I was only twelve, and all mom cared about was me not making a scene at her perfect funeral."

"She was grieving too, Nate," Linh said.

"She's always been so practical and driven; get better grades, haircuts and manners."

"At least she makes the best brownies," Linh said.

"Yeah, well you eat them. I want my dad back. He was the gentle one. He was always encouraging me, more like a friend. Everyone loved him. Two hundred and twenty people jammed the restaurant for the funeral... and they all knew he was dead because of me."

"No," Kyle said.

"You weren't there. The only one who understood was Dustin. Some lady said that my mother was *never* going to be able to handle two teenage boys on her own. She nailed that. It started right then: Mom and I got into a huge fight, in front of everyone."

"What about?" Linh asked.

"I don't even remember. Dustin swooped in and told Mom our aunt Rose was looking for her. A minute later, he and I were outside laughing. I can still see his funny dunce expression when he called the funeral another episode of *The Ryder Family In Crisis* reality show." Dustin had always taken care of me like that. I smiled just talking about it.

I tried not to think of the funeral, but that day replayed regularly in my head. It was a line that marked the end of my childhood, of my family. The ever-growing chasm between Mom and me started then. It was the last day we were allowed to see Aunt Rose, Dad's sister. And, it began the brutal march toward the loss of Dustin. In truth, I'd been a basket case ever since the funeral. The Outviews were just the final piece to shove me over the edge.

Something else happened at the funeral, something that would make going on without my dad and even the Outviews seem trivial. Of the more than two hundred guests listening to eulogies that day, two were destined to impact my life like colliding comets. One would attempt to kill me many times, and the other would try equally hard to save me... but I didn't know any of that then. I was just a kid trying to get through my shock and guilt.

I was happy to escape the car once we arrived at Kyle and Linh's house. It was a restored Victorian near the Southern Oregon University campus where his uncle was a physics professor. His aunt, a secretary at the Oregon Shakespeare Festival, always got us free tickets. We'd seen every play for three seasons. I liked them, but Bà, Kyle's grandmother, made me a little nervous. She was an old medicine woman or something, and during the Vietnam War, she took care of soldiers with herbal remedies. For the past two years, they'd been my "normal" family.

"Nate, when my parents were killed in Vietnam by that explosion, I was twelve, like you when your father died."

"I know," I said suddenly feeling selfish.

"Everything was taken from me, too. Everything." He looked at me across the car's hood, pulling the cigarette from his lips. "I spent almost a year in an orphanage, before Bà and Linh's dad got me out and brought me to America." Lihn's father was Kyle's biggest hero, and he was whom Kyle named himself after once he decided his Asian name was holding him back.

"Sorry man. I'm not a Zen master like you." I knew he was reminding me of his story to make the point that I didn't have it all that bad. Kyle had been holding me together for a long time, but even his great patience had an end.

I followed him into the house. We were on the steps to the attic when Linh caught up to us, tapping my waist. "You okay?"

I turned to face her. She stepped up so we were inches apart on the narrow staircase. "No, not even close. Are you happy I'm finally admitting it? And surprise, today is the day you get to find out how *not* okay I really am." I had to tell them; the Outviews were a secret I couldn't carry any longer.

A harsh glance told me she was hurt but her answer came softly sweet. "Yes." She touched my hand. The innocence of her face countered the knowing in her dark eyes. "It's your fear making you lash out." Linh was intuitive that way. "Don't worry, whatever it is, we'll help you. I promise." She took two deep breaths as if coaxing me to do the same. I got one done before Kyle called to us.

Kyle's room was in the attic, or rather it *was* the attic. He and Linh's dad had converted it into a spacious loft that occupied the entire top floor of their old house. It was one of my favorite places to hang out. Other than the dormer windows, all the available wall space was lined and stacked with thousands of books. His computer lived on a glass desk near one end, his bed at the other end. Three couches filled the middle of the space, all facing each other with a large triangular coffee table in the center. Giant posters of Hubble Space Telescope images covered the slanted ceiling above the bookcases, along with some of his more intricate drawings. I walked past his five thousand-piece all white jigsaw puzzle and the matching black one next to it. He'd been working on them for years. "When are you going to give up on these puzzles?" I asked. Each was a little more than half done. "It gives me a headache to look at them."

"It's meditative. They help keep me balanced, yin and yang." As if he was telling me this for the first time.

I scoffed.

"You just don't have the patience for it," Kyle said.

I laughed. "Neither do you, or they would have been finished a couple of years ago."

"You can help any time you want."

As usual, Linh, Kyle and I each sat on our own sofa.

There'd been almost no sleep in two nights while I tried to avoid Outviews. My brain was hardly working so I avoided the subject, scared of their reactions. I fell asleep in midsentence.

Saturday, September 13

Eleven hours later, I woke up. It was two a.m. Linh was gone, and Kyle was crashed in his bed. I stretched and stood up; a note fell to the floor. I read it by the light from his computer screen. Kyle had sent a text to my mother from my phone telling her I was sleeping over. I realized that I'd slept for all those hours without any Outviews. Sitting there in the dark, the tears flowed like they hadn't since I was a child. I used a pillow to muffle the wails because for ten minutes I cried, curled up in a fetal position until exhausted, sleep captured me again.

Some time later I awoke, still in darkness. The familiar sick feeling came, my eyes got heavy, and the room blurred. Not again, I begged, as the spiral and mist of an Outview started to take me back to a place I didn't know but knew I did not want to go.

The woods were thick with smoke and gunpowder. My faded uniform was unmistakably Union, and off in the distance canon fire boomed. Somehow I'd been separated from my company. I checked my musket and bayonet and continued toward the battle. Halfway down into a ravine I spotted a lone rebel soldier, filling his canteen in the stream, and trained my rifle.

"Hands up, you filthy reb!"

He turned slowly around. "My God, Henry, is that you?"

"Kent?" I said. We'd grown up together in the mountains of Virginia but wound up on different sides. I looked around again to be sure we were alone and then shuffled toward him. "Damn, Kent, I hoped we wouldn't meet again until after the war."

"Is it ever gonna end?"

I shook my head. Suddenly there was noise above us.

"Those are your troops," he said, panicking.

Through the grime and dirt were the eyes of my friend, my childhood. "Go! Get on out of here."

His eyes flashed silent thanks, then instantly he turned and escaped down the creek. I reached the top of the ravine and a captain's boot kicked my face sending me rolling back down. Two fellow Union soldiers quickly retrieved me.

"I just watched you let the enemy go. You some kind of spy, private?" the captain asked.

"No sir." I spit dirt, blood, a tooth.

"You're lying!"

Before I could respond, a bayonet pierced my groin. Blood gushed with my agonized scream. Another soldier set a pistol to my head before the captain stopped him.

"We don't waste bullets on traitors." They tied ropes around my legs and dragged me behind their horses. Underbrush, rocks and fallen branches gorged and ripped at me.

I heard a familiar voice from somewhere else.

"Nate, Nate, are you all right? What's going on?" Kyle was shaking my shoulders. He had saved me again. I pushed myself up. The light was on.

"Oh God, Kyle, you brought me back. Thanks, man," I said, trying to find my bearings.

"Back from where? What are you talking about?"

"I wish I knew." Then I realized Kyle was Henry. It didn't make sense.

"You're really worrying me. You've been acting seriously strange," he said, as if his stare could pull the answer out of me.

"I need you to help me do something... it's probably illegal, maybe even dangerous."

Kyle stood up and looked down at me, tossed a fresh cigarette in.

"We're friends. You know I'll help but you need to start talking. Illegal? Dangerous? You better talk a lot." His look showed what I already knew. He had an extreme fear of authorities. A siren could make him hyperventilate, and seeing someone in uniform would send him into cold sweats and near paralysis.

I didn't want to mix Kyle up in my troubles but couldn't get out of them without him. It was all so fantastical. I was scared that telling him might harm our friendship or worse, that speaking it out loud would make the insanity real. Kyle was the smartest person I knew. He was in every advanced class our school offered, even taking a few college courses. If anyone could help me with my wild plan and figure out what was causing me to lose my mind, it was Kyle—but only if he believed me.

Linh came in, carrying a large tray of food. She was like out of a dream, breezy and glowing. The digital clock showed it was just after six.

"Bà and I have been cooking since five, so you better like it."

"What did we do to deserve this?"

"I told her you've been sick and stressed. She said good food would fix you up."

"Is it safe to eat?" I teased.

"Nate, don't be mean. Bà loves you."

I took a few bites of Xoi Trung, sticky rice with egg. "It's so delicious I might actually start to believe that."

"Talk, Nate." Kyle grabbed a Bành Bao, a Vietnamese cake.

The food and especially the perfect sleep had momentarily improved my outlook. Although still reluctant to reveal too much, I began with the question that had consumed me for months. "How do you really know if you're crazy or not? I mean, if you're crazy, are you in any kind of state to know you are?"

"What are you talking about?" Kyle squinted his eyes.

"I think I might be going crazy, lock-me-up-because-I'm-insane kind of crazy."

"Why?"

"For at least a year I've had these nightmares, and they're not your regular wake-up-heart-pounding bad dreams. They seem completely real like I'm different people all the time. It's totally schizophrenic. And I hear voices, too."

"What do the voices say?"

"Mostly they say my name, like an echoing whisper, but there's a lot of other stuff like 'listen' and 'remember.' Usually not more than a word or two at a time."

"They aren't telling you to kill anyone or yourself or anything crazy?"

"No."

"Nate, you're stressed out. You think you killed your dad. I mean hearing things, nightmares, not sleeping, and what happened to Dustin… why don't you go talk to someone, a counselor?"

"I don't want to wind up like Dustin."

"That's what this is all about isn't it?" Kyle asked. "You think you're turning into Dustin? Listen, Nate, that doesn't make *you* crazy. If you were crazy, I would know. You're a little strange, actually a lot of strange, but not crazy. Besides, you're worse than crazy: you're a teenager."

"Does your mom know what's going on?" Linh asked.

"She suspects, but I can't trust her."

"Why?"

"Mom's the one who did it."

"Wow. I thought it was a court-ordered thing," Linh said.

"Yeah, she got the court order."

"That must have been so hard for her."

"Hard. How does a mother even do that? All I know is every time I've tried to bring it up she cries and refuses to talk.

"Why?" Linh asked.

"For the same reason she won't let me see my dad's sister. Because she only cares about herself." I paced the length of the room. "I mean, she hears me waking up in the night screaming. Even in daytime you know how I get, zoned out, freaked out. She's gotta be thinking I'm going crazy like Dustin did, but she pretends nothing is happening."

"Your mom must be terrified it's going to happen to you," Linh said.

"I am too. But she's never even around. She only cares about the restaurant."

"Bad dreams and your subconscious mind talking to you," Kyle interrupted, "I think you need to start meditating." Although Kyle occasionally talked about how important meditation was, this was the first time he suggested it. "I'll show you how. It's a challenge at first but becomes easier. It's is a beautiful thing, and it will help clear these troubles, I promise."

"Anything is worth a shot. But they're not just bad dreams."

"What then?" Linh asked.

"It's like Death is bullying me."

"That's just your guilt talking," Linh said. "Don't you get that?"

"Sure I do. My dad is dead, it's my fault, and you're the only two who don't believe it."

"Meditation is better than counseling. It keeps me sane in this crazy world," Kyle said.

The "troubles" I told them about were only a sliver of the horror, but this wasn't the time for full disclosure. If Kyle and Linh became as overwhelmed as I was, there might be no way to escape the madness.

5

Kyle raised his voice an octave and said, "It's a scandal."
Linh rolled her eyes.

Starting in eighth grade, Kyle and I began making fun of all the gossip in school by talking like two girls, in high voices, "It's a scandal. John broke up with Cathy, then went out with Carol, but Cathy was kissing John's friend Brad. It's such a scandal... " We'd crack each other up.

We were both giggling when Linh said, "You two should grow up! There's nothing funny about this." That of course sent us into a fit, but eventually we calmed down.

"I told you my secret. Now you said you'd help me."

"Nate wants us to do something dangerous and illegal," Kyle told Linh.

"*Potentially* illegal and dangerous," I corrected.

"So I'm going to wind up in jail for hanging out with a couple of nine-year-olds."

"Tell us," Kyle urged. I was sure he sensed there was more going on, but he was patient—Zen patient. He knew the rest would come in time.

"I want to go see Dustin."

"That's illegal?"

"I want to get him out."

"Oh."

Kyle looked at Linh.

"It's understandable you want to see your brother, but you're sixteen. They aren't going to let you take him home. Do you actually want to break him out?" Linh asked.

"Yes. He doesn't belong in an institution."

"How do you know?" Kyle challenged. "Why's he in there?"

"Awhile after my dad died, Dustin started getting paranoid. He was smoking a bunch of pot at the time, so I thought it was all about that. But it got real bad, and my mother was very worried. He'd have conversations with himself—more like arguments—and heard voices." I glanced at Linh and saw it register in her eyes. She knew where I was coming from. "He stopped sleeping, started blurting things like 'they won't leave me alone,' and was always talking about coded messages and secret meanings in everything."

"How old was he when it started?" Kyle asked.

"Fifteen."

"And you started seeing things and hearing voices at fifteen, too?"

"Yes."

They both stared.

"I remember what he was like. And it's been increasing a lot since I turned sixteen."

"But he smoked tons of weed and who knows what else. You won't even take aspirin."

"Yeah, he's the main reason I don't. Maybe drugs and alcohol made everything more intense for him, or he might have been using them to numb himself or to escape the voices and visions."

"You're not Dustin."

"Not yet, but he was fine, too." I paused to hold in the emotion. "Then at some point he lost touch with the real world, or at least my mom thought he did. I need to talk to him. I need my brother. We have to get him out."

Linh saw me fighting tears.

"What was the final straw that got him committed?" Kyle asked.

"He freaked out, said he had to go back and take care of some things. The only way he believed he could get 'there' was to kill himself."

"He tried?"

"The day after he turned sixteen he drove to Mount Shasta, did some coke and started hiking higher and higher in just a t-shirt and shorts."

"Was he going to jump?"

"No, he was going to freeze himself to death. He said that's the way the Incas did it."

"Wow, that's almost cool if it wasn't so tragic," Kyle said. "So what happened?"

"The coke kept him up so he continued hiking and climbing almost all night. There was only a crescent moon, so mostly he was stumbling around in the dark, but he kept heading up. Sometime before dawn, he finally collapsed and fell asleep. And he would have gotten his wish and froze to death if it hadn't been for two hikers who found him a few hours later."

"How'd he get to the institution?"

"He told my mother the whole story and said he was going to find another way to get back. She didn't know what to do, so she had him committed."

"Putting her own son in a mental institution. That's totally cold," Kyle said. "Even so, tough lady."

"I heard her on the phone right after it happened, when she didn't know I was listening, telling her friend about how terrible it had been. Mom said Dustin kept screaming for her to help him while they worked to get the straitjacket on. He flung the orderlies and doctors off like blankets, crying 'Mom, Mom, I'm not crazy. Don't let them do this.' Mom told her friend that it was worst than the day our dad died."

"That's so sad," Linh said.

"For Dustin."

"For all three of you."

"She said it was only temporary, but every month I asked her when Dustin is coming home."

"And?"

"After twenty-four evasive answers, it's pretty clear his 'temporary' hospitalization is permanent."

"And she won't allow you to visit? You've haven't seen him in all this time?"

I shook my head.

"I'll take you to Dustin, but why do we have to break him out?" Kyle asked.

"Because my brother might be the only one who can understand. I need to know exactly what happened to him. He'll never reveal his secrets while medicated in an institution."

"What secrets? It sounds like he may have really needed professional help."

"Whatever. Don't you get it? He's my only brother. He was my great protector, and I watched him twist into a desperate, hollow, angry stranger. We need to help him." I raised my voice, hands shaking, "We need to *save* him."

"Don't you mean help *you* and save *you?*" Kyle asked.

"Yes!" I shouted. "If he's crazy then that means I am, too." I smeared my eyes before tears could escape. "You guys gotta help me, please!"

"Where is he?" Kyle asked. "Why don't we go visit him and then decide what to do after we know what we're dealing with? I mean, you haven't seen him in two years. He could be a raging lunatic."

"I don't know where he is."

"Seriously?"

"She won't tell me where he is. She's afraid I'll try to find him, and it's true. I would have run away but there was nowhere to go."

"How are we supposed to find Dustin?"

"Whenever my mom goes, it's always a day-trip. So how many mental institutions could there be within a half-day's drive from Ashland?"

It turned out there were four. After a few minutes on the Internet, we narrowed it down to a private facility in Roseburg, the most obvious choice, and about a two-hour drive.

"Mountain View Psychiatric Hospital, Providing Quality Care Since 1957. Inpatient psychiatric services for children, adolescents, adults, and geriatric patients, providing a safe place where compassionate, quality care supports recovery from mental illness and addiction," the description read.

"Sounds like a great place. Maybe they're helping him," Kyle said.

"Two years? It doesn't take two years," I said.

"Kyle, Nate's our best friend, Dustin's his brother. It's family. We have to go," Linh said.

"Road trip!" Kyle shouted. A three-day weekend was coming up at school; it would be the perfect time. Early in the summer we'd all gone camping and were sure our parents would let us go again.

"Visiting hours are 8 a.m. to 8 p.m., seven days a week," Linh said, looking up from her iPad. "Shouldn't we call to make sure he's there?"

"Yes, you should." I dialed the number and handed my cell phone to her. "Tell them you're Jennifer Ryder and you'd like to speak to your son, Dustin Ryder."

"What if they put me through to him?"

"Not a chance," I said. It took less than three minutes to prove me wrong, as she shoved the phone at me and I said hello to my brother for the first time in more than two years. "Dustin, it's Nate."

"Long time, Dude. How's it going, brother? Is something wrong with Mom?"

"No, Mom's fine. She doesn't know I'm calling. Hey, you sound normal."

"You caught me at the right time of day. I'm at my clearest in the morning but they're gonna hit me with a round of meds in a few minutes. Why doesn't Mom know?"

"She won't let me visit or contact you. It's like she's afraid I'm going to catch what you have."

"Isn't that why you're calling?"

"What do you mean?"

"You know what I mean; you're seeing things all the time now, aren't you?"

I was too surprised to answer.

"And you hear the voices?"

"How did you know?" I whispered.

"I've been waiting for you, brother. How are you handling it? Better than me, I hope."

"It's gotten kind of crazy lately."

"Hey, don't say that word around me."

"Sorry."

"Nate, I'm kidding."

"I'm coming to see you next weekend."

"It might be a rough trip."

"What do you mean?"

"I wish I had time to explain, but I hear the nurse coming to drug me up right now. Just be extra careful. I won't be in any condition to help."

"What are you talking about?"

"And Nate, whenever it get's really bad, you have to let go and trust yourself. That's where the good is. If you feel it inside and it soothes you, then you know it's okay. Trusting anything else gets tricky." I heard something in the background and then he said, "Bye, Mom, see you next weekend."

"What do you think he meant?" I asked after filling them in.

"He may not have meant anything *real*. He is in a mental hospital." Kyle raised his eyebrows. "Not to be rude, but he could actually be crazy."

"I know my brother, and he sounded totally sane. He shouldn't be in there."

"I hope you're right."

I did, too.

Our parents agreed to our camping trip. All I had to do was keep my head together for another week.

Talking to Dustin had made me feel much better. Maybe he really wasn't crazy, which meant maybe I wasn't. But his warnings worried me. What did he mean by "it could be a rough trip?"

6

The Outviews came almost nightly, but they had begun invading my waking hours, too. Linh and Kyle didn't understand they weren't nightmares. I hadn't either, but that hope shattered on a beautiful morning last July. Digging a hole in the backyard for a new fence post, I was suddenly standing over a freshly dug grave in the rain. I turned trying to figure out what was happening. It was still a sunny day; the backyard and our house were normal. I looked back at the ground, and there, instead of my posthole, was the grave and a muddy puddle at the bottom as the rain grew heavier. It was a nightmare in broad daylight. Both scenes were happening simultaneously. Which one did I belong in? When I focused on the grave, the backyard faded away. Looking back at my house, the grave receded. I had an eerie feeling that the "me" standing by the grave wasn't really me. I mean, it was, but not Nathan Ryder. It was another time. There were three horses tied to nearby trees and two men with rifles a little farther back. A third with a pistol was yelling at me.

"Jump on down there, Wesley," he said motioning to the grave.

"Hell no! You ain't burying me alive, Brett," I shouted back. The voice startled me because it vibrated inside my body, but I heard it as clearly as my neighbor's radio at the same time.

"Yes, I am," he yelled angrily. Water dripped from the brim of his cowboy hat.

I started shouting at him louder. "If you've got to kill me then I reckon that's what you're gonna do, but have some decency, man." The rain picked up. "How dare you talk about decency!" He pulled the trigger. The "me" by the grave and the "me" in the backyard both went down when the bullet tore into my knee. I looked back toward the house and up at the blue sunny sky, but my references were blurring because, at the same time, I was wet from the rain. Brett shot my other knee. I screamed out in both the past and the present, and then he pushed me down into the grave. Crashing hard in two inches of muddy water, one of my arms snapped under my weight. A scraping sound competed with the falling rain while dirt came from above as they dumped in shovels full in a slow steady rhythm. My agony gave way to the terror of being buried alive. Once the earth covered my face I stopped screaming, unable to tell what was up or down. The pressure from the mud numbed all pain, as the crushing force stole my breath and finished me off.

Kyle found me passed out next to the fence. I lied to him and said something about the post hitting my head. It took almost two days to stop favoring my right arm and walk without a limp. I still haven't gotten over the emotional impact. That was the day the Outviews invaded my real life, and being awake hadn't felt safe since.

I wasn't just being vague about the Outviews. I hadn't told Kyle and Linh many other things. No matter how close we were, if they knew everything, the only way they'd agree to go to Mountain View Psychiatric Hospital would be if I stayed as a patient. I'd seen "pops" over people's heads all the time—sudden bursts of color the size of a pencil eraser would go off like a tiny firework display, bright and vivid, highly saturated. They even occurred when I was alone and just thinking about things. I was figuring out if there was a pattern to the colors: red pops seemed to be a warning or happen around anger, while hanging out with Linh usually brought clear or bright aqua pops. I wanted to keep a list, but there was too much going on.

I sat in my room feeling guilty for not being completely open with my friends. I often thought out my problems while cropping and enhancing photos on the computer. Everyone knew me as a photographer because I always had a camera with me. The summer after sixth grade I started selling photos online and in a few shops around town, making enough money for regular upgrades to my cameras and laptop, plus some savings for a car.

Staring at a recent photo of several deer reminded me of shapeshifting. We studied it in eighth-grade history class. Shapeshifting was a big deal in Native American song and dance ceremonies, hunting, healing, and warfare. With me it was different; hallucinations were attacking my sanity. Out of the corner of my eye, there'd be a large deer with a full rack of antlers, but then looking again, it turned out to be simply a brown bush. An eagle in a tree would really be an old trash bag caught in branches. A running lion was actually corn stalks rippling in the wind. The first look was fleeting but crystal clear—no question I'd just seen a giant tortoise, but it was really a small dumpster. When it started happening twenty times a day, every day, I knew there was more to it. Either I was crazy or I really did see a coyote in the school cafeteria or a giraffe in my front yard. If no one else saw those animals, then I had to face the explanation: insanity was closing in.

I was unable to concentrate on the photo. My thoughts continued to seek meaning in the shapeshifting episodes. I got up from the computer and paced the room.

The rushing sound of a tornado sent me to the floor. But as usual, nothing happened, no air moved and it didn't last long, it was just the "wind noise." The first time I heard it was about two years earlier and maybe a week before Dustin went up Shasta to kill himself. He and I were hiking together. We did it less and less as he became more estranged, but this had been one of his rare clear days. We were about two miles into a three-mile hike when I heard the sound, a strong wind whizzing past my ear. My hair even moved, but other than an inch around my head, the air was still. After the third time, Dustin noticed me rubbing my ears.

"I keep getting this sort of sound in my ears," I said.

"You, too? Get used to it, little brother."

"What do you mean?"

"I started hearing it when I was fourteen, too. I asked Dad about it. And it was the weirdest thing." Dustin stopped walking and looked at me. "Dad started crying."

"Why? What did you say to him?"

"All I said was, 'Dad, I keep hearing the wind in my ear and I feel like a hummingbird is flying around my head.' He pulled me in a hug and started sobbing, saying, 'oh no, oh no, I'm sorry, Dusty, I'm sorry.' I didn't know what he was talking about or why he got so upset."

"Didn't you ask him what was wrong?"

"Course I did. He said I hadn't done anything wrong and we needed to have a long talk, but it would have to wait because he was late for work."

I grabbed Dustin's shoulder. "And?"

"He said he wanted to take me somewhere and show me something, that we'd talk on the way." Dustin's eyes were filling. "We never had that talk, Nate. Dad died two days later."

The guilt was nauseating. Dad had wanted to take Dustin on the Grizzly Peak hike alone. I begged and begged to go until he finally gave in. Not only had I caused his death by going, but I had prevented him from telling Dustin some great secret, from showing him something important. I sat down on the trail. "What was he going to tell you? Show you?" I asked weakly. My head throbbed.

"I wish I knew. He was pretty upset when I asked him about the sound. I had the feeling that he heard it, too. Like he was all torn up because he passed it on to me or something." Dustin was looking up at the trees but seemed to be staring much farther away. "He was distraught. You would have thought I'd said the army was shipping me out to fight some horrible foreign war." He paused and spoke softly, almost to himself, "And in a way that's what it's been like."

Looking at Dustin was like looking in a mirror, same hazel eyes flecked with gold, and sandy brown hair, but he was taller and solid where I was lanky. I could almost see him fading away as he stood there, battling memories and angst.

"Dustin, what's been going on with you? You've really been freaking Mom out."

"Mom's been a wreck ever since Dad died. She thinks she's going to blow it and disappoint him or worse, let *us* down."

"She's doing okay."

"Glad you think so. The problem is she doesn't believe anything I say. She thinks I'm just a burnout and tripping all the time."

"Well, aren't you?"

"Only when I need to."

"That seems like all the time." With that he sparked a bowl and offered me a hit. "Whatever," I said.

"You have no idea what it's like. Everything's coming in at me, and now I have you to worry about on top of all that."

"Don't worry about me," I said. "Try getting your own life figured out."

"You sound like Mom. Neither one of you knows what's going on."

"Because you won't talk about it. Why don't you try telling me?"

"Why don't you try growing up and not be such a mama's boy? Then maybe you could make up your own mind. Anytime I try to talk about it, everyone thinks I'm crazy."

"I don't think you're crazy, I just think you're a big freak."

"How did you get to be so immature?"

"I'm fourteen, what's *your* excuse?"

"Never mind, Nate, they'll come for you, too, and you'll have a chance to deal with all this. Maybe then you'll understand your older brother isn't such a crazy freak."

When we got home, Dustin split off and headed toward town. I had a chest pain and curled up next to a sequoia until it went away. After that, I only saw him a few times before he got committed. Today was the first real conversation we've had since that day in the woods.

I continued pacing in my room, switched back to working on photos, read about the San Francisco 49ers online and did almost anything I could to avoid sleep. Mom saw my light on and came in. She appeared to have aged ten years in the four years since the funeral. There was a little gray mixed in the long blond strands. Her thin face was still pretty, but lines had etched a history of recent sorrows.

"Make sure you email me your route, which campsites, Kyle's plate number and all that good stuff." Mom was efficient. "Hey, when you're next in town, come by the restaurant. Josh would love to see you."

"Sure, I'll try."

"You know, Josh and your dad were good friends, more than just partners. He has always adored you and hardly sees you anymore."

"I know Mom, I said I'll try." The truth was I thought Josh was a pretty cool guy. He and my parents started the restaurant together before I could walk, and I literally grew up in the place. Mom probably thought I was avoiding him, but it was actually the restaurant I was avoiding. Dad died there.

It was located near the university campus and although its official name was The Radio Station, everyone called it "the Station." It served healthy sandwiches, gourmet burgers with each dish named after a different musician, from Adele to Townes Van Zandt. It may have been most famous for wild desserts like Caramel Crisis, Chocolate Disaster or Die By Pie. The ceiling was covered with authentic album covers from old vinyl LPs. Framed concert posters, ticket collections, and other music memorabilia decorated the walls. An authentic radio broadcast studio, complete with an on-air light, sent tunes out to the dining area. Huge screens showed vintage concerts, and a marquee out front listed them as if they were live, like "THE BEATLES tonight." The place was usually packed with college students and hip locals; the kids at my school considered it a cool spot.

Her once soft eyes were now hard. I wanted to tell her I was scared. Couldn't she see how lost I was? But Dustin had tried talking to her, too.

"I've been worried about you," she said. "Do you want to talk?"

"Not tonight, Mom, I'm really tired."

"Okay, let's find time though." I thought she said we should talk only because she believed it was what a mother should say and was probably hoping to coast to my eighteenth birthday so her job would be done. She'd be rid of the responsibility of both her sons.

I lost another duel with sleep and was out soon after she left. I was a grown man, running along a beach. The sea was an odd shade of purple. Some kind of drone, the size of a six-pack of sodas, was chasing me as yellow marble-sized projectiles rained down. Another drone closed in from the opposite direction. I darted toward a cliff, dove into a small cave, and waited until the craft flew in after me. I threw a stone and smashed it. More drones flew to the cave, but I was already half way up the cliff on an old, primitive trail. When I reached the top, the sight was stunning. A futuristic city of pale reds and blues, silver towers rose out of an expansive, manicured forest that looked like an endless garden. "Where am I?" Or, rather, "When am I?" More attackers came from the beach, yellow marbles zinged at me. Desperate to escape, I ran toward the cliff's edge. The yellow buckshot ripped across my arms and back. I fell for what seems like minutes before my head split open on a boulder.

Instantly, I was in my room, heart pounding, reeling from the pain in my back and an intense headache. "My name is Nathan Ryder, I'm sixteen, I'm in eleventh grade... " I repeated my mantra. Why do I always see death? What are the Outviews trying to tell me?

*S*unday, *September 14*
Kyle pulled up as the sun lit the morning sky, and we headed to the park. There were a few joggers and an old man walking a dog, but otherwise we had Lithia Park to ourselves. A hundred acres of shallow canyon land, an enchanted forest stretching around rushing Ashland Creek, seemed from a Tolkien book. Trees made me feel safe, and sometimes when the Outviews were especially bad, I thought about sleeping in the park. The ponderosa pine bark smelled of vanilla and reminded me of my mom. The strong, smooth cinnamon-colored bark of the madrone felt like my dad, and the scrub oaks had always been Dustin in their tough scrappy gentleness. The alders, laurels, conifers, willows, maples, and sycamores were friends. Even though I'd grown up in the park, I usually found new places to explore but not that morning. I knew where Kyle was headed as soon as we crossed the road at the second duck pond: the Japanese garden.

The park had history. It was known how each trail had been created, who designed the duck ponds a hundred years ago, even why a certain flower was put next to a stonewall. But lost to time was the origin of the Japanese garden. Black pines, red pines, Japanese maples, persimmons, isu, and other exotic trees and shrubs looked a thousand years old.

Kyle explained that his daily meditations were split between the garden, an abandoned pear orchard, and home. He also did regular walking meditations, which I didn't know were possible.

"Let's see if we can calm down those voices of yours. Meditation is the art of silencing the mind," he said softly. "When the mind is quiet, your concentration is increased, and you experience inner peace."

"That's all I want."

"It can be elusive. You have a lot of turmoil."

"You're telling me."

"Before she died, my mother taught me to meditate. I'll teach you the same way." He pointed to a rock at the base of a Japanese maple. "Sit here and keep your back straight. Try to concentrate on only one thing; it's harder than you think. Focus on this flower. No matter where your mind goes, keep bringing it back to this flower."

I tried for almost an hour, surprised by how difficult it was to empty my cluttered mind. Every time I got close, the words "family" and "past" echoed in my head. Then came waves of deep sadness and a harsh feeling of loneliness.

On the way back to his house, Kyle repeated that, "getting to silent mind is very hard, it will take time."

"Kyle, I gotta say I didn't enjoy that."

"You'll learn to. Did you like it when you first fell in the river? No, but now you love to swim. Does a baby like her first breath of air? No, she is terrified, but there is no life without breathing. Meditation is like that."

"I might be in trouble then."

"Practice. Everything is practice."

"Kyle, are you really seventeen? Sometimes you seem more like seventy-seven."

"You can take control of your mind," Kyle said, ignoring my question. "You need to throw unwanted thoughts out. You're not a bunch of thoughts. They aren't in charge."

"Then what is?"

"You are, your real self, your higher self."

"I'm not sure, but aren't those just different ways of saying my soul? Are you getting religious on me?

"Religion isn't real, but you are."

Driving to his place, Kyle suddenly pulled into a random driveway gasping. I turned just in time to see an Ashland patrol car cruise past. Kyle closed his eyes and breathed deeply. He wouldn't talk about it, all I knew was he'd been treated roughly in jail with his parents not long before their deaths.

Back in his attic room, he handed me a copy of *The Essential Writings of Thich Nhat Hanh*. "Read this. He's a Vietnamese Buddhist monk and peace activist who lives in exile. Martin Luther King, Jr. nominated him for the Nobel Peace Prize and the Dalai Lama said, 'he shows us the connection between personal inner peace and peace on earth.' I think he's one of the most important people on the planet."

Linh joined us, and we told her what had happened at the garden.

"I just kept hearing the words 'family' and 'past.' I couldn't make them go away."

"Often when I meditate an answer comes to me." Kyle's eyes gleamed.

"You're like consumed by these voices and nightmares and your brother went through some of the same stuff, right?" Linh said. "Maybe it's a family thing. Let's search your family's past online."

"My mom was adopted."

"Then it'll be easier because we only have one side to research."

"My dad had a sister, my aunt Rose, the one we're not allowed to talk to."

"What a scandal." Kyle and I started laughing.

"Why are boys so immature?"

I grabbed the flip-flops off her feet and tossed them toward the stairs. "Who you calling immature?" She couldn't help but giggle.

We looked up the name Montgomery Ryder. Before long, a page showing his date of death came up.

"What was your dad's middle initial?" Kyle asked.

"It's 'B,' why?"

"Because a few Montgomery Ryders died around that time… Look at this." Linh pointed to the screen. "Including your dad, eleven different people named Montgomery Ryder died within five weeks of each other!"

"Unbelievable!" Kyle said.

"That can't be right," I said.

"Yeah. See, Montgomery A. Ryder, sixty-three, from Baltimore, June 19; Montgomery J. Ryder, thirty-four, from Poughkeepsie, New York, June 23; Montgomery F. Ryder, fifty-six, Sarasota, Florida, June 25. It goes on to the last one, Montgomery L. Ryder, fifty-one, died on July 27 in Wichita, Kansas. It has your dad's date of death as June 28."

"That is way spooky," I said. "I mean, eleven Montgomery Ryders—it's not like John Smith or Tom Johnson. It's not a common name."

"Let's see how many died the year before," Kyle said, as he navigated the page.

"None," I said reading the results, "check the year after."

"None again," Kyle said. After checking all the years since and ten years prior, we found only one other Montgomery Ryder death nine years before my dad died. Then we checked for any Montgomery Ryders currently living.

"Oh my God," Linh said, as we all stared at the monitor. Not one Montgomery Ryder was alive today.

"It's too weird," Kyle added.

"Guys, I think something is really wrong here." I felt sick. "Come on, there were only eleven people on the planet with my dad's name and they all died when he did? All of them?"

Kyle started pulling up obituaries. Within half an hour we had printed copies of every one of them. Their ages ranged from thirty-one to seventy-four. Three died in accidents and eight of natural causes, either stroke or heart attack. "Nate, how exactly did your father die? Like where was he and who was he with?" Kyle pressed.

8

M onday, September 15
Every month during the school year I had to meet with my guidance counselor, Mrs. Little, whose duty was to make sure I was coping with all my "problems": the death of my father, being raised by a single mom, and, especially, having a brother in the nut house. Today was our first meeting of my junior year. She had also been Dustin's counselor, so she was extra worried and cautious about me.

"Good morning, Nathan. How are you doing, pal?" She must have been my mom's age but dressed and acted like a generation or two back. Her brown hair done in a *lovely* 1950s style always amused me.

"Fine."

"Are you really?"

"I'm good, really good."

"Okay. And how's your mother?" she asked in an uncaring tone.

"She's good, too."

"Did you enjoy your summer?"

"Yeah, it was nice."

"Okay. I need to ask you some serious questions. Just take your time and try to answer truthfully." She started typing as she talked, turning the monitor so I couldn't see it. "You know we've touched on these issues before, but now that

you're the same age, well, at that age when your brother's difficulties got out of hand, we need to keep a close eye."

I nodded.

"Nathan, do you think you are able to easily tell the difference between real and unreal experiences?"

Absolutely not, I thought. "Yes ma'am," I answered.

She stared for a moment to be sure she believed me. I
didn't think she was convinced. "Okay, and have you experienced any instances of seeing things that were not there?"

Just about every day. "No."

"No hallucinations of any kind?"

"No."

"Good." She half-smiled and continued to peck away on
the keyboard. "What about hearing things? Voices? Strange
music?"

"Mrs. Little, I'm a teenager, I hear strange music all the
time."

Another half smile. "Not what I mean, Nathan. I think
you know I meant inside your head, voices or sounds that
weren't real, that no one else could hear, just you."

What would happen if I told her about the voices? Just
ask Dustin. "No, ma'am."

"You look tired. Are you having trouble sleeping Nathan?"

"No, I stayed up too late over the weekend."

"Are you using drugs of any kind?"

"No."

"Are you sure, Nathan, because your brother sat in that
very chair and said no to the same question less than a week
before he was, well, sent away."

"I'm not Dustin, Mrs. Little."

"Of course not, but do you ever think you are him?"

Oh my God. How did she get this job? "Aren't you supposed to be *helping* me?"

"Do you believe I am trying to hurt you? Do you believe
anyone is trying to harm you? Do you think people are out to
get you?"

"That's not what I meant."

"Nathan, the fact is that your grades are not what they should be. You test well, but the last few years you've barely maintained a C average."

"I've always gotten As in history."

"Yes, well…" She dismissed it as if history didn't count for some reason. "You're having trouble paying attention in class, and some of your teachers say your thoughts jump around and that you seem distant. Schizophrenia has been found to occur more frequently in teens with a family history of the disease. It's much better if we can catch it early, not when it's too late." She paused to make eye contact. "Like with your brother."

"Do you have any more questions for me, Mrs. Little? I'd like to get back to class."

"You can go, Nathan, but please try and remember I'm on your side. You can come to me anytime."

Faking a "thank you, Mrs. Little" would have been a good idea, but not slamming the door behind me was as much as I could muster.

After school I rushed over to Sam's house, a geologist who lived across the street, two houses down. I'd taken care of his lawn since I was eleven or twelve. With everything going on, I completely forgot to cut his grass over the weekend. It wasn't like he would fire me or anything—we were buddies—but I wanted him to know it would be covered.

"Hey, how was school?" he greeted me, while pulling a laptop case out of his car.

"Sam, sorry I didn't get your grass done this weekend." I pushed my mower up his driveway.

He looked over his yard and shrugged. "I don't think they'll kick me out of the neighborhood. No worries."

"How was Canada?" He was often going to exotic locations around the world—the Ukraine, Alaska, South America, North Africa—always in pursuit of oil.

"Cold. I'm home for a couple of weeks and then back out again."

"Where you headed next?"

"North Dakota, I'm afraid," he sighed, as if it was the most awful place he could think of. He was away more than he was home and in addition to paying me to do all his yard work, he gave me an extra fifty dollars a month to keep an eye on the place, take in mail, water house plants, feed his fish, that type of thing. But it was cool because Sam had a massive DVD collection and didn't mind me borrowing them. We were both huge classic film fans—Hitchcock, Spaghetti Westerns, Steve McQueen—our taste identical.

"Is Lisa going to be staying here next trip, or do you need me?"

"No, she's coming with me and... it's Liz."

"Sorry, I can't keep them all straight," I said, half serious, but we both laughed. Sam was a bit of a womanizer, and sometimes one of them would stay at his place when he was away.

"Hey, let's catch up later. I've got to get changed for a date."

"Liz?"

"Kristy."

"Hope you keep them all on a spreadsheet." I laughed.

"Good idea." He smiled, as he went inside.

It was always nice when he was back home. Sam filled in for my dad and older brother in the most relaxed way. And there were plenty of weeks when I saw him more than my mom. He was in his mid-forties, about the same age my dad would have been. Other than his short hair, he even looked a little like him, six-one, six-two, a fit, avid jogger. Dustin used to say, "Dad probably sent Sam to keep an eye on us."

*T*uesday, *September 16*
    Amber Mayes was seventeen and one of the prettiest girls at Ashland High. She was a senior and I, a mere junior, so she was out of my league even if she wasn't the daughter of a movie star. Everyone seemed to know that her father had bought her a perfectly restored vintage 1969 VW convertible bug on the day he filed for divorce. Because her mother, Ivy Mayes, was a well-known actress currently on a TV series shooting in Portland, most of the horrible divorce details were covered on the Internet, cable news, and worst of all, in the local newspaper. Amber and I had been in classes together for half our lives but were never really close. I was walking a block from school when she pulled over in her turquoise bug, "Nate, you need a ride?"

    I didn't mind walking, but Amber was truly irresistible, even if she was only being nice to me because her older sister had been dating Dustin at the time of his breakdown. Now we shared the bond of "broken home, family in crisis."

    "I'd never miss a chance to ride in the coolest car in town." I regretted my words as soon as they were out. She didn't think the car was cool.

    "How long 'til you get your license?" she asked, as we cruised up the street with the top down.

    "In like nine months. My mom is making me wait until I'm seventeen on account of Dustin freaking out right after he got his." I knew it was precisely 264 days, but I didn't want to sound like a ninth grader.

"Well, if I still have this guilt-mobile on your birthday, maybe I'll sell it to you cheap."

"Cool." Just then a moose jumped in front of the car. "Watch it," I yelled, as I braced my hand on the dashboard.

Amber stomped the brakes, "What?" she shouted.

I don't know what it really was, a sign for the park, a low-hanging branch, it didn't matter; I'd clearly seen a moose, but nothing was there. With just about anyone else I would have made up some excuse, but for some reason I found it impossible to lie to Amber. "I thought I saw a moose."

"A moose in downtown Ashland? Do you see moose often?" she asked, with not a trace of sarcasm. She resumed driving and turned off the main road to cut over to my street.

"No, first time it's been a moose."

"You mean this happens often?"

"Yeah, well, it's no big deal. My eyes just play tricks on me every so often."

"Have you ever looked up any of the animals?"

"Why would I?"

"To see what they mean. Animals all have meanings. Maybe your guides are trying to give you a message," Amber had a bit of a reputation, some kids called her "New Age Mayes" because of her not-so-secret obsession with psychics, reincarnation, and crystals.

"You've lost me."

Amber pulled over and started playing with her iPhone. "Here you go," she read, "The moose is predominately a solitary animal known to have an uncanny ability to camouflage itself, otherwise known as shapeshifting." She looked up at me. "It's the symbol of creativity and dynamic forms of intuition and illumination. This is the important part. The moose teaches us the ability to move from the outer to the inner world."

"Why is that the important part?"

"I don't know, Nate. Do you?" Amber's green eyes filled with excitement. But this was nothing new. They always looked like she was seeing some spectacular party that only she'd been invited to; it was part of what made her so dazzling.

"How would I know?"

"Nate, I don't think about things before I say them. I just let it flow. You should try it. I feel like you're always censoring yourself."

"Look, I'm dealing with a lot of stuff right now, and I don't need a bunch of recycled Hollywood psychological garbage thrown at me."

"Wow! There you go. Does that feel better?"

"It would take a lot more than that to make me feel better."

"How long have you been seeing animals?"

"It's no big deal."

"Yeah, you said that already. That's how I know it *is* a big deal."

"I don't want to talk about it."

"Why, what are you afraid of?"

"I'm not afraid."

"Do you think you're going to end up like Dustin?"

"Do you think you're going to end up like your mother?"

"I think I liked you better when you censored yourself."

"I'm sorry."

"Let's go to my house."

"No, I really should get home."

"Too bad because I'm kidnapping you." Her mother wasn't home; she never was. Her sister was a freshman at the Academy of Art University in San Francisco, studying acting. Amber mostly lived by herself with an old housekeeper who had come by three times a week since she was six.

The house was fancy but not overdone. The real money came from her father. He was a "money manager," and several of his clients were well-known Hollywood stars. They also had a place on the Oregon coast, a condo in Los Angeles, and something in Mexico. "Dad's been living in LA for a while now."

"Sorry about the divorce and everything."

"Me too, but Dad isn't the deepest guy in the world, and Mom was born a messed-up drama queen, so it was bound to happen."

I started to nod then stopped. "Now who's censoring themselves?" I said. "That's like a quote you'd give to a tabloid reporter."

"No, I'd tell tabloid reporters to go screw themselves."

I couldn't help but laugh, even though she wasn't being funny. We climbed the stairs and sailed down the hall to her bedroom. It was big with its own bathroom and balcony. "Nice scenery," I said, surveying the whole town and the mountains beyond.

"Tell me the last animal you saw before the moose."

"Why won't you let this go?"

"Because I want you to know you're not crazy."

"You mean not like Dustin? Well, I know I'm not crazy."

"Do you?" She stared into my eyes so long that I wanted to run away, I wanted to hug her, I wanted to cry. "It's okay, Nate. You can tell me. I can help." She took my hand in both of hers. It was jarring. I was sitting with the hottest girl in school on her bed, alone in her house, and she was holding my hand in hers and talking softly to me. If I wasn't days from losing my mind, I might have thought I'd won the lottery, might have tried something I shouldn't have.

Instead I started to tremble. "Oh God, I wish you could." My voice was shaking.

"I can."

And I believed her. She wrapped a blanket around me, and I realized in my crumbling weakness that strangely Amber Mayes might be my last chance. "What do you most want, Nate?"

"Ashland."

"What do you mean?"

"Sometimes, it's like my life is slipping away. Not like I'm dying but that who I am, in Ashland in the present time, this sixteen year-old," I said, pointing to myself, "is fading out."

"To where?"

"It's like I'm losing my life in Ashland and falling into a web of nightmares."

"Tell me about them." She had her arm around me rubbing my back. "Just breathe slow and deep and let it go." I told her about three Outviews before I was too drained to say more. She went to her bookshelf and pulled down a book. *Twenty Cases Suggestive of Reincarnation.*

"Do you know what it is?" she asked. "Do you believe in it?"

"I've never really thought about it."

She looked at me, bewildered. "Well, I do. And I think you've been seeing your past lives."

"Is that even possible?"

"Read that book."

"Why is everyone giving me books to read all of a sudden?"

"I could give you two dozen books about it, but this one is by a scientist. Dr. Ian Peterson was a biochemist and professor of psychiatry at the University of Virginia. He spent decades traveling the world, interviewing kids who had memories of past lives."

"You mean there are more like me?"

"Well, his work focused around children between two and four. A child would start saying things to his parents or siblings about a life he led in another time and place. And these kids want to go back to those other lives because they miss people or need to finish something. When the parents start looking into the facts and descriptions the child has given, they find out he is right. Some of these kids are two, and they can perfectly describe places they have never been to and people they have never met."

"That's crazy."

"No! It's not. And you're not crazy. You're doing the same thing. Somehow a channel has opened up, and you're able to tap into your past lives."

"So, how do we keep living all these lives?"

"Because we're energy. We're not the flesh and bones sitting here. Our souls go on and on. They just keep switching vehicles. Your body is nothing more than a vehicle for this particular trip called Nathan Ryder."

"You're blowing my mind, Amber."

"You're blowing *my* mind. You don't know how lucky you are to be able to see what you see."

"You call it luck. I call it a curse."

"I wish I could do it. The kids Stevenson studied—and he investigated hundreds of cases—are too young to know how to develop it. They lose their abilities about the time they start formal schooling."

"Yeah, they probably have counselors like Mrs. Little."

"I'm serious. This is real. Stevenson followed strict scientific protocols. He was published in prestigious journals and released like six books. He's a modern Galileo."

If she was right and reincarnation was real, then maybe I wasn't going crazy, and that was a relief. Waves of tension left my body. She made it all sound so believable. But if I was falling back into past lives, then where was that going to end? What was that going to do to me?

"Nate, you have to start writing down your Outviews."

"Why?"

"It'll help you get to the point where you can control them. I've read other books where people are able to regress themselves at will and even choose where and when to go."

"Why would I want to do that?"

"Why *wouldn't* you? There are so many things you can do once you figure out how to handle this."

"How am I supposed to handle or even understand this monumental metaphysical stuff when I can't even handle being a teenager?"

She took me home, making me promise to keep a journal of Outviews. After the time spent in Amber's bedroom, I knew my life would never be the same again. She had opened a new world to me, given me something other than insanity to explain what was happening. And, my God, what if it was true?

Ten minutes later there was a knock on my door. I thought it was Amber returning, but it was Linh. She had walked over to check on me. "Tell me about what happened the day before your dad died, why you think it was your fault."

Normally I would have refused and changed the subject—it had come up before—but this time I was drained from the session with Amber, and it just came pouring out. "Dad, Dustin, and I had been hiking up Grizzly Peak. As always, Dustin wanted to go off trail, and we made our way down into a steep bowl and up the other side to a far ridge where the terrain got tough. An area of scree caught me by surprise, and I sprained my ankle pretty bad. Dad carried me on his back all the way to the car. The next morning at work, he had a heart attack."

"Oh, Nate. It wasn't your fault. I know as a twelve-year-old it may have seemed like it, but he—"

"You sound like Dustin. He told me over and over that it wasn't my fault."

"Dustin was there, and he was older. Why didn't you believe him?"

"Because he told me at the funeral that we would get through this and that he wouldn't let me forget about Dad. And he lied. We aren't getting through it. Our family is destroyed. And I can't remember everything. My dad is fading away. All the hikes he took us on, camping, the music he made us listen to, it's all lumped together."

She held me without saying anything. Minutes passed.

"I'm sorry I'm such a mess. I didn't want you to see me cry." I rubbed my eyes.

"Don't be dumb."

After she left my plan was to search reincarnation on the Internet, but I was fried, so I put my iPod on shuffle, turned up the volume, and went for a walk. Unwell, an old Matchbox 20 song came on and immediately threw my thoughts back to Dustin.

I was convinced that before Dustin was locked up he must have been going through the same stuff. He couldn't deal with Outviews and voices, and then drugs complicated his reality-bending fog. For two years he'd been shut away and wasn't even crazy. What had they been doing to him all that time? How much of him was left? Did he still have Outviews or any of the other "problems" that I hadn't been brave enough to share with Kyle, Linh, or even Amber? Tomorrow it was time to tell them everything.

Sam was getting mail from his box. I pulled out my earbuds when he waved.

"Look what I just got in the mail." He ripped open the bubble mailer. "*Blindman.*" He held up the DVD. "1971. Starring Tony Anthony."

"I've always wanted to see that. You know one of the Mexican outlaws is played by Ringo Starr!"

"I know, fresh off the break up of the Beatles, and it's supposed to be a pretty cool movie. Want to borrow it?"

"Yeah, thanks! But you see it first; I won't have a chance until next week sometime. Hey Sam, can I ask you something?"

"Sure." His look reflected confusion in my sudden change of mood.

"Do you believe in reincarnation?"

"Wow." He chuckled. "Little early in the day for such a deep subject."

"Seriously."

"Seriously? Okay. Yes, I think I do."

"Really? Why?"

"Why do people believe in anything beyond this life? Fear. Faith. I don't know. I think there's too much going on in our heads to just have it end when we die. You should read this book, hold on." He ran inside his house.

Great, someone else giving me a book to read, I thought. He jogged back out and handed me the book, *Reincarnation, An East-West Anthology*, edited by Joseph Head and S. L. Cranston.

"Do you remember Mindy?"

"That pretty blond you were dating for a long time?"

"That's right."

"What ever happened to her? I always thought her name was Mandy."

He laughed. "You really can't keep them straight can you? That's funny. She married a chiropractor in Medford last year. But anyway, she was big into reincarnation and said this was a great intro into the topic. This book is a collection of thoughts and writings of well-known people throughout history—scientists, statesmen, theologians, philosophers, and poets. It's definitely enlightening."

"Thanks!"

"Hey, Nate, are you all right? Everything okay?" Sam knew what happened to Dustin, and I could see the concern on his face.

"Yeah. I've been having some strange dreams lately, and then I met this girl at school who's all into reincarnation... "

"You, too, huh?" He gave my back a little shove, laughing.

I laughed, too. In the right circumstances, Sam could have a serious conversation. We'd had some about my dad and Dustin in the past, but this wasn't the time for either of us.

11

ednesday, September 17
W   After school I made the dreaded walk to the Station to meet Amber, Kyle, and Linh. I arrived early to talk with my parents' old friend and partner, Josh. The scents of my child-hood— fresh-baked bread, chocolate and pastries, ground coffee and musty beer on tap—relaxed me. It seemed like Dad was in the back doing inventory, as if he might walk out any minute.

Seventeen years earlier, Dad had been thirty and Mom just twenty-six when they started the place with Josh, who was still at the university then. He'd been their college con-nection ever since, keeping the Station relevant and popular, staying up on the latest music, having a knack for harnessing hip and cool.

"Nate, wow. Six months?" Josh grabbed my arm.

"Yeah, sorry I haven't been around much."

"Jeez, you've grown." He stood back. "I can't get over how much you look like your dad." Only in the last year had he stop sporting a ponytail and kept his beard trimmed close. Jeans, fluorescent tees, and a ball cap from some nearby vine-yard were his uniform. Even at Dad's funeral, he showed up in a faded black pair but substituted a black shirt. "If I was your age, I wouldn't be hanging out at my mom's business either."

"How's it been going anyway?"

"We're busier than ever. Bet you don't see your mom much because she's constantly here putting out one fire or another." He'd always been skinny, but I noticed the beginning of a beer gut or, knowing the desserts at the Station, maybe a cake gut.

"Josh, can we talk about something for a minute, in private?"

"Sure." He motioned for me to follow him. We walked passed Mom's office. She smiled and waved, clearly pleased that I had listened and had come to see Josh.

I closed the door behind me. "When my dad died, you were here with him, right?"

"Yeah," he hesitated.

"Did you find him?"

"Yes, I did."

"Can you tell me about it?"

"Nate, what's going on?"

"I want to know. Please."

"All right. It was early on a Monday morning. I think there were only three or four of us here. Your dad came in from out back and was moving kegs around, then there was a clatter-banging noise. I ran back to see what happened, and there he was, collapsed on the ground. A couple of kegs had tumbled down. One was still rolling. Your dad only lasted another minute or so while I was yelling for someone to call 911."

"Did he say anything?"

Josh got up from his chair and came closer to me, leaning on the edge of the desk.

"No, I mean I don't think he could have. It was a massive heart attack, and he was gasping a little but was already gone. I'm sorry. You know it was just awful."

"Why was he outside? You said just before it happened he came in from out back."

"I don't know. Maybe he was taking some trash out to the dumpster. I never really thought about it." Josh walked over to look at a picture of my parents and him, taken on the opening day of the restaurant. "We were all so young."

I got up to look at the photo I'd seen a million times.

"Was anything strange happening in the weeks or months before he died?"

"What do you mean?" He studied me.

"I don't know what I mean, Josh."

"There was something that always bothered me. Your dad was pretty edgy one day, so I asked what was wrong, and he told me that a very close friend had just died. The strange part, though, was that this old friend was a day away from going public about something and—"

"What was it?" I interrupted.

"He didn't say, just that the guy was going to blow the whistle on some huge corruption or cover-up. He mentioned a name. It was kind of unusual, so I've remembered it. 'Lightyear.' Anyway, he said his friend died of a brain aneurism the night before he was to give testimony or be interviewed by the media or something. You know your dad; he didn't believe in coincidences."

"When was this?"

"About three weeks before your dad died, I guess."

"Did you tell my mom?"

"I didn't see any reason to bother her."

"Didn't you find it strange that his friend died on the eve of blowing the whistle and Dad dies a few weeks later? Maybe Dad was involved, too."

"No, come on, don't turn this into some cloak-and-dagger thing. Your dad wouldn't even take part in a poker game. There was an autopsy; everything was kosher." He saw my expression of concern. "I did do an Internet search on the guy's name, but nothing came up. It was just a coincidence."

"I thought you didn't believe in coincidences."

"No, it was your dad that didn't believe in them. Just because something is strange doesn't mean it's wrong. You know what I mean?"

I didn't know what he meant. Something was wrong.

"Do you remember Dad's friend's name?"

"Sure. Lee Duncan."

"Do me a huge favor? Don't tell my mom we talked about all this. It might upset her."

"Yeah, I've got your back. But listen, she's been worried, and your dad would want me to be here for you. And I am. Is everything cool? You'd tell me, right?"

"Everything's fine."

"Come to me anytime about whatever. I'm not your mom; I'm your friend. Okay?" He patted my shoulder.

"I know." I pointed to the monitors. "My friends are out there. I'm gonna join them."

Mom was still on the phone. Another wave and smile; I was back on her good list.

12

Amber, Kyle, and Linh were filling out music requests for the DJ. The waitress carried them off to a slot in the studio as I joined them.

"So?" Kyle asked.

"Josh said a few weeks before his death, Dad was worried about a close friend who was planning to go public or testify about something big and then died of a brain aneurism the night before."

"It keeps getting weirder," Kyle said. "It's like a conspiracy."

"You have no idea," I said. "You guys are probably wondering what Amber's doing here. She can explain it much better." They both knew who she was, but we'd never hung out. Amber talked for more than ten minutes before anyone else spoke. Kyle and Linh had studied enough Buddhism that they were more open to reincarnation than I was. Our food came, Kyle had a Tracy Chapman, Linh the Pearl Jam, Amber the Adele, and a David Bowie with extra cheese for me.

"I call them Outviews because it's like I go out of myself and see a view of another person, another place... another time."

"How many have you had?" Linh asked.

"Hundreds, I don't know."

"Are they always awful?"

"Pretty much. I die in each one."

"It's like a punishment," Kyle's voice became low, "to have to relive a hundred deaths. Why?" he looked at Amber.

"I've been reading nonstop since Nate told me, and it seems that the most common entry point into a past life is through its death, a kind of backdoor. But with practice, he can get deeper into the lifetime. Eventually he could go to any point in a life and not even need to bother with the end." Amber's light strawberry blonde hair fell below her shoulder, and her cheerleader looks belied her knowledge of the esoteric subject. "There's a ton of research and case histories of people doing just that."

"That sure would be easier because Kyle's right, they do feel like punishment, actually more like torture," I said. "Maybe now you're less likely to think I'm whacked out, so I can tell you everything else that's been happening to me."

"There's more?" Linh asked.

"I was hoping," Amber added.

Kyle rubbed his hands together. "It's a scandal."

"Scandal," I added.

Amber looked confused.

"Don't mind them Amber, they're really a pair of clowns."

"I always liked the circus," she grinned.

"Trust me, this one's not Ringling Brothers; it's more like Dingaling Brothers."

Everyone laughed. Normally I would have tossed one of my fries at Linh, but I didn't want to act so juvenile in front of Amber.

"We're waiting," Amber said.

"I remember feeling different from other kids even before kindergarten. It was as if everyone else knew what to do and how to fit in except me," I began.

"I still feel that way," Linh said.

"But at the same time I used to think that everyone saw and heard what I did. When I figured out they didn't, I was around six or so. That's when it stopped, or I stopped paying attention, and it went away."

"Like what?" Kyle asked, sipping his tea.

"Movement, almost seeing someone in the trees. Shadows moving independently, lights, hard to describe but like little points and trails of light in the woods, the grass, shimmering around people and plants. I don't remember everything, but I can still recall the feeling. It was joyous, magical, like discovering where you left a treasure you'd forgotten about."

"I can just picture you as this cute little kid playing among the fairies," Linh said.

"Then a couple of years ago the premonitions started. At first I hardly noticed them. A thought would flash into my head for no reason at all, like Rick Barnes isn't going to be at school today. Sure enough, he'd stay home sick. I would always look at the phone three seconds before it rang. Or knowing which nights Mom would be home late. Recently though, it's been bigger stuff and farther in advance. About a month ago, a picture of an older woman in the hospital came into my head. It was our neighbor, a crazy artist with about twenty cats. Two weeks ago, an ambulance picked her up. For a while, they weren't sure she was going to live, but I knew she'd be fine because there was an image of her coming home in my head almost a week before. And I see colors around people and—"

"You see auras?" Amber asked.

Kyle was doodling on a napkin, only his doodles always looked like they should be framed.

"An aura is your psychic energy body," Amber explained. "Edgar Cayce, a famous psychic, called it the weathervane of your soul. It's like a halo that surrounds your whole body. Everyone has one, even nonliving things."

"They're in motion and change colors. Sometimes… " I stopped as the waitress came over, "they're an inch thick but they grow and contract so they can be like two feet in places."

Then I told them about the pops and the shapeshifting. It was a lot to take in, and for me too, hearing it all at once.

"Anything else? Can you read minds? Time travel?" Kyle demanded, smiling.

"Nothing really useful like that." I said.

"Give yourself some time, Nate," Amber said. "You don't know what you're capable of yet. You're awesome."

I caught Kyle and Linh exchanging a look; they didn't seem convinced.

"It's not like I'm a comic book superhero. I just want to know why this is happening to me. Why not you, Kyle, with all your meditating and quantum physics? Or you, Amber, with your million new age books and palm reading?"

"I don't read palms."

"You know what I mean."

"You can develop all these abilities into something so powerful," Amber said.

"I think he'd be happy to just have the Outviews stop," Linh said.

"Why would he want them to stop?" Amber was shocked.

"They're not fun!" Kyle shot back.

"Let's talk about Lee Duncan and Lightyear," I said, trying to change the subject.

"It's exhausting being your friend, Nate." Kyle had a strangely amused yet serious look.

Mom stopped by and scooped up the check the waitress had left. Everyone thanked her. She scoffed. "You kids come as often as you want. Nate's friends are always welcome. Besides, we've got out-of-towners who eat here more often than my own son." She was smiling, but I still felt the zing. Mom called a server over with a tray of desserts and wouldn't take no for an answer. It'd been a long time since I tasted a Vanilla Waterfall and missed them. Amber and Linh split a Sunrise Cake Sunset, and Kyle had the Mint Happiness.

Once Mom was safely back in the employee area, I told them everything Josh said. We explored possible explanations, but with the timing of Lee Duncan's unexpected death, his telling my dad secrets before he also suddenly died along with everyone else in the world with his name, it was extremely suspicious. Fifty minutes later, we walked out of the Station very tired and each convinced that my father had probably been murdered.

13

Just as Josh had said, nothing useful came up when we searched Lee Duncan, even when adding the word Lightyear. Kyle suggested I meditate on them, but nothing happened. "Patience," he said, more than once.

Maybe I wanted to alleviate my guilt of being responsible for my dad's death, but there were too many coincidences. Obviously, someone killed him and Lee Duncan to silence them. The facts that he died with people around who apparently didn't see anything unusual and the autopsy confirmed cause of death as a massive heart attack made me feel like a crazy conspiracy theorist. But I was getting used to being crazy, so I decided to figure out what Lightyear was and learn more about Lee Duncan.

I started meditating four times daily, in the morning, before bed and two other times whenever it could be worked in. Amber suggested calling on my guides. She said we all have them, but most people use the name guardian angels. Some think they are dead friends and relatives, but Amber thought it was deeper than that. Apparently, entities from another dimension are able to help us. Amber was hitting me with so much information that it occurred to me that "New Age Mayes" might be a little nuts herself, but at this point I didn't have any other great options. Besides, for the first time in years, something felt right. Finally, who I was started to make sense.

Later, while bringing our trashcan in from the curb, I saw Sam again. He walked across and asked if I'd read the reincarnation book. "I skimmed it but haven't gotten into it yet." "I know how much you like history. You may be surprised to know how many famous people believed in reincarnation. Benjamin Franklin, Napoleon, Gandhi, General Patton, Thoreau, Socrates, Henry Ford, on and on."

"I had no idea."

"You're not alone. You're not crazy. For some reason you're able to see something most of us can't."

In the middle of the night I woke to whirling stars and the spinning trees. When had I fallen asleep? When had I woken? Was I awake? Nothing mattered. I was going again. Amber's sparkling eyes shined across times that I did not remember I had forgotten. The Outviews were a familiar strangeness now, and the distant screams that always accompanied them had taken on a musical quality. This one was the first time I knew someone going into it. Where was I going and could I stop? Would I get back? That was the question that terrified me most: what if I just didn't come back to this lifetime?

14

Thursday, September 18

Third period was English with weaselly Mr. James, who held the distinction of being the least favorite teacher of my entire school career. What are the odds that Dustin sat in the same chair and also had him during third period, two years earlier? Most of the time Mr. James called me Dustin, but he said it almost like "Dis-gus-tin." He would call on me only when he was sure I couldn't answer, like that day. "Dustin, in the *Adventures of Huckleberry Finn*, Huck uses several aliases. Will you please tell me one of them?"

There had been no time to read this when Kyle expected me to consume Thich Nhat Hanh, Amber had four books she said must be read, and then there was the book from Sam. "It's Nathan, Mr. James, and I—"

He cut me off, "Incorrect Mr. Ryder, Huck Finn did not use Nathan as an alias. Who can tell Dustin the right answer?" And I thought I was crazy.

Luckily fourth-period history was my favorite subject with the best teacher, Mr. Anderson. He had a way of making history cool and exciting, not like some boring stuff that already happened. He showed us how events, even thousands of years ago, not only affected us today but were similar to current events. "The same things keep happening again and again," he'd always say. "It takes humans a very long time to learn." He was my youngest teacher—I'm sure he wasn't thirty yet. Sometimes I'd miss lunch because he and I would get into a long conversation about the Vikings or the American Revolutionary War. Kyle told me I was Mr. A's favorite student.

I was leaving the cafeteria to head for fifth-period French class when Mrs. Little stopped me in the hall. "Nathan, there's some testing I'd like you to come in for next week."

"Is it required?"

"What does that mean?"

"Is it voluntary or mandatory?"

"It's something I think could give us some insight... something that would benefit you."

"No, thanks."

"What does that mean?" For a high school guidance counselor, she sure had a hard time understanding high school kids.

I gave her my best incredulous look. "I'm not interested in your test."

"You don't understand. This isn't anything that would affect your grades. I'm simply recommending—"

"I'm going to be late for French." I moved away, enjoying her exasperated look.

After school, I again searched unsuccessfully for Lee Duncan online. It was time to see if anything in my dad's stuff might help. A dream the night before showed an image of his desk. It whispered something just before a huge red wrecking ball completely demolished. It had to be a message, I thought. There must be something in there that can help me.

A few years before, Mom had cleared out a lot of his things but pretty much ignored the study, a small room off their bedroom still stacked with books and papers. His desk was more like a dresser but the slanted top folded down. I searched for a while, finding nothing of interest until a thought popped into my head to look behind the small drawers that held paper clips and rubber bands. There seemed to be too much space between them and the back of the desk. My fingers touched a tiny metal circle in the wood that I couldn't see from the front. I pushed it and a false panel swung open. It was a small cavity, maybe big enough for a paperback book.

Pulling out my discovery, four small pieces of gray stationery written in my dad's handwriting. Three were in some sort of foreign language. The fourth was a list of names I didn't recognize except for Lee Duncan. I was ecstatic, like Sherlock Holmes. There was also a very small gold box with jade inlaid circle and diamond patterns, about the size of a matchbox car but light and obviously hollow, but no latch or any way to open it. The final item was an intricately carved piece of tube-shaped dark wood maybe three inches long. Knowing Dad had hidden these items, it was as if we were unraveling the mystery together.

I carefully closed the secret space, neatened his desk and took the treasures with me. Even after rummaging through the rest of the room, the garage, closets, nothing else surfaced. It was impossible to get the box open without destroying it so I decided to wait and see if Kyle had any ideas about what the objects were or how to decipher the papers.

Kyle called as I was finishing the search.

"Good timing, I said. " Wait until you see what—"

"I'm in your driveway," he interrupted obviously agitated. "We need to talk right now." I ran down. He was backing onto the street before I'd even closed the car door.

"What's wrong?" I asked.

"I'll show you in a minute."

"Can't you just tell me now?"

"No. I need to show you." A minute later we were pulling into a parking space next to one of the bridges leading into Lithia Park. Once in the trees, Kyle stopped walking and put his hands on my shoulders. "This is getting scary, Nate."

"What are you talking about?"

"Some old Spanish woman came up to me and said she had a message for you."

"What woman? When?"

"About twenty minutes ago. I don't know who she is. I was about to get into my car in front of my house, and this old woman walks up all friendly and says, 'Hello Kyle, my name is Amparo. You don't know me, but I have a message for you from someone who wants to help you and Nate.' She looked, you know, friendly enough, and it's broad daylight. With all this crazy stuff going down, it didn't seem so weird even though I knew it was."

"What did she say?"

"That we're in danger, serious danger."

"Hold on. Tell me *exactly* what she said."

"Her name was Amparo. She was delivering a message from a guy who knew your father and Lee Duncan for like twenty years; they'd been very close. He needed to warn us about the serious danger we're in and wanted to explain some extremely important things to you, including the truth about your dad's death."

"All right, I'm sorry, but doesn't this sound creepy?"

"Of course it does, but so does everything lately. She said to meet the guy in Brookings on Sunday at Tea Leaf Beach at the first low tide, and he'd be waiting for you."

"Meet him? How do we know this Brookings guy isn't the one who wants to hurt us? How did they find us? How do we know we can believe them?"

"She said you would ask those questions, and I'm supposed to tell you that the person who sent her can tell you why Brett shot Wesley."

"Jesus!" I choked. I hadn't told anyone about that Outview. I leaned against a tree wrestling with fear and amazement.

"Who are Brett and Wesley?" Kyle demanded.

"Do you remember last July when you found me on the ground in my backyard?"

"Of course."

"Well, it wasn't the post that knocked me out. I'd had an Outview, and in that lifetime I was Wesley and a guy named Brett shot me."

"You mean you actually physically feel what happens to you in a past life?"

"Yeah, it's not as severe, but it's still real."

"Incredible." His eyes deepened and at the same time were distant.

"Sometimes I think crazy might be a better alternative."

"Maybe we shouldn't rule that out yet." He sat on the ground and fumbled with his pack of cigarettes. "What do you think?"

"No one on the planet knew about Brett and Wesley. I mean how could he possibly even know those names?"

"This Amparo was really old, like a sweet great-grandmother, not the type to send us into a trap."

"But it could be trap," I said.

"Why? Who would want to?"

"The same people who killed Duncan and my dad."

"If someone wanted you dead, why couldn't they just do it here. Why Brookings?"

"I know, right. And if he knew about Wesley and Brett, then something wild is going on. I want to know I'm not crazy and if my dad was murdered. I have to meet him. It's riskier not to."

"Yeah, but then what? We have to come home sometime. We have school on Monday."

"Kyle, don't you think school is the least of our worries?"

"Maybe yours, but I need a perfect GPA to get into MIT."

"MIT doesn't admit dead students."

"Don't get carried away!"

"Kyle, listen, all the dead Montgomery Ryders, Lee Duncan confiding in Dad and dying the next day, now this old lady shows up to set a clandestine rendezvous with some mysterious mind reader... *and* I found two strange objects and hidden papers concealed behind a *secret* panel in my Dad's desk, one of them with Lee Duncan's name. I mean, it's like we've fallen into a Hitchcock movie."

"I know. Add all that to New Age Mayes' theories of your past lives, you and Dustin seeing and hearing whatever it is you do, and I think it's more like the *Twilight Zone*."

"Welcome to my world! You can check out any time you like, but you can never leave."

"Huh?"

"It's from an old Eagles song... Never mind, I always forget you and modern music aren't acquainted. But I could use your other considerable mental talents to help me figure out the stuff from my dad's desk. It's all codes and symbols, pretty weird."

"Of course it is," he forced a laugh. "We'll look at them on the trip."

"You think we should be scared?"

"I didn't before Amparo showed up. Oh, she also warned that anything we say on our phones can be heard and our online activity is being monitored. She said not to travel with our cell phones or computers."

"It sure as hell sounds like we should be scared!"

15

Later that night, I was home packing a backpack, including the objects and papers from Dad's desk. A bad feeling that I might not return came over me. It was probably a combination of the Amparo woman showing up and the concept of my dad and his friend being killed by some mysterious person powerful enough to make their deaths appear accidental. I looked around at my favorite photos, books on great photographers, and fiddled with a few of my old matchbox cars that lined my bookshelves. The sense of doom worsened, so I meditated.

A sudden knock at the front door jolted me, and I carefully peered out the window. Amber's turquoise bug was parked next to my dad's old Toyota silver 4x4 pickup truck. Mom had saved it for Dustin, who had driven it for one day before his suicide run to Shasta. I used to think she was keeping it for when he got out, but now it seemed more likely she was saving it for me, if she ever let me get my license. But I was determined to see Dustin drive it again.

"I'm glad you stopped by. Can we go for a drive?"

"Sure." She smiled. Amber was wearing a purple tank top and white shorts, thin leather sandals. She must know how distracting her looks were.

I told her about the message from the guy in Brookings. We forgot about a drive and just sat there talking. She listened to the whole story, the concern on her face clear. "Oh, Nate," she finally said, casually putting her hand on my thigh. "It's exciting and scary at the same time!"

"Yeah, I don't know what's going on."

"But maybe after seeing Dustin and the Brookings guy, the mysteries will unravel."

"Or get deeper."

"Think positive."

"I'll try, but just in case, I want you to know the meeting is at the first low tide on Sunday at Tea Leaf Beach in Brookings. You're the only one I'm telling." I fidgeted with the beads hanging from her rearview mirror.

"I've never heard of Tea Leaf, and I've been going to Brookings forever."

"Well, if someone's trying to set a trap, why wouldn't he just grab me here. I'm not hiding. And he knew about that Outview."

"I know; that's so amazing."

"Frightening is more like it, that someone's been inside my head."

"Maybe he wasn't in your head. Maybe he's from that lifetime."

"Great, maybe Brett's come back to finish me off. Not only is there danger in this lifetime, but people are traveling through time to kill me."

"I doubt it. I just know it's someone trying to help you. I can't wait to find out. Do you want to stay at our beach house?"

"Could we?"

"Yeah, no one's there." She told me where the key was hidden.

"I wish you could come."

"Me, too, but my mother gets back tomorrow for a long weekend of 'quality time.' It's a joke; my mother's only close to her make-up mirror. But my sister will be home, too."

"I had another Outview today." I waited until her eyes found mine. "You were in it."

"Really?" She couldn't hide her pleasure. "When was it? Where was it?"

"We were sisters. It was at least a hundred years ago because you were driving a horse-drawn wagon. I was lying in the back in dirty blankets and straw, cold. But there were wildflowers. You spoke in a language that sounded German, but I don't think it was. My body was brittle on the rough road, like a vase rattling in a crate, and I begged you to stop."

"You were dying?"

"Yeah, like always. You started crying when you finally stopped the wagon."

"How old were we?"

"Hard to say. We looked sixty, but I think we were really thirty-something. So you were crying because you knew we weren't going to get any help. Even if we did, it was too late. You could tell I'd be dead very soon."

"Tell me about the way an Outview comes to you. How do you see it?"

"It's almost like watching a movie, but the screen has no defined shape. And only pieces are in focus as I look at them. Sometimes just part of a face is clear, but what I can see is in 3D. I'm like an observer floating right there, but at the same time I'm one of the participants, experiencing and feeling everything they do."

"Like a dream."

"But with actual physical pain."

Her face saddened.

"They're so real, like I'm there but pressure from all the years between pushes away everything that isn't in my immediate view. But lately, the area in focus has been getting larger."

"How did you know it was me?"

"That's what's cool about this one. I saw your eyes going into it and knew you'd be there. That's never happened before. But it's hard to explain, a recognition in the eyes."

"Have you ever seen anyone else you know?"

"Mom, Dustin, and Kyle at various times."

"What happened next?"

"An agonized tragic scream from you as I died." Amber reached over, put her arms around me, and pulled me close, her wet tears on my cheek, the warmth of her breath in my nose, the slight fragrance of apples as we melted together, embracing sisters across a century of absence. I know we stayed like that for several minutes, and when we fell back to this time Amber was staring into my eyes through blurry tears. She gave me the softest kiss, our lips touching like the brush of a feather. We sat in the car for a while longer, not in an awkward way, just warm silence. "I should go," I said, getting out, surprised how drained I was.

"Promise you'll call me from Brookings."

"If not before." I leaned into the window a moment, then turned and jogged to my house.

Later, I walked over to Sam's. "You have to watch *Blindman* tonight. It's great!" He handed it to me once we were inside.

"I won't have time until next week. I'm leaving early in the morning on a camping trip. That's why I came over, to tell you I won't get to your lawn again until Monday after school."

"Great weather for camping! Where you headed?"

"Me and a few friends are going to Crater Lake."

"I love it there. Forget the grass. It'll be here."

"Thanks. Hey, could I ask something without you thinking I'm crazy."

"Try me."

"The reason I wanted to know what you thought about reincarnation is because I keep seeing visions of what I think are past lives I've had, and it's almost like I'm there. They happen a lot, and I'm afraid I could be losing it."

"You're not crazy Nate. You're about one of the most well-adjusted kids I've ever met, mature, responsible, great taste in films." He tapped the copy of *Blindman* I was still holding. If you're having visions like that, you should explore them, maybe keep a journal. Have you talked to your mother about them?"

"No. I don't like how she handled things with Dustin. That's why I wanted to ask you. I've told a couple of close friends, but I'd like an adult's point of view. And, well, you've been all over the world and dated Cindy, who was really into reincarnation."

"Mindy," he corrected, smiling. "It's not as unusual as you think. In fact, in India and that part of the world, it's pretty common. In Tibet, they believe every Dalai Lama over the last seven hundred years has been the same soul reincarnated, each being an incarnation of the last. That way they retain the spiritual wisdom acquired over all those lifetimes. If you thought you were the Dalai Lama, I might wonder, but seeing pieces of prior lives is fascinating. Write it all down. What a cool movie it would make: teenager relives past lives." A great weight lifted as Sam spoke. He was a successful adult and talked like what was happening was normal. We spoke for another half hour, and he even gave me Mindy's number in case I wanted to talk to someone else.

*F**riday, September 19*

*F*riday, September 19
By the time the sun made an appearance, we had Kyle's car packed with sleeping bags, tent, piles of schoolbooks, three backpacks, two iPods, and a jammed cooler. Mom was still asleep when we left. Kyle and I reluctantly left our phones, but Linh brought hers in case something went wrong but kept the power off. She rode shotgun, while I worked on meditating in the back seat.

Each time my mind got close to clarity, the depths of my situation obliterated it. How could we get Dustin out? My dad hadn't died of a heart attack; he'd been murdered and his killers might be after me. Clear, clear, clear. What is happening—the pops, auras, paranormal visions, voices, and shapeshifting? Focus, focus, focus. All at once there was a shift and control. I was unprepared for the calm, a feeling of vanishing into the universe yet being connected to everything. It's hard to say how long that state lasted, probably no more than ten minutes. Next, a voice spoke like the ones I'd been hearing for so long, but it was clearer and saying more than one word, much more. It was like hearing three voices at once, with the words condensed so four words came in the space of one. Surprisingly, it was easy to understand, and what it said was almost too fantastic to believe.

"Where were you?" Linh asked.

"How long was I gone?"

"Almost half an hour," she said.

"That was a good meditation," Kyle said slowly, unlit cigarette dangling from his mouth.

"Do you ever hear voices when you meditate?" I asked.

"Sure."

"But like a bunch, all talking at the same time, and you're able to hear everything?"

"No, that sounds like a Nate original. What did they say?" he asked deliberately.

"They said I could do anything."

"Sounds like my uncle," Kyle eyed Linh.

"Yeah, but they meant stuff we think is impossible. If I remember my soul, the universe will be there and all human limitations will vanish."

"Do you have to die for that to happen?" Linh asked.

"They said there are many things coming and that I must be ready." I sounded possessed, and wondered if they believed me.

"Go on," Kyle urged.

"They said I needed to be ready to face evil."

Kyle's eyes widened. "Then let's get someone to buy us beer."

"I'm serious," I said.

"So am I."

"No, you're not," Linh said. "I believe you *heard* it, Nate."

I couldn't tell if she meant she believed it happened or just that I thought it did.

"I believe you, too," Kyle said. "I'm just not ready to fight off Hannibal Lecter this weekend."

"I wish I could explain how it feels to know something so bizarre with absolute certainty. On an incredibly deep level I know it's all true, and I'm not just worried, I'm terrified."

"These will help." Linh tossed me a pack of almond M&M's.

"That, some Twizzlers, and a Coke will almost have the same effect as beer," Kyle said.

Everyone laughed.

I passed the stuff from my Dad's desk around, but beyond a cursory glance, Kyle couldn't really focus on them because he was driving, and Linh was as baffled as I.

A state trooper passed us. Linh put her hand on Kyle's shoulder. For the next mile or two, he checked the rearview mirror compulsively. We were riding through thick forest now. Linh commented on the beauty of the trees. I knew she was still trying to lighten the mood, but it was my topic and I took the bait.

"Do you know what the world's largest, oldest and tallest living things are?"

"Haven't you told us this before?" Kyle's quizzical eyes narrowed.

"I haven't heard it," Linh said.

"Trees," Kyle said.

"It's no surprise the tallest living thing is a tree, a *sequoia sempervirens*, better known as a coastal redwood not far from here in northern California. Its name is Hyperion."

"It has a name?"

"Most of the tallest trees do. They're important. But the largest living thing is a grove of aspens in Utah called Pando. They count as one thing because all the trees in the stand are connected by a single underground root system. Pando covers over a hundred acres and is probably eighty thousand years old. Some say it could be much older because when one tree dies, others grow up out of the same roots."

"So that's the oldest?"

"Not technically because each individual tree only lives like a hundred thirty years. The oldest single tree is a bristle cone pine called Methuselah, also in California. It's almost five thousand years old."

"Wow!" Linh said.

"There was an even older one in Nevada named Prometheus, but some grad student cut it down in 1964 to find out how old it was."

"You're kidding!" Linh said. "Was he arrested or anything?"

"No. There are different accounts of whether he actually knew what he was doing but... I mean it's really a crime what we do to trees. The cure for all our diseases is probably in the rainforests, but we may never know."

"It's sad," Linh shook her head.

It was just after eight a.m. when we arrived. I'd been to Crater Lake before, but something was different this time. The glassy indigo water reflecting cotton clouds and two thousand foot volcanic cliffs disoriented me. Only the pines, firs, hemlocks, and the solitary Wizard Island rising out of the incredibly deep lake kept me from falling down. Gravity also helped. It was cooler because the elevation was over a mile higher than Ashland, and, although it was a beautiful day, it smelled like snow as always because the lake was filled almost entirely by snowmelt. The silence sounded like meditation, but slowly I began to hear a rush of water, lava, and steam. It grew so loud that I screamed to Linh and Kyle, "What's that noise?"

"What noise?" Kyle asked, just mouthing words because I could hear nothing above the roar, which increased to the point I believed the lake might erupt. A shimmering ripple crossed the surface of the water, then instantly, complete silence. A tall, Indian-looking old man emerged from the trees, scruffy, leathery, long, thin, tangled gray hair, light gray pants and white shirt faded and worn.

"You boy, you shouldn't be here."

"Excuse me?" Kyle answered.

"Not talking to you. It's that one." He waved a spindly finger at me. "He shouldn't be here yet."

"Why not?"

"You're not ready to be *here*. You've not studied; you've not practiced. You ain't even awake yet."

"I think you're confused," Kyle said gently.

"Confused? I'm way beyond confused, but you're not even up to confused yet, so maybe you should mind your own business." The old man wasn't aggressive or threatening, but he didn't look like he was going to leave. I was uncomfortable, but at the same time he was magnetic, like a bristly, cranky old college professor adored by his students because of his sheer brilliance.

"Look, could you just please leave us alone?" Kyle tried once more.

"There are three of you, so even if I did leave, you wouldn't be alone. I belong here, so I'll not be leaving." He threw a stick at me. "What about you, Nathan?" Linh gasped, and Kyle looked at me with stunned concern.

"How do you know my name? Who are you?"

"If you were supposed to be here, you would know my name already. I'm the Old Man of the Lake."

"Okay, old man, how do you know his name?" Kyle asked.

"Listen to me. I'm not just some old man; I'm *the* Old Man of the Lake. And I already told you to mind your own business, Dac." He called Kyle by his Vietnamese name, which almost no one knew.

"Seriously, who are you?" Kyle was looking around, worried. I was scanning the area as well, remembering Amparo's warning that we were in danger.

"Could you just tell us who you are and how you know our names?" I asked.

"Nathan Ryder, everyone knows your name, just not yet." We stared at him. He looked straight at me.

Linh broke the silence, "Do you want us to leave?"

"Doesn't matter what I want. He just ain't going to understand this place yet."

"Would you explain it to me?" I asked.

"Sure thing, Nayyy-thonn, then I'll teach you about the origin of the universe, how to walk on water, and the trick to time travel." More silence. Linh took a picture of him.

"Don't do that," he said firmly. Linh put her camera away.

"Why don't you want me here? I need to know. Please, will you help me?"

"See where you are," he said, waving his arm in a circle over his head. I gazed out at the lake. "Not with your eyes. See it, don't look at it." I stared back at him. "You're just too early to understand." His expression softened, but not by much.

"I'm sixteen, I don't understand any of this."

"Because you think you're sixteen. You believe that. Too bad, because you're not."

"How old am I then?"

"How old are you? How old am I? How old is the sky? Why don't you ask me a question that is important to know right now?"

"Like?"

"Why am I here," he offered.

"Okay, why are you here?"

"You boy, not me. I know why I'm here. You're here because this is one of the great earth vortexes."

"An earth vortex?"

"A portal. A crossroads of multi-dimensional fields. It occurs here."

"What does?"

"So much."

"What do you mean?"

"You're not ready, boy. Come back when you are. Come back in a week." He tossed something at me. As I caught it, I looked up at the old man, but he was gone. In my hand was an almost black but tinted blue stone, smooth and round, a little smaller than a poker chip and nearly as thin. Kyle and Linh were looking for the old man.

I showed them the stone. "It's from the bottom of the lake," I said.

"How do you know?" Linh asked.

"I don't know, but I do."

"Where did he go?" Kyle looked around.

Hastily, we got back to the car all weirded out and shaken by the encounter. It was their first experience of something unexplainable. No one wanted to talk about it. A couple of minutes later, we found the next overlook along the rim road. Linh read from a guidebook she'd borrowed. "'At 1949 feet, Crater Lake is the deepest lake in North America. But if you go by average depth, it is actually the deepest in the world that is entirely above sea level.'"

I wasn't paying attention. I was still thinking about the old man and wondering what a vortex was while considering the possibilities of a multidimensional portal.

Linh read, "'The lake was formed by the cataclysmic eruption of Mount Mazama in about 5680 BC. Geologists estimate the mountain was 12,000 feet high when the top 5,000 feet of it blew into the sky in one massive blast of rock and earth.'"

"It's enormous," Kyle said, looking out over the lake.

"No rivers or streams flow in or out of it," Linh said. "It's probably the purest water on the continent. They've found plants photosynthesizing three hundred fifty feet down."

"Yeah, even from here I can see down pretty far into the water," Kyle said. "But where does that unreal blue color come from?"

"Listen to this!" Linh said, looking up from her book. "'One of the most fascinating mysteries of Crater Lake is a floating tree trunk. This remarkable ancient hemlock has been bobbing, absolutely vertical, for as long as Crater Lake has been documented. Its earliest known reference is from 1896, and it was first photographed in 1902.' It's like an iceberg, hiding most of its bulk beneath the surface; those who get close to it can see some thirty feet down into the depths of the lake. This is so amazing; it's completely straight as if it's growing right out of the lake."

I wasn't sure what the big deal was until she added that it was called, "The Old Man of the Lake."

"Let me see," I said. The picture showed a bleached gray and white tree trunk sticking four or five feet out of impossibly blue water. The reflection was perfect but also visible was a branchless tree towering deep below the surface. "It's him," I whispered.

"Okay, now I'm starting to think you *are* crazy," Kyle jabbed me.

"Come on, you saw him, we all saw him. It wasn't just me this time, right? He came out of nowhere and disappeared right back into the trees," I challenged.

"So?" Kyle volleyed.

"He gave me this stone, see it looks like the lake, same shape and color. He said this place is like a door to other dimensions."

"Kyle, he knew your real name," Linh shot back.

"I know," he conceded.

"Wait, I took his picture," Linh said. She fumbled with her camera. "Guys, you won't believe this." The shot showed me on one side but where the old man had been standing there was nothing, only trees behind where he had been. "He was there when I snapped it, I saw him in the screen, I swear," Linh said. Even Kyle believed her. The angle of the shot would have made it impossible for him to have not been in the picture.

I read, "'It's a mystery how the Old Man of the Lake floats upright, freely traveling over the entire twenty square miles of the lake, sometimes at great speeds. Once rangers recorded it moving almost four miles between dusk and dawn. Some think it is the guardian of the waters.' Listen to this; 'In 1988, when scientists were exploring the lake by submarine, they decided the floating trunk could be a dangerous hazard, so the Old Man was tethered where they found him on the east side of Wizard Island. Restricting the Old Man's freedom had immediate repercussions. A storm quickly descended upon the lake and only subsided after the Old Man had broken away from its anchor and was able to glide the lake once again.'"

I took another look at the photo in the book and then handed it back to Linh. "He's the ultimate shapeshifter."

18

We continued around the rim road, stopped at a few more overlooks where I snapped some nice shots of the scenic lake, ate lunch at the pinnacles surrounded by towering pumice swords rising from the mist, and took more photos. Mom had sent delicious sandwiches and desserts from the Station, prepackaged party assortments grouped as: Grammy Winners, Solo Artists, Number Ones, and Girl Bands. For us, she sent their largest called Rock and Roll Hall of Fame, with all the sandwiches named after inductees.

I pulled out the gold box and carved wood again and handed them to Kyle, then gave four small pages to Linh.

"I agree with you. If this box was solid it would be much heavier," Kyle said, "but I can't see how to open it."

"It's gotta be those jade inlaid designs."

"I think you're right. If it opens, that pattern is the way."

"What about the carved wood?" I asked.

"It's almost like a language, and there are ten words," Kyle said. "The rest of it is just pretty flowers or vines for decoration, I think."

Linh had been studying the writing on one of the four sheets. She read the list of names out loud. "There are nine names, but one of them is the word 'you.' Your dad wrote these, right?"

"Could it be for you, Nate? Are you the 'you' on the list?" Kyle asked.

"I have no idea who he wrote it for."

The other three sheets were no help. Although they appeared to be just gibberish, Kyle was positive they were really English written in a kind of scrambled code. We weren't able to decipher anything.

Driving again, eager to get to our campsite still a couple of hours away, I detailed several recent Outviews.

"Do you think we've all died in such horrible ways like you have in all your Outviews?" Linh's voice was thin.

"The world's been a rough place for most of its history. Even in the last hundred years when we've supposedly been our most civilized, more than two hundred million people have died in wars, genocide, or man-made disasters. Brutal diseases have taken millions more, auto accidents, fires… life is hard," I said.

The campground stretched along the southern bank of the Umpqua River where lichen-draped cedar, Douglas fir, and deciduous trees provided a dense canopy. That, combined with the thick understory of fern and thimbleberries, gave the area a lush, semitropical feel. We found an ideal site atop a slight rise on the bank of the river. The rapids were loud and frothy. Linh thought our site was too close, but Kyle and I convinced her it was fine.

A guy selling fruit boxes of firewood walked up while we finished setting up the tent. It was the Old Man! Kyle and Linh actually backed up a little.

"You're the Old Man!"

"And you're a young kid. Need some wood?"

"Don't you remember us?" Linh asked.

"Yeah, I think I saw you on the trail somewhere."

I dug the blue stone out of my pocket. "Remember this?"

"I do," with a glint in his eye, "but you're still too early."

"What happened to you before? Where'd you go?"

"Had business to tend to."

"Are you really the floating tree?" Linh blurted out.

"You know my people, the Klamath tribe, witnessed the eruption and were here at the formation of the lake. It's a sacred site. We still use Crater Lake in vision quests. Our war-riors climb the caldera walls, as they have for centuries, and dive from the high cliffs. The strongest and bravest are re-vealed to have extraordinary spiritual powers."

"Will you tell me about the lake being a portal?" I asked.

He considered me for a moment. "The legends say that ancestors come and go from there and that the living can sometimes find a way through if they are pure of heart and reasons for the voyage are good."

"It sounds hard to believe," Kyle said.

"This river, these trees, and the great blue lake have taught me there is nothing I should not believe. Everything happens in cycles, over and over again."

"You sound like my history teacher," I said.

"School teachers are wise in the world of what can be seen, but that's only a tiny stream that flows into the river of what really is." He moved his arm away while wiggling his fingers.

"I think I know what you mean," I said.

"There is ten thousand times more in the invisible world, more that we don't understand than what we do. It's all around us, and we are too busy to see. Most of my people have forgotten the way, lost the ability to see beyond the mate-rial world. The whites lost their way many generations before they even found this continent."

"I'm trying to figure it out," I said.

"I see things written on your face; your struggles are just beginning, boy."

"That's not real encouraging." It was similar to what the guide told me during my meditation in the car. "What do you see?" Up close, his face suddenly seemed even older than when we first met.

He studied me again. "Great learning. You will begin to swallow knowledge. That is something I've not seen until you. You'll find lost spirit dances. But be cautious, boy, there's darkness waiting, a very strong force that will stop you if it can." His face contorted into despair. "There is a tiny hope, maybe even a chance, you could fight past this battle."

"Nate!" Linh gasped. A week ago what he was saying would have seemed like the ramblings of a madman, but with each passing word his message resonated deeper within me.

"What should I do?"

"There are many who will help you. You're not alone. Some will appear real, but remember, the ones you can't see can help the most. They are around you now."

"You can see them?" Kyle asked.

"I don't have to. They are there."

He was looking at his old truck full of boxes and scanning for the next tent. I could tell he wanted to go.

"Thanks" was all I could think to say.

"And Nathan, you are going to buy a box, aren't you?" he asked.

I gave him four dollars.

"You asked me what you should do. You need to remember. And once you do, think of the lessons from your previous conflicts. Sometimes it is the Great Spirit who pushes you, or earth guides, but in any kind of battle, strategy is not to be overlooked."

He handed me the box of wood.

"Thanks, Old Man." Our eyes met briefly before he turned. Strategy, I thought, would be a good thing to think about. While watching him make his way to the next campsite, I hoped we'd meet again.

"Wow!" Linh said.

"Strange dude," Kyle said, "but not a floating tree."

"I don't know," I said softly.

Kyle rolled his eyes.

We had started to build the fire when I spotted a huge bull with gray horns. "Look at that bull coming at us!"

"Where?" Linh shrieked in alarm.

Kyle scanned the trees casually. "It's not real, is it?" He held out his arms and lowered them, looking from side to side. "Let's not attract attention."

He was right; it was gone. "It's just the roots of that fallen tree," I said, pointing. "That's how the shapeshifting happens." Two raccoons appeared from behind it. "Do you guys see those?" I asked quietly.

"Yeah, but they're not flying or anything," Kyle joked. "Ever hear about the boy who cried wolf?"

"I know. I'm a mess," I said, looking at the ground feeling sorry for myself.

"Don't worry." Linh hugged me. "I'm good at cleaning up messes."

Dinner was around the campfire, eating more great food from the Station.

"I just don't understand how the Old Man disappeared, how he wasn't in the photo. None of it makes sense," Linh said.

"A taste of what I deal with daily," I said, adding wood to the fire. It was getting cold and dark. Stars glittered.

Kyle heated up some water and squeezed in a couple of lemons. "To best friends and the hope that our journey is good," he said. We all touched metal cups. "And now, you meditate." He pointed at me. Kyle and I went off to find spots. Linh stayed by the fire, writing in her journal. I found a friendly feeling fir and sat on its bed of needles, cleared my mind fairly easily, and was still for half an hour. The moment I came out of my meditation, Linh looked up from her journal and smiled at me.

Any meaning held in the things from Dad's desk still eluded us. Just before dark we laid out our sleeping bags in the tent, with Linh between Kyle and me. She always smelled of lavender, and I enjoyed being next to her. We talked briefly about our plan for the morning. The river's mesmerizing churning took us quickly to sleep. My final thoughts were wishing Amber had been able to come with us.

B eams of light broke through the night. Snapping twigs and voices—someone was coming. I slid out of my bag and un-zipped the tent flap. Figures were weaving among the trees, but it was hard to know how many. They were getting closer. I slipped on my shoes, leaving Linh and Kyle asleep. The fire was just a cluster of glowing coals, but there was a moon and I could be seen. A light crossed my face and one yelled, "There he is!" I took off, looking for cover in the foliage and hoping they would follow and leave my friends alone. The river was louder and more violent than before. I sprinted along the now high and steep bank. Bullets ricocheted off the trees ahead, my adrenaline surged. They were trying to kill me; they were going to kill me.

Dogs barked. "How did they find me? Where can I go?" The river was raging, lights flashed all around, and heavy steps pounded through leaves. I dashed into the dense forest and left the thundering water behind. I was trying to dodge trees, but branches and undergrowth whipped and slashed my face and body. Backtracking toward the tent, I looked back more than ahead. Suddenly a tree limb smacked my shoulder hard and knocked me off my feet. I landed on an elbow but somehow didn't yell out in pain; instead I laid on the ground, catching my breath and tried to figure out where I was and where they were. The dogs were louder.

I ran again, wanting to reach Kyle and Linh and the car. A crushing blow slammed into my waist from what felt like a two-by-four. "You thought you could escape?" he spit.

I was unable to move and could only see his silhouette. "Who are you?"

He laughed. "You're full of surprises. Too bad you've forgotten the name of the man who is going to kill you." He raised a rifle, put it to my forehead, and pulled the trigger.

I heard Kyle yelling, "Linh, over here." A noise had woken them, and they discovered I wasn't in the tent. It took ten minutes to find me. "Are you hurt?"

"I thought I was dead. He shot me." My head felt split in half.

"You've been shot? Where? Should I get help?"

It was morning. Kyle came into focus. I checked my body—quite a few scrapes and cuts, and my left shoulder and elbow were tender. No gunshot wound. "I was sure he shot me."

"Who? Nate, are you all right?"

"I think so." I was trying to put the pieces together.

"Is he okay?" Linh was there now.

"He thinks someone shot him but can't find where."

"Did you check him?" she asked. "The noise that woke us sounded like a gunshot."

"I'm okay, I think it was an Outview on steroids. People were after me, like it was happening right now." I rolled over, my voice strained. "It just didn't seem like an Outview. I can't believe I'm alive."

Kyle helped me up. I saw him and Linh exchange concerned glances. They packed up camp. We didn't talk for the first twenty minutes of the drive. I was torn between times, hunted, haunted, and bewildered.

Saturday, September 20

It only took forty-five minutes to reach Mountain View Psychiatric Hospital. I shook off the Outview as best I could. It was nothing compared with what Dustin was going through. Nonfamily members had to be at least sixteen to visit, and Linh said she didn't mind waiting in the car. Just before eight, we were done signing in and directed to a very nice outdoor courtyard, where flowers and wood benches were drenched in morning sun. A few minutes later, Dustin entered from a door opposite us, gaunt and aged. He'd always seemed so much taller than me and at six-one still was, but now he seemed small somehow. We hugged. "Nate, you've been growing. Not sure I can call you my *little* brother anymore."

He remembered Kyle.

"You look good," I lied. For the first time he was skinnier than me, sickly.

"That bad, huh?"

"No, really. And this place is nothing like I pictured. You know, it's almost tranquil."

"Yeah, it's a real goddamned vacation resort. Should I see if they have any vacancies? You all want to check in for a couple of years?"

"Sorry, all I meant was I was expecting it to look like a prison."

"Don't be too disappointed, it's worse. At least in prison your mind is free. Here, they lock up my brain every day with meds that are stronger than iron bars."

"Sorry."

"Stop apologizing. You didn't put me here."

"How much time do we have until they drug you up again?"

"About forty minutes. So you better tell me why after two years you finally got brave enough to disobey Mom and show up." His voice was weaker than his words.

"I know you're not crazy, and we need to figure this all out."

"I'm not crazy now because it's happening to you too, right?"

"Something like that."

"How do you know *you're* not crazy, Nate?"

Kyle scrunched his face but didn't want to get in the middle of this.

"I thought I was for a while, but now I think that you and I have some ability to connect with the other side, like maybe the voices we hear are from dead people or guides. And somehow we can see into our past lives, you know, re-incarnation." His lips were moving at the same time I spoke, mouthing the words a split second before I said them. "Do you know what I'm saying before I say it?" I demanded.

"Only an instant before. How could you tell?"

"Your lips are moving."

"Oh, I didn't realize."

"That's cool. Kyle, watch his lips while I talk. Can you do it with other people, too?"

"Yeah, as long as I'm not on Epidol, Sciliden, Kaperdane, Dardax or any of the other chemical-cocktails-from-hell they force feed me."

"So, what do you think about my theory?"

"Nate, where were you two years ago? Of course I know this stuff. I get about seventy minutes of clarity every morning and that adds up to a lot of time to think over a period of two years. And I've had a little help, too. Aunt Rose comes to visit at least once a week."

"Does Mom know?"

"Of course not. You know Mom was never a fan of Rose but then, with what happened at Dad's funeral… Well, let's just say Mom told her she wasn't welcome in her boys' lives anymore."

"I never did know what happened, just that they had some big fight or something."

"Mom sure has worked hard at protecting you. The way Rose tells it, she told Mom that Dad had been murdered. Not something you should spring on a widow with two kids at a funeral. Anyway, she didn't stop there, she warned Mom that you and I were going to develop psychic powers, and it would be much easier on us if Rose taught and tutored us through it."

"How did she know all this?"

"She's psychic, too."

"Of course she is," Kyle said.

"Maybe not the best one," Dustin said with a chuckle. "Not sure where she was coming from on Dad's death, but she definitely has some abilities, and it must run in the family. She said Grandma and Dad did, too."

Kyle's eyes met mine. Before I blurted out that she was right about Dad being murdered, I remembered where we were and didn't think Dustin needed that information just yet.

"You have to go see her," he said. "She lives like an hour from here in Merlin."

"Your psychic aunt lives in a town called *Merlin*? Oh, that's appropriate," Kyle said.

Dustin cackled loud and almost looked good for a moment. "He's funny, Nate, better get him out of here, or they'll want to keep him and straighten out his humor."

"How do I find her?"

"She's in the book. Merlin, you know it's just north of Grants Pass. Anyway, drive down the main drag—it's a tiny place—and you'll see this little brick house with a neon sign out front saying 'Psychic' and 'Palms Read.' You can't miss it."

"Seriously, she's a roadside psychic?" Kyle asked.

"Yeah, want to know who you're going to take to the prom? She'll tell you," Dustin said.

Then he went quiet and stared at the brick wall for a long time.

"Dustin, are you all right?"

"As lone as God, and white as a winter moon, Mount Shasta starts up sudden and solitary from the heart of the great black forests."

"That's beautiful. Who said it?"

"I did. Didn't you just hear me?"

"I mean, originally."

"I don't know, some dead poet. We need to go to Shasta, Nate... soon. I have to show you something. Something you have to see to believe."

"What is it?"

"There'd be no way to describe it. I wouldn't even try. I have to take you there."

We walked laps around the courtyard for twenty minutes, chatting small talk, trying to avoid the awfulness of what his life had become.

"Did you drive my truck?"

"No."

He looked disappointed.

"We're going to figure out how to get you released."

"Just bring my truck up here, leave the keys under the mat. I'll find a way out to it." He was serious.

"We need to do it so they don't come looking for you, where they will leave you alone."

"Are you going to tell Mom you saw me?"

"I don't know yet."

"If you do, ask her what Dad would think of me being here!"

"Dad wouldn't have let her put you here."

"I know. That's my point. Maybe she'll listen to you. Or maybe she's ready to lock you up here with me."

"What did you mean when you told me on the phone it might be a rough trip?"

"Meet any strange people? Anyone come screaming out of a past life trying to get you? And the trip ain't over yet, Nate."

"How do you know this stuff?"

"I'm psychic, remember? Or wait, I'm crazy... psychic, crazy, psychic, oh, I keep forgetting which it is. I'm so confused." He laughed heartily.

"You said you wouldn't be able to help."

"Meds."

"I know, but how could you help otherwise?"

"Man, we got to get you some proper teachin', little brother. It's not just about peering into past lives and hearing random things. You can see into this life and hear things that actually mean something."

"How?"

"Get me out of here and I'll show you."

"If you can do all that, why can't you get yourself out?" Kyle asked.

"Who invited him?" Dustin asked, pointing to Kyle. "How'd he get in here?"

"Fair question."

"Look at me. Just look at what the meds have done. If not for Rose, I wouldn't even be able to have this conversation. Can you see me sweating? Do you know how hard this is for me? I'll be in bed for a week after this visit."

"I'm sorry, but if you still hear the voices and see past lives—"

"It's less and less, the meds really fog it all out. I guess that's what they're supposed to do. But there are other things that I've been working to develop during my brief mornings of fragile clarity."

"Like?"

"That's gotta be a topic for another time. Our seven minutes remaining isn't near enough to even begin." He gave me a long pleading look. "Nate, you have to get me out of here. It's a slow death, I swear."

"I know."

"No, Nate," his voice hushed but firm. "You do *not* know." He leaned close to me, still talking in a loud whisper. "These pills make me seem all calm for Mom so she thinks I'm getting better, but the only thing wrong with me is *these pills*. She just won't believe the chemicals are destroying me from the inside. Destroying me." The last words came out as a desperate hiss.

"We did a bunch of research online, and now that you're eighteen, they have to review your case within nine months. If they think you're ready to re-enter society, then Mom can't stop them. I'm sure they'll let you out then."

"In nine months it won't be worth bothering with me anymore. I'll be a puddle of a man. Nothing but mush, Nate." His hand reached gently to the back of my neck and slowly pulled me to him until our foreheads were touching. His eyes did more talking than his mouth. "Find a way, Nate. Please find a way to save me."

"I will Dustin, I will," I whispered. He squeezed the back of my neck and nodded slightly. His lips trembled and eyes filled. He nodded again. We sat there a minute until the orderly came to take him away. Just before the door closed behind him, he looked back and nodded again.

"Are you okay?" Kyle asked, as we were walking back to the car.

"How could I be? I might have been the one in there. Do you realize how close I came? They're killing my brother, maybe not like my dad, but don't kid yourself, they *are* killing him, too. They're just doing it in some slow and terrible way." I had to kneel on the ground. Linh saw from the car and ran to us.

"What happened?" she asked.

"We have to get him right now," I said.

"Nate, we can't," Kyle said.

"What happened?" Linh repeated.

"There's nothing wrong with him. My brother has spent two years being tortured for no reason."

"He hasn't been tortured," Kyle said.

"What do you call it? Two years of chemicals and confinement. You heard him; he'd rather be in prison. They've kept him from his mind. They've methodically been stealing his sanity. You know all these pharmaceuticals have brutal side effects. Who knows what the meds are doing to him physically. It *is* torture."

"Okay, I'm not going to win that argument. I have no interest in defending what they're doing here. I sure wouldn't want it done to me or anyone. But we can't just go and grab him," Kyle said impatiently.

"Let's figure it out and make a plan."

"Let's talk to Rose."

"Who?" Linh asked.

"My Aunt Rose has been helping Dustin deal with his psychic gifts without my mother knowing. Dustin said that she and my dad and my grandmother were all psychic, and Rose knew Dustin and I would be, too."

"And she told his mother," Kyle added.

"Your mom knew?" Linh asked.

"Well, knowing and believing are two different things. My mom must be afraid of all this for some reason."

"Do you blame her?

"Yes, I think I do," I said.

"Nate, let's get out of here. We can't save him today. Let's go find Rose," Kyle said, putting his arm around me, urging me to the car.

"All right, but either way, I'm going to get him out. Not in weeks or months but in days."

"Here, I wrote this for you," Linh said handing me a sheet of paper.

> brother to brother
> sun to sun
> side by side
> forever young
> I look into your eyes
> I see a thousand worlds
> of which I am familiar
>
> we share that secret
> that violence
>
> and unlike the weather
> we are consistent

with what we have chosen
brother, dearest friend
enemy, confident
can you know
this love that forever binds
as blood connects
embroiders the earth we walk on
together this march
this passive remembrance
of shoelaces learned
music played, cigarettes burned
we are the image I hold —
a longing to know
why this separation
this other-worldly beckoning

an outcast to our souls

Brother, hear my cry
I am here, in front and beside
like Tolstoy, or Gandalf
like a tree,
or a dog

A unt Rose looked at the three of us a moment before screaming, "My God, Nate, that's *you*, isn't it, honey?"

"Hi Aunt Rose, it's been a long time."

"It's been ages! Oh, aren't you handsome like your father. What are you doing here? What am I talking about? What are you doing out there? Get in here." She pulled me in the door. "And who are your friends?"

"These are my best friends, Kyle and Linh."

"Come in, come in all of you." Inside the foyer, she led us through open double doors to a room with a carved round wooden table and matching cushioned chairs. I was pretty sure Rose was about five or six years younger than my dad, which would make her around forty-one.

"I'm so flustered to see you, Nate. I just got back from the beauty parlor." Her hair was reddish brown, which probably wasn't her real color because I recalled seeing several other shades over the years.

"It's very pretty." Linh smiled.

"Oh, you think so, Kitten?" Rose beamed, playing with her long wispy strands.

"Is that a crystal ball?" Linh asked.

"Sure is," Rose said, pointing us to the sofa under the window. The coffee table was fashioned from thick planks of redwood and pine and contained several dazzling rocks. I recognized a rather large amethyst cone. She'd given me a smaller version on my tenth birthday, knowing that I loved rocks. There were also geodes and crystals in yellow, clear, pink, and green. "Nate, it's been four damn years since your mother excommunicated me from my own family. I'm tickled the universe finally brought you back to my door, but I hope everything's okay."

"We just came from seeing Dustin. He suggested we pay you a visit."

"Is Dusty okay?" she asked, sitting behind the crystal ball dressed in flowing layers of multicolored scarves similar to the ones that adorned the room around her table. From our angle, it was difficult to see where she ended and the room began, which is probably the effect she wanted.

"As well as he can be in that place."

"I know it's awful. I can't stand to see him there. I'm a little surprised because I didn't think you'd visited him before."

"I've been seeing past lives and hearing voices."

"Of course you have, honey," she said, looking at Kyle and Linh. "Does your mother know?"

"Does she know what? That I went to see Dustin? That I'm here now with my black sheep, forbidden aunt or that I'm some sort of psychic freak?"

"Oh, Nate honey, you're not a freak. It only feels that way because most folks don't remember how to be open to the universe."

"My mom doesn't know anything."

"Don't be so sure. Your mother is smarter than you think. That's how she got my brother. He always went for the smartest girl. Your mother is pretty, but Montgomery didn't care a thing about that. All he wanted was brains."

"If she's so smart, why did she lock her firstborn in an asylum?"

"She's scared, Nate, like a lot of folks, just plain terrified. Your mother always has been."

"What's she afraid of?"

"Oh God, I don't know. What *isn't* she afraid of? She's scared of anything that might disrupt her white-bread view of the world. She doesn't want to know what's on the other side of the veil because she just barely manages to keep things straight on this side."

"That's no reason to doubt your own son."

"Fear's a powerful thing; it can be blinding. Dusty didn't help his cause with all the drugs, which sort of ruined his credibility with her. I'll bet she's mighty worried about you, though. Dusty was always tough, anyone could see that, even when he was little. But you were the sensitive one, always lost in your thoughts and worrying over folks."

"Do you know who murdered my dad?"

"Goodness, you get right to it, don't you? Did I mention you were always forthright as well?"

"I don't know how to be polite about someone killing my dad. I want some real information."

"I know you do. I miss him so much, but I don't know who did it or exactly why. If I did, I don't know what I'd be capable of, but let me tell you that I do know for a fact he was murdered."

"How do you know that?"

"He told me."

"Who?"

"Your daddy."

"My dad told you he'd been murdered?"

"He came to me just hours after he died, long before your mother even called to tell me. He was right there," she said, pointing to the doorway. We all looked, I almost expected to see him standing there. "He was out of breath like he'd been running and just as solid looking as you or me. But I cried, 'no, no, Montgomery, no,' because I knew right away he'd crossed over. You may not know this but your dad and me were close. We talked three or four times a week our whole adult lives. It was the gift that bound us. But we'll talk about that later. He looked at me and said, 'It's not what they say. Don't believe I died.' For a minute I thought he was trying to tell me that his soul was still there, you know, that none of us really die. But he knew that I knew, and his face was so distressed. 'Murder again,' he said. I got real calm because I knew it was taking so much energy for him to appear to me like that, and I needed to understand everything he was trying to get across. I asked who and why, but he just shook his head, and then I realized he was gone. I hadn't even seen him go."

"How do you know you didn't imagine it?'

"Please, Nate, this is what I do, this is who I am." She waived an arm around at the candles, crystals, colored scarves, and trinkets hanging about. "Do *you* think I imagined it?"

"What'd my mother say when you told her?"

"She didn't get the full version, just that I'd received a message from the other side telling me Montgomery was murdered, that the autopsy was faked or missing something. And, well, she always thought I was nutty and she was still in shock, so it didn't go over too well."

"You told her that Dustin and I have psychic abilities?"

"Yep. I guess I might as well have told her that you two were alien witches and her husband had been killed by the Lord of Darkness trying to save Princess Leia."

Linh giggled.

"So, you've been visiting Dustin ever since he got to Mountain View?"

"No, I didn't even find out he was there for four or five months. I kept hearing these voices that said, 'help Dusty, help Dusty,' over and over again. Then I found him, and I've been trying to help him as best I could, between the drugs they have him on and the restrictions of where he is."

"How'd you find him?"

"There are ways. I found him on the astral. My mother had this gift too, but my father forbade her to talk to us about it or use it. She still did, of course, just kept it to herself. About the time your dad and I started coming into it she died. You never did know your grandmother, Nate, but you would have liked her, and she would have loved you to pieces. She had a way, I'll tell you. Anyhow, she was able to help us enough to keep us from getting locked up or killing ourselves, which is what happens to so many who find the power."

"What did my dad do with his?"

"Your dad rejected it, which isn't easy because it keeps coming up. Still, he managed to keep it under control. Not me. I embraced it, but I've had a tough time with this human dimension. I'm the kind of nutty psychic who gives nutty psychics a bad name. Married four times, I like my wine a little too much. Messed up my life pretty good, I guess. It can be hell keeping it all straight with worlds always colliding. I've been trying to make amends by seeing Dusty through his dark time."

"How's he doing? I mean, really?"

"I gotta tell you, honey, it's not all peaches and cream. I've been able to keep him somewhat sane by showing him ways to control his past life visions, and he's also been able to do some very limited astral traveling. But he's drowning in toxins, and we're going to lose him if he doesn't get out of there very soon."

"That's what I think. We're going to figure out a way. Will you help?"

"You betcha. I'll lead the charge, honey."

"What about showing me some of those tricks about controlling past lives. I call those visions 'Outviews.' And astral traveling? My friend Amber mentioned something about that, but is it really possible?"

"Nate, I'll give you as much time as you're willing to devote. I'll show you everything I know. And Kyle, don't worry, I'm not as kooky as I look," she said, smiling at him.

"No, I don't think you are, I mean—"

"Didn't you read the sign out front? I know what you're thinking. I also know your energy is very powerful. And Linh, you need to study your dreams, for you it's the way to your soul. I'd love to read some of your poetry."

We all looked at each other.

"How is it I've never known you were a psychic?"

"Your mother didn't want you boys to know, so your dad made me promise never to mention it."

"What part of my life is true?"

"Honey, is *any* part of anyone's life true or real?" She sang the word "real" as she said it.

"I'm obviously not the one to ask. Aunt Rose, can I borrow a phone?"

"Sure, my cell should be out on the hall table."

"How about I do a reading for you, Linh?" Rose said as I was walking out.

I found her phone on the table next to a deck of tarot cards and a stack of her flyers. "Amber, it's Nate."

"You called! How are you? Where are you?"

"We're at my aunt's house in Merlin. You'd love her; she's a psychic."

"Your aunt's a psychic? Why am I not surprised? She should be able to help you a lot. How'd you run into her?"

"That's a long story. Actually my aunt's a long story. I'll tell you all about her when we get back."

"And Dustin?"

"I have to get him out. He's as sane as me."

"I'll resist the joke." She laughed. "What's the plan?"

"I'm still working on it. How's it going with your mom and sister?"

"It's been nice, really. We're having a good time. I miss you though."

Rose did a reading for Linh, while Kyle and I raided our stash of candy. Linh said later that Rose told her stuff no one else knew about her and that Rose even described some of Kyle's past in Vietnam. She said Linh would come into her own spiritual power, beginning with dream messages. "Nate, she said you would be my teacher, that you would teach Kyle, too. She said you're very powerful. Actually, she stressed *extremely* powerful."

22

Rose insisted on buying us lunch. We ordered Chinese, delivered while she explained vortexes. "You've heard of Sedona?"

"In Arizona?" Linh asked.

"Good girl. It's probably the best-known area for vortexes, even though they're doing a good job of crowding out the energy with condos, golf courses, and tourist traps. But still, they're there. Earth's not just a rock moving through space with a bunch of water, trees, and people. It's energy. And up until a few thousand years ago, we used to interact with that energy."

"Then a vortex is a place where we interact with the earth?" I asked.

"Yeah, that's putting it simply but accurately. Vortexes are spots where the concentrated energy from the planet and the universe is really present."

"What comes from the interaction?" Kyle asked.

"Healing, transformation, awareness, great and positive things. Even if you don't believe in anything, a vortex feels intensely powerful because it's like a direct connection to the power of your soul."

"How do you find them?"

"They're not secret. I'll give you a list of all the known ones, but many, many more haven't been rediscovered."

"What about dimensional doorways?"

"That's a little beyond me. I believe it's where you can *physically* move from one place to another, even to a whole different dimension. But I've never done it. I have had luck on the astral, though. That's the connection of souls, the unconscious minds as one, our closest plane. We are wrapped in and surrounded by it. The astral is the invisible stuff that binds this material existence and connects it to all else."

"So, you can travel through your mind?"

"Oh, yes. Everything is connected, so once you tap into your subconscious, you can go almost anywhere, even to past lives, like what you call Outviews. You're actually astral traveling."

"But I could do it within this life, too?"

"Sure, I visit Dusty that way sometimes. It's the same way your dad told me he'd been murdered. Anyone can do it."

"How?" Linh asked.

"Like anything else, sweet one. Practice."

"Can you show us?" Kyle asked.

"I'd love to, but it takes time, so why don't we do that on another visit? You all come up early, and we'll spend a day. I'll get a little course prepared."

"Can we bring another friend?" Linh asked Rose. "Nate, Amber would love to learn."

"Bring a whole party if you like," Rose said. We were all very excited and decided on the following Saturday.

We left around two-thirty, which meant we'd make Brookings by five o'clock. Back on the interstate, I couldn't shake the strangeness of the Outview from last night. Rose's talk of vortexes and the astral made me wonder just where we were on the plane. Or what was actually happening. "What if this is all a dream?" I suggested.

"We can't all be having the same dream," Linh said.

"How do you know that? Nothing really seems certain anymore."

"We could all be insane," Kyle said. "I saw this movie once…"

"Even with all that has happened to me recently, last night seemed extra weird."

"Last night? What about the Old Man of the Lake? And Aunt Rose seeing your dad? This whole trip's been weird," Kyle said, pulling into a gas station to fill up.

Heading into the convenience store, I was stopped by an attractive young woman coming out who dropped her purse. Its contents spilled onto the sidewalk; I stepped on a stray quarter.

"Here you go." I handed it to her as she pushed a hairbrush into her bag.

"Thanks." She looked up at me. "Do you ever feel like it's all a dream?"

"What did you say?" A wave of dizziness hit and my vision blurred, as if someone had just smeared a streak across the whole front of the store. Everything ran in reverse. Her purse emptied again. The coin flew back under my shoe and then rolled backward. All her stuff jumped from the ground back into her purse and she went backward into the store. A jolt, a smear and she came out again as if nothing had happened. She smiled at me and was going to walk on without a word.

"Excuse me," I said. "Do you know me?"

"Don't be silly, Nate, of course I do."

"Where do I know you from? What just happened?" I asked.

"You wouldn't remember. But don't worry, you will. I'll see you soon."

"Wait," I said.

"Don't worry so much," she repeated. "Once you're open, everything is visible. Keep looking; you'll be amazed."

She walked behind a delivery truck and was gone once it moved. I went in for a soda and a couple of packs of peanut butter cups, but it took a long time for me to make up my mind whether to get them with or without crunchy nuts, jumbo sized, minis, regulars or the white ones. Picking a soda also proved difficult. I walked into a display of sunglasses and bumped into a truck driver. Linh came in to check on me, but by then I was in line. She gave me the "we were worried you might have been chased by ghosts again" look and escorted me back to the car. I decided not to tell them about the woman with the purse and also didn't mention the leopard or gazelles that made appearances along the way.

It took more than an hour to locate someone in Brookings who could tell us how to find Tea Leaf Beach. We were beginning to think it and the guy we were supposed to meet didn't exist. The guy at the outdoor shop was surprised. "Not too many people know about Tea Leaf," he said, and then shared the secret closely guarded among locals. It made sense no one knew about it, the only access was hidden behind a guardrail along the busy coastal highway. After that, a steep path down takes about twenty-five minutes to navigate.

Finding Amber's beach house was much easier. Up a winding road through a security gate with a four-digit code, still set to the year her divorced parents married. The wooden house sat on a ridge. You couldn't see the ocean until you were inside or on the deck, but then the view was sweeping.

I called Amber to let her know we'd found it and how much we all loved the place. But really I wanted her to know that Aunt Rose was going to teach us about astral traveling and more on the following Saturday. "Can you come?"

"I can't wait!" she squealed.

While eating the last of our Station food and watching the sun go down, we speculated about our mysterious morning meeting, which was quite early because low tide was at 7:19 a.m. and sunrise at 6:43 a.m. In case there wasn't enough light to see the trail, I put flashlights in our packs.

We looked over the stuff from my dad's desk again. Linh thought her dad might be able to help with the coded writings, and Kyle said he had some tools at home that could pull the inlays out of the box. We had no good ideas about the carved wooden piece but thought of taking it to an antique dealer. I still had the bluish-black stone from the Old Man. It was beautiful but otherwise didn't seem important.

Kyle went to sleep first, but I was reluctant. Linh stayed up, and we wrapped together in a blanket on the deck. The ocean was far enough away that the surf couldn't be heard, but there was enough moonlight to see it churning out to the horizon. Unaware that everything was about to change, we talked at length about all that had happened before falling asleep.

23

Sunday, September 21 (Equinox)

After going up and down the highway several times, Kyle finally spotted the correct section of guardrail. There was barely enough room to pull the car off the road. We'd been expecting to see another vehicle belonging to the man we were meeting, but there was none. The trailhead was nearly impossible to see among the thick ferns, lush undergrowth, and dim light. Our flashlights lit the narrow path through the primeval forest. Large banana slugs left slimy trails, and sticky spider webs grabbed our sleeves. No one spoke except for the occasional, "This is so beautiful." The forest hushed us. Everything was fantastically green, in so many different shades. The trail dropped more than five hundred feet in about a mile, making for a steep and slippery descent.

A mountain lion crossed about sixty feet in front of us. "Whoa!" I said, holding out my arm to stop Kyle who was right behind me.

"I saw it, too," he said.

"What was it? I just caught a blur of something." Linh asked.

"A mountain lion," Kyle whispered.

"Should we turn back?" she whispered. Just then the sun broke though in shafts of white light fully illuminating parts of the forest that had been hidden.

"Let's just start being a little noisier from now on," I said. "I'm glad I wasn't the only one who saw it this time. You guys would have thought it was just another shapeshifter."

"Maybe it was. I'm not sure of anything anymore," Kyle replied.

Around the next switchback, a stream joined the trail and we crossed crude log platforms. The sound of waves filled the quiet forest, glorious. A few minutes later, we emerged from the trees and walked along an edgy cliff, the path, no more than a foot wide, but thick foliage acted as a railing. The trees retreated as the ocean came into view, a breathtaking sight. We sipped water. Below was a spectacular cove, with huge black monoliths rising from the surf like guardians of the coast. Their exotic shapes, the cliffs framing the beach, and the tropical-like forest felt like a coastal jungle of Mexico. Photos didn't capture the scene, and I was too nervous anyway to get anything good.

There on the sand, a solitary person sat on a large black boulder surrounded by driftwood. He was staring out to sea so intently that I expected to see whales or a ship. Nothing but waves danced in the early sun. He didn't move until we were right in front of him, blocking his view.

I guessed he was probably in his late forties. His shaggy gray hair blew in the ocean breeze, eyes a remarkable pale turquoise, light blue pants rolled up mid-calf and a faded green, long-sleeve shirt, gave the impression he'd been walking the beach for hours. Inexplicably, the sight of him relaxed me.

"Nate, thanks for coming." He spoke immediately in a deep soft tone, which reminded me of my dad. "I know you have many questions. I'll try to clear up as much confusion as I can."

"Maybe you could start by telling me who you are."

"Of course, forgive me. My name is Copeland. Spencer Copeland."

Linh, Kyle, and I exchanged glances. He was one of the names on my dad's list.

"Nate, I feel I've known you all your life, so I'm delighted we can finally speak face to face." He turned to my friends.

"Kyle and Linh, you're somewhat newer to me, but I'm most pleased to see you, too."

"Okay, Mr. Copeland," I began.

"Please, you must call me Cope."

"Cope? That's my middle name," I said.

"Yes, it is."

"So you're the old friend my dad named me after."

"Yes."

"How come we've never met?"

"We did a few times when you were younger, but life took me in a different direction."

"How about I just call you Spencer?"

"As you wish."

"Why did you ask us here today and to such an out-of-the-way spot?" I looked around still a little nervous.

"Perhaps that is as good a place as any to begin." He smiled. "Let's walk." He rose and we followed. "The people who are looking for you cannot easily hear us at this location. The high cliffs and narrow beach afford almost no area for their electronic surveillance to pick us up. Likewise, the water adds great difficulty to their remote viewers."

"Who's looking for me?"

"Let me go a bit further back to answer you. I first met your father and Lee twenty-two years ago. We were at a retreat in northern California. Synchronistic events brought us together; we were grappling with our gifts."

"So, you see things and hear things, too?"

"Yes," he said, staring out at the ocean. "I have the same burden you do."

"And my father did, too."

"Oh, yes, but he turned away from it. He wanted to be normal. I think he did a pretty good job at that, too. Actually, anyone can see and hear what you do. Kyle and Linh will begin soon, now that they are open to it."

"You mean it's contagious?" Linh asked.

He laughed. "Yes, thankfully, in a way it is. Everyone possesses these extraordinary senses. But as you can see just by watching what Nate has gone through, it is a challenge to deal with, and society discourages it, so virtually all simply close off to the glimpses and glimmers. But let me go on— we only have so long before the tide comes in. The three of us became instant friends, brothers, really. After the retreat, we stayed in touch and got together at least once a month, helping each other develop our abilities and dealing with the many things we saw and heard. At some point your father met your mother and decided that he didn't want to try incorporating other dimensions and a thousand lifetimes into his world with her."

"So, she broke up the gang?"

"No, no. Your father and I haven't missed a week without some sort of contact. It was Lee who really broke up the gang, to use your words." Something in his tone conveyed his great sadness. It was as if he had to watch friends get killed while he was chained to a wall or something. And that feeling of frustration seemed to pass right from him to me.

"Lee was recruited into Stargate," he said.

"The TV show?"

"I wish it had been as simple. Stargate was the codename for a highly classified program between the CIA, DIA, and FBI. It started in the late sixties during the Cold War, when the U.S. was afraid the Soviets were gaining the upper hand on psychic research, specifically, remote viewing."

"What's that?" Kyle asked.

"The short answer is ESP, extrasensory perception. The government initially used it to find out if the viewer could give impressions about distant or unseen targets, sensing with the mind to see in places where satellites couldn't. At least that's what they told the Senate Select Committees responsible for their funding. But there was quite a bit more to it."

"And they used your friend, Lee Duncan?" I asked.

"They used Lee, yes, that's a good way to put it. There were many others, too. And they had a lot of success. You'll never read about it in the history books, but it was key to ending the Cold War and bringing the Soviets down, and it still affords this country a variety of foreign policy victories to-day." We walked along the sheltered beach littered only with driftwood and a light scattering of shells and river rocks. Linh found a sand dollar. "Then back in 1995, word of the pro-gram leaked, and people thought this was a complete waste of taxpayers' money on what most saw as a silly fortune teller program. So an independent evaluation was ordered. Days be-fore the review was to begin, the CIA opted to simply close down the Stargate project—but not really, that's just what they told Congress and the press. They actually kept it alive in a Langley basement until just after the 9/11 attacks when it was secretly folded into the Department of Homeland Secu-rity, expanded and renamed Lightyear."

"So that's what Lightyear is?" Kyle said.

"Yes. But it becomes more."

"What happened to Lee?" I looked up at a small waterfall emerging from the trees, pouring over the cliff ahead of us.

"The administration took hold of Lightyear and got more aggressive with it. That was an awful time. When the new president came into office, there was some hope, but that quickly faded. By then, it had matured into a powerful tool. They put a new director in charge of the program who was well-connected, and he decided to use it for other means, such as the accumulation of wealth and power for himself and a few of his cronies. But they're so well hidden within the CIA that they're able to do things no one knows about. We're talk-ing immense corruption."

"And Lee was going to blow the whistle?"

"Yes, he was."

"So they killed him?"

"Yes."

"And my dad? Lightyear killed him, too, didn't they?"

"Yes." He stopped and turned to me, the turquoise eyes full of memories I'll never know. "I'm more sorry about your dad than you can understand. Lee at least wandered know-ingly into the cobra's nest, but your dad was just trying to live a normal life. He wasn't bothering anyone."

"Who killed my dad? I pleaded.

"I don't know his name."

"You don't know who's running Lightyear?"

"It's ultra classified, buried so deep inside the CIA that it might as well not exist."

"Can't you find out? You knew Kyle and Linh's names. Can't you use some of your magic to find this bastard?"

"I'm sorry, Nate, it doesn't work like that."

"How does it work then? I can see into lifetimes from hundreds of years ago like it's happening now. I hear voices from other dimensions. People see military bases and terrorists plotting on the other side of the planet in their minds, but you can't figure out a way to see who killed your two best friends?"

"I'm not saying it's impossible; it's just not that simple."

"Then why did you ask us here?" I shook my head, disgusted.

"You're in danger, Nate."

"The guys from Lightyear? What are they going to do, kill a sixteen-year-old kid?"

"At the very least. Yes, they will kill you."

"Why?"

"Several reasons. As soon as you did an online search with Lee Duncan and Lightyear in the same query, that was reason enough."

"How do they know I did that? Is some psychic honed in on me?"

"There's a little-known government agency called the NSA that monitors all Internet and phone traffic. Someone from Lightyear had them looking for that phrase along with Lee's name. The NSA doesn't even have to know why. They just send the data to the CIA, and it filters back to Lightyear."

"So my own government wants to kill me? It's too unbelievable to believe."

"Nate, haven't you learned in the past few months that the most unbelievable things are often the things that are actually the most real?"

"No."

"I find *that* unbelievable."

"I don't care what you think," I said.

"Spencer, you said, 'at the very least they would kill him' what did you mean by that?" Kyle asked calmly. "What else would they do?"

"Kyle, I'm sorry to say that you're all in danger, not just because you're Nate's friends but because you searched for information on Montgomery Ryder on your personal computers. That's reason number two for taking Nate out, but it definitely puts you in some jeopardy. The only reason Nate is still alive is that it took a while to get the report to Lightyear. The government's big and routine information moves slowly, but now it's a priority."

"Are you going to help us?" Linh asked.

"I'm going to do everything in my power to help you," Spencer promised. "But perhaps their most important case for killing you, Nate, is a reason they don't even know yet."

"Great. What is it?"

"Your abilities to tap the powers of the universe may be the only thing that can bring them down."

"Aren't you being a little melodramatic here?"

Spencer grabbed me. "Listen to me, Nate. You have *no* idea what you're up against! Lightyear is run by the nastiest people you can imagine. They're using remote viewing to manipulate events and advance an agenda of cruel greed. They won't just kill you; they will kill your friends and family. Haven't they already proved that? They'll kill a whole school of children if they need to. Melodramatic? I haven't even begun to tell you what's going on at Lightyear. These people are vicious. This is nothing less than an epic battle of good versus evil." He let me go.

"I'm sixteen," I screamed, running toward the ocean. Kyle and Linh ran after me. Spencer sat down in the sand. "This is too much," I yelled above the surf. "What does he want from me? What does the universe want me to do? What can I do?"

"Nate, you need to chill out," Kyle said. "Get hold of yourself. We need to know what Spencer is telling us."

"Do you believe him?" I asked.

"Yeah, do you?" Kyle answered.

"Every word."

"So, why are you giving him such a hard time?"

"Because I don't want to hear what he's saying. I want to go to sleep and dream of cars and football games. I don't want voices whispering in my brain. My dad didn't either. He turned away from this stuff, and that's what I'm going to do."

"I think it's too late for that, and it didn't work for your dad; they murdered him anyway. Didn't you hear Spencer? *You* may be able to stop us *all* from getting killed."

It was then that I noticed the tears streaming down Linh's face. "Linh, are you okay?"

"Everyone's talking about us being killed like it's no big deal," she was shrieking, "like if we do this we could get killed or these people might just kill us or our families! *Our families*, Nate!"

"Linh, we'll be all right. Somehow we'll all get through this," I managed to say.

"How do you know that? He said these people don't care about blowing up a school. He said they're vicious!"

"I don't know what we're supposed to do," I said.

"Yes you do, Nate. It's all right here." Kyle was so calm. Linh and I both waited for his next words. "We need to go back and listen to Spencer. He will help us." Kyle pointed at Spencer, sitting, once again, concentrating on the ocean. "He didn't bring us here just to scare us. He must have some plan on how we can survive this. And Nate, you need to stay calm from now on, and you have to keep meditating. It *will* help you."

"I feel like my head is going to explode."

"I know," he said, "but it won't."

We headed back to Spencer. He stood as we approached. "I'm sorry, Spencer, I'm pretty freaked out by all this."

"Perfectly understandable, Nate. I came on a little strong."

"So, I'm supposed to save the world?" I asked.

"That would be helpful, but my first goal is to just keep you alive," he said.

"*That* would be really helpful," I forced a laugh. "Kyle thinks you have a plan. Is he right?"

"Thank you, Kyle, for your vote of confidence. I do have some ideas about a plan, but it isn't my plan per se. It's your plan."

"That kind of worries me," I said.

"It shouldn't. Let me explain. You're all familiar with destiny and its meaning?" We nodded. "Now, imagine that the major events of your life are set up before you are born. You have free will in between, but the big stuff is preordained for your life's plan." More nods. "Now, the fun part: Try to comprehend tens of thousands of these life plans for each person overlaid on top of each other and all intersecting at various points."

"You're losing me," I said.

"Yes, this is incredibly complex. No one gets it, but try to have a sense of the setup. What it means is there was a plan for the exact situation you find yourself in right now, but it all changes with each decision you make or anyone else in your world makes or anyone in theirs and so on."

"That clears it up," I said sarcastically.

"What I'm doing such a bad job explaining is dynamic destiny, meaning, there *is* a plan. We just have to find it."

"Who sets up the plans?" Linh asked.

"We each set up our own plans. This is simple stuff for our souls. Trying to get our human personalities to understand it is basically impossible."

"How do we find the plan?" Kyle asked.

"I'm going to help Nate remember some tricks so he can connect with his power."

"Like magic?" Linh asked.

"Oh Linh, this is so much more powerful than magic. The long-forgotten powers of the soul are the inspiration for all the magic that has ever been."

"I don't think we have that kind of time," I said.

"First lesson: everything can change in an instant. Truly, it is possible to learn everything that has ever been known in just an instant."

"That's a trick I would like to learn," Kyle said.

"Me, too," added Linh.

"Something tells me it isn't going to be quite that easy," I said.

"Probably not," Spencer said. "But you have to know that if you can get yourself to a certain point, it could be. We'll settle for some fraction of that, for now anyway."

"You're asking an awful lot from me."

"I'm not asking anything. I'm only here to help. Look, Nate, I know you're only sixteen, and an avalanche has come down and you don't know how to handle it. Don't even think you can handle everything that's needed from you. But you can. Believe me, you have it within you."

"I appreciate the pep talk, Spencer, but I'm not convinced."

"Think of it this way then. You have no choice. There is no alternative. If you do not rise to the occasion and remember who you are, then you will be killed. And have no doubt, Nate, you won't be alone."

"Stop putting all this pressure on him," Linh said.

"Linh, I would much prefer to spend years and years teaching him and showing him what he is capable of, but as Nate said, 'we don't have that kind of time.' This is not a game, and there is no guarantee the good guys will win. But I wouldn't be here if I thought this was hopeless. And Linh, I am willing to die in this effort. This is more important than you can know." The sound of the crashing waves took over for several minutes. I knew he was right about one thing. I didn't have a choice. If the people who killed my dad and Lee were really after me, then it would take more than magic to save me, to save us all.

Spencer explained that Lightyear's director was using the vast powers at his disposal to do everything from manipulating food prices to starting small wars. "They are monitoring or have people in all major law enforcement agencies and governments worldwide. Scores have been assassinated at his direction. The stakes are enormous. It's hard to know their true size or how far they will go. But ironically, Lightyear is probably the biggest force preventing a real awakening. The church isn't helping either, but that's another topic."

It was just before ten o'clock when Spencer told us that he needed my complete attention for the next twenty hours. A crash course, he called it. The three of us took a walk, leaving Spencer to watch whatever it was he saw out there. None of us liked the idea of splitting up, but he insisted there was too much to go over and so little time. Although still anxious, we believed he could be trusted.

Kyle and Linh would go back to Amber's beach house and pick me up in the morning. We'd all have to miss a day of school, but they could spend the afternoon studying and I could catch up on the drive back. We walked them to the trail. I gave Kyle my camera. Linh hugged Spencer and then me.

"I don't want to let you go," Linh said, tearfully.

"I'll be fine. We'll all be fine." I didn't want them to go either.

"I want to believe that," she said.

"Then, do."

Kyle stepped in. "Promise me you'll keep calm. Thich Nhat Hahn says, 'Every time we make a step we are moving with all the cosmos, and all our ancestors move and take steps with us.' Think about that. I love you, brother."

24

I turned to Spencer, "So now what?"

"There's so much more than seeing past lives and hearing things. It's overwhelming really. Let's go through this in steps. What you call Outviews are just a window. Imagine being able to actually walk in the door. You can wander through past and future lifetimes, drop into any specific time or place."

"Not just the deaths?"

"You'll never have to see a death again if you don't want to. But you must know by now that death is really just a transformation. It's like passing through a veil to a new experience, quite marvelous really."

"Yeah, well, you should have seen some of mine. There wasn't anything marvelous about them."

"You'll see what I mean later."

"My Aunt Rose mentioned astral traveling."

"Yes, right now you could watch your mother at work or your brother sleeping, anything, anywhere."

"Seriously? And you think I can learn to do this?"

"That and so much more. You've already been doing it. Outviews are just a form of astral traveling. We just need to show you how to control it."

"Why do you think I can do all these things?"

"You know everything. That's what people forget, literally. Everyone already knows everything, it's just a matter of getting our personalities to remember."

"How many years of study does it take?"

"There are many levels. There are nuances that can take a lifetime to master, even for you."

"What do you mean even for me?"

"See, Nate, you're from a long line of *special* people. These abilities run in your spiritual DNA."

"I thought you said everyone could do these things."

"Everyone can, like everyone can play the piano or hit a baseball, but some people are born with a little extra talent to do it more easily."

"And I'm one of those people?"

"Yes."

"And you, too?"

"Yes, but not on your level. Normally I would want to ease you into this, but time is very short. I don't have the luxury of bringing you along as you become ready."

"So I'm not ready?" A particularly large wave crashed into one of the giant black monoliths trying to hold the sea back.

"Let's just say this might not all go as smoothly as it would if you were a little older and we had more time, but you *can* do this. You weren't just born with extra talents. Every generation produces tens of thousands of people who have heightened abilities. I call them 'the wave.' But of those, there are seven who are born with a channel so open to the universe that they can impact tremendous change, historic change." The ocean took his attention again. "And while it's true that even if someone is not one of the wave they can still develop extraordinary abilities, it takes so much discipline that it's extremely rare. I'm one of the wave, but *you* are one of the seven."

"What are the odds?" I asked, trying to make light of something I couldn't grasp.

"One in a billion." His answer didn't help since I couldn't really fathom a billion. I remember my history teacher saying that a billion hours ago man was living in caves.

"I don't care about changing the world. I just want to get my brother out of the institution and see my dad's killer in jail."

"That's what your human personality wants, but your soul has a different plan. Once it's awakened you'll find it incredibly hard to put the genie back in the bottle, so to speak."

"You said yourself I'm not really old enough to do all this."

"I need you to not be sixteen now. I need you to be who you really are."

"How old am I really?" I asked, repeating the question the Old Man of the Lake didn't answer.

"We're all as old as the universe. For now, just try to think like some five-hundred-year-old wizard," he replied, very seriously.

I thought of my father and me walking quietly in the old growth forest of western Oregon. "I'll try."

"Nate, I'm going to show you some extraordinary things that you have forgotten you can do. To any average *human* they will seem like super powers, and they are. But our souls can do them effortlessly. The most important part is for you to believe they are possible. So I want you to think about this: if the soul exists and it can really survive human death and come back again in another body… "

"We both know it can."

"Exactly, but are you taking for granted what that means? Simply put, if reincarnation is real, just imagine the power that is required to pull it off… a million times, a billion times. And you're tapped into that." He looked at me. "*Anything* is possible."

"You're saying some exciting stuff, but these concepts are pretty tough to get my head around."

"Maybe this will help. Watch that driftwood." He pointed to a log about two feet long. It began to move, spinning in the sand and then, taking off like a rocket, soaring into the surf.

"Cool! How did you do that?" I asked excited.

"Now, you do it."

"Just like that, no explanation?"

"What if I told you that I didn't really make the driftwood fly but that you did because you expected it to?"

I concentrated on another piece, willing it to move, but after a few minutes nothing happened. "I can't do it."

"Remember it's not just Nate doing it. You're a channel for all the power that has ever existed. Everything is possible."

I tried again. Nothing.

"Stop concentrating on it. It's energy; you are energy. You and the wood are connected. The air between you is full of energy. The power moving that ocean is the same. Don't think about making it move. Just move it. This is easy for you. Make the wood fly."

It started slowly, moving slightly. It spun. Faster. It shot straight up in the air. I ducked so it wouldn't hit me on the way down. Spencer didn't flinch. "I did it! Did you see that? I did it!"

"Now do you believe?"

"Yes. I mean I'm not sure what I believe, but I sure believe something." I was breathless.

Spencer laughed. "That's a start. If someone saw you doing that they might call it telekinesis, but you'll learn it's more than just your regular ol' telekinesis. What we're doing is part of one of the five great powers. Moving things is a form of 'Gogen.' It means to manipulate space, in the ancient language."

"Which ancient language?"

"One you've never heard of. A language that predates all known history."

"Why was it so easy?" I asked.

"Everyone on this planet is capable of doing this if they would just clear themselves of all the junk and practice."

"What junk?"

"Prescription drugs, inoculations, chemicals, processed foods, pesticides, possessions, debt. The list is long. But it is simple for you because you're one of the seven. All you need to do is believe and be shown what you're capable of, and you can do almost anything."

"Was my dad one of the seven of your generation?"

"No, he wasn't, just one of the wave."

"What happened to those seven?"

"Earth is a minefield for these messengers. The asylums got a couple. Three fell into drugs and alcohol. Another committed suicide, and politics took the last one."

"Politics?"

"His gift made it easy to rise to power, but sadly corruption crept in on him."

"What about the other six in my generation?"

"Similar story—Ritalin, illegal drugs, institutions, or death. It's the same for the tens of thousands in the wave. The vast majority wind up blocked. Our soul may be the most powerful force there is, but in modern civilization we've created so many ways to blind us to the universe—cell phones, wireless networks, EMFs, microwave ovens—all weaken our ability to connect. Organized religion, the public education system numbs us to our true selves. The message gets buried. Not to mention this horrible food we've had the last fifty or sixty years. It's killing us."

"I've got a lot to learn," I sighed.

"It'll be much easier for you now." He tossed me a book. I have no idea where it came from. "Hold on to that for a while."

"Okay," I said glancing at the title, *The History and Origin of the Solar System*.

"There are many different ways to handle these gifts. Lee pursued a path trying to integrate his with work in a way he thought was doing good. Your father decided to ignore his to have a regular family life. Rose uses hers to earn a living."

"What about you?"

"I've spent my life in study, contemplation, and practice."

"Why? What will that do?"

"Maybe it was all for this day, all so I could guide you through the fog and keep you alive to fulfill your destiny. For many decades an increasing number of people have been waiting for the promise of the New Age to transform the human race. And many are questioning if there's still time. Have we screwed it up beyond saving? I don't think so. Nate, what is the age of the sun?

"What?"

"Answer the question."

"Approximately 4.6 billion years old."

"What is its diameter?"

"About 1,392,000 kilometers."

"And Nate, where is the sun located?"

"The sun is currently traveling through the local interstellar cloud within the inner rim of the Orion arm of the Milky Way galaxy."

"How far is that from earth?"

"About 149.6 million kilometers."

"Good. How much hydrogen does the sun fuse?"

"Stop it!" I shouted. "What the hell?"

"All you need to do is keep your hands on a book for a short time and you will absorb all of its information."

"No way!"

"There are some nice tradeoffs with this 'burden,' yes? You just have to remember that everything written isn't necessarily true, so just because you know what the books say doesn't mean it's accurate. Reading is not the same as understanding."

"Okay, but this is very cool."

"Yes it is. Quite the little timesaver."

"Oh, by the way, the sun fuses 620 million metric tons of hydrogen each second," I said, handing him the book.

"Very good. Reading a book that way is a form of 'Vising', another of the five great powers. This one is a method to transform energy. You'll learn other uses of it soon enough. But right now, you need to practice Gogen."

After using Gogen to move objects ranging from piles of sand to decent-sized boulders for several hours, I was ready to go out into the real world and have some fun. I couldn't wait to show my friends. But I was surprised by how tired it made me.

"I haven't eaten since breakfast. When can we go and get something to eat?"

"Tomorrow. I'm sure Kyle and Linh will take you for breakfast. You'll be fine until then."

"No really, I'm hungry."

"Food will only get in our way. After what you've just done, what's a twenty-four-hour fast? Think about that. You've still got some water, and when you run out, there is a lovely stream in the woods."

"Great, I'm in psychic boot camp," I grumbled. "So what's the biggest thing I can move anyway?"

"How do you think the pyramids were built?"

"Really? So there's no real limit?"

"There are no *real* limits to anything we can do, but there are often complications. Moving a building, for example, brings into play many other forces and soul destinies. Therefore, it might be too complex to make it worth attempting." He was silent until I looked at him. "I'm giving you the keys to the most awesome power there is. These are all just parts of it. Even if you were much older and wiser, it would be an astronomical responsibility. Maybe your youth will prove to be an asset because I'm sure you'll admit that even the most sophisticated sixteen-year-old doesn't have the level of maturity to be up to this."

"You mean, will I use these powers to play tricks on my friends?"

"No, I have to trust you're beyond that kind of nonsense. What I'm saying is, if you use it for good, for the purpose of spreading love and reminding everyone who they really are, it will grow stronger in you. If you let ego get in the way or turn the other way, it will weaken and your life will sour."

"I'll need help to stay on track. I think I could mess this up pretty easily. I mean, I barely passed biology with a D, and chemistry isn't looking any better."

"All you need to do is remain open and pure, and the help you need will be there. It's up to you, Nate." I tried to let it all sink in but didn't know if I could. "We should move on," he warned.

"Wait, I have some questions. Can I move myself?"

"If you mean can you levitate, the answer is yes, but that will come much later. It's more complicated."

"How long do I have to hold a book to get the info out of it?"

"I don't really know. Depends on the size I guess, not too long. You'll figure it out."

"This seems like a wild fantasy story."

"There is no such thing as fantasy. It is all real somewhere. Even the most far out reaches of your imagination are actually happening in some dimension. Now, let's get into healing. I have a feeling you're going to need this skill."

"Another thing to worry about."

"Rub your hands together," he said, ignoring my sarcasm. "You're moving the life force. Remember, it's there in every living thing."

"That's why it's called life force?"

He smiled. "We all have the ability to heal ourselves and others by using it. This is how it was done before the techniques and knowledge were lost to the ages. This is part of the third great power, 'Foush', to enhance the human senses."

"What are the other two?"

"'Timbal', is used to view time. It is how you see Outviews. 'Solteer' is the final power, it's a way to control consciousness, but we'll get into that another time."

Spencer showed me how to use visualization, and soon I could feel a slight vibration in my hands as they warmed. But as soon as it happened, he said, "Let's get to your next lesson."

"Don't I need to practice?"

"Yes. Practice is one of the most important things you can do. And it's the only way you can master anything. But you'll have plenty of opportunities to work on your healing abilities very soon." His tone was more serious than I would have liked.

"Should I be afraid?"

"Fear is nothing you should voluntarily enter into. When fear arises naturally, you pay attention to it as a warning, but never go looking for a reason to be afraid."

"I think I understand."

"The next door we open is very useful. Something you'll need tonight in fact."

"What's tonight?"

"Let's not get into tonight yet. Now, you understand that everything is energy. The patterns of energy, the attraction and exchange of it all leaves a story. It's always there. What this means is everything can tell you everything. Where something is at a specific time in space, how you make the connections and the distance you're willing to travel are the only limits on what can be revealed. It's all energy, one big energy."

"Fascinating. What does it mean?" A warm salty breeze passed.

"Put your hands on that rock. Now close your eyes and try to look for something in the darkness of your mind."

After half a minute I started seeing things—a guy running on the beach with a golden retriever; next, a group of teenagers laughing and playing on the sunny beach. One of them passed a joint to the other. A girl declined. The other one accepted. Then, a different day, this time foggy, a young couple walking the beach, another with a small child using driftwood and tarps to build a shelter from the sun. They played and looked for shells. The father took pictures.

"What's all this I'm seeing?"

"It's the energy that has moved past this rock."

"Incredible! How do I know what happened when?"

"That's the tricky part. You could easily spend the rest of your life exploring this single ability and still not master it, but with time you'll develop considerable control. As it is now, the images you saw could have been yesterday or a decade ago."

"What do I do with it?"

"Just work on it as often as you can. It's another form of Vising. You'll discover so many uses for this talent that you'll wonder how anyone survives without it. Survival is actually a useful benefit, as this will literally save your life more than once." I didn't need more incentive than that. It was fun in a voyeuristic way, much more exciting than any reality TV show could ever be. I wandered the beach touching rocks, trees, even the sand. I peered into the lives of people like a hidden video camera. My favorite was watching the tide roll in during a long-ago thunderstorm. Then the rock was engulfed by the surf while I remained dry. It was addicting. Spencer finally made me stop.

"Aren't I going to forget how to do all this stuff?"

"No, you won't lose any of it. It will just keep getting stronger. You've always had these abilities, and now that they've awakened again, you own them." He stopped and stared out at the ocean for a minute. "And Nate, remember not to discuss your father, Lightyear, or any of the things you're learning with anyone. No matter how much you trust them."

"Okay." His words made me nervous.

I noticed more and more seagulls landing around us. I looked at Spencer.

"Animals are open to the universe. They have filters to block themselves. They aren't trying to make sweeter soda or pills to make their pain go away. They don't want the biggest TV. Animals just are. And because of that they are open. They immediately sense when a human is also receptive. And since this is happening right here in their domain, I think they are kind of welcoming you or saying hello. It's hard to say, actually. There sure are a lot of them, aren't there?" he said, turning and taking in what was now untold thousands of birds filling the beach around us.

We watched in silence as they landed. The black monoliths contrasted the countless white birds covering them. The hysteria of white wings against swirling blue waves crashing on the rocks was mythical. The area suddenly became warm and hopeful, as the beach was now more feather than sand. "What should I do?" I asked.

"I'm not sure really. I've never seen anything quite like this," Spencer said. We continued to watch the beautiful spectacle, and then, as if by some secret cue, they lifted in a flutter of wings, soft yet deafening. Spiraling above the beach and out to sea, masking the sky, they quickly dissipated in all directions and were gone.

We walked on the narrowing beach as high tide culminated and made our way around a jutting cliff that was practically in the waves. I wondered if we would make it back.

"There are some things your Aunt Rose can teach you quicker because of your relationship."

"Do you know her?"

"Oh, we met a thousand years ago."

"You mean when you were both younger?"

"No, I mean we actually knew each other as Anasazi Indians around 1100 AD at Mesa Verde. We've also met a few times in this lifetime through your dad."

"What should I ask her help with?"

"The color sparks you see, auras, and prophecy," he said.

"Prophecy?"

"She uses a crystal ball, I believe. Any reflective surface will work. You can do it without any props, but it's easier to use something. She's also good at helping with guide writing, which is writing or typing what your guides are telling you. Especially early on, you'll find this a great way to communicate with the other side."

"So you still talk to my dad?"

"Yes."

"Can I?"

"Not yet, but you'll learn. He's with you always. You've had many lifetimes together."

"So, is he waiting to reincarnate again?"

"No. He's currently alive in several different incarnations. There are no limits to the soul. We don't just do one life at a time. We're almost always living multiple lifetimes simultaneously, dozens."

"Talk about schizophrenic."

Spencer smiled. "We can cross-communicate between all these different existences and even knowingly, but usually unknowingly, interact with one of our other selves. It can be more than the mind can handle. Your dad's soul can be with you, talk to me, watch over Dustin, follow every moment of your mother's grieving struggles and live forty other lives all at the exact same time."

"So he could be a cab driver in New York, a rice farmer in Thailand, a housewife in London and a homeless person somewhere else, all right now?"

"Yes," he said. "And guiding you from the other side without any of those incarnations knowing about any of it."

I couldn't wait to tell Amber. "Speaking of all these lifetimes, you said you were going to show me how to control the Outviews so I wasn't always dying."

"We'll meet back here again on Friday. It'll have to wait until then."

"No, I can't take many more deaths."

"Okay, it's a huge topic, but I'll tell you now how you can avoid that. Whenever you feel you're about to enter a death, in your mind just turn around sharply."

"That sounds pretty simple."

"It's not. It can be quite messy, but at least it should let you stay away from the deaths until we have time to go into it more. Explaining the time navigational aspects of astral traveling within the split realities of the multi-dimensional, soul-connected universe is time consuming."

I looked up at him, then away. "Whatever."

"We've just touched on some things, abilities that will help you manage the dilemma you're in. There is so much more to explore. Eventually, you'll be able to teach Kyle, Linh, Dustin, Rose and many others who are part of the wave. You are like the moon. As you do things that affect the wave, everyone on the planet will feel the effects of the tide."

"I can't believe how much I've learned today."

"Don't let your newly awakened abilities fool you. There are enormous powers swirling around in the world. You're nothing near invincible, Nate. You need to practice avoidance, not confrontation."

"Believe me, I don't feel invincible."

"Maybe not on this beach with me while all of this is still so new, but there will be times soon when you're with your friends or your mother, and you feel like your abilities can allow you to do anything, like you're a god. Watch for those thoughts and banish them. They will bring more trouble than you can dream. You are not a god, just a small fraction, incomplete without the rest of us. I know you think that you'll never feel that, but you will, and that's why you must spend the night alone in the woods. It will give you perspective. And when those feelings come, then you will have this night as part of you. It'll give you something to draw from to stave off the erupting ego."

"Are you crazy? I'm not spending the night *alone* in the woods. It's not safe. And it's totally unnecessary, I'm not like that." I couldn't believe he really wanted me to stay in the forest overnight!

"Nate, this is no small thing. I told you earlier today that this is an epic battle between good and evil. What I'm talking about is the technology of man with all its materialism and greed suppressing the power of our souls. It can go either way at this point. The numbers are on their side, in the short term anyway, or at least in this dimension. Neither side is organized in the battle, neither side acknowledges the war, yet it *is* happening."

"What's that got to do with me sleeping in the woods?"

"Your dad asked me to help you. I'm asking you to do this. You need to do this."

He had shown me so much. I would have done anything he asked. I just needed to contain my fear. "Okay, Spencer."

"Thank you," he said. "Then it's time. You need to spend the night in the trees and not on the beach."

"What if I need you before Friday?"

"Trust the universe."

"What am I supposed to do tonight?"

"Make it to sunrise."

"Am I going to?"

"You need to talk to your guides. Ask for their help and protection. Tell them you're ready. They will help you."

"What about a tent, sleeping bag, food?"

He shook his head.

"Seriously?"

"You won't need them."

"And where will you be?"

"Somewhere else. You will not need me either."

"Wait, I saw a mountain lion in the woods on the way down," I said panicked.

"Remember, animals are open."

"So they won't hurt me."

"I didn't say that. A mountain lion is still a mountain lion and will eat you if it needs to. I'm just saying that you're not defenseless against the animal instinct. There is more to it than that."

"There's always more to everything it seems."

"Now you're getting it."

"So how do I stop the mountain lion or bears or whatever else from eating me?"

"Get that channel clear and keep calm. You should feel more at home and safer the deeper you are in nature. It will always be like that. Besides, the lions and bears will be the *least* of your worries tonight."

"So this is goodbye until we meet again Friday," he said.

"You're leaving now? I won't even see you in the morning?"

"I'm hungry. I need to go get a good warm dinner." He laughed.

"No, really, I'm nervous about all this."

"You aren't scared?" he asked.

"Yeah, I'm scared. Falling-off-a-cliff kind of scared."

"The only way you'll get into trouble is if you let that fear control you."

"How the hell do I avoid it?"

"I can't teach you that. You have to figure it out. The trees are kind," he said pointing toward the forest.

I looked up at the imposing verdant canvas stretching along the cliff as far down the coast as I could see in either direction and headed in. The sun was already touching the ocean. I had maybe an hour of twilight left.

The trees did look gentle and ancient, wise giants protecting the coast. Moss covered lower trunks, fallen trees, rocks, everything. I crouched on the narrow trail, touching and reading the trees that bordered it, using my new Vising ability, watching who had come and gone over the days, months, and years before, not knowing when was when. I smiled, seeing Kyle and Linh as they had passed earlier.

Spencer had suggested heading north up the coast, so I navigated through thick undergrowth until darkness stole the last visibility. There was a trace of moonlight, but almost none filtered into the forest, and my sight was limited to less than three feet. "What am I doing?" I thought. It had been around seventy degrees during the day, but nighttime temperatures plummet to the low forties. There would be total darkness for more than nine hours. The clock was ticking. I had hiking boots, long pants, a T-shirt, and a fleece but was starting to feel the chill; there would be no sleep.

The coyotes announced their presence first, singing their manic songs. There were other animal noises and bug sounds I didn't recognize, didn't want to know. I tried to meditate to fight the growing tension and fear, and I reminded myself to breathe. "Go to the beach," I whispered, the rumble of waves soothed me. Just walk downhill. "Was it high tide or low?" I wondered. No, Spencer was adamant that this was needed. He had said something poetic about it Linh would like; what was it? "You need a dark night of the soul."

"It couldn't be much darker," I thought.

Then I remembered his parting advice, "Talk to your guides, stay in the trees."

"Guides, I'm unsure how to do this, so I'm going to assume you can hear me. I'm just going to say that I need help. I'm scared. I've camped and hiked a lot, but staying out here all night alone with no light is kind of different. Really very different." Then it hit me. I had a light, the one from that morning. I pulled the pack off my back, unzipped the outside pocket and "Yes! Let there be light!" I surveyed the area. It gave an extra ten feet but when turned off, nothing. It was five minutes before my eyes adjusted again, so I pledged to use the light only for emergencies.

"Back to you, Guides. Maybe you reminded me about my light. I sure would have felt stupid finding it tomorrow. Anyway, as I was saying, anything you can do to help me get through this night would be great. But I also could use help getting Dustin out and finding the guy who killed my dad. And you probably know I really need the most help figuring out how to do all this cool stuff Spencer has been teaching me or reminding me or whatever. I don't want to blow it. I really think he might be wrong about me being one of the seven. Maybe he just said that to give me some extra confidence because I just don't think I'm smart enough to do all this." I waited for an answer. Nothing came.

My senses fell into crisis, a stunning feeling of fire grabbing, so hot, I tore at my fleece, wanting it off. A terrible haunting noise broke the night, drums echoed through the woods, loud, ceremonial, driving. I was running again, stumbling and dodging trees. What was this punishment? How many lifetimes have ended with me being chased to my death? Was it now or long ago? No way to know, I just had to run. Pursuers were closing in. Voices ordered a strategy to trap me. It was blisteringly hot, my skin slick with sweat. Running. Running. Why weren't they shooting? The mob was so close now. Torches appeared in front of me. More came from the sides. I was surrounded. Surely they were about to kill me.

The heat stifled my thoughts. A desperate attempt at escape occurred in my last wisp of consciousness. In case this was a past life and not the present, I tried Spencer's method of avoiding death in Outviews. I consciously and abruptly turned around. Instantly, moving back several years earlier in that life, I was younger and hiding in a tree. It was no longer night in the Outview; instead, the warmth of a balmy morning felt cool after the burning heat from before.

Seeing my hands holding onto the branches, dark and dry, I was African. Slave traders had just captured my parents, who were being loaded—chained and shackled—into wagons; a large ship waited in the distance. Although it was probably sometime in the 1700s, the devastation was total, as if they had taken Dustin and my mother. The modern-day me understood what awaited my African parents at the end of their voyage on the slave ship, if they were unfortunate enough to survive. The "me" in the tree just knew his parents were gone forever; it was a death.

A deer jumped over me so close that its hoof grazed my shoulder. I was no longer in the tree but back in modern-day Oregon. Before I had time to figure out why, the mountain lion was there. It stopped from its pursuit of the deer and faced me. I could see it from the outer limits of my vision, which was now maybe ten feet. I thought of the light in my pocket. It growled and shifted its weight. Our eyes locked. There wasn't much time. I couldn't outrun it, and climbing a tree to escape a cat is not an option. Suppressing panic became harder each second. Could I Gogen an animal, maybe a big log, a rock? Get it between us? No, too risky. I'd have to divert my attention for too long. Why would Spencer put me in this position? What had he said? Clear the channel and keep calm. He said I should feel safer in nature. The cat was moving now, a few feet to my left, stalking me. I kept my eyes on it and began to speak softly.

"I'm not afraid, you're not my enemy." It sounded corny and I'm not sure where it came from, but at least I was doing something.

It screamed as if to say, "You *are* afraid."

"I'm not sure how to end this standoff. I'm only here for a night. This is your home. May I stay here tonight?"

It leaped toward me. In the millisecond I had, my only thought was, move. The mountain lion landed at least six feet to my right. Either I moved it or I moved. I had no idea which. Without stopping it turned and came again at full charge, screaming.

"Stop!" I yelled. And it did. What now?

It growled.

Something pushed me to walk toward it. There was no time to think of alternatives. I kept eye contact as I approached. With trembling hands, I slowly reached behind its ears and petted the big cat, sensing it was a female. Our eyes were just inches apart now and hers suddenly closed. When they opened the cougar screamed right in my face. She moved and through the momentum or some other force, my hand gripped the fur behind her ears flinging me around onto her back. I locked my legs around her and used all my strength to hang on as she went tearing into the blackness. I managed to get one arm around her neck. My vision adjusted just as we were sailing across a wide, deep ravine thirty feet in the air. Her speed was shocking. I'd ridden on a motorcycle once with a friend of Dustin's and this was similar. The lion was silent as she navigated the jungle, her muscles tensed and flexed, indescribably pure power. We came to a cliff wall, the first pause since my ride began ten minutes earlier. My thoughts caught up as I was about to get off she leaped straight up onto a ledge and was running again. I could now see about fifty feet ahead and the ground was less steep.

Flashes of the lion's life came, a long series of hunts and kills. There had been cubs at some point, maybe two litters. Only one survived but was grown and gone. We ran another ten minutes. She stopped for no apparent reason and seemed to be waiting. I dismounted. A quick look at me, then she ran in the direction we'd been going, into the darkness.

I stood there wondering about the encounter. Would anyone believe I'd ridden a mountain lion? Did I believe it? It was impossible to imagine a greater thrill. But there was much more to it. A spiritual connection occurred between us. How did it happen? Do we reincarnate as animals? Was it real? If not, then why was I now so far from Tea Leaf Beach?

The questions would have to wait. It was suddenly very cold. How far had we come? I didn't know it at the time, but mountain lions can travel thirty-five miles an hour. In twenty minutes at top speed, we could have gone ten miles. Hopefully, it was less than half that. A daunting task lay ahead, with so much ground to retrace through a black forest. At least now I could see farther; it was a useful new power that had surfaced without Spencer or my prompting.

I headed back with Spencer's warning replaying, "Lions and bears are the least of your worries tonight." My steps quickened, out of a mixture of needing to stay warm and concern about *everything*. Every few minutes I stopped briefly to listen. There was so much to hear: the distant ocean, crickets, and always the rustle of things moving, some a few feet away, others farther. I distinctly heard footsteps that stopped whenever I did. Animal? Human? Something else? I didn't know but moved a little faster each time it happened. Soon I was running. After what seemed like hours but was probably fifteen minutes, I had to rest. My breath rapid, legs burning, I heard the steps stop again. Keeping my thoughts light to alleviate the rising fear wasn't working. I got my flashlight and positioned it in my hand so any pressure from my thumb would turn it on. I had no other weapons, but in a dark forest a bright light could possibly save me.

It wasn't difficult to find the way back to Tea Leaf Beach as long as I kept the ocean on my right. I drank some water—there was not much left. I started my gentle jogging until a small clearing opened, which the lion hadn't brought me through. The break in the trees allowed moonlight to illuminate the meadow, and three deer on the far side were startled as I lumbered in. It seemed safe, maybe because I could see something coming before it was too close. I knelt down in the middle of the field to rest and think about something more than survival. My hands, wrists and face were cut and scraped by the five million branches over the last few hours. Rubbing my hands together generated warmth of my life energy and I took turns moving my palms over my injuries. After a while the soothing healing put me to sleep.

Why was I back at the African coast? Watching the slave ship being loaded, my mother crying, father defiant but frightened; however, this wasn't being viewed from my perch hidden in the tree as before. Now I was holding a gun. I was white, one of the slave traders. "No!" I screamed and vomited bile. It was the cruelest of fates. My soul experiencing two simultaneous lives, which crossed as both slave trader and the son watching his parents torn from his existence. It was impossible to comprehend living as such a horrific person.

I jerked violently awake, shocked I'd fallen asleep. How long? I surveyed my surroundings, happy to see the small meadow and my Oregon moon. I needed to be as far from the slave trader as possible. There must be some way to wash that existence from my soul, which had always seemed so pure to me but now was dirty and ugly. All I wanted to do was claw my skin off and rip the slave trader out of me.

I headed back into the woods, not caring if I made it to dawn. Could I ever forgive myself? In how many other lifetimes had I been evil? Only the thought of freeing Dustin gave me hope, a step toward some kind of redemption. What a joke! How many lives had I ended or put into torturous forced servitude as the slave trader? How could I ever redeem my soul?

It was good to be back in the trees. They had sympathy; they did not judge me as a slave trader, even though I was certain they knew. If I couldn't live with myself, I would come back and stay among the trees as a hermit until I could face a mirror again.

Any inkling I had of what time it was evaporated with the nap in the meadow, but I knew it would be darkest and coldest before dawn. I went on without thinking of the slave trader and then without warning collapsed to the ground sobbing. Screams I couldn't recognize as my own wrenched out of me. It was too much. The ferns and undergrowth enveloped my body, and my face buried into moss and dirt. I don't know how long I was there. The damp, numbing cold was more dangerous than lions or bears, and so was the slave trader. I didn't care.

My thoughts were in a different world, following a slave's journey when something nuzzled the back of my neck. I turned over, hoping for the mountain lion. It was a medium-sized buck. They wander into Ashland all the time. But this one was different, gentler and somehow wiser. He looked into my eyes as if I was the first human he had ever seen, and waited until I understood. When I rose, he leisurely moved away but looked back, to be sure I followed. This went on for quite a way. He walked slowly through the forest, continuing to look back every so often.

I was shivering uncontrollably. Walking was not helping, and my steps were increasingly difficult. He led me into an area of thick brambles and bushes. Two doe rose, startled as we entered the small space, flattened out with only enough room for the deer. The buck pushed at me in a way that I sunk to my knees. I couldn't believe it but he actually wanted me to sleep with them. Their gentle warmth, as they curled around me, didn't just save my life but gave me hope. If these special creatures cared, then how wretched could I be? When I woke, they were gone. I was warm, dry, and renewed.

Later, I came to the ledge the lion had leaped onto. It wasn't the exact spot we'd come through; it was much higher here. I saw no way down and reasoned it was probably highest near the beach, which was lined with cliffs, so I moved in the other direction. The cliff went on forever, and I was getting cold again. In order to get back to where I started, I had to try and climb down.

It was probably only ten or twelve feet, but there wasn't much to hold onto. I was doing pretty well until a rock crumbled in my hand. The fall wasn't far, but the ground was rocky and uneven. Nothing seemed broken, except my ankle was twisted, legs and arms were bruised and it hurt to breathe. Lying on the cold hard ground, injured and shivering, I knew I was in trouble. I rubbed my hands together to begin healing but it was beyond my novice skills. I could move, even walk, but not far. There was dry kindling in this area as a break in the trees had allowed the sun to dry things out. Unfortunately I had no way to light a fire.

My dad had taught Dustin and me a trick to start one using a mini-mag flashlight and although my light was in my pocket, steel wool and a small wire were also required. The memory of camping with my dad brought the distinct feeling that he was nearby. "Dad, are you there? Can you help me?"

No answer, but I was sure he could hear me.

"*Your* friend Spencer got me into this mess."

Nothing.

"Spencer can hear you, right? Could you go tell him I'm lost in the wilderness and maybe he could rescue me? Spencer, are you out there?"

The spiral of an Outview began to take me.

"Not now," I said too late.

There I was in a bombed-out village. A German Panzer tank passed by the open doorway of the building in which I was hiding, making it obvious this was the Second World War. Thank you, Mr. Anderson, you taught me well. Two friendly soldiers approached from another room speaking in French, which was nowhere near as easy for me as history. Still, it was clear they were discussing some kind of plan to either attack or escape. Knowing the pattern of my Outviews, I figured we were all about to get killed. Then a third soldier approached. He was smoking a cigarette and offered me one. I looked up to accept and saw my father's eyes. He handed me the metal tin of matches, winked and smiled. Seconds later came the unmistakable whistle of an incoming shell. We didn't even make it to the floor. I rolled out of the Outview back into the cold night, onto the steep ground above the beach, coughing. It took a moment to realize that clutched tightly in my hand was the small tin box of matches. Stunned, I couldn't take my eyes off them. "Thanks, Dad," I whispered, tears streaking my cheek. He was with me. Lost in that moment was the fact we had died together in France during World War II. There would be time to think about that later. Right now, all I could do was bask in the miraculous happening of my dad coming back.

I was shaking again and needed to get warm fast. Taking a sharp rock, I dug a shallow pit and surrounded it with stones. After quickly gathering dry grass and twigs, I struck a match against the embossed striker on the bottom of the tin. Soon there was warmth and light. I made a good pile of wood to supplement the fire for some time. "Thanks, Dad," I repeated several times before moving on to my wounds, concentrating on my ankle. Two hours must have passed. I drank the last of my water and kept very warm. Slowly the healing took affect. The bruises and new scrapes did not take as long as the ankle. The difficulty in breathing was the last to go. Because I didn't know what was causing it, I channeled the healing energy around my torso and trusted it would cure what was needed. It did.

Exhausted, all I wanted to do was sleep but there was too much ground to cover, and I wasn't interested in seeing the slave trader again. After piling dirt on the fire, I reluctantly began walking. How far to go? I tried to will my mountain lion to return, to carry me back. I called her with my mind. Soon the ravine that was so easily crossed on her back was before me, deep and wide. It was passable, but even in daylight if I was well-rested and with a full canteen, it would take more than an hour to make my way down the steep grade, one-hundred-fifty feet or so, then back up the other side. "Dad, you there? Got a bridge up your sleeve?"

No one came. No lion, no deer, no Outviews. Just me and the struggle. It must have taken two hours until I finally crawled out of that hellish ditch. But I did it. It's the part of the night I remember least. As the sky lightened, I found the path to the road. Twenty-four hours earlier, I had descended this trail with Kyle and Linh. It was a *long* time ago. I was different then.

26

Monday, *September 22*

Kyle and Linh were leaning against the guardrail as I came out of the ferns. Would they see the change, the absence of the confusion I'd worn for so long? I wondered how much to tell them.

Linh wrapped her arms around me.

"Got any water?" I asked.

Kyle handed me a full bottle.

"It's all so incredible. You won't believe any of it," I said.

"Of course we won't, but you have to tell us anyway," Kyle said.

"Yes, we have the whole car ride to Merlin. We can't wait to hear."

"I'm sorry, guys. I just have to sleep," I crawled into the backseat.

"No fair," Linh said.

"Where's Spencer?" Kyle asked. "Does he just live down there on the beach? Where's his car?"

"I don't know," I said.

Two and a half hours later they woke me as we pulled into Aunt Rose's driveway. "Did you guys eat?" I asked. "I'm starving."

"We went to a drive-thru," Linh said. "You didn't even move."

Rose was dressed in a purple and emerald green frock-kind-of-thing. "Tanya and I were just sitting down to eat. Any interest in bacon, eggs, and pancakes?"

"Aunt Rose, you *must* be psychic," I said "Did I ever tell you that you're my favorite aunt?"

"You're sweet as caramel, aren't you, Nate?" Rose led us through to a spacious kitchen. "This is my stepdaughter, Tanya Phelps, the best part of marriage number three, or was it four? Oh, who can keep track of these dramas?" she said, waiving her hand.

Tanya held up three fingers indicating she was from the third marriage.

"Tanya's taking accounting at the local community college," Rose added.

"It's not like I'm going to Harvard or anything," Tanya corrected.

"Accounting is math and that makes you smart enough for Harvard in my book," Rose beamed.

"I'm turning twenty-three tomorrow," Tanya said. "I've decided to give myself a gift. I joined a weight loss clinic, and I'm going to try and lose twenty-three pounds by New Year's, right after I finish these pancakes." Her short curly brown hair and green rectangle eyeglasses made her look more serious than she was. I liked her right away.

After breakfast we moved into Rose's "reading room," as she called it. I was eager to talk to her about my time with Spencer. Kyle and Linh couldn't wait to hear, but I was hesitant to say anything in front of someone I'd just met.

"Tanya is a double-Scorpio and my best friend on the planet. Anything I know, she knows," Rose assured me.

Tanya's large, soft brown eyes seemed to have only three settings: surprise, amusement, and mockery. She was harmless.

"Do you remember Spencer Copeland?" I asked Aunt Rose.

"Sure, course it's been forever ago, twenty years since I heard his name. He and your dad were inseparable, and their other friend, Lee, I kind of had a crush on, but was in the good part of my second marriage so I let it alone."

"Spencer said he knew you during a lifetime at Mesa Verde."

"Did he now, well, that's very sweet. Ask him to come by for some lemonade next time you see him, will you, Nate? Now that I think of it, maybe *he* was the one I had a crush on."

I told them about the healing lessons and my long night in the woods but left out the mountain lion, World War II, the slave trader, and the deer. "And then there's this," I said, pointing to the crystal ball.

"What?' Kyle asked.

"Watch." I stared at it. The ball started rolling in its stand and then floated above the table. No one moved. It traveled quickly in a circle around Rose and then fell gently into Linh's hands.

"Oh, Nate!" Rose cried.

"Amazing!" Tanya laughed.

"You're Harry Potter!" Linh shouted.

"I guess this settles it. You're not crazy, Nate. The rest of us are," Kyle joked.

They were staring at me. "How long have you been able to do that?" Rose asked.

"Since yesterday."

"It's telekinesis," Rose said.

"Sort of, but Spencer says it's more complex. It's called Gogen."

Doing it for them made it real, and I sat there as amazed as they were, wondering what it meant, imagining all the possibilities, and remembering Spencer's warnings about ego.

"Aunt Rose, can you tell me about the wind noise?"

"It's the ancients," she said. "They're opening the channel. They wish to speak to you."

"Do you hear it?"

"Not since I was younger."

"I've got a million questions."

"There is so much to discuss, so many things to show you. When you come next Saturday, we'll spend the day getting into things. I promise."

Kyle said we had better get going soon since we were going to stop at Mountain View to see Dustin again and then still make it back by a decent hour.

"We've got to get him out," I said. "There has to be a way to use my gifts to get him out."

"Nate, even before you showed up the other day, I've thought about every way possible to get Dusty out of there. And the only option that doesn't bring a world of trouble with it is to get your mother to do it."

"She won't."

"It's easy for her. All it takes is the stroke of a pen. She'll listen to you," Rose said.

"Just raise her car up in the air and she'll rethink the whole position," Kyle suggested as we said goodbye to Rose and Tanya.

Dustin came through the same door as he did just two days earlier but was quite different. His words slurred and eyes glazed. "Are you okay?" I asked.

"This is your brain on drugs."

"We'll get you out this week, one way or another."

"Is there a plan?"

"Yes, but you don't want to know it."

"I have to get back to Mount Shasta. Can you take me?"

"What do you need to do there?" I asked, concerned.

"Show you something. You won't believe me if I tell you. I need to show you."

"You'd be surprised by what I can believe."

"I just need to show you," he repeated, agitated.

"Okay, we'll go."

"When?"

"Let's get you out first."

"Get me out first, good idea. Did you see Rose?"

"I did. She said to give you a kiss for her."

"I'd have died long ago without that woman." For a moment he looked like I remembered him when we were kids, innocent yet brave.

It was a two-hour drive home to Ashland, straight down I-5. We'd hit Ashland about five thirty and meet Amber at the Station for dinner. We stopped on the shoulder for about fifteen minutes after two National Guard military vehicles came up behind us. Kyle barely got the Subaru off the road; soldiers were his greatest fear. After a brief meditation, and a fresh cigarette in his mouth, he silently pulled back into traffic.

"You two are such a part of all this, I can't imagine not having you with me. School is going to feel so weird tomorrow," I said.

"What are you going to do, Nate?" Linh asked. "The people looking for you, won't they still be there?"

"Spencer didn't even want you coming back to Ashland."

"What am I going to do? Live at Tea Leaf Beach? I've got to convince my mom to get Dustin out. It's the most important thing in the world to me."

"Are you sure you don't *want* to run into these guys? Do you think that your new powers can somehow make you immune to their tactics?" Kyle asked.

"No, really, that's not it."

"Maybe you'll get all cocky and start looking for a showdown with your father's killer to avenge his death."

"I won't! That would scare the hell out of me. Don't worry."

"We *are* worried, Nate," Linh began. "None of us knows what to expect back home."

The Station was busy for a Sunday night, probably because the "concert" playing on all the big screens was a U2 show from the mid-eighties.

Josh, wearing an electric green T-shirt, waved me over. "Hey, welcome home. Your mom had to run to Sacramento for a used restaurant equipment auction we just heard about yesterday. You know we're redoing part of the kitchen. It's going to be so much better. Let me show you."

"Yeah, Josh, how about another time? I really need to use a phone, and we're starving."

"Oh sure, use your mom's office. Anyway, she'll be back around three tomorrow."

"Thanks." I headed to her office and called Amber.

I looked suspiciously around the room as I made my way to our table.

"We got you a David Gray and some fries," Linh said.

"Perfect, thanks. Amber's on her way. My mom's in Sacramento until tomorrow afternoon, so I guess the Dustin talk will have to wait until then."

Mostly we just watched the concert and waved to a few people from school. Kyle asked what Spencer said about the stuff from Dad's desk, but with everything that happened at the beach I totally forgot about it. I would do it at our next meeting on Friday.

Amber slid into the booth next to me. Even here, with so many college students, heads actually turned when she came into the room. Everyone noticed her sparkling beauty, but she never flaunted her looks. It was more about energy for her, as if she was always seeking the magic she believed existed in every moment. She was as passionate about New Age and metaphysics as Kyle was about philosophy and quantum physics. I sat there for a minute while the others talked. I'd read an article that described her mother as alluring and magnetic on the screen, attributes that Amber inherited, but where did she get her sensitivity? Not from the parents I saw profiled in the tabloids.

"Can I crash at your place tonight? They're watching my house."

"If you promise to tell me everything that happened this weekend," she said.

"I'll give it a shot, but that'll make for a long night."

"Who needs sleep?"

"It's a scaaandal," Kyle chimed.

Amber must have seen me tense up as we pulled up to her house and found its front door open and a strange car in the driveway. "Don't worry, it's just my sister's boyfriend. They're heading back to San Francisco."

"Hi Rod," Amber said as we passed him.

He smiled and nodded, then tossed a couple of bags in his backseat.

"Bridge, you remember Nate?" Amber said to her sister in the front hall.

"Sure, Nate, hi. How's Dustin?" Bridgette Mayes wasn't quite as beautiful as her younger sister, but by any other measure, she was gorgeous. She'd been crazy about Dustin, and his breakdown hit her hard. As far as I knew she hadn't seen or talked to him since. Other than looks, I never understood what he saw in her. Where Amber was engaging and sincere, Bridgette was more like a cardboard cutout that talked in sound bites.

"He's hanging in there," I said.

"Good to hear. Okay, we're out of here, Amber. I'll call you tomorrow. Now you two don't do anything I wouldn't do."

"So anything goes then?"

"Pretty much." She was laughing as the door closed.

Amber let me grab a shower, which I desperately needed. After talking more about Lightyear, Spencer, and the weekend, we read to each other out of her growing New Age library. She was in awe of how, while I was reading something to her, I was absorbing the entire volume at the same time.

"We took our textbooks on the road trip, and not only did I memorize all of mine but Kyle's and Linh's, too!" I said.

Around ten my exhaustion was winning, and Amber set me up in the guest room. "The doors are all locked and I even set the code on the driveway gate so it can't be opened except from the house. No one from Lightyear has a clue you're here, so rest well," Amber said.

The Outview was long and tragic. I tried to turn away from the death, but like the slave trader episode, things got uglier. I was a kid fighting and stealing food from other children during the Black Plague of Europe in the mid 1300s. Death, disease, hunger, and violence were everywhere.

"Nate! It's okay. You're okay." Amber was there. "You're at my house in Ashland. You're safe."

"Oh man, it was awful," I said trembling.

"Come on," she took my hand and led me to her room.

"What?" I asked standing next to her bed. The blue light of a digital clock announced 3:18.

"Get in. You're sleeping with me." Before I could argue she got under the covers and pulled me beside her, hugging against my back, a leg between mine with her arms wrapped around my shoulder and waist. I had on only a pair of sweat-pants, she was wearing the lightest sleep-shorts and matching spaghetti-strap top.

"Do you want to talk about it?" she whispered.

"No. I want to forget about it. I want to forget all my past lives."

Amber felt like sunshine when you come out of a cold lake. The Outviews, Lightyear, and everything else vanished in her softness as she pressed into me. Neither of us spoke, but I knew she was awake, her warm breath somewhere around my neck. I could turn and kiss her easily. I thought about it. In fact, that's almost all I could think about, which was a glorious change, liberation from the hauntings of my mind. That's probably the only reason I didn't make a move. I was afraid to stop the wonderful pause from my crazy world. Amber was protecting me. And out of my ordeal somehow I learned that the purity of her gesture was better than any sex.

The next thing I knew it was 5:51. Amber was still asleep, one arm across my waist. We needed to get moving, but I didn't want this to end, didn't want to go back into the world. Today I needed to convince Mom to get Dustin out. I had more confidence since the night in the woods and my time with Spencer, but I decided not to tell her about my powers or Dad's murder yet. That would certainly confuse the issue of bringing Dustin home. I couldn't see her until after school and that was assuming the Lightyear guys didn't get me first. By 5:59 the stress destroyed the soft mood Amber had created in the night.

"Amber," I said gently. "We should get up."

"All right. Are you okay?" she said, sleepily.

"Yeah. Thanks for last night."

"De nada."

"Hey, how come you don't have a boyfriend?" I asked. It was almost a minute before she answered, and I thought my question offended her.

"Because no one really knows the real me." We were quiet and then she asked, "How come you don't have a girlfriend."

"Because *I* don't even know the real me, and handling one more thing right now would be impossible."

28

Tuesday, September 23

We drove by school twice and decided everything looked okay. Spencer's warning that these people would kill a whole school full of kids kept me alert. "I'll be fine," I said, but I wasn't really sure.

Pop quiz in Algebra II. The groans around the room normally would have included me, but it was enjoyable, and the test in chemistry was fun. The only problem was not finishing too early. Vising changed my whole outlook on school. I was excited about English class, where I knew Mr. James would call on me because he was sure I hadn't read the assigned book, *Catcher in the Rye*.

"Dustin, could you tell me who Luce is?"

"Sure, Mr. Jim." Laughter from the other students.

"Hold on, funny man, my name is *not* Mr. Jim."

"I know. And mine's not Dustin."

"It's not?" He looked at his attendance book. "You are correct, Nathan, isn't that unusual? Now see if you can tell me who Luce is."

"Luce is a friend of Holden's. They talk a lot about girls. Holden thinks Luce is cool. And Luce told him to get a girlfriend."

"Where did they meet?"

"In a bar."

"I see you have read an online summary of the book, Mr. Ryder. I frown on that. I consider it cheating."

"I didn't read an online summary."

"Cliff Notes, then."

"No. Ask me any question you want." He asked me thirty-seven questions until the bell rang ending class, each one answered correctly.

"Nice to see you finally read a book, Mr. Ryder. I'm not surprised *Catcher in the Rye* appealed to you. We'll see how well you do with Shakespeare. Class dismissed."

Amber found me at lunch. "Are we going to sleep together again tonight?" she whispered.

"The scandals if anyone heard what you just said," I teased. "I might just start the rumor myself." I could hear Kyle saying it now in a falsetto.

"I'll just deny it, and who do you think they're going to believe?" She laughed.

My French teacher called on me and asked in French if I'd done my homework.

"Oui," I answered.

"Très bon. S'il vous plaît dites-moi quelle est ta couleur préférée?" she asked.

"J'aime la couleur grise,'" I answered. She was quite surprised.

"Quels aliments que vous aimez?"

"J'aime la pizza et des frites françaises et des tasses de beurre d'arachide, mais seulement pour le petit déjeuner."

She laughed. We talked like that back and forth for five minutes. Several students started clapping. When they settled down, she called on someone else and we got back to a normal class. At the end of the period she asked me to stay.

"Cela était tout à fait une démonstration de la fluidité. Comment avez-vous fait cela, Nathan?"

"Vraiment, c'est pas une grosse affaire que je viens de passer beaucoup de temps avec ce livre," I said.

She gave me a disbelieving look but then said in French that she might have to transfer me to French IV.

Kyle was waiting in the hall. "Do you really think that was a good idea?"

"Probably not, but it sure was a lot of fun."

Linh ran up to us. "There's a black SUV with government plates out front, and I just saw some guy wearing a suit go into Little's office."

"That can't be good. I'll cut my last class and get out of here. I'll see you guys later at the Station. Make sure you aren't followed." But as I shut my locker, I realized they could find me anywhere. If I'd known I was never going to return to Ashland High School again, I would have said goodbye to my history teacher, Mr. Anderson.

Before going into the restaurant, I went behind the building and tried Vising to read a large tree that was across from the loading dock. If I could just see what happened the day my dad died. Instead, I saw him several times, but all were weeks or months before his death. I headed in to see Mom.

"Hey Nate," Josh said, looking up from his paperwork. "Out of school a little early?"

"Yeah, I blew off gym."

"I don't blame you." He laughed. "Your mom should be here any time now."

I asked to see the plans for changing the kitchen. Afterward he showed me some photos from a recent trip to the Southwest. Josh gave me my first camera for my ninth birthday. Mom thought I'd break it—being tough on toys was a habit—but that digital camera woke me up to the details of the world. I took hundreds of shots a day. Eventually the shutter button wore out, but by then I was hooked. Josh helped me start selling my early photos. I think he and Dad actually bought the first twenty or so, but they told me strangers did.

When Mom showed up, Josh excused himself. "How was your trip?" she asked, putting down her briefcase and water bottle.

"I saw Dustin this weekend."

"You what?" she gasped. "How did you find out where he was?"

"It wasn't hard. You should have taken me to see him a long time ago."

"Nate, I don't like you being dishonest with me."

"Don't you think not letting me see my brother for more than two years qualifies as dishonest? Maybe even cruel and unusual."

"I don't have to defend my decisions to you. I've done what is best for both of you."

That was highly debatable, but it wasn't going well and I needed to stay calm. "That doesn't matter anymore. All that's important is getting Dustin out."

"He's not ready."

"That's a lie. I talked to him. He's perfectly fine. You're just trying to lock your problems away."

"How dare you, Nathan! If your father was alive, you would never speak to me this way."

"If my father was alive, Dustin would not be wasting away in an asylum."

"That's not fair." Her voice shaking, "Dustin's a mess. If he gets out of there he'll start using drugs and end up trying to kill himself again."

"So it makes more sense for him to choose the drugs he wants instead of the poison they give him? Better to kill himself than let those stupid doctors do it."

"You don't know what you're talking about. Everything isn't so simple. If you think he's fine that's because of what Mountain View has done for him. He has complex problems, brain disorders, addictions, serious issues. We're not equipped to handle that, I'm hardly ever home as it is."

"I've noticed."

"That's a cheap shot, Nate."

"I don't even want to get into that."

She wiped tears from her eyes. "I've really tried to do a decent job with you boys. It's not easy. I'm sorry if you think I'm no good."

"If you're really sorry, then get him out of there. What kind of mother lets her son be tortured?" I tried to soften my tone.

"They're not doing electric shock therapy on him."

"Not with electricity, but the chemicals are doing the same thing. Don't you think it's hypocritical that you eat organic food because you don't want chemicals and pesticides in your body but you let them do that to him?"

"It's not the same thing."

"Tell me how it's different. I mean, Mom, you don't even use nonorganic here at the Station. But then, we all know your precious restaurant is more important to you than your kids."

"Nathan, you're so far over the line I don't even know how to talk to you anymore. What happened to my sweet little boy? When did you get so angry?"

"When I got old enough to realize you're screwing up my life."

She just looked at me. There was a long silence. So much for me remaining cool. I think she glanced at the picture of my father on her desk. When she began to speak there were fresh tears in her eyes, but her voice was calm and gentle, "Nate, what's going on?"

"I want Dustin out of that place."

"I know, but what else is going on?"

"You mean, am I on drugs, going insane, a serial killer? You sound just like Mrs. Little."

"That's not what I asked. Please, just talk to me." She walked around her desk and sat in the chair next to me. "You can trust me."

"Trust is earned Mom. You can't expect me to trust you after what you did to Dustin."

"You were twelve when Dad died and fourteen when Dustin was committed. You don't know everything that was going on. If I hadn't committed Dustin, he'd be dead now. That much I know for sure."

"What if you're being sure isn't enough? What if there's another way? He's older, I'm older, you are, too. Let's bring him home and try."

"I can't handle it, Nate. I'll screw it up, and Dustin will be worse off than ever."

"Fine, he can stay with Aunt Rose."

"Oh, Jesus, Nate. Your Aunt Rose is loony tunes. She and Dustin will wind up as some tragic tabloid story if I let that happen."

"Nothing can be as awful than where he is now. Just let him try. Give it a week. Take it a day at a time. You owe him a chance."

"I know." I could barely hear her response.

"I'm begging you, Mom. I need my brother—we need each other."

Another long silence. "Okay, Nate, I guess." Defeated, she went on. "I could sign him out for a temporary home visit and see how it goes." Her eyes were strained, tired.

We hugged for the first time since Dustin went away. She agreed that I could go with her to get him first thing in the morning. "We need the talking time," she said.

We were going to get Dustin! I couldn't wait to see the look on his face when we showed up to bring him home.

"I'm going to stay at Kyle's tonight. We're working on a research project, and because I'll be missing school tomorrow, we need to get ahead."

"Okay, can he drop you here on his way to school? I have a couple of things in the morning, real quick before we leave." That was perfect because I couldn't go near the house with the Lightyear guys out there, and I was looking forward to another night with Amber.

I was out of clean clothes from the trip and didn't want to wash them at Amber's, so walked to the "Suds and Save," a couple of blocks toward campus. A few college kids and some old ladies were the only ones in the place so it seemed safe. I pulled the weekend's clothes from my backpack and got the wash going.

"Nathan, I thought I might find you here," an old Spanish lady said to me.

"Not again," I said out loud, certain I'd never seen this woman before in my life.

"In this life, no," she said, reading my thoughts. "But we've known each other many times, you and I."

"Are you one of my guides?" I asked, trying to move farther away so no one would hear.

"You are so young this time. I have traveled a long way to see you."

"Where did you come from?"

"There are many stories from our past that you should know about. There is danger for you soon, no time today."

"What danger? Do you know specifics?"

"It was on a ship the first time we met. And do you know that seven or nine lifetimes we knew each other in between, and then, the last time I saw you, on a ship again. Isn't that something?"

"It would be interesting if I knew what you were talking about, and I don't want to be rude. I mean I don't know if we were married or brothers or maybe you were my mother. But that's just it, I don't remember. So, I'm sorry, but I'm pretty stressed right now and then you show up and you know me and maybe you could help. But you aren't answering my questions."

"It feels different. But you know I've been needing to see you since before you were born this time. More than twenty years ago I started the search to clear the karma. It wasn't just for me, but because of what happened, Ignacio has suffered."

"Just tell me what you're talking about," I begged.

"You know, I could have come last year, but you would have just thought me a crazy old woman, and so I waited."

"You are a crazy old woman." I laughed. "What do you want?"

"Forgiveness."

"For what?"

She just stared, deep and sorrowful.

"Yes. I forgive you everything," I said.

"I wish it were that simple, but you must know the stories. You must understand where it began and the last ending.

When you remember all of that, the agony of it, the rage," she steadied herself against a dryer, "that is when you can decide if you will forgive or not."

"Look, um, what's your name?"

"I am Amparo."

"Amparo?" I looked at her. "You're the one who told Kyle about meeting Spencer?" The dryer whirred.

"Yes," she stared long at me. "A very small favor to help you."

The implications of her being the same person who helped Spencer contact us multiplied beyond what I could handle. The dryer stopped.

"Okay, thanks. But listen, you really don't know me. If whatever you're talking about happened in another lifetime, then I'm over it, okay? Really, you could have cut my head off with a butter knife, and I wouldn't hold it against you anymore, okay? I don't hold grudges. You're all right, really, it's over."

She smiled one of those wise, all-knowing smiles that only old people are able to pull off. "You are young." She put a finger to my cheek. "I will wait. But you and I may yet have little time. Karma is forever."

She was quiet. "You shall see it as a vision. It will come because we have met. I am so very sorry for what you are going to see, Niño. And then we will meet again because we must."

I took my clothes from the dryer and said goodbye. It would have been easy to forget about her because my brain was on complete overload, but the pain in her eyes was unlike anything I'd ever seen before, even in all my Outviews. I needed to understand karma better, needed a book.

I dialed Sam's cell from the payphone outside the Laundromat.

"Sam, it's Nate."

"I didn't recognize the number."

"I'm at a payphone. Listen, I'm mixed up in something. I don't want to talk too much about it over the phone, but maybe tomorrow afternoon, if you have some time, I could come over?"

"Sure, anytime, but what's this about?"

"My dad didn't die the way you think. And there are some people who want that fact to remain a secret. And they may be after me."

"Are you serious? Are you saying what I think you are?"

"Yes. And I can't go to the FBI because it's people within the government."

"You really are in a mess, aren't you? How did you learn all this?"

"It's a long story. I'll tell you later."

"If you're right about all this, then what you need is a good lawyer. And my sister's one of the best. She's a top criminal defense attorney and sues the government all the time. I couldn't tell you how many corruption cases she's been involved in. We can trust her. If you want, I'll call her and see if she can be on the phone with us tomorrow. What time do you want to come over?"

"Oh Sam, that would be fantastic. I'll be back by three." Once again Sam, unlike Mom, believed me right away.

"Good. I'll set it up."

Walking back to the Station, I was relieved. An experienced lawyer would know how to navigate this. But they'd want proof, and I wasn't sure how to provide that. There must be a way. Maybe the things from my dad's desk held some answers.

Kyle was waiting in the parking lot at the Station when I got back. Linh was home safe with Bà. Heading to Amber's, we talked about karma.

"In Buddhist teachings"—it was one of his topics—"for every event that occurs, there will follow a reciprocal event. It can happen in this lifetime or in another."

"So, if I did something bad in my last life, I may have already paid my karmic debt in *that* lifetime?"

"That's how I understand it. Like if you steal something from me today, you should try to clear that within this life so you don't make your next incarnation more difficult. And if you do many good deeds, then it can make things easier for this life and others that follow."

"Seems like a fair system."

"It is one way to explain all the inequalities in the world."

"So all the rich people were really charitable or poor last time around, and this is their reward?"

"I don't think it's nearly *that* simple."

"Now you sound like Spencer."

"I'd like to hear how he explains it."

We backtracked several times and crisscrossed up side streets to make sure we weren't being followed.

30

Amber was sitting on her wide front porch reading *The Seat of the Soul* by Gary Zukav. She hugged us both, then handed me a phone and gave Kyle two, one for Linh. "Prepaid. Untraceable. We have to be able to communicate." She wouldn't let me pay her back. "I've programmed in all our numbers."

"Amber, this is great. I've been going through cell phone withdrawal." I laughed. Kyle pointed out that the NSA could still pickup key words so we agreed not to use names, even Lightyear or anything specific.

After Kyle left, Amber cooked a fancy dinner with help from the housekeeper. Luckily her sister phoned, which gave me a break from Amber's nonstop questions about Spencer, Rose and my "powers." Kyle called to say everything was fine. No sign of anyone. I convinced Amber we needed to give all the New Age talk a rest. "It's too much sometimes. I just want to feel normal."

"Let's talk about football," she said.

"I didn't know you liked football."

"I got it from my dad. He's a Raiders fan, so I like the Chargers."

"That must be hard being a Chargers fan."

"Shut up. Who do you like?"

"The only California team that matters, the 49ers, of course." She knew more obscure stats about players than I did.

We were still talking football when the housekeeper stopped in the living room to say she was leaving.

Around 7:30 Amber went into the kitchen for drinks. I started sweating, like someone had cranked the temperature up to a hundred. She returned with two sodas just as I realized this was the same warning heat I felt before the mountain lion showed up. Looking at Amber, I held my finger to my lips and went quietly to the window.

"Come on," I whispered.

"What? Is someone out there?"

"I don't see anyone, but Lightyear agents are definitely here." I slung my pack on and headed toward the back.

"Where are we going?" Amber asked.

"We have to leave," I said firmly.

She hesitated.

"Now!" I grabbed her hand, and shot across the backyard into the trees. Behind a scrub oak, I looked back at the house; there was still no sign of movement, but my temperature had not cooled. "Do you know where these woods come out?" I asked her.

"It connects to Lithia Park," she said.

"Let's go." We tore through the trees and twenty minutes later entered the southwest side of the park. I called Kyle and asked him to pick us up where he taught me to meditate.

By the time we got to the Japanese Garden, Kyle was parked in his aunt's car. I climbed in the front. "What happened?" he asked, pulling away.

"Someone came to Amber's."

"Who? How did they find you?" he asked.

"We didn't actually see anyone," Amber said.

Kyle looked at me.

"They were there. You guys should know by now that I'm not just paranoid," I said.

"You *are* paranoid, but even paranoid people have enemies," Kyle said.

"Why your aunt's car?" I asked.

"I thought it was a good idea because they know mine."

Amber reluctantly agreed to sleep at a friend's house, and a few minutes later Kyle and I were alone.

"If they came for you at Amber's, then they'll find you anytime now, and then what?"

"I don't know, but right now I need a place to stay tonight by myself. I don't want my friends in any more danger than they already are."

"I've got my aunt's keys to the theater on this ring."

"The Shakespeare Theater? Isn't that a little unusual."

"And you're not!"

"I guess it's one of the last places they would look."

The Oregon Shakespeare Festival is huge in Ashland. They do 750 performances across three theaters, with an annual attendance of about 400,000. The Elizabethan theater has a traditional open roof and is modeled after London's original Fortune Theatre and the famous Globe of 1599.

"Look at the stars," Kyle said. "It'll be just like camping. Too bad your sleeping bag is in my car. But you can find something in wardrobe and sleep backstage anyway. Just be out by six in the morning. I'll call your phone to wake you."

Once Kyle was gone I questioned my actions. What the hell was I doing? People were after me! They knew I was at Amber's. How long would it take them to pick me up? The federal government was massive, and there were departments no one knew about. The motives and manipulations of the darkest parts were frightening. And, as Spencer put it, the people wielding the power from those places might be the closest thing to evil. "The universe is beautiful, peaceful and loving. But there are people who are something else entirely," he had said. And those were the ones hunting me.

31

The backstage area was actually a three-story building over a maze of dressing rooms, storage areas, and steps to the towers. The place smelled like plywood, make-up, roses, and sweat. I found the wardrobe area and a pile of blankets, then discovered a side room filled with all types of props and four mattresses. I tipped one flat and lay down, apparently going out instantly because when I checked my phone it was 3:28 a.m., almost six hours of sleep, with just one Outview—Amparo and me on a fishing boat, of course ending in my death. She failed to save me, but it didn't seem to warrant her pain and desperation for forgiveness. I wandered around looking for a Coke machine or even water and found myself back in the amphitheater under dazzling stars.

I stared up into the universe and tried to raise my guides, meditating and begging. I desperately wanted someone to talk to me in clear and simple terms. Spencer had said humans are on about the slowest vibration, that guides and more evolved entities have to slow their vibration extremely just to get to a human level of understanding. Because of the substantial reduction in the original vibration, much of their actual message is lost in translation. He also had explained that information from guides is so far beyond our comprehension that when we begin opening up to our soul and the universe, we become easily confused and overwhelmed. I knew just what he meant.

But my guides must be protecting me somehow because I was still alive and free.

Then I heard her voice. "It reminds me of another time long ago… "

"Amparo, what are you doing here?" I was startled. "How did you know?"

"I'm just waiting, hoping… "

"Until you get my forgiveness?"

She nodded.

I let out an exasperated sigh. "I saw you, Amparo. You and I were on a big fishing boat somewhere in the North Pacific. It seemed to be in the 1960s, so either you're not really alive right now or it was a simultaneous incarnation."

"Yes, my soul is living five lives in present time."

"Okay, so there was a tragic accident, but you tried to help me. I mean, you struggled and even though you didn't save me… You couldn't hold on any longer; our hands slipped apart. I was looking right into your eyes as that piece of equipment crushed me. It wasn't your fault, but I forgive you."

"No, Niño, there is more."

"Fine, we've had other lifetimes, you told me that. It doesn't matter to me what happened. I'm only concerned with this life and staying alive."

"You are mistaken. There is much that concerns you that has little or nothing to do with this incarnation."

"Please, let's leave it in the past."

"It cannot remain there, Niño. It will not stay in the past until there is understanding and forgiveness." Her eyes carried the injuries of centuries.

"What do you need me to do?"

"Take my hand and look back between us. See what is there, and then do what your heart wants."

"I forgive you."

"You may decide to kill me."

"You've got to be joking!" But I could tell she was not.

"There were three great betrayals. They were all my doing. You have never retaliated in any way, although you had opportunities."

"I guess you were never a slave." She didn't know what I meant.

"Please." She gave me her dry, wrinkled hand, I closed my eyes and the Outviews took over, catapulting across time into ancient dwellings of my soul.

The first encounter occurred more than two thousand years ago. We were peasant oarsmen on a Roman merchant ship somewhere in the Mediterranean. Amparo stole a small amount of food and was caught. Rather than take the punishment, "she" claimed to be working at my direction. In the hours that followed, another accuser, Amparo's friend, stepped forward and charged that I was responsible for earlier thefts. That man also reported me for attempting to recruit him in my "gang of thieves." I was thrown overboard. After treading water for half a day, I drowned.

I had done nothing to deserve that awful fate. The peasant I was had never wronged Amparo, didn't even know "him." Furious, I wanted to scream and tell her what she had done. Amparo didn't know of the peasant's family—his sisters, nieces, and nephews who loved him and always waited for his return, wondering what happened. I wanted her to know all about the life she took. But still, I could forgive her.

Another meeting of our souls occurred during the late thirteenth century in northern Italy. Amparo was my mother, and I, not yet eighteen, was a married woman, Helna, with a two-year-old child. It was during an early and particularly brutal era of the Catholic Church's Inquisition. It was the pope's way of putting down competing religions by forcing the heretics to convert or face prison, torture, and death. This would continue in various forms for six hundred years. My mother was charged with heresy and kept in prison for several years without trial. And trial was not how we understand it today but a public humiliation where only a full confession would offer any kind of reduced punishment, meaning avoiding death. But since that required implicating others, it was its own kind of cruelty. Amparo (my mother) falsely accused me to avoid more torture. I never saw my husband or son again. And that was worse than the different tortures the Church inflicted upon me before my death in prison.

The pain of never holding my son again left a gaping emptiness of longing, I was lost. As Nate, I relived the betrayal of my mother from that time and knew Helna's complete rage as she suffered away in a crowded dungeon. The anger flowed through the modern me. Helna needed revenge, and I wanted to give it to her. I had to destroy the person who caused the agony. It was a consuming narcotic; I was ready to kill her.

What I saw next would take a year to retell in enough detail so that one could begin to understand the layers of emotions and drama that led to the third betrayal. I lived it all that night, suffering as if it had happened to Nate today in Ashland, Oregon, rather than to Erich in the Harz Mountain region in Germany during the peak of Nazi power. Prior to the war, I had lived in Halberstadt and fell in love with Rachel, a beautiful Jewish girl. Neither family approved, but we stole moments and were planning to marry. The rise of the Nazis changed all that, and, within the turmoil of the SS rounding up our friends, we managed to escape to the mountains with twelve of her relatives, including her eight-year-old brother and ten-year-old sister.

My late grandfather had once had a small cabin deep in the forest high above the Bode Gorge in the Harz Mountains. I'd only been there once as a young boy but had his handwritten map and after more than a week in the wilderness found it. He had spoken of a woman, Marlene, who lived in the village, eight miles from his cabin, and my mother said she could be trusted. She turned out to be our lifeline, selling us several chickens and a goat, and occasionally sending her fifteen-year-old daughter with flour and grains. That, along with hunting and gathering in the forest, kept us alive. A small stream, two miles away, supplied water. The treks were long and we couldn't do it in the winter, but then there was plenty of snow to melt. We were able to build a second room onto the cabin so it wasn't quite so crowded.

We lived that way for seventeen months before the SS discovered us, led by Marlene's daughter, who I now know as Amparo. I never found out why she betrayed us. Everything quickly disintegrated into horrors. Rachel's father was beaten to death, and I had to watch Rachel and her sister raped before we left the woods. Three days without food ended at Dachau. It would take more than two years for all of us to slowly die as part of one of the worst nightmares in human history.

It wasn't like watching a movie of these lifetimes. I actually relived them in full 3D suffering. It would be impossible for me as Nate to ever get the sadistic guards from the death camp out of my mind. The things I witnessed in the Italian medieval prison would have been enough to steal the beauty from my life. But then Amparo sent me to Dachau, and I would never again, in any lifetime, be able to enjoy a peaceful existence without being haunted by those images.

Amparo would have to die. How could anyone cause such misery? And she certainly couldn't be trusted. She had probably already contacted Lightyear. They could be waiting outside, or maybe they'd just come in and shoot me. But didn't she like me to have long tortuous deaths? A simple bullet wouldn't do—better to dream up a nice slow painful way to go. Surely the folks at Lightyear could handle that.

I did not want to open my eyes because if I did I may have never stopped crying, and I needed to decide the best way to murder the old lady next to me. Her hand was still in mine and my disgust made me want to squeeze so tight her bones would snap.

"Please look at me." It was the voice of the peasant sailor who'd gotten me tossed into the Mediterranean.

My eyes flew open, and I ripped my hand away. It wasn't until I jumped to my feet, ready to defend myself and ready to fight, that I saw him on his knees before me. He caught my eyes in his, and I experienced his life. It had all been lived in fear. Everyone he ever loved—his parents, siblings, a woman, children, and friends—had been murdered by invading Romans, all, except Ignacio. Amparo mentioned him in our first meeting at the Laundromat, the one also affected by our karmic crisis. He had been the other guy on the boat who corroborated Amparo's story and was his only remaining friend. Ignacio was about to take responsibility before Amparo thought to blame me.

He looked at me so full of regret and agony that I knew his soul had carried the heavy burden for two millennia. It wasn't a decision made by Nathan Ryder but rather by my soul.

"I forgive you," I told him. Instantly, a release occurred making me lighter and freer. So great was the high that when I next heard the voice of Helna's mother, I welcomed her.

The peasant morphed into her as I watched. Remaining on her knees she looked up into my face so lovingly that I must have appeared not as Nate but as Helna. Her life before I was born played between our gaze, and again I witnessed our experience together as mother and daughter. This time I was seeing all the sacrifices and missing parts from her point of view. Next came her time in prison, not much different from my own, but she lacked youth and rage to carry her through. In the end, there was no excuse for turning me over to the Church; they had just worn her down. The act of surrendering your child to end your own pain is not natural, and it had distorted every life she had lived since.

"You are forgiven," I whispered. The surge of joy in me was immediate, powerful, and transformative—my thoughts were clearer and my whole being calmer.

Then she became Marlene's daughter, who was sixteen by the time she brought the SS to exterminate us. When she found my eyes, her face displayed pure terror. She had no idea what she had done until it was too late. It would take many more years before she learned the whole truth of what consequences had resulted from her actions. She was merely trying to impress a young German soldier she had a crush on stationed near her village. She thought we would be sent home to work in some kind of internment camp until the war was over. Her mother was the first to explain what she had really done, but it would take eight more years before the full repercussions became known. Consumed by unbearable guilt, she had taken her own life at twenty-four.

Even then, forgiving her would have been out of the question without the first two forgivenesses. I looked at her for a long time, trying to see past the atrocities of Dachau, and although those ghosts would never release their grip on me, I fought through my conflicts. Taking her hands, I raised her up never losing eye contact until tears flowed.

"I forgive you," I said, hugging her tight. Instantly ecstatic euphoria overtook me, and we both started laughing. Then she was Amparo again.

"Thank you," she said through tears. There was something different about her appearance. She was healthier, younger, happier.

We didn't share many more words, as I was suddenly completely fatigued and needed sleep. She sat in the chair next to me and found a blanket somewhere. I slept as peacefully as I could remember; forgiveness was a deep, soft, comforting place.

32

ednesday, September 24

At 5:30 a.m., my phone rang. "Hello Mr. Ryder, this is your wake-up call." Kyle snickered. "We hope you enjoyed your stay at the Shakespearean Inn and Campground." I quickly re-arranged my backstage bed and removed any trace. I had to get out before the first workers arrived, but waited until the last moment. Outside worried me. I was excited about getting Dustin, but something about the day ahead made me uneasy. In fact, the future in general was beginning to feel claustrophobic.

It was a typical brisk late September morning in Ash-land, heading fast toward warm. Clouds didn't exist, and the sun seemed to know its annual three-month battle with fog was still six weeks away. Rounding a corner, on the ten-min-ute walk from the theater to the Station, I almost tripped over one of the town's rare homeless. With dirty hair matted in dreads and clothes worn and soiled, the bearded man looked ancient but, if cleaned up and shaved, was probably only fifty.

"Watch it, kid."

"Sorry, I didn't see you."

"Yeah, pretend we're not here, the invisible, scavenging downtrodden. Look the other way—you may catch leprosy," he said with a glare. "You high and mighty people can't abide by the scourge of us lost and forgotten souls. Careful, I might touch you!"

"Maybe other people are afraid of you or want to pretend you don't exist. I just think you've got an attitude problem."

He laughed so hard, for a minute I thought he might die coughing. About to leave, I waited to make sure he lived through the spasm.

"I wasn't always like this," he said.

"Of course not. No one is born that filthy."

He laughed again, this time rolling over.

I started to walk away.

"Hey, could you spare a few thousand dollars?" he called.

I couldn't help but laugh.

"How about more then? I could really use a million. I need to buy a house," he cackled. "I'm homeless, remember? You know that fancy neighborhood above the boulevard? I'd like a house there. It would make those uptight people *very* nervous. I'd have my hobo friends over, and we'd dress like this and live out on the lawn. Never even go in the house." He was hooting now.

I handed him a five-dollar bill. "Well, start saving."

"Hey, what do you know? Kid's funny *and* has a heart. See, here's the thing." He produced a wooden match from somewhere and struck it with his tooth. "This money isn't even real." He lit the five-dollar bill.

I reached for it, but he swung it away. "I guess you're not eating today then, or drinking," I added under my breath.

"Why, because that money's gone? It wasn't real in the first place. If I'm hungry, I'll eat. And if I'm thirsty, I'll drink!"

"Hard to do without money."

"Money, why are you so obsessed with it?" He fanned five-dollar bills, hundreds of them.

"Where did you steal that?"

"People give it to me."

"So you can burn it?"

"It's mine. I can do what I want with it. Want yours back?"

"No." I started to walk away again.

"Good because *yours* is just a pile of ashes." He lit the others.

I thought of stomping on the pile. It was probably more than a thousand dollars; he was obviously out of his mind. Instead of leaving, I watched it burn. "Were you rich once?"

"I've been everything once," he hesitated. "But none of it really matters. Nothing matters but this moment. People get weighed down with money and all that it buys. Stuff, everyone has so much stuff. It ends up ruling them. A man with possessions is not free."

"A warm dry house with a roof over your head and food in the kitchen can be nice."

"Then why did you sleep in the theater? It has no roof."

"How'd you know that?"

"It's easy to see where people have been. Once you're not mired in the muck of the material world, everything is apparent."

"Who are you?"

"My friends call me Crowd."

"Funny name for a guy who doesn't like people."

"Who said I don't? I like them. I just don't want to be around any. I feel sorry for them."

"Why?"

"Because the unseen world is all around us. It's where everything really happens, where everything originates. But ninety-nine percent don't see it. All they see is TV and Walmart."

"Sure sounds like you don't like them."

"People passing by me every day think I'm dirt. For all they know, I'm a Pulitzer Prize–winning writer, a Nobel Laureate or someone's grandfather, but they don't know because they never bother to stop. Busy, busy, busy! What if talking to me could solve all their problems? Answer all their questions?" He kicked at the ashes of the money. "When someone goes into a shop, a bank, or a restaurant, clean, nicely dressed people serve them, but they're still indifferent or even rude, downright mean to their servers. And the thing is they have no idea what is going on in the clerk's life or the teller's or the waiter's. For all they know, that morning the clerk found out her father had a stroke, or the teller discovered his wife was leaving him, or the waiter is waiting for test results on whether he lives or dies. Maybe one of them lost a child a few weeks earlier. No one knows; no one cares. How did this happen that strangers got so strange?"

"Am I supposed to be able to answer that?"

"It's a shame you have so much to do. What with all the older generations screwing everything up so bad. The youth, as always, is our only hope." He held a hand up offering me a five-dollar bill again.

I shook my head.

"I'll see you again sometime," he said, grinning. "Think about what I said. Ask, seek, think. One day you may need to understand people better. Teenagers don't know everything; they just think they do. The difference is they're more open than the grown-up sheep."

During the car ride with Mom, I tried to keep the conversation light. I didn't want her to change her mind. "Josh offered to help with Dustin once we get him home," she began. "They were so close. Dustin used to hang around the Station every day after school, helping him and your dad."

"I remember. I was there, too."

"Just younger."

"Yeah, I've always been younger than Dustin. That's why he's my older brother."

She broke the tension with a quick laugh.

The woman at the desk said, "Good morning, Mrs. Ryder."

"Hi Kristy, I'd like to sign Dustin out for a family visit."

"What do you mean? I thought you knew," Kristy looked very concerned.

"Knew what?"

"Dustin's no longer here. They transferred him."

"Transferred? Where? Who?"

"It was some government thing."

Her words nauseated me. "When?" I demanded.

"Just a few hours ago."

"Kristy, what is going on here?" Mom was losing it.

"Let me get the administrator."

"You better get someone. I want to know what the hell you've done with my son!"

Moments later a man in a white coat was there. "Mrs. Ryder. I'm sorry, I was planning to call you this afternoon."

"Dr. Crane, you had better tell me where Dustin is right now."

"He's been transferred to St. Elizabeth's."

"Where is that?"

"Washington."

"You let someone take my son out of state? Where is he, Seattle? I'll drive there right now."

"Not Washington state, Mrs. Ryder. St. Elizabeth's is in Washington, D.C."

"What? You've moved him to the other side of the country? Under whose authority? Why wasn't I called?"

"The Department of Homeland Security."

"Are you kidding?" she asked. I found a chair and fell into it.

"Mrs. Ryder, their paperwork was all in order."

"What are you talking about? How do you know their paperwork was in order? Does Homeland Security come in here *regularly* and take your patients? Is this common?" Mom was angry but clearly thought this was some classic government snafu. All I could think was the faceless man who killed my dad now had my brother. I didn't know what to do. He might not even be alive anymore.

"I did call Washington and verify."

"Let me see the paperwork, I want to know who to call to fix this mess." He handed her a clipboard. "Look right here," she pointed to the form. "This is obviously a mistake. It says here he is being moved because of national security reasons. And the box next to "threat" is checked. Dustin has been locked up here for more than two years, before that he was playing high school baseball and Little League, before that he was in goddamn diapers. He's no threat to national security." She actually laughed. "You people are the crazy ones around here. Make me copies of these and get Homeland Security on the phone," she demanded, as she pushed the clipboard back to the doctor. "Don't worry, Nate, we'll get this straightened out." She looked at me. "Nate, are you okay?"

"No," I said, too upset to cry.

Before she could respond, the doctor handed Mom a phone. More than half an hour later Mom slammed it down. "I've never been so frustrated in my life. They slid my call around to six different people and finally told me this case is classified. I'm his mother, and they tell me it's classified. They're sending me forms to fill out. They've got my boy and they're sending me flippin' forms. Dr. Crane, you better lawyer up because I'm going to close you people down." She scooped up the papers Kristy had copied. "Come on, Nate, we're going to hire the meanest son of a bitch lawyer we can find."

"Can you believe this?" she said once we were in the car. "And don't start with me because I know you're going to tell me this is all my fault."

"It's not *your* fault, it's mine. They're using Dustin to get to me."

"Who is? What are you saying?" she shrieked.

"Mom, we need to talk."

"I'm right here. Start talking. Are you somehow in trouble with the federal government? What on earth is going on?"

"I can only do this if you promise me that you won't say anything until I'm done and that you'll keep an open mind."

"Okay. I'll try."

"Dad was murdered."

"Oh, come on, Nate. Did you get that trash from Aunt Rose?"

"Mom, you promised."

"There was an autopsy for God's sake? Who'd want to kill your father? He was the kindest man on earth. You're making me very upset."

"Jesus, Mom, the autopsy was faked. Do you believe everything they tell you? Dad was killed by someone in the CIA because he knew too much."

"You've been watching too many stupid spy movies with Sam. What would he have known? How to design a menu? What inventory to have on hand for Super Bowl weekend? The only thing your father knew about the CIA was the time he spent at the Culinary Institute of America! This is ridiculous."

"He knew some serious secret stuff. He was psychic. That's where Dustin and I got it, and Grandma had it, too. Are you going to tell me you *really* didn't know about his powers, our powers? Why do you have such a hard time believing your sons?"

She started to cry.

I took the papers and held them in my hands. A minute later I knew every thing they said. The only part that mattered was they had been signed by Agent Sanford Fitts. My enemy now had a name.

"I don't know, Nate, I don't know. I'm not completely blind. Your dad tried to tell me some things around the time I was pregnant with Dustin. I never wanted to hear it. I loved your dad, but all this witchcraft stuff, it isn't natural."

"It's not witchcraft, and there's nothing more natural than connecting to our soul. It's the human world that's not natural."

"I grew up a good Catholic, and it's hard for me to not think of ESP, reincarnation, and talking to the dead as wicked and sinful or plain silly."

"What if I told you the Catholic Church taught reincarnation for its first five hundred years? It was a Jesuit priest, Pierre Teilhard de Chardin, who said, 'We are not human beings having a spiritual experience; we are spiritual beings having a human experience.' Dustin and I have special abilities. You can't deny what is true, Mom."

"I'm listening."

"Are you?" I stared. "Good. Then hear this. The CIA has psychic spies, and the corrupt man in charge of them is using ESP to get money and power for a small group. Dad had a friend who was working for them, but once he discovered the truth, he was about to go to the media with the whole story. They killed him, but not before he told Dad. Only they didn't know which Montgomery Ryder he told, so they killed all eleven of them."

"Oh my God! How do you know this?" She was pale, but I repeated it again so she could not miss how horrific it was.

"They killed eleven innocent people just to be sure they silenced one. Four years later, Kyle, Linh, and I searched the Internet with the code name of the agency along with Dad's friend's name. And suddenly they're after me. They couldn't get me easily, so they took Dustin."

"Is it true?" she asked through tears.

"I'm afraid so. And at the same time this is going on, I'm fighting for my sanity. I've seen visions of hundreds of deaths from past lives. Spiritual guides whisper in my ear, and I can see images and things you couldn't believe."

"Like Dustin."

I nodded.

"Oh God, what have I done to Dustin? To both of you?" She sobbed uncontrollably now. I held her.

"Mom, get it together. We need to go."

"Can you ever forgive me?"

"I'm working on it. You really need to ask that question of Dustin." This set off another round of crying. But relief surged. She finally believed. More than Sam or Spencer or anyone else, that made me know for sure I wasn't crazy—*my mom* believed me.

Any joy from the resolution between us was quickly replaced by awful thoughts of what was happening to Dustin. We had to find him. "Mom, we need to see Aunt Rose. It's not safe for me in Ashland, and Rose can help us." She was in no condition to argue. I explained how Rose had visited Dustin regularly to try and keep him sane.

"We'll fix this, Nate," my mother repeated every time there was a lull in our conversation. But she, like me, was in over her head. I told her more about the people after me and could see her struggle to concentrate on driving. Mom's face showed emotions ranging from confusion to real fear. Would she have a breakdown once it had all sunk in? We needed her strong. She had to have hope, or the weight of her mistakes and the potential loss of her sons could engulf her.

"Mom, pull off at the next exit. There's something I want to show you."

"There's more?" she asked wearily. We pulled into a rest stop and started to walk. Once in the trees I used Gogen to move a rock the size of a basketball and let it float slowly up to her face.

"How?" She looked in disbelief. I made it float around her twice. It landed far from its original location. "That's the most amazing thing I've ever seen!" She laughed and laughed.

"I want you to know we are not powerless against these people," I told her. "We're going to find Dustin and bring him home."

She wrapped her arms around me. "Promise you'll be careful. I can't lose you, too."

34

Without knocking on the front door, I burst into the reading room, finding Rose with a client. "They took Dustin," I shouted.

Rose stood up. "I'm sorry, Tina, we'll have to finish another time. Forgive me, it's a family emergency."

"The government grabbed him. Some garbage about a national security threat," I continued.

The startled woman collected her purse and left quickly with a slight bow. Mom pushed past her at the door.

"Jenny! Hello... uh... " Rose stammered. They hadn't seen each other in four years.

"Homeland Security took Dustin out of Mountain View this morning. You're supposed to be the great neon psychic, so why couldn't you see this coming?"

"Mom, stop it. Aunt Rose, look into your crystal ball and tell me where they have him. Is he okay?"

I sat across from her. Mom paced behind me.

"The ball is for prophecy, seeing images of the future and sensing things. In order to find him, I'll need to go on the astral."

"What does that mean?" Mom asked impatiently.

I silenced her with a look.

"He's alive," she said, after a few minutes. "He's clearer; maybe they haven't given him meds today."

"Thank God!" Mom said.

"Where is he?" I asked.

"A house. A green brick house in trees."

"He's not on a plane? Or in a big hospital?" Mom asked.

"No. It's a lovely sage green residence, and that's a very healing color."

"They said he was being transferred to a mental hospital in Washington D.C.," Mom said.

"Well, they haven't done it yet. I think he's still in Oregon."

"Then, we can get to him," I said. "Can you teach me how to see where he is?"

"Concentrate," she told me. "Just think about Dustin. Picture his face. Hear his laugh. Look for him."

"I don't see anything."

"You're too upset. If you can meditate for a while, we can try it later when you're calmer."

"Rose, can't *you* see where he is, I mean exactly where is this green house?" Mom demanded.

"I'm not getting anything beyond a house in the trees. My talents are a little cloudy these days, but even at my best, it's hard to get perfect details. It's not like watching TV, Jenny."

"I need Nate to stay with you if that's okay," Mom said. "Someone is trying to hurt my boys." Her voice broke, and the sobs began again.

"Of course, Jenny, as long as he wants. You're welcome too."

"Thank you, Rose. But I'm going to find a lawyer and start looking for Dustin in the physical world. No offense, but I can't leave his fate to what you all see or don't see in that silly ball." Mom left a short time later, promising to get a prepaid cell phone on the way home. She said she would bring me some clothes, my computer, and other stuff in a few days. I told her about Sam's sister, the lawyer, and she said she'd go by and see him.

I called Kyle and Amber. They were stunned and shaken by how close we came to being picked up the night before. They would come to Rose's on Saturday, as planned, if I was still there and still free.

For the next few hours, Rose told me everything she knew about the astral, but it wasn't working for me. After that, I spent a long time with her going through what she considered the best New Age books. She was blown away by my ability to "read." Mom called from the road on her new cell phone.

I explained that Rose believed I was too tired and stressed to effectively see anything on the astral.

"I want you to know that I believe in you and love you very, very much." Her voice betrayed the strength in her words. She was barely holding on. I knew in that moment that if Dustin died, my mom would cease to be, even if she survived.

Thursday, September 25

I couldn't believe the clock as I awoke from a deep sleep. It was almost noon, which meant for more than twelve hours there had been peace. Aunt Rose was with clients. I went into the kitchen, made a sandwich, grabbed a Coke, and called Mom.

She had talked to five or six lawyers. "It's like they only let idiots pass the bar," she said. "They keep telling me there isn't much I can do. The government has all kinds of powers to detain citizens if they are suspected of aiding terrorists. Never mind that Dustin hasn't done anything. The lawyers say not knowing where he's held makes things even more difficult. Talk about stating the obvious. One of them suggested I should contact the media."

"Bad idea. Dad's friend Lee had the same plan. That's what started this whole nightmare."

"I can't just sit here waiting."

"We'll find him," I said. "As soon as Aunt Rose is done with her clients, we'll get back to our search. Have some faith, Mom. This psychic stuff is for real."

"I'll try." She sounded distracted.

"Sam said his sister is involved in some big case right now in New York but that she should be able to talk tomorrow or Monday at the latest," she said.

"Damn it! Did you tell him about Dustin? Can't he get her on the phone in the evening or sooner? She's his sister!"

"He was appalled about Dustin being abducted. Thinks it's gotta be a mistake or, he said, if you really did stumble into some corruption, then it's a blatant act of harassment and his sister will make a huge case over all this. But he did say that proving your dad was murdered may be difficult unless we have some evidence."

"I haven't told him about the other ten Montgomery Ryders dying or the whole Lee Duncan story. I'll fill him in, but what about Dustin in the meantime?"

"That's why I'm still calling people. Oh and on top of everything, Mrs. Little called a few minutes ago. She said that some of your teachers have suggested you might be cheating. You were perfect in algebra, aced a chemistry quiz, embarrassed your English teacher, and had a conversation in fluent French."

"Not a bad day's work."

"I'd say. Then she wanted to know why you weren't in school. I told her that I didn't like her accusing my son of cheating, that you've been working with a private tutor, and that your results clearly show that the school was not adequate for your needs."

"Way to go, Mom!"

"Back when Dustin was having all that trouble, she was the one who really pushed me to have him committed. I'm not buying what she's selling anymore. I told her we were pulling you out to be home-schooled by private tutors."

"What'd Little say?"

"That we should meet to discuss options and legal requirements. I said I'd be in touch."

"She probably wasn't very happy."

"That woman is never happy."

After more practice, I could see Dustin but not on the astral. Instead, I was just getting glimpses of him using prophecy. For some reason, using a dark pan filled with water was easier than the crystal ball. I was getting pieces and visions, which Rose said were indications of the future that only meant he was alive right now. Interpreting prophetic images was an art, she said, handing me a book about a famous seer named Nostradamus.

Aunt Rose saw more on the astral—a green brick house in the trees, high on a hill with a deck overlooking orchards, almost certainly Oregon, and maybe somewhere in the Rogue Valley but it wasn't possible to pinpoint. Dustin was alive, but he was looking pale and feverish, "like someone going through withdrawal from drugs," Rose said.

"What about his getting to us on the astral? You said you had taught him."

"I always helped him. I think he could probably do it on his own by now, if he stays off the meds, but he'd have to get over the withdrawal first."

"Then, what can we do?"

"You're seeing Spencer Copeland tomorrow. He can find Dustin."

"By then it'll be more than forty-eight hours since they took him."

"I know it, honey. But at least he seems to be nearby. The best thing is for me to teach you all I know."

Rose started explaining colors, her favorite subject. We went over chakras, auras, the colored pops, color meanings, symbols, and reflections. For hours, she told me what she knew. At the same time I held onto books on each topic. The colored pops, she said, were like shorthand between the universe and our human personalities. Understanding the significance of each color and its many shades would require meditation, but her books on colors gave me a strong head start.

She taught me to read faces, saying you don't have to go into the clutter of peoples minds to find out what they're thinking, feeling, where they've been, what they've seen. "It's all on their faces and in their eyes. Everything gets record-ed in lines, tones, shape of noses, the hue of cheeks, pattern of forehead lines, thickness or thinness of eyebrows, dryness of lips. You can spend hours reading a face." Then it was on to body language and what our movements reveal. When I thought that lesson was over, she told me how best to conceal what my own face and movements could give away.

It was easy to understand her humor-filled lectures. The astral was a huge topic, but she gave more of the basics, adding details to the brief introduction she'd given me the prior weekend. Still, it was overwhelming at times, and once when I expressed my frustration, she took my hand in hers. "Honey, always remember that understanding this spiritual stuff is far simpler than understanding people and their personalities. The soul at least makes sense."

Then we moved to guide writing. This was more difficult than I expected. Rose had me sit quietly in front of the computer with my fingers lightly resting on the keyboard. She did it with a pen and paper. "It's how I learned," she said. "It's easier for me, but your generation hardly knows what a pencil is anymore." I cleared my mind as she instructed and waited. Later, she said, I could ask specific questions, but for now I was to just let my guides talk about whatever they deemed most important. Nothing happened for half an hour. I decided this was not for me and gave up, but Rose said, "Stay put, honey." Ten minutes later, words began to flow.

"This time is for something to you that may not be easily understood but so much of what you are open to now has shown that this is possible so that you can find where the place is and the things that you are to do will be possible in your mind because they have already happened in the universe the planes of existence and crossing times play a role in each other but this should not stop the efforts of where you are heading it is sometime to see any place to feel what must be in this now a chance has come to grow all the remaining but obstacles may be too many depending on the number that find the openings and see the shows... "

Three pages like that before I made it stop.

"It'll get easier to understand what they're saying. Read it a few times and it may become clear," Rose said, after reading it. "But you get a sense they know what's going on and have a lot to say about it."

"I should hope so." The feeling of a spirit guide communicating with me through my mind was not new, but seeing it so clearly on the screen was very exciting.

Tanya, deciding it wasn't the best time to start her diet, brought pizza for dinner. We discussed every theory we could think of on where they were holding Dustin and what we could do to find him. The answer was always Spencer; we needed his help. Rose had several clients the next day so Tanya offered to drive me to meet him. "I love the beach," she said, taking a sip of her sugar-free soda as she scarfed down the last slice.

After dinner, I called Mom and promised her answers tomorrow. She was still going around in circles with the lawyers. "Josh suggested we talk to one of the Ashland cops who frequents the Station. It would all be off the record, but we could get some advice."

"No way!"

"I told him you'd say that. He wants to come up to Merlin to talk to you about it."

"We're dealing with a rogue element in *our* government. There's nothing normal about this situation, and we can't address it in normal ways. If Josh wants to come up here for a history lesson, fine. Otherwise, tell him to stay in Ashland and don't talk to anyone."

"Nate, I'm not going to tell him that."

"Well, think of something to stop him, or we'll all end up arrested."

Kyle reported that both he and Linh had seen a van watching their house. Linh saw it at the Station, too, and wondered if they were looking for me or if they knew I was out of Ashland and were just keeping friends and family under surveillance. Amber had also seen it driving past her driveway in the morning, then again at school around lunchtime. They were all nervous.

It was hard for me to sleep that night. Thoughts of Dustin swirled in my mind—where was he? Maybe trying to get to us on the astral? What was Agent Sanford Fitts doing right now? Would he find me? I thrashed in the sheets until morning, waking out of an Outview; my dad and I were friends in the same Mayan lifetime that I had died by a conquistador sword, falling into the sacred pool. But this time, we were in the seaside town of Tulum, plotting with seven others how to get the artifact safely to the only person who could save our people. It ended abruptly, and although I knew they/we had failed to protect the artifact or preserve the Mayan civilization, I was oddly left with a sense of optimism.

36

Friday, September 26

Rose made her famous bacon, eggs, and pancakes. "Glad I decided to postpone my diet." Tanya laughed. Rose told us she had already checked on Dustin on the astral, he was still not looking well. She'd had no luck communicating with him yet.

"You tell Spencer Copeland that I said he needs to find Montgomery's first son," Rose ordered me.

"I've got a good feeling that Nate's going to find his brother," Tanya said.

She handed me three Spanish books "Here're the books you asked for. All those years toiling in high school Spanish and all I can remember is how to count uno, dos, tres, cuatro. Maybe you'll do better."

Linh called just before we were going to lose cell coverage, driving along the Smith River. "The van was out there again this morning. I'm really worried about all of us."

"I'm on my way to see Spencer right now; by the end of the day we'll have a plan to rescue Dustin and keep everyone safe. Just be very careful. Don't go anywhere alone. They obviously don't want any publicity, and it doesn't seem like they're willing to just snatch any of us in the light of day."

"I had a dream last night—" Linh began before we lost the signal. Tanya offered to turn around so we could finish the call, but we had to get to Spencer.

I meditated until we got to the coast, then directed Tanya to the guardrail.

Entering the forest that separated the road from the beach was like going home. The trees greeted me, my name in the breeze. I traversed the steep trail with memories of that night mixed with the sights before me. The woods made me feel strong. Spencer was right; nature was the power place. These trees were extra special. This was the place of my "vision quest." It would always be sacred.

Spencer was waiting in the same spot where we first saw him, as if he was part of that rock, part of this beach.

"What do you see out there?" I asked, interrupting his view.

"The problems of humanity."

"In that beautiful ocean?" I asked. Then I saw his eyes, troubled, sorrowful.

"I'm torn, Nate. To show you the things you need to know is to steal your childhood and burden you with more than a person should carry."

"My childhood ended the day my dad died."

He stared into my eyes. "They got Dustin."

"I knew you'd know." I tried to read him, but it was impossible. "Right now, all I care about is getting Dustin back. Can you find him?"

"I can help *you* find him. They're using Dustin as bait. They want you to come for him."

"How do they know I can find him? Do they know I have psychic powers?"

"I believe so."

"Then for sure they want me dead."

"If they can't convince you to 'work' for them, then they will have to kill you."

"You're always so full of good news."

"Nate, don't take it lightly. You may not survive this."

"You don't understand, Spencer. If I take it too seriously, if I dwell on all that's at stake, then I'll run away and hide. I'm not some brave hero. Linh thinks I'm Harry Potter; I'm not. I don't understand what's happening. I don't know what to do. And every other word out of your mouth since we first met is how the weight of the world is on my shoulders and how at any moment, I could be killed; my friends and family, too. Now they've grabbed Dustin and are stalking me and the people I care about. I can feel the freaking pressure! Okay? It's there with every waking breath, and I don't even want to talk about how it is when I sleep. So, don't worry about me taking things too lightly. I'm just barely hanging on, all right?"

"Okay. Fair enough," his whole face softened. His eyes apologized. "Let's get started."

"I'm ready."

"Good. But I will need your patience once more. We won't find him right away. There is an order to how we have to do this. I need you to trust me."

"Fine, but you're not going to ask me to spend the night in the woods again, are you?" I smiled.

"No. You've done that. Did it better than I could have hoped, as a matter of fact. You should know your father is proud of you."

"I felt him that night."

"He was with you." He nodded. "Now, do you see that seagull up there?"

"Yeah. Where are his ten thousand friends?"

"They may show up yet. But we're only concerned with that one. You need to connect with him and then put him to sleep."

"How?"

"Remember everything I'm showing you is knowledge you already have. These are things your soul has been able to do for millennia."

"So, you're saying you're not going to tell me how to do it?"

"It's enough that I've told you that you're capable of it."

I watched the bird for a moment, then closed my eyes and flew with him in my mind. We became one. 'Sleep,' I whispered in my head. I opened my eyes and instinctively ran to where the seagull was dropping out of the sky. My arms extended as it fell softly into my hands.

"Easy, huh?" Spencer asked.

I gently cradled the gull and said, "Wake up now. Fly," as I tossed it into the air. My bird circled once and then flew away.

"It's harder with people. But you'll practice."

"You mean I can put people to sleep?"

"Yes, it's a subtle form of mind control, part of Solteer. You can do all sorts of things."

"That's frightening."

"Yes, it can be. Use it wisely."

I nodded. My thoughts raced with possibilities, then a nervous feeling arose, what if Sanford Fitts and the other Lightyear agents could also use Solteer?

"Don't worry about that," Spencer said, reading my mind. "If people use these powers directly to cause harm, then they weaken considerably."

"What about someone from the dark side?"

"The dark side is a myth, made up by religions to keep people in fear."

"Why?"

"So they could be controlled easier. In the modern world, Hollywood has perhaps done more to propagate the presence of a dark side than the Church." Something I couldn't see out in the ocean took his attention for a couple of minutes. Then, he turned to me staring intensely into my eyes. "There is no evil in the natural universe. It is a creation of man, and they do it extremely well. One could say the human race has mastered the art of evil."

I thought about his words. It was a revolutionary idea to me, and he was not presenting it as a theory but as fact. And if the only evil that existed in the world was from ordinary men, then I might have a chance against them. After all, I had the power of the universe at my disposal.

"Yes, it is a fact," he was reading my mind again. "And yes, you do have all that power within you. But you're still a mere mortal, just like them, and they have all the power of the U.S. government at *their* disposal. That's no small thing,

especially because the battle is being waged on earth, a decid-
edly human place."

"But earth is part of the universe, and it's inhabited by
souls, right?"

"Yes, but most of them are trapped in the amnesia of
their human existence. Earth may have once been one of the
jewels of the universe, but man has been doing a good job of
burying its beauty and power in layers of filth and mayhem
for the past few thousand years. And with each passing decade,
their rate of destruction has been expanding exponentially."

"But I have a chance. A good chance."

"Yes, you do. And the more people you help to awaken,
then the better your odds."

"When can I read minds like you do?"

"Much later. If we are both among the living, I will help
you remember more of your lost powers next summer. And
still more a year after that."

"And if we're not among the living?"

"Then you won't need reminding, you'll already know."

"What if I'm alive and you aren't?"

"Someone else will help you. There is never a shortage of
help. *Always* remember that."

"Finally some good news from Spencer."

"What I'm about to show you may appear to be a weapon, but of course it's not. You can use it for protection, but
there are many other uses, as with all knowledge. But this is
most often used as a healing tool." He cupped his palms in
front of him, looked slightly toward the sky, and then focused
his gaze on his hands. Slowly, he worked them back and forth
as if forming a ball out of clay. And then, there it was, nearly
invisible but there nonetheless.

"What is it?"

"This is a healing orb called a 'Lusan'. It's made using
Foush *and* Vising. It even mixes in Gogen." He placed the
grapefruit-sized ball gently on the sand and rolled it. Tiny
green sprouts formed in its wake. Then, he pushed it softly
against a small scab on my hand. No blemish remained when

he removed the sphere and hurled it against a nearby boulder where a ten-inch chunk of the rock obliterated.

"Incredible!" Beyond that, I was speechless. The first thing that came into my mind, "Does the military have this?"

"It's hard to say how far things have gotten at Lightyear."

"But they can't use these powers for harm, right?"

"Not directly, but they manipulate the people into believing they're doing good. And they believe it. They think they are protecting their country from terrorists or enemy nations, and so the power is real."

"In other words, if they convince an agent I'm evil, then they can use powers against me."

"Something like that. Back to your training."

I watched him make another Lusan and throw it into the ocean producing a momentary geyser thirty feet high. "Now, you do it. Gather your thoughts. Pull the energy from the universe, focus it in your hands, then just imagine making the perfect snowball, keeping your focus until the ball becomes independent of your energy."

It was surprisingly easy. Once I found the moment the ball no longer required my kneading, I couldn't help but laugh. The feeling was invigorating, warm, and tingling. It made me want to jump up-and-down like an excited kid. "What should I do with it?"

"Follow me," I walked with Spencer to where the narrow trail left the trees to meet the sand. "Walk up the trail four or five feet, then roll it down slowly."

I did and was amazed. The trail vanished as greenery of all kind from ferns to wild flowers grew before my eyes and filled the worn path. "Wow! That's unbelievable!"

"Turns out the most unbelievable things *are* the most believable." He smiled.

"How have we forgotten all of this knowledge?"

"That is a story as long as human existence. And not really worth telling even if I knew all the reasons, which I don't."

"Imagine what the world could be like if we all remembered."

"Yes, imagine."

And I started to, still caught in the euphoria of producing the Lusan.

"Not now though. Time for that later. There is much to do," he said.

I picked up the ball and walked to the water, rolling it on the surface like I was bowling. It sliced a shallow gutter through the surf for several feet before being swallowed by a wave in a sizzling bubbly stew.

"Your next lesson won't seem as flashy as a Lusan, but it will prove to be one of the most profound things you'll learn in this life." He paused to insure the impact of his words resonated. They did. After everything Spencer had shown me, I was open to anything and intrigued by what he would attach so much importance to. "You know how to hug people?"

"Yeah." I laughed.

"Good. Next time you hug someone, close your eyes and picture their eyes in all the detail you can. And hold that image with the thought of finding their soul. I find it useful to silently but passionately ask, 'who are you?' And then you should begin to see their past. Their whole life will flash before you in a matter of minutes. The longer you hold on, the more you will see."

"No!"

"Wait, there's more. If you continue to embrace them, you will see a brief few seconds of blackness and then a review of their prior lives will begin to flood in. It will accelerate so that you can go through a thousand years in a minute."

"How would I digest all that information?"

"Your soul will process it. Remember, you'll be potentially seeing hundreds of lifetimes. This is all part of your Vising power."

"I don't know if I want to know anyone that well," I said, thinking of the slave trader.

"It can be a difficult thing. You'll find it easier if you can remove judgment from your personality traits."

"How hard could that be?"

"Just when I forget your age, you remind me quite nicely."

"Can I try this out on you? Can I see your past?"

"I think that would complicate things considerably right now. Try it on Kyle or Linh when you next see them. It's time to visit the astral."

"Really? I'm ready?"

"We're going to find out."

"This is going to be so cool."

"Before we go into this. I want you to know there are two reasons why we are progressing this way." He picked up some sand and let it slip from his hand into the wind. "As I said earlier, there is a logical path that makes each step easier than the last. But I'm balancing that with what I anticipate you may need on your *immediate* journey."

"You can see my future, can't you?"

"Only parts, and it changes as I watch it. It's not like the past; the future is fluid. It is constantly in flux and rearranging based on what we do, think, see, and hear and by what billions of other people do, think, see, and hear as well. So, if I see something of the future right now, five minutes from now it could be very different."

"What good is it then?"

"As one gets more proficient with Timbal, one begins to develop a knack for deciphering it and an ability to guess what the ramifications of a subtle change in the present will do to the future. Obviously, the farther out in time you go, it becomes more difficult to rely on anything we see."

I dug my toes into the sand, looked beyond the ocean, and squinted into the sun for a moment. "When will I be able to see the future like that?"

"Sometime in the future."

I laughed, but he wasn't being funny.

"Astral traveling is one of the soul's core abilities, and it's accessed through Gogen. It's like being on a highway of sorts. But what I just said may be the greatest understatement ever spoken. Still, it will give you a reference point to try to grasp the unfathomable. Through the astral, you're able to move within your lifetimes as in your Outviews. You can also move between time and dimensions to any place or moment in the universe."

"My head hurts. I don't think I can handle this."

"Do you remember lesson number one?" he asked.

"Everything can change in an instant. Everything can be learned in an instant."

"Close enough. Don't worry. You don't need to understand it. You won't ever anyway. I don't, and if I try too hard, it hurts my head, too. All you need to do is know how to access it."

"Can I get lost out there in time?"

"You can temporarily get stuck in between, but you should eventually return to where you started from."

"So what do I do?"

"It'll be different when you teach other people, but since you're one of the seven, all you need to do is get yourself in a slight meditative state and disengage your personality by feeling pure love. Surround yourself in white light, and you will feel a moving sensation, kind of like how it feels to fly in a dream. Soon that will be gone, and you will just be at places and times."

"But how do I choose the places and times?"

"That part takes considerable trial and error. Initially, what your soul needs you to see will be your destinations, but you can begin to control it by focusing on what you want in your meditations."

"So, why has my soul needed me to see a hundred of my past deaths?"

"You tell me."

"I don't know."

"Yes, you do. But you can answer yourself later. Are you ready to go?"

"I want to find Dustin."

"I know."

"Will I?"

"I don't know. I hope so."

37

I sat on a warm boulder near the trees, closed my eyes, and let the sound of the waves take me into a deeper state. The surf sounded like his name, "Dussss-tin, Dussss-tin."

Suddenly, there he was, sitting on a wooden chair inside the green house. His face was pale; dark circles under his eyes. He was thin, wearing a blue sweatshirt and sweatpants that were a size too large. "Dustin," I heard myself yell. I was sure his expression changed. Was it possible to communicate with him? "Dustin, can you hear me?" His lips moved with my words. I repeated and his lips moved again, saying his own name. I moved right in front of his face. He mouthed my words as I said them. "Nate is coming to get me. Nate is coming to get me," I said. I saw a look of recognition on his face, and then a smile.

Then he said out loud, "Nate is coming to get me." He couldn't see me, but he could somehow feel what I said.

Not knowing how much time remained, I moved away from his room. I needed to know where he was—a locked door, an agent in the next room, two more on the deck. Drifting away from the house with an aerial view, I saw a highway and recognized the mountains. My God, he was just outside Ashland! The roads were familiar. Looking around and seeing the green house, I knew it would be easy to tell someone how to drive there. I had command of the astral!

I glided back into his room. "Nate knows where I am. Nate knows where I am. He's coming." He repeated my words. Then he looked around the room trying to see a sense of me. "I'll see you soon, brother," Dustin whispered.

Then I was back. Spencer was walking toward me from the ocean.

"I found him," I yelled. "Spencer, I saw Dustin."

He smiled.

"I know right where he is. Let's go get him."

"Nate, I need you to listen to me now." I could tell I wasn't going to like what he was about to say. He had that look my dad used to get when he had to tell me we couldn't free the tiger from the zoo or paint our minivan yellow.

"No, Spencer. Don't you dare tell me we can't go get him. If that's what you're going to say, I don't care. Tanya will take me tonight. I'm not waiting until tomorrow."

"Listen to me, Nate. You aren't ready for that. If you go now or even tomorrow, you will die and so will Dustin."

"You don't know that. You said earlier the future is changing all the time, so you can't know that for sure. You don't know."

He looked at me, his eyes trying to calm. I wanted to turn away but could not.

"You just want to make sure I save the world or something. You don't care what happens to Dustin. You don't want anything getting in the way of *the plan*."

He shook his head.

I stared at him.

"Have I ever betrayed your trust?" he asked.

"I've known you two days, Spencer."

"Do you believe that?"

I closed my eyes, finally breaking his gaze.

"Nate. If you can't trust me, trust the universe."

"Damn it, Spencer. I just want my brother safe."

"I know."

"When? When can we get him?"

"Soon."

My face told him that was not an acceptable answer.

"That's all I know. Nate. We must trust the universe."

"Do we have more to go over?"

He nodded.

"I need a break." I got off the boulder and walked down the beach, ripping open a pack of almond M&M's. If I had so much power, why couldn't I make a Coke machine materialize when I needed one?

I wasn't much good for our remaining time. I was too distracted by Dustin's physical appearance and how close he was. My mother could be there with the police in about fifteen minutes. But what would the police do? Arrest him and turn him back over to Homeland Security. That might be a little better than his current predicament but probably not. The truth was I didn't know what could happen or what to do. And I didn't know about trusting the universe. My dad probably trusted the universe; it didn't work out well for him. All I could do was trust Spencer.

He started explaining vortexes to me, building on what I already learned from Rose. I knew they fell under Gogen. But his normally simple explanations were not working on this topic. "Vortexes and dimensional doorways are often located at sites considered sacred by indigenous cultures around the world. They're almost always beautiful places. Even unaware people will feel something at these spots: an increased optimism, heightened energy, euphoria, some kind of awakening, healings. You get the idea?"

I nodded.

"You'll find large trees grown in a spiral, boulders in strange configurations, anomalies of vegetation, geological formations, or a marked absence of what is otherwise all around the area. There are usually physical characteristics; they aren't meant to be secret, but most have been lost since no one is really looking."

"Crater Lake? Mount Shasta?"

He nodded slightly, but his eyes held a combination of wonder and awe. After a few seconds he continued. "And with your increased awareness, you will find many of the less significant ones throughout your travels. But remember… " He paused and then whispered, "Oh no." A rainbow appeared, seemed to liquefy and spill into the clouds. They immediately blackened and it started raining heavily. It stopped as quickly as it had started. I wouldn't know until later, when it was too late, what he had seen.

"I was saying, even the less significant ones are important. They will—"

"What just happened?" I interrupted. "Did something bad happen to Dustin?"

"We need to stay focused. Dustin is fine."

I exhaled.

"Now we have little time remaining, and it's crucial that you understand this."

"Can't you just give me a book to absorb?"

"There is no book written that comes close to addressing the realities of this subject. If there were, we wouldn't have the troubles we do on this planet."

"So, why don't you just write one?"

"It would not be understood. Perhaps *you* will one day."

"Are you seeing something in the future that says I'm going to write about vortexes and other dimensions?"

"No, I am merely attempting to get back to the topic we should be concentrating on."

"Vortexes."

"Yes. Every vortex is different, and two people will react differently to the same one. But it is a charger, a transformation tool and—"

"Can we switch to dimensional doorways?"

He looked at me exasperated for a moment, but it quickly passed. "Dimensional doorways are located near every vortex. They are found less often without a vortex, but those are nearly impossible for anyone other than the most evolved."

I was half-listening.

"Where the astral is accessed by your mind, dimensional doorways are entered physically."

"You mean I can walk right in?"

"Yes."

"Where do they go?"

"Everywhere."

"That's a little vague."

"Okay, it isn't as though you come to a heavy wooden door with a big brass knob, open it and find yourself anywhere you want to be. Going on the astral is better for that type of need. Every dimensional doorway is different, and they are almost completely invisible."

"How do I find them then?"

"You'll learn to feel them, but if you know where one is, you can recognize it. The ones you know will appear like a shimmering circle, kind of like the heat you see coming off the hood of a car on a hot day."

"There's so much going on that people aren't aware of."

"They used to be aware of everything. It was something then. The unseen world is enormously deeper and much more exciting than the human world, but when the two were combined it was a million times more fascinating."

"Are we trying to get back to that combination?"

"In a way. But let's stay on track here. Dimensional doorways are a bit of a double-edged sword in this war. The access they provide to power and knowledge is unmatched. If Lightyear gets—"

"Lightyear? You mean anyone can wander into one of these things."

"Yes."

"Whoa! But you said they couldn't use powers for harm."

"That's not exactly what I said. Powers diminish if they are used for harmful purposes. That's why there's almost no true knowledge of our souls left, no connection, no access to our powers. They diminished, were lost and then forgotten a long, long time ago. But dimensional doorways are there. They are open and do not depend on individual powers. Perhaps a great shift could close them or open them wider, but even a mass murderer could stumble into one. They are not without defenses however. They're virtually invisible, generally located in remote places and, even then, an entrance is not something you could normally accidently walk into. They're in odd spots that usually need to be climbed to. Many remain lost, even to the most evolved."

I kept seeing Dustin's face. He would come for *me* no matter what anyone said. I didn't know what to do.

"I think we've done enough today."

"But we just started on doorways."

"Yes, and it's a critical topic requiring total concentration."

"But—"

"You have considerable things to ponder and practice."

I knew his mind could not be changed. "How and when will we meet again?"

"I'll get word to you."

"Thanks for the lessons."

"You know all these things now, but they take *practice* to be truly useful. Right now they can be more dangerous than helpful."

"I'll be careful." I started up the trail.

He shouted after me, "Don't go near Dustin! They want you to come for him. Dustin will be kept alive until you're either in their custody or dead."

38

Tanya was waiting as I came out of the woods. "I was about to call you."

"I read your mind."

"Really?"

"I'm joking."

I didn't want to talk about anything spiritual; my brain was about to short circuit. For the two-and-a-half-hour drive Tanya and I discussed music, movies, food, and anything I could think of to keep my mind off the universe. Even so, my thoughts kept returning to Dustin, and I continued to resist the urge to have her drive straight to him.

Red poppers and an unusually high number of shape-shifting animals kept me on edge. At one point hundreds of crows flew out in front of us. Even Tanya saw them. "That's called a murder of crows," she said.

"I know. Not a good sign," I thought of the melting rainbow, black clouds, and instant storm earlier. Something was wrong.

When we got to Rose's just after eight, she was nowhere to be found. Her car was out front, but the house was unlocked and empty.

"That's odd," Tanya said. "Wonder where she is?"

"Maybe she's out for a walk."

"That would be a first," Tanya was concerned.

"Call her cell," I suggested.

Tanya dialed the number, and we heard Rose's phone ring in the hall. "Now I'm really worried. Rose leaves her cell by the door with her keys so she won't forget to take it."

We agreed to wait an hour before panicking, but it was very strange. Rose knew we would be home in the evening and wanted to hear everything. I used Vising to read the bushes, yard, and front door. Unfortunately, I still couldn't control the time I was seeing, so it was just a random jumble of images, which could have been years before. Nothing unusual, but I kept trying.

By nine all doubt was gone. Tanya said Rose hadn't stayed out past nine as long as she'd known her. Tanya came into the reading room while I was looking into the crystal ball.

"The police already knew she was gone and said she's not a missing person. They consider her a fugitive."

"A fugitive? Are you kidding? Do they know we're talking about Rose?"

"They said there is a warrant out for her arrest."

"For what, telling the future while under the influence?"

"I'm serious, Nate. We used to be neighbors with this cop, and I called him for advice. He pulled her up on the computer to make sure she hadn't been in an accident or something. Then he was like, 'Tanya, how well do you know your stepmother?' and said 'the Department of Homeland Security through the FBI issued a warrant on charges of terrorist activities.' Does *terrorist* ring any bells, Nate?"

I'd been telling myself that this couldn't have anything to do with me, that there would be some logical explanation. But now, she wasn't just missing; Sanford Fitts had her. "This is outrageous! We're living in a police state!" The sick feeling growing inside won out over my anger.

"Nate, what are we going to do?"

"I've got to warn my mom."

Tanya was distraught.

Mom answered. "The people who have Dustin took Aunt Rose while we were gone today! They issued a warrant claiming she's a terrorist. They said she fled," I said.

"Nate, are you sure? Could she have fled? What if she found out about the warrant and went into hiding somewhere?"

"I guess that's possible, but I think she would have let us know somehow. Either way, you need to stay away from the house. I think you could be next."

"I'd like to see those bastards come knock on my door. They would—"

I cut her off. "Mom, these are not the kind of people to mess with. You'll suddenly have a heart attack or a car accident. Don't be crazy! They got Dad, Dustin, and now Aunt Rose. I don't want to be alone in the world. Go stay with someone. Don't be by yourself. Promise me."

"Okay. Okay. I'll go to Barbara's. But what about you? They want you most of all."

"I'm not staying here tonight. I'll keep moving."

This time I read the front walk and within a few minutes I saw them, two armed men. Viewing from behind, the agents in blue DHS parkas and matching ball caps, looked at Rose's face, which expressed no surprise.

One of them said, "Rosemary Ryder Phelps?"

"Yes," said Rose.

"Ma'am, I'm Agent Dandon and this is Agent Fitts. We have a warrant for your arrest." He handed her papers. She didn't even glance at them. She must have known something. There was no struggle; she hadn't fled.

Surprisingly, other images burned into me at the same time; I was suddenly staring at my dad behind the Station restaurant. A man in a ball cap was talking to him the morning of his death. It was a quick glimpse from behind, but it had to be Fitts! Why else was I seeing it now? They were laughing, and something flicked from Fitts' hand that my dad didn't see. He swatted at his neck like a mosquito bit him, but it was too late. Whatever Fitts had shot into his bloodstream was already moving through his veins. He had been murdered! Then a second realization hit me: Fitts was the same man who had, in the Outview from the campground, chased me and shot me in another lifetime.

I was reeling in despair and rage when Tanya interrupted me. "What should we do?"

"Leave here now! They could be back any minute. We need some place to stay tonight."

"They don't know me. Why wouldn't my house be safe?"

"Let's go, we've been here too long!"

As we were rushing out, I saw Rose's phone again and grabbed it. Tanya zipped out of the driveway and swerved dangerously into traffic. I dialed Sam's number.

"Now they took my aunt Rose!"

"Nate, slow down, who took your aunt?"

"Homeland Security arrested her just like Dustin. They're claiming she's a terrorist. Once again we have no idea where they're holding her. We need your sister now!"

"They can't just do that. This is getting out of hand. What the hell is going on? Sounds like we may need more than just my sister. I'll call again, but my guess is even with this the soonest we'll get her involved is Monday at nine. Can you be here?"

"Why not now? Or this weekend?"

"She's slammed. This case is eating up every minute on research, witness interviews, whatever lawyers do in big litigation. She couldn't do much over the weekend anyway."

"Mom's after me to go to the media, which I think is too risky. She's also talking to other lawyers, trying to get someone to help."

"Don't worry. I'll talk to your mother, and I'll call my sister again right now."

I tossed Rose's phone on the dash and turned to Tanya.

"I saw them arrest Rose. The agents, one of them killed my dad... and me! I'm sure they took her when I saw the rainbow spill into the clouds on the beach. Spencer must have seen it happen. Why didn't he tell me? Why couldn't he find a way to stop it? Why didn't they wait for me? How did they find us?"

"Nate, what are you babbling about? Are you going to freak out on me?"

"No, no. I'll be okay." But I wasn't sure; it was too much at once. Fate was pushing Fitts and me together in the cruelest imaginable karmic catastrophe. I phoned Amber.

"Bridgette?" Amber asked, sleepily.

"No, it's Nate."

"Nate? Oh, I fell asleep talking to Bridgette. Are you okay? What time is it?"

"They got Aunt Rose! Arrested her for being a terrorist."

There was silence.

"Amber, are you there?"

"Yeah. Why would they take Rose?"

"It's not safe for you to stay alone. Can you go somewhere?"

"Not this late. I'll be fine tonight. Even bad guys have to sleep."

"I'm not so sure. Go to a hotel. Tanya and I are heading to her place now. I don't think they know about her, so it should be good for a night. Call me the minute you're up."

Another sleepless night. It was ironic; all I wanted was sleep, when only ten days before it had terrified me. But my mind was churning with the conspiracy that had taken over my entire existence. I tried to block it out; I had to sleep.

I quizzed myself on my new abilities and the five great powers while passing time in the night. Outviews and prophecy were done under Timbal. Colored pops I now knew were signals from the universe. The wind noise that came when spirit guides announced their presence, channeling through guide writing, and seeing shapeshifting were all part of Foush. But Lusans, the holographic-like healing balls were the most exciting part of Foush. They felt more magical than any of the other stuff. Manipulating space, or Gogen, allowed me to move objects, which was super fun and continued to amaze me each time. Also part of Gogen was traveling the astral, which was a whole mind-boggling trip all its own. Reading objects and people were different forms of Vising and totally surreal. My new way of "reading" books might be the most practical thing I ever learned because it opened up all of human knowledge to me. How was I going to remember all these powers, and how much more was there? The technique for putting people to sleep was part of controlling consciousness known as Solteer. I wondered if there was a way to use that on myself? It was all quite fantastic, but the real powers were still to come.

*S*aturday, *September 27*

Kyle, Linh, and Amber arrived at 8:30 a.m. They would have been earlier but were extra cautious to make sure no one was following them. The strain on Kyle's face was evident. Authorities were after me, and he was involved. I recognized the look of no sleep. Amber hugged me first; she held on so long I was afraid of accidently reading her life.

"I'm just glad you're safe," she said.

"Any luck seeing Rose?" Kyle asked.

"Nothing," Tanya answered for me.

Linh looked tired and sad. "What's wrong?"

"Them taking Rose is tragic. And who's next?"

"It's so screwed up. They can call anyone a terrorist and take them," Kyle said.

"They're the terrorists," Amber said. "Lightyear needs to be exposed."

"I know where Dustin is."

Everyone looked at me. "He's being held in a house just outside of Ashland."

"Let's go," Amber said.

"Is Rose there?" Tanya asked.

"Not as of this morning. Dustin's well-guarded. We can't just storm in," I said.

"I think we could," Amber said.

"This isn't some Disney movie," Linh said. "It's the government we're up against."

I hadn't told them about any of my new powers and believed we really had a shot at getting in and out of there safely. Spencer had to know I wouldn't wait long before doing something. I worried that each day we didn't act, Dustin was that much closer to getting killed. And where was Rose?

"For the moment Dustin is okay, and we know where he is. Aunt Rose is missing without a trace. I can't see her. Everything that works with Dustin comes up blank with her."

"Could that mean she's dead? I mean would you be able to see her if she were dead?" Tanya asked quietly.

Linh ran out of the house in tears. Kyle started after her.

"I'll go," I told him.

"I could have saved Rose." She was crying when I caught up to her. "The dream I tried to tell you about yesterday before we got cut off; Rose was running across a giant dartboard and big darts kept landing next to her. Each time one hit— and they were big and sharp—she would turn in the other direction. She was scared, and the darts kept coming. Finally she got to a place when the darts stopped."

"Is that it?"

"Rose looked down and realized the place she stopped at was the bull's-eye. She looked up and screamed just as the dart hit her. It was terrible," she sniffled.

"Linh, you didn't know that was a warning."

"But I did. As soon as I woke up I knew something bad was going to happen to Rose."

The guilt was mine. If I had turned back and listened to Linh's dream instead of racing toward Spencer in my pursuit to save Dustin, I could have told Rose about it. She might have been able to hide. Whatever happened to her was my fault. Even before the dream, it was me who put Rose in jeopardy the minute I went to her house. "You're all in danger because of me."

"It's not your fault. You didn't do anything wrong."

"I need to be more mindful."

"You've been reading too much Thich Nhat Hanh." She smiled.

"More like not enough."

"You love history so much you should know that truth always prevails in the end."

"Maybe, but sometimes 'in the end' can take centuries."

"Are you scared?"

"Yeah." Impulsively, I took her hand. "Linh, even if I die, I'm not really dead. You know that, don't you?"

She nodded, fresh tears falling.

"I'm not frightened of death." I was telling myself as much as her. "What I'm scared of is not triumphing over these killers. It's not just Spencer's words anymore. I'm starting to sense how much is at stake. It's everything." My words were crystallizing what I'd been feeling. There was more to it than saving Dustin and finding Dad's killer. Spencer wasn't training me just for that. I was beginning to admit that to myself. He was right. It was a war, and I couldn't walk away if I wanted to as I'd been drafted lifetimes ago.

Kyle came out of the house. "Wanted to make sure you two were okay."

"We're not," I said. "But I guess no one is."

He gave me a strange look.

"I brought you those books you wanted." He opened the hatchback and handed me the box holding dozens of volumes by Thich Nhat Hanh, and twice that number from his uncle's library on quantum physics, astronomy, and philosophy.

I took the books inside and held them one by one. The others sat around watching, totally amazed that in such a simple way I could quickly absorb so much information.

"I didn't know Rose, but she was psychic," Amber began. "What if she's using some technique to block you so that you won't look for her?"

"Why would she do that?" Tanya asked.

"I don't know. So he'd concentrate on saving Dustin instead of her? Or maybe because it would be too dangerous to try and get her. Or what if she has some trick to get away on her own, and we could mess that up?"

I was about to tell Amber that she was grasping, but I saw the hopeful look on Tanya's face and said, "Yeah, maybe."

Once I finished the books, we went for a walk. Tanya lived in a rented cramped two-room guesthouse on a pretty piece of land overlooking the Rogue River. She led us carefully down a path to the river. We followed her, single file, as it wound down the very steep grade through a series of switchbacks.

The trail widened a bit along the water. It was a rugged and scenic section of the famed river. Amber had never been on the Rogue. Tanya explained to her that its source was near Crater Lake where it begins a 215-mile dash to the Pacific Ocean, ending at Gold Beach, just north of Brookings, like a thread weaving through my own spiritual journey.

At Amber's request, I moved stones from around the banks and dropped them in the river using Gogen. I told them it was good practice, but in truth I was just showing off. It turned into a little freak show as they all started naming things for me to levitate and move. Only Linh didn't play. Instead she wrote in her journal among some wildflowers, the rest of us were laughing and joking.

"What *are* we going to do?" Tanya suddenly blurted out. Everyone turned to her. "While we're screwing around here, Rose needs us."

"We just needed to let go of some of this tension," Kyle said.

"Someone has to find Rose. And since we can't go to the police, the only hope we have is Nate being able to see her somehow."

"I've been trying, Tanya," I said.

"Not while your wasting your powers playing in the river with your girlfriend."

"Wait a minute, Tanya, you were telling him to Gogen stuff, too, and—" Amber started.

"It's okay," I said, quieting her. "Tanya, I know you're worried about Rose. We all are. But I can't look every minute. I barely know what I'm doing. Spencer and Rose are the two who have been helping me. There's no way to get ahold of

Spencer until he contacts me, and obviously Rose can't help right now, so I'm kind of out here winging it. Monday we're going to talk to a top attorney who is great at these kind of cases.... We'll get her back."

"He's not a machine," Kyle said, biting down on an unlit cigarette.

"It's just… " Tanya said, beginning to cry, "if I hadn't taken Nate to Brookings yesterday, I would have been with Rose at the movies. We go every Friday afternoon and then to dinner."

Linh put her arm around Tanya. "The truth is we're all in danger."

"True," Kyle said. "But they could have picked us up already. They've only taken people with psychic abilities: Dustin, Rose, and they've tried for Nate."

"Maybe," I said, "but let's not get any false sense of security."

"No chance of that," Amber said. "I think we're all scared senseless."

"Let's go back. My mom's coming soon to try to convince me to go to the FBI," I said.

We made our way up the trail in silence.

"I'm going to take this, it's Bridgette." Amber flipped her phone open. She stayed outside as the rest of us went in.

A few minutes later, my mom came in with Amber.

"Hope you guys are hungry," she said unpacking a spread from the Station. Amber had an Adele, Kyle a Bob Dylan, Linh took half a Fleet Foxes, Tanya grabbed the Tracy Chapman, and I had a Ray LaMontagne with no mustard.

"Rose phoned me just after lunch on Friday. You know we had a rocky relationship," Mom said to everyone. "Rose said how sorry she was about all our misunderstandings, and since both of us loved the same three people more than anything, we should have been best of friends. It was like she knew something was going to happen. That's possible, isn't it, Nate?"

"Yeah."

"I mean she went on to say that we should work hard at being friends in the future and help Nate through all this. But it was just the timing, you know, after what happened."

"If she'd known she was going to get taken, she would have hidden somewhere, left town or something. She would have called me," Tanya said.

We were all quiet for a while, eating and thinking. Mom brought out a few large containers. "Strawberry Secrets, Fudge Crumble Invasion and Marshmallow Dream Moose Cake for dessert." Even Tanya applauded. Once everyone was stuffed and the conversation found another lull, Mom was ready to exit.

"Nate, walk me to my car. I'll see you all soon," she said to the others amid unanimous thank-yous for the food. She tossed her purse in the front seat. "Nate, I've been talking to Josh about all this, and he agrees with me that we can't just let you run around waiting for these agents to get you. They have Dustin and Rose. We have to go to the FBI or CNN or something."

"Why do we keep having this conversation? Give me a couple of days."

"Surely, you don't think the whole government's corrupt and all the media outlets, too?"

"No, but I don't know which ones aren't. It's too risky. This is about so much more than Dustin, Dad, and Rose."

"Well, of course it is, but all I care about is keeping my family safe. I've made a lot of mistakes with you boys since Dad died, and I don't want this to be another one. What am I supposed to do if you go missing tomorrow? Do you think I won't go to the FBI then?"

"Mom, follow me."

Once we were above the river, I made a Lusan and handed it to her.

"Oh, that's incredible!" she said.

I nodded and held out my hands. She gently placed it back in them. I threw it into the river producing a large geyser that lasted almost a full minute. Mom's mouth fell open.

"You have to understand I'm not a kid anymore. I can do amazing things. A week ago I was in a French village with Dad during World War II. I can see the past in incredible detail, speak three languages fluently, and can recite the laws of quantum physics to you."

"Its hard for me, Nate. I'm astounded and impressed but terrified all at the same time. It's tough enough for me to think of you graduating next year. You saw your father?"

"No one really dies."

"In spite of all the horrible aspects of this mess, that's really a beautiful thought."

"It's breathtaking, Mom. Trust me, okay?"

"All right, Nate. I want to, but it's already been three and a half days. I know he's supposed to be in federal custody, but we really aren't sure. I'll give this until the end of the day Monday." She wiped a tear. "You stay in touch and don't be a hero. There are good people who can help us when the time comes."

"You got it." I handed her a sheet of paper. "That's the address where they have Dustin, and some other details about the place and guards that I noted. Nothing's going to happen. I just don't want to take any chances with Dustin's safety."

"I have to stop thinking now. I want to leave with images of that beautiful ball and geyser in my head." She fumbled in her purse and handed me two hundred dollar bills out the window.

"Thanks, Mom." I still had some cash from selling photos and my savings were untouched, but the money would help with all the extra gas and food.

Amber came out before I made it back inside. "I just promised my mom everything would be fine, but I'm not really sure."

"It will be. This isn't happening by accident."

"No, but that doesn't mean I can't screw it up somehow. What if Rose is dead?"

"Do you think she is?"

"I don't understand why I can see Dustin almost effortlessly, but not a trace of Rose comes through even with prophecy."

"You just told us that you hardly know what you're doing. Give yourself a break. There are so many possible reasons why you're not getting anything from her—you're still learning."

"I just think she'd be trying to get a message to me… even if she were dead."

"I've read plenty of famous cases where it can take months or years for someone to get word from the other side."

I shook my head. "It's so frustrating. I've learned more this past week than in my entire life, and I still can't—"

"Here's a little more." She pulled a book from the backseat of Kyle's car. *Animal-Speak: The Spiritual & Magical Powers of Creatures Great & Small* by Ted Andrews. "It's my favorite book on understanding the meanings of animals. Remember the moose?"

"Our first date, how could I forget?"

"It wasn't a date," she said with a laugh.

"Tanya seems to think you're my girlfriend." I smiled.

She put her arm around me. "We'll see about that."

"Why is everyone still giving me books to read?" I joked. "Thanks." I handed it back to her as we went into the house.

"You already memorized it?"

"Want to test me?"

"I believe you. And, I certainly don't want to start that circus up again."

"All right everyone, I'm not saying you have to leave, but you can't stay here." I announced.

"What?" Kyle asked.

"I don't want anyone staying where I am. It's not safe."

They all protested.

"Nate, if you think I'm going to leave," Tanya said, "then you aren't the great psychic everyone thinks you are."

"Tanya can stay because, well… it's her house, but the rest of you can't. I mean it."

They reluctantly agreed and decided Amber would stay at Kyle's and Linh's. I would have preferred them in a safe hotel somewhere but lost that debate. Linh handed me a folded sheet of paper. "It's something I wrote for you. You can read it later."

I stuffed it in the back pocket of my jeans and pulled her close. She was soft and warm. "It's not your fault," I whispered.

Once they were gone I spent more time searching for Rose on the astral and in my pan of water with no success. I asked Tanya if she would allow me to read her life. "It might help me find Rose. And even if it doesn't, I could really use the practice."

She was fascinated by the prospect. "Can you see my childhood, like when I was three?"

"Vising can even let me see your past lives if you want."

"Oh my God. I do. I want to know everything."

"You may think you do. But believe me, our past lives aren't always what we'd like."

I held her, and Tanya's life showed itself to me. Mostly mundane, but the wonderful parts centered around Rose; they adored each other. Tanya's father had been strict and abusive when she was young. Nothing worse than beatings, but some were severe. He'd belittled her, too, and there weren't many friends. Her mother didn't wake up one day after taking a mixture of pills. Tanya was about three years old and lay with her dead mother all day until her father came home and found them. No one ever told Tanya it was suicide. I sure wasn't going to break that news.

I pulled away and looked at her. She was the first person I'd read, and it was so personal I could barely handle it. I'd seen all the laughter and tears, anger and fear. The emotions were still flowing through me even after the images stopped.

She smiled at me sweetly.

"You've done really well," was all I could think to say.

"Did you see my past lives?"

"No, but we can."

She nodded.

I held her again, quickly flying through her life. It was just as Spencer had described, a few seconds of darkness and then lifetime after lifetime unfolded. We talked for more than an hour, as Tanya asked an unending stream of questions about those previous incarnations. Nothing was too exciting, but she had once been a princess; she liked that. And we both thought it was cool that in one life she was a sailor on the Pinta, one of Columbus's ships in 1492. I didn't say anything about her three other *current* incarnations; one actually lived in Los Angeles. I wasn't sure how she would take that information, and I was too tired to find out.

"I'm wiped out but wired at the same time," she said. "I'm sure I'll never get to sleep."

"I think I can help with that. Spencer taught me a way to calm people or put them to sleep. Well, technically he didn't teach me, but he reminded... never mind."

"Does it hurt?"

"Of course not. Very gentle."

Twenty minutes later she appeared wearing sweats and a T-shirt. Once in bed I looked at her for a few moments, closed my eyes, and pictured her having a deep peaceful sleep.

"Did it work?" I whispered.

When there was no answer I went though the dark house, stretched out on the couch, fully clothed, and read Linh's poem by flashlight. Reading in the dark was possible but not pleasant.

> Its beautiful music
> This war of the worlds,
> Of the time, the dimension
> You think you are the body
> That holds these wings
> You think you are the message
> Held tight, in the bottle
> Upon that ocean of colors and dreams
> So hot, from too many hands
> Changing sharp things
> Over and over again
> It is history
> It is a dream

It is life, dear friend
Humor the butterflies
Whose path is lined with death
Whose whisper is only heard
Within a silence
Deep in the core of a forest
For that magic,
Sustained involuntarily
Is the essence—
Or the beat,
Yes, the raucous sensual love
My friend,
That is the stamp you must stain
Upon this land
That is the print you must
Leave upon the faces
Of all of us innocently moving
Toward whatever light is brighter
And you, the chosen one?
Perhaps, take my hand
I am empty and I will not hesitate
To open to this velocity—
This fresh start,
This embrace.

Sleep came easy.

40

Sunday, September 28

The heat woke me. I jolted up panicked, thinking the house was on fire. While shaking off sleep, the warning hit me. We were in danger. I grabbed my backpack and pulled on shoes in one motion while lunging toward Tanya's bedroom. "Tanya, wake up!" I snatched her sneakers.

"What? Huh?"

"We have to go. Right now."

"Why?" she asked, following me.

"Someone's out there. Let's go."

"I don't have shoes," she said, as we went out the back door.

"Here." I pushed them into her hands as we sprinted across the yard toward the river. The sun wasn't up, but the sky was beginning to lighten.

"This is Federal Agent Fitts. Stop or I'll shoot!"

"Tanya, go, go," I whispered, turning to face Sanford Fitts. My night vision was still adjusting, and all I could see was his silhouetted figure. "You won't shoot," I yelled, taking off after Tanya.

"Damn it," I heard him say, then footsteps. Fitts was a trained agent; he could catch us.

I found Tanya on the second switchback; she had stopped to put on her shoes. The trail was steep, but she knew it well and I could see in the dark. Moving as fast as we dared, we were on the third switchback when she asked, "Where are we going?"

"To the river."

"Then where?" she asked.

"I don't know. How far along the river can we go?"

"The trail ends where we went today. We'll be trapped."

Before I had time to consider our predicament, Fitts crashed down on us from above. He was on top of me, and I could feel his strength. We went over the edge locked together, rolling and smashing through brush, tumbling onto an outcropping of rocks. I managed to separate myself from him and stiffly got to my feet. I was bleeding in several places, battered and bruised, but nothing was broken. I looked down on the creature who had murdered my father, face down in the scrub but slowly beginning to get up. I kicked him hard in his ribs.

"Oooff!" he cried out.

"You killed my dad, you bastard!" I screamed, kicking him again and again. "I'll kill you!" I shouted, out of control, looking for a rock to smash on his head.

"Nate," Tanya's voice, pained and weak, called from somewhere below us. "Help me, help."

I had no choice but to leave Fitts. But, I figured, he was in no shape to go anywhere, "I'll be back," I spit, landed a last kick on his neck, knocking his DHS hat off, then raced down toward Tanya's voice.

I found her tangled in a fir tree. When I tried to move her it was obvious by the screams that at least one leg was broken. Rubbing my hands together, I began to heal her leg, but there wasn't going to be time. Instead, I concentrated on making a Lusan healing globe. The instant I moved it across her leg she cried in painful relief. I heard other agents' voices above us. They had found Fitts. My vengeance was denied, but more critical at that moment was escaping. Their voices went silent. They were moving down toward us. Tanya was a long way from being healed.

"Can you move?" I whispered.

"I don't think so."

"They're coming. We have to move."

"Leave me. It's okay, Nate, you go."

I pulled her up, supporting her weight with her arm around my neck. She screamed, but I kept pushing towards the water. They were near. I looked back and saw two men; Fitts must still be down. They were very close now. I still had the Lusan I'd been healing Tanya with. We were almost to the river. They'd be able to grab us any second. Obviously, their orders were to take me alive, or I'd already be dead. I pushed Tanya into the water as gently as I could. She screeched loudly. I turned and threw the Lusan at the agents. There was a flash, dirt and rock flying… and screams. I didn't wait to see.

I dove in after Tanya. The current had us both. Her head was above the surface, and the cold water was hopefully cutting her pain. I forgot all my aches. Still, the cold would become an enemy. After a few minutes, the rapids eased some and I could get to her, working us over to the other side. It took forever to navigate the rocks, but it got shallow enough that I could pull her out onto the opposite bank. There was no way to know how far down we'd come, easily a mile. If the agents survived, and Fitts must have, it would be tough for them to find us before morning. I hoped so anyway.

Tanya was in bad shape. Her teeth were chattering; she tried to speak but wasn't making any sense. I was shaking, freezing, and wet. The exertion and fear left me unable to make another Lusan. Somehow we stumbled forward. The bank was flat here and after a few dozen excruciating steps we almost fell into someone's tent. A guy came out ready for a fight, but his flashlight revealed trauma victims who were no threat. We were in a large campground along the river. I'm not sure what happened next, but somehow people got us into a car and soon we were at the hospital in Grants Pass. The sun was coming up.

I told a story that we'd been looking for my lost dog when Tanya slipped and fell down the bank into the river. The nurse said I was a hero for going in after her—crazy, but a hero. Aside from a few gashes that only required bandages, I was pronounced good enough to see Tanya.

"Once you visit your friend, come on back, we need you to stay until we reach your mother." The nurse handed me my dry clothes and shoes. "We're not supposed to use the dryers for patients' clothes, but seeing how you're a bona fide hero and all… "

I high-fived her.

Tanya was going to be fine, too, although a rather large cast would be on for six weeks along with crutches. "Don't worry, I'll figure out how to heal broken bones way before that," I promised her.

She smiled. "You better not stay, Nate. They'll probably look for you here."

"I just wanted to see you first. I'm leaving now."

"Nate, how did they find my house?"

"I've been trying to figure that out myself."

"Do you think they'll try to get me?"

"I don't know. You're not a relative, and so far they've left my friends alone. They could have grabbed Amber, Kyle, or Linh at any time. If I stay away from you, I think they might, too."

"Where will you go?"

"I'll figure something out. And don't worry, we'll find Rose."

"I heard you yelling at that man, the first one who came after us. He killed your dad?"

"Yes."

She squeezed my hand.

"He's got Dustin and Rose, too. I wanted to kill him. I was going to kill him. It feels horrible."

"Don't let it eat at you. He deserves it. What about the other ones? What did you do to them?"

"I don't know. They might be dead."

"You better find a good place to hide."

"I called Kyle, and he's on his way. We'll find somewhere." I'd given him a quick rundown of what happened and told him to come alone.

"Thanks for saving me."

"I'll see you soon." I hoped it was true. I hurried to the hall, knowing it was possible Lightyear was already in the building.

41

I was looking for an exit when I heard Josh's voice!

"Nate, how did you get here?" His shirt was the color of a yellow highlighter.

"Some guys from a campground brought me. How did you know I was here?"

"I didn't. Your mom has me listed as an emergency contact. The hospital phoned me forty-five minutes ago. I drove straight here. I've been trying to call you, but it keeps going to voice mail."

"Wait, what are you talking about? My mom's here?"

"Isn't that why you're here?"

"No, a friend broke her leg." He couldn't see the bandages under my clothes. "What's wrong with Mom?"

"Oh Nate, you don't know. God, I'm sorry. She was in an accident."

I couldn't breathe. In that moment, I questioned everything. Not Mom. It was all coming apart.

"Nate, are you okay? Here," he moved me into a chair.

Josh shouted to a nurse passing by, "Can you get him some water?"

"Nathan, what happened?" she asked; it was my nurse.

"Your mom's okay," Josh said. "She just came out of surgery. I spoke with the doctor. He said he expects her to make a full recovery."

"When did it happen?" I finally managed.

The nurse went for water.

"On her way home from seeing you. Not far from here she went off the interstate. No other vehicles involved."

"Take me to her!"

"She's not awake yet. As soon as they get her into a room, we'll go up there."

Josh hugged me. I buried my face in his shoulder. I was sobbing. The nurse set a cup of water on the window ledge and draped a warm blanket over me. "Is he all right?"

Josh nodded.

"I'll come back and check on him soon."

Josh began talking calmly to me. I don't know what he said, nothing important, but soon he had me distracted enough that my thoughts could connect and I stopped crying.

My nurse came back and gave directions to my mom's room. Mom's face was badly swollen and cut. The seatbelt and airbag saved her but there had been lots of flying glass.

"Mom?"

She opened her eyes. Almost a smile, but the pain canceled it quick.

"Nate, sweetie."

"I'm here, Mom," I took her hand. Her eyes closed.

It was five minutes before she woke up again. In the meantime, a doctor had come in and told me she would, in fact, live. It was hard to believe looking at her bloodied face, but he said she could go home in two or three days.

I still had her hand when she said, "There was this big light, I couldn't see—"

"Headlights?"

"No. Driving fine, then blinded by big flash of light right at me."

Josh came into the room.

"We can talk about it later." No one could have convinced me that Lightyear wasn't involved. They were trying to wipe my family out of existence.

"You've needed some time off anyway," Josh said to her, smiling.

"If you're here I must be dying."

"No. The doctors guarantee a full recovery."

Kyle showed up. We left Mom with Josh and went into the hall. "I asked for you at the nurses' station, and they said you were up here in your mom's room. What happened to her?"

"She went off the road on her way home from Tanya's."

"Was it Lightyear?"

"I can't prove it, but I have no doubt."

"You know you shouldn't be here. They're going to figure it out pretty quick, if they haven't already. Your mom, Tanya, they put them here. They know you'll come."

"I can't leave my mom."

"Listen man, do you think your mom wants you dead?"

I pushed him out of my way.

He grabbed my shoulder from behind. "I'll tell her everything that happened tonight. I'll walk in there and tell her agents are on their way to kill you and that you're just going to wait for them at her bed."

I was furious, knowing he'd do it, knowing he was right. I had to leave. Frustrated, I couldn't even take care of my mother.

"Damn it!" We started down the hall. Josh called after us.

"Josh, say bye to Mom for me. I'll call soon. We *have* to go."

"If you need a place to stay…" He caught up to us. "And you really should talk to the FBI. You're in pretty deep, buddy."

"Mom agreed to let it play out a little longer."

"Think about it. And here," Josh handed me a fifty.

"No Josh. I'm good. Mom gave me some cash yesterday."

"Just take it."

I thanked him and stuffed the bill in my jeans. "We gotta go."

We flew out a side door and raced around the building to Kyle's car. His eyes darted back and forth as he sped out of the lot.

"Where are we going?" Kyle asked.

"Brookings. I've got to find Spencer; this is out of control! And I can't reach him any other way, so he's got to be at Tea Leaf."

"Sounds like a long shot. What about Dustin?"

"One thing last night taught me is that Lightyear definitely wants to take me alive. Spencer's right. Dustin is safe as long as I am."

"When did you last meditate?" Kyle asked.

"Yesterday morning."

"That's too long."

"Yeah, well, I've been kind of busy trying to stay alive." I gave him the whole story including the Lusan. "They may all be dead."

"It's the government. They can't ever *all* be dead."

"The ones at Tanya's could be, and no one might know yet. I wish I'd made Fitts tell me where Aunt Rose was."

"How would you have done that?"

"I don't know. I was so filled with rage I couldn't think straight." I put the papers from my dad's desk on the dash to dry. I was glad he always wrote using Fisher Space pens because, even after being in the river, the ink was barely blurred.

"You had those with you?" Kyle asked pointing to the carved piece of wood and gold box in my lap.

"Yeah, in my pocket. My camera, too, but it was lost in the river."

"You should memorize the sheets, in case next time you go for a swim you're not so lucky."

"Good idea." I held the sheets for a minute and it was done.

"Did you get a chance to ask Spencer about them?"

"Yeah, he was strange. I *know* he recognized the box, but he said he didn't. He thought the carved piece was a message of some sort that would reveal itself at the right time. I don't think he knew what it meant. The pages, though, I swear he could read the ones in code, I mean I watched him and he was reading, but he just shook his head."

"How about the list with his name on it?"

"I asked if he knew any of the other names on the list or why my dad would have written it, and he got lost somewhere for like two minutes, staring off into forever. Then said no. It was like he didn't want to give the pages back to me, but he finally did. Spencer's a riddle wrapped in a mystery inside an enigma."

After a few minutes of silence Kyle asked, "What's going on with you and Amber?"

"No comment."

"It's a scandal," he said in a falsetto voice.

"We're just friends. But I should call her to see if we can crash at her beach house."

I knew Kyle was worried about missing school. I told him I'd help him study. We stopped for some snacks and sodas. I called Amber and Linh and caught them up. Amber wanted to join us at the beach house, but I refused.

Far ahead, a mountain lion lumbered across the road. "Did you see that?" I asked. "Pull in up there."

"What?" I wasn't surprised he didn't see it. The lion, or maybe a shapeshifter, had run into Jedediah Smith Redwoods State Park, one of the last uninterrupted forests of old-growth coastal redwoods left on earth.

"Something important to me. A mountain lion."

"Why's that important?" He drove down one of the narrow dirt roads that accessed a small part of the 10,000 acres of giants. "Because we saw one the morning we first met Spencer?"

"Yeah." I opened the car door. "Park and catch up to me. I'll be right back." I jumped out and pursued the ghostly animal. This was the first time a shapeshifter had lasted more than a few seconds. Finding the narrow primitive path he'd taken, I was small and hushed by the three-hundred-foot trees. The scent of pine and dark organic earth filled me. Negotiating through lush ferns towering over me, there was another glimpse of the lion, so I increased my speed.

A woman was on the path ahead, and it was not clear where she came from. A flowing blue skirt with a jagged hem and bare feet made her look out of place in the trees.

"Hello." She appeared older than Amber but younger than Tanya.

"Hey, you're the one with the spilling purse from the gas station."

"Of course I am, Nate. Why would you be talking to me otherwise?"

"Did you send the mountain lion?"

"What lion?" she asked, alarmed. Then she dismissed it. "I have some things to show you."

"I should get my friend."

"Kyle can wait. This will only take a few minutes."

"Who are you?"

"Names, names, names. Why on earth is everyone so hung up on names?"

"Where are we going?"

"Just be in this moment right now. What happens next is of no concern, at least not until it happens." She giggled.

The redwoods had always been special to me, but something had changed now. I could hear them. It wasn't like they were speaking English; they were communicating their energy. Quietly growing, breathing, absorbing sun and moisture, it was all around, gentle and powerful.

We weren't really following a trail, but she seemed to know where she was going. The earth sloped toward a small clearing, a stand of redwoods bigger than the rest, in deep greens, reds, and browns.

"Welcome to the Grove of Titans." She introduced them, "This is Lost Monarch and here is El Viejo del Norte. This beauty is Screaming Titans, and there are Aragorn, Sacajawea, Aldebaran, Stalagmight and that one over there is Del Norte Titan." She looked at me smiling. "Takes your breath, doesn't it?"

"Yes," I whispered, and walked over to Lost Monarch. Its magnificent trunk was nearly thirty feet wide. I learned later Lost Monarch was the largest living tree by width *and* height. I stretched my arms against the thick, twisting bark. In a few minutes twenty-two centuries drifted into me. Very few people had been here in all that time, mostly animals, and the seasons shifting in this isolated place. I saw the tree grow from its first year, when it shot up seven feet, and the eventual climb to where it was today. Then Lost Monarch invited me to climb.

"It wants me to climb," I said. "How?"

She was standing next to me when all at once she half ran and half floated up and then disappeared into the canopy. Even with the powers I'd accumulated, it was an awesome display.

"Where are you?" I yelled.

The trees were quiet. A few minutes later she came down another tree. "Now you."

"I think I'll need a six-week flight training course before I could attempt that."

"It's not flying, silly. It's 'Skyclimbing,' easy in nature, hard on buildings, even for you."

"Even for me? You say it like I'm special."

"We both *know* you are."

"You must know Spencer."

"Spencer-nencer, Silly-nilly. Never heard of him. Ask another question."

"You're weird."

"Is that a question?" She laughed. "Okay, I'll tell you. The constraints of gravity are looser than scientists would have you believe. So all you do is this." She ran between trees gaining speed and momentum and soon was skipping from the ground to the lower branches and then from tree to tree. "It's one of those things you just have to know you can do."

"Are you sure you don't know Spencer? You teach just like him."

"The soul is more powerful than any earthly laws of physics. Mind over matter and all that. You use Photoshop to modify your photos, right? By rearranging pixels you change the look of a picture—remove a flagpole, take out red eye, enhance colors, on and on."

"Yeah."

"Good, now stay with me. Atoms make up everything. Think of atoms like pixels. You can rearrange the atoms on this canvas. Your mind is like your computer's mouse: just point and click." She waved her arms to frame in the trees around us. "It's really nothing you need to think too hard about. Just know your hands and feet can find something more solid than leaves and air. This won't be difficult for you. Lost Monarch invited you *personally*." She seemed proud.

It turned out not to be hard at all and for a while I was convinced it was a lovely dream. I only needed the briefest contact with a branch, or even the pine needles, in order to take off. Later I learned it was done using Gogen and Foush.

"How do you like Skyclimbing?" she shouted.

"Is this real?"

"Is anything?" She laughed.

"It's like that Chinese movie where they fly around on bamboo trees, sword-fighting."

"Where do you think that idea came from? All creativity comes from the soul. When you read something in books or see it in movies, it's all expressions of soul memories."

Branches obscured the ground, and sky was also impossible to find; it was another world. The redwoods were so huge that other trees, some surprisingly large, grew right on their limbs. Dried leaves, sticks, and plants on many of the branches made it look like the lower ground. Dirt was several feet deep in places. Rabbits and other small animals made the upper reaches their homes. Each time I climbed higher, a new mini-forest revealed itself.

Unexpectedly, she was by my side again.

"It's like a great floating forest. Where are we going? I can't stay up here too long, Kyle will be wondering where I am."

"Kyle is fine. Time's a funny thing and of no use to your soul. It is a human invention."

"Like evil."

"The only evil in the world is chocolate." She laughed and Skyclimbed into another tree.

Wondering if nature could help me in my search for Rose, I sat down and got into a meditative state, disengaged my personality by feeling pure love, surrounded myself in white light. But instead of Rose, there I was in Dustin's room.

"Nate, you're here, aren't you?" Dustin said quietly.

"I am. You're looking better."

"Are you allowed to lie when you're on the astral?" he asked, knowing he looked bad.

"Apparently."

He smiled. "When are you getting me out?"

"I'm working on it. Any day."

"It can't be sooner? I guess I'll have to trust you on the timing. At least my head's clearing, but going off these meds cold turkey is a new twist in the torture."

Then I was in Rose's empty house and quickly back on Lost Monarch.

"Hello," I yelled. "Hello." I didn't know her name.

"Hello, hello, hello," she sang, emerging from somewhere below.

"Could you please tell me your name?"

"This whole name business is an issue for you, isn't it? Make one up."

"You can't just tell me your name?"

"A name only matters for now, and I don't want to carry anything that heavy around. If you need one, give me one."

"How old are you?"

"Now you're pulling age into it. Is that another issue for you? Is that information necessary to pick out a name? Age, time, names, these are silly things."

"No. I just wondered because you seem so wise but look so young."

"Why, thank you. Am I blushing? I must be blushing. You're such a charmer. I like you. Yes, I like you very much."

"You're so peculiar."

"More compliments. Sweet, sweet you are."

"Can I call you Gibi?"

"Of course, it's a lovely name. But I'm curious why you picked it."

"When I was little, I had an imaginary friend. It freaked my mom out, but one of the cooks at our restaurant, an old Turkish immigrant with about a hundred kids and grandchildren, told her it was just a 'gibi', a pretend friend. I haven't thought about Gibi for years, but you remind me of her.

"I wasn't imaginary, Nate."

I studied her closely, "*You* were Gibi?"

"I am."

"Where have you been for the last ten years?" It astonished me.

"I never left."

"So, how come you stopped talking to me?"

"It was the other way around, Nate. But it's not your fault. When babies are born, they're more a part of the spiritual plane than the material world. As they grow up, society takes over, and around age five all is forgotten of what took place before this lifetime. Kids begin to think of the beauty in dreams and any connection to the powers of their souls as make-believe."

"Why is that allowed to happen?"

"Allowed? Such a strong word, as if someone's in charge."

"Isn't there someone in charge?"

"Everyone is."

"How can that be?"

"How can it not be?"

I stared at her. She occupied my earliest memories, and the feelings washed over me.

"Why did it take you so long to come back and help me?"

"The day at the convenience store wasn't the first time. I stopped in many times through the years… your dad's funeral, the fourth-grade field trip when you were lost, whenever you were lost, as a matter of fact, or really scared."

"Like now."

She started giggling and grabbed my hand. "Come on, let's play!"

"Shouldn't you show me what you brought me here for?"

"Yes but… I mean it's extraordinary. It's just, you'll never be the same again."

She said it sweetly with a trace of nostalgia, like when Mom talks about me riding my tricycle. Did I really want to see something that was going to change me forever? Yes.

"Let's go."

She pointed up.

W e made our way up to the crown of the tree; the sky came into view, deep blue with a strong bright sun. Balancing on the thin upper branches of Lost Monarch, thirty-two stories high, the breeze kept us bobbing back and forth.

She pointed out other trees. "Do you see how they make a sort of circle?"

"Yeah, Lost Monarch completes it."

"Exactly. Now look down between them."

There was a shimmering circle about fifty feet down. It was translucent and would have been invisible except for the subtle rainbow of colors radiating from it. I remembered Spencer's description.

"A dimensional doorway?" I asked.

"Yes, but 'portal' is a much nicer way to say it, don't you think?"

"Where does it go?"

"Don't you want to see for yourself?"

"How do I get into it?"

"You jump."

"You're not serious."

"Quite." She nodded smiling.

"You want me to dive off this tree into thin air?"

"I don't want you to jump, but if you want to see what's inside, it's the only way."

"I can't do it."

"You can do anything."

We stood there shifting in the breeze as I pondered my nerves.

"Isn't there one of these on the ground somewhere I could try?"

She laughed. "Not like this one."

"When will I see you again?"

"I'll be here when you come out."

"So I do come out?"

She nodded, smiling.

"Talk about a leap of faith... " I gave her a glance that said you had better be right, then did my best imitation of a professional cliff diver I'd once seen on TV.

It would have been impossible to miss even if I tried. Some force pulled me into the center of the portal. The greenery, brown branches, and trunks of the trees were blurred streaks that became a light brighter than any known radiance, and yet it was not blinding. I soared into warmth. Landing isn't exactly what happened—I was all at once walking in what I imagined a cloud would be like. My feet never really touched anything solid, but I seemed to be moving forward. It was difficult to really know. Gold light glowed all around. My mind unlocked, instantly recalling memories in vivid details—soul memories.

After no more than thirty steps, I could see an opening in the portal and before me was a green alpine meadow. I was on the slope of an 18,000-foot mountain, at the top of a black cliff more than a hundred feet above a rocky, moss-covered valley floor, encircled by snow-capped peaks. Melting ice plummeted over the cliff into a tiny stream.

Somehow, I knew it was the Andes Mountains of Peru, at the first few drops of the world's largest river, the great Amazon. The headwaters begin an epic 4,000-mile voyage to the Atlantic Ocean, one-fifth of the world's river flow. It's no coincidence that this mighty river travels through the largest rainforest on earth, producing twenty percent of our oxygen and home to half of the planet's species. The Amazon rainforest has existed for more than fifty million years, but in just five decades, man has brought unprecedented destruction and radically reduced its size.

Within the portal, I understood this to be a crime against humanity. It became clear to me that trees protect the human race, most often from ourselves. They guide and heal; without them we could not breathe. Trees do have souls, and we are connected to them, but unlike us they do not do bad things. The more trees we destroy the more difficulties we face, as there is less pure energy in the astral. Clear-cutting forests weakens our species and trouble follows because the balance is disturbed.

Rose had tried to explain about the souls in other living things, but I think even she would be surprised by the interdependency of all things. What would Rose think of this portal? It was a million times more than what she told me about the astral. Did she know? Could I use it to find her? I'd have to ask Gibi. Instead of learning about the trees, I should have been looking for ways to save Rose and Dustin.

Before I could fully digest my thoughts, I was on top of another mountain, this time in Nevada, where a grove of bristlecone pines huddled against the wind as they had for thousands of years. It was the site of the awful murder I'd told Linh and Kyle about. On August 6, 1964, the death of Prometheus, the world's oldest living thing took place, by chainsaw. The portal opened above where the tree had lived for almost five thousand years; its void was vast and desperate. A mere few days after it was cut down, the U.S. Congress passed the Gulf of Tonkin Resolution, officially entering the U.S. into a long and bloody war, resulting in more than 58,000 U.S. deaths and as many as a quarter of a million Vietnamese fatalities. The U.S. military also dumped millions of gallons of poisonous herbicide on the incredible forests of Vietnam, causing thousands more Americans to eventually die of cancer and an estimated four million Vietnamese civilians to become victims of dioxin poison.

What would Linh have thought if she could have seen the sacred trees around the former home of Prometheus? More startling would be Kyle and Bà's reactions to the possibility that cutting down Prometheus had started the U.S. to slide into the horrendous Vietnam War. How different their lives would have been.

I'd been away for a long time, and Kyle would be searching. And I needed to get to Dustin. The portal was allowing me to physically go to places, so there must be a way to get to him. I needed to return to Gibi and find out how.

Back in the portal, another corridor, I stumbled out into a tragically filthy and primitive slum somewhere in Africa. I was standing on a sheet metal and tarp roof. The portal entrance was almost five feet above me. Raw sewage ran everywhere. I saw malnourished children with bloated bellies, vacant eyes, dying mothers, AIDS, malaria, contaminated water—a perfect collection of the world's miseries. They came begging: a naked and exhausted child no more than six with a dirty orange plastic car in one hand and a stick in the other that he used to dig through trash piles, sought any crumb. I had nothing to give. Maybe two hundred more began climbing on the shanty. I Skyclimbed into the portal, escaping dozens of reaching arms just as the shack collapsed.

Would anyone believe how important trees were if they hadn't seen what I had? Could they see a correlation between war, poverty, disease, despair, and the killing of trees? Not likely. They would think I was crazy and lock me up like Dustin. How many misunderstood people were wasting away in institutions? I needed Dustin. We had so much to do together. The profound depth of what I had witnessed in the portal was crushing and left me physically drained.

Coming out, the upper branches of Lost Monarch were within reach, and I quickly moved to the top of the tree. More stars than I'd ever seen were visible. I could easily tell differences in sizes and colors that were impossible to see before, jewels of pink, pale-blue, and gold. I realized it had been a suicide of sorts: the innocent earthly boy Nate ended with the leap from the tree and my soul had emerged.

44

Where was Gibi, I wondered, and then she was there. I took her into my arms, and we held each other floating on the trees, drenched in stars.

"What do I do?" my words choked out.

She held me.

"Gibi, what am I supposed to do?"

She stroked my hair.

"What have we done?" I clung to her, dazed and inconsolably grieved. Steadied in the branches of ancient treetops, high above the ground, having just traveled ten thousand miles in a handful of steps, I possessed the power of the universe in my mind, and yet I wept out of total frustration and inadequacy.

"The slum you were at used to be part of a great coastal African forest," she whispered. "It was destroyed decades ago by logging, oil exploration, agriculture, industrialization, development... the usual reasons all belonging to greed."

"Why did I see that? What am I supposed to do?"

"It's too soon to understand, but don't you feel the possibilities of what you can do?"

"All I feel is our whole planet heading for a future right out of a dystopian novel."

"That process was started more than a hundred years ago."

She went on to explain that this portal was not the one for getting to Dustin or Rose. I pressed her for any information on Rose, but she had none. Gibi told me of several other portals, but none was more famous among seekers and mystics than the Calyndra Portal.

"Many have been lost that we may never find again, but Calyndra is legendary. It's somewhere along the Skyline-to-the-Sea Trail, which descends from the ridge of the Santa Cruz Mountains to the Pacific Ocean. The thirty-mile trail winds through two California state parks, Castle Rock and Big Basin Redwoods, but it's thought to be in Big Basin."

"What's special about it?"

"Supposedly, no one has been in Calyndra for more than a hundred years, but they say it can transport you to any specific time and place in the *past*."

"Can you change things once you get there?"

"I don't know. I've never been but maybe. Time's a funny thing." We talked for the remainder of the night about things I'd seen in the portal and what they meant. The sun returned, clearing the possibility that it was just a dream.

"It's time to go. You must continue your journey, but if you hide in towns they will find you. When you're in trouble, the only place you can possibly escape is in nature. You must get into the trees where you can be concealed and protected."

"I wish I could stay here."

"Redwoods are truly mystical. Normally, it would be best to remain here, but you cannot. You still need to do many things out there."

"Do you know what will happen? I mean will Lightyear succeed in killing me?"

"I can't tell."

I searched her eyes and saw both sadness and joy.

"In the meantime, you need to go back to Crater Lake."

"Is that why I haven't been able to get it out of my mind?"

"Yes, your soul knows. It's a powerful spot, like a supernatural confluence."

"What do I do when I get there?"

"What do you most want right now?"

"To free Dustin."

"That answer is waiting for you at the lake. Before you go, I have something else to show you. Let's get back on the ground."

What I'd seen in the portal, although debilitating, put my personal problems into perspective. For the first time in my life, I understood just what wisdom was and the texture of it expanded my mind. Touching the forest floor again was an odd sensation, like the feeling of coming off an extreme amusement park ride. The emotional baggage of my young life returned with that first step, but it was muted and diminished. I was stronger.

"Do you see that bridge over there?"

"It's extraordinary!"

"Come on," she said, grabbing my hand.

The bridge was narrow, two skinny people could just walk side by side and we did. It was a beautiful arch carved out of a fallen redwood. A thin strip of copper oxidized long ago to a soft green, covered the outside of the railings. Midway, we stood above a swift shallow stream, filled with colorful soft round rocks, parted lush ferns. It was all so lovely, but none of it real. The bridge and the creek vanished, and we were once again standing among the trees.

I looked questioningly at Gibi.

"I sent the suggestion into your mind using an old power known as Solteer. Now it's your turn."

"Can you give me a *little* more instruction?"

She giggled. "Yes, if you're going to be a baby about it. Imagine something you want me to see. Picture it in as much detail as possible. And then see my eyes, feel the presence of me. Send it to my mind. Simple things are best, but eventually you can create very complex ones."

I tried but nothing happened.

"You have to feel me. Our conscious minds may be separate, which is where we live as humans, but the subconscious is connected and that is where you must go; it's the way to your soul. It's how you Skyclimb and how you make Lusans. It's the same with everything your soul does; it is just manifested through the mind." She twirled around, her blue skirt spinning. "Now, make me something pretty."

I wasn't sure how to make something more beautiful than where we were but I tried again, and she squealed even before I saw it.

"It's fantastic! I love it, thank you, thank you." She clapped her hands.

The waterfall came down from between two redwoods, and we could not see the top. A misty pool not far from where we stood was surrounded by wildflowers of every shade of blue and purple. She hugged me and ran into the flowers and splashed in the water, even kicking some of it on me. A minute later it was gone.

"Is there a way to make it last longer?" I noticed we were both dry.

"Oh yes, with practice you can make them last as long as you want, but only if you're near the person. They won't remain after you've left a place."

"I can't believe everything that's been happening."

"Your journey is just beginning. It's *very* important."

"When do I get to understand it all?"

"When it's over... if you're lucky."

I pondered what she said. "Why me?"

"This life is your time. It's true that you're young in human terms. Awakenings are much more common around age thirty. But, Nate, you've had so many varied lives, and that evolution has brought you very near to returning to your soul."

I was quiet again. "I was a slave trader."

"I know."

I saw something in her eyes. "Oh no, were you there?"

She nodded. We looked at each other for a long time.

"I killed you? Please, tell me I didn't kill you."

"I forgave you long ago."

"I don't know how you could."

"Forgiveness is powerful. You may think it benefits the other person, but it is all for the forgiver."

I thought about Amparo and knew she was right. It made me feel better. "I don't ever want to live another life like that."

"We've all had many lives where we weren't nice. Everyone needs to go through the good and bad, as it's the only way to experience everything so that there is total understanding." She placed her hands on my cheeks and softly kissed my forehead. "Now, get out of here, silly. Kyle's looking for you."

"Oh my gosh, Kyle." I started jogging. "When will I see you again?"

"I'm around." She laughed as I raced away.

After the last turn in the trail, Kyle was walking toward me.

"I'm sorry. I had no idea I would be that long. So much happened."

"I wasn't going to worry until you were gone at least eleven minutes," he said sarcastically. He looked at me strangely, a look I was getting used to from him.

"How long was I gone?"

"It's been like five or ten minutes since you got out of the car."

"Are you sure?"

"Of course I'm sure. I'm not the one chasing hallucinations."

I tried to grasp how two days of my life could squeeze into ten minutes of his. It was beyond bizarre.

"So did you catch up to the mountain lion?"

"No, but it got me where I needed to go." For the next twenty minutes I gave Kyle the highlights of my two days in the redwoods. Despite his usual sarcastic comments, he believed every word.

45

"Here's for gas," I handed him one of Mom's hundreds.

"Cool. We'll fill up in Brookings."

I still wanted to find Spencer before we headed back to the lake. He knew more about Lightyear, and I needed his help in order to free Dustin. I was incredibly hungry, but there was nothing until the beach. After seeing the slum, I promised myself I'd never complain about being hungry again.

After filling up with gas, we stopped for fish and chips and a six-pack of Coke then drove straight to the guardrail above Tea Leaf Beach. The trail was vibrant in the midday sun. I couldn't help but think that a few hundred years earlier this forest connected to the redwoods. It was about one o'clock; Spencer was not on his boulder. We walked the beach in both directions calling out loud and silently. I meditated, asked seagulls, and went to the astral. Dustin was sleeping, Rose was as lost as ever, and Spencer Copeland was nowhere. He told me to trust the universe, but it wasn't providing answers.

We drove to the beach house after picking up supplies. Our plan was to return to the beach at sunrise. All I wanted was sleep.

At the security gate, Kyle had punched the first two digits of the code into the keypad when the heat rush hit me.

I grabbed his arm. "Something's wrong."

"What?"

"When there's danger, I get outrageously hot, like walking through fire. Get out of here, now!"

He threw it in reverse and sprayed gravel as we flew backward and hit a neighbor's mailbox. I looked up at Amber's house fearing they heard us but saw no movement. Still my temperature didn't return to normal until we were well down the coastal highway.

"How would they know you'd be at Amber's beach house?" His voice shaking.

"I don't know. How do they know anything?"

"Amber knew we were going there," Kyle said. "She was the only one who knew."

"So, you think she's a Lightyear agent? Linh knew, too."

"We need to figure out how they keep finding you."

"They have freakin' psychics working for them, so how hard could it be?"

"Maybe."

"Either way, they know we're in Brookings, so let's head to Crater Lake."

"You're kidding, right?"

"We can be there by eight and get a tent up before dark."

"Why don't we just sleep near Ashland so I can go to school? Remember school?"

"You can leave the lake early in the morning and still make first period."

"Sounds fun," he said sarcastically. "I guess I can handle it. But why back to the lake?"

"Gibi said the answer to saving Dustin is there."

"Maybe we'll see the Old Man again."

"So you do believe he was real?"

"Sure. The Old Man was, but him being a floating tree trunk, that's something else."

"Trees are mystical, and the lake is a vortex. It's all part of the journey."

"Where's this 'journey' going to end?"

"Ask Spencer. In the meantime, let's hope Gibi's right about the lake." I was silent for many miles. "Amber gave me a book on animal meanings, and it says when a mountain lion appears, it's time to learn about your power. The mountain lion I saw is like a sign, a message from my guides. Her book talks about young cats learning by trial and error. So when a lion reveals itself, it gives its energy and traits to a person—in this case me—and says it's time to assert and show my power."

"How are you going to assert your power?"

"The mountain lion is one of the few animals capable of killing a porcupine without injuring itself. It's developed a special trick of flipping it on its back to expose its vulnerable belly. It teaches that it's time to make a choice, something we must do quickly and strongly. We can use our power to defend ourselves or attack with equal effectiveness."

"So, what's your choice?"

"Sanford Fitts is the porcupine."

"You're going after Fitts? That's crazy! I knew you were going to get all cocky."

"That man killed my dad, he's holding Dustin hostage, my mom and Tanya are in the hospital, and who knows what he's done to Aunt Rose!"

"What are you going to do?"

"I'm not sure yet. I'm only just now deciding this. The mountain lion teaches decisiveness in the use of our power."

"Nate, this is a trained government agent and by the very nature of him being that, it means there are others, lots of them, backing him up."

"I'm not going to wait anymore. He's come after me three times. It's only a matter of time before he succeeds. Spencer is wrong to wait. Where the hell is he anyway? It's not like I'm going to do anything dumb. I've picked up a few centuries of wisdom in the last week. There are things I can do that I haven't even told you about."

"Like?"

I didn't answer right away. "See that fire truck up there?"

Kyle stepped on the brakes. "Where did that come from?" he yelled.

"From your mind."

"It's not real?" he shouted.

It disappeared just before we passed it. Kyle pulled the car off the road.

"Don't mess with me, Nate." He got out of the car and stormed to the trees.

I went after him. "Kyle, I'm sorry, wait."

He turned around as angry as I've ever seen him. "Listen to me. I'm your friend, and I'll help you and back you up. I've put myself and my family in danger for you. I'm with you in this supernatural, science-fiction world you've dragged us into. But you have to tell me right now that you will never again mess with my mind. I need to know that whatever I see is real."

"I'm sorry. You wanted to know what I could do, and I needed to practice and—"

"Don't practice on *me*."

"Never again, Kyle. I promise."

"My mind, Nate, it's all I have."

"I'm sorry, I get it."

He gave me a shove. "Let's get back on the road. Did I mention I'm also your stupid chauffeur?"

"I know, and I never say thanks. I take you for granted, and I'm an all-around ungrateful, immature, self-centered jerk."

"You're not a jerk, at least not all the time. Ungrateful and immature, maybe."

We both laughed and went back to the car.

"So, you can make people see things that aren't there?"

"Yeah, it's done using one of the great powers called Solteer. Pretty cool, huh?"

"As long as it's not on me."

46

I fell asleep for the last half of the drive. Kyle woke me as we pulled into the campground at Crater Lake just after eight. With not much daylight left, we got to work on the tent, and hammering down the last stake I heard a familiar voice.

"It's the boy with many guides," Old Man said.

"Hey, Old Man, I was hoping we'd see you."

"Because you need good wood?" he asked, holding out a box.

"I need some advice, and yes, we want wood, too." I fished a five out of my pocket, handed it to him and waved off his attempt at making change.

"What advice could you need, Many Guides?"

"It's kind of a long story... "

"No, no, something has changed," he interrupted. "I see the mountain lion in you, very strong."

Kyle looked at me and then at Old Man. "Unbelievable."

"Yes, you have been through fires since we last met." He smiled slightly. "And now you return to the volcano."

"You know about the mountain lion?"

"It's your totem, one of the animals that will guide you throughout your life. Mountain lion's traits are part of your power as you walk forward, wise leadership without ego and great intuitive ability. The mountain lion carries messages from humans to the higher spirits, a link to Mother Earth and Father Sky."

"Sounds about right," Kyle said.

"This totem means you're a leader. Others will see your power and follow you. The lion in you tells them to go in your direction, if they choose, but not in your footsteps. The path they follow must be their own. A mountain lion pushes her young toward independence. She remains vigilant if they need help but allows them to find their own way. This is how to lead."

"I've never been a leader of anything," I said. "Can animals really pass on their traits?"

"Mother Earth and all her creatures will teach if they're honored. Mountain lion has granted you nearly perfect balance, shown the way to conserve your energy and how to recognize the importance of timing. A mountain lion does not hesitate when it attacks. Do you know what I'm saying, Nate? It goes for the weakest place of its target."

I moved my gaze to Kyle; we both knew what he meant. Sanford Fitts was my target. Where was he vulnerable? Could I choose the right time?

"I have more wood to sell. But you and I have an appointment tomorrow. Don't be late," he said and walked off.

"Wait, when? Where?"

"You'll find me." He was gone.

An hour later Kyle and I were sitting around the fire, pondering the two objects from my dad's desk, determined to figure them out. I'd already tried reading them and again with no luck. Kyle held the wood piece and I the gold box when Old Man showed up again. He'd finished his wood-selling rounds.

"Here are a few scraps I had left over." He handed over some old two-by-fours. "You may need them, going to be cold tonight."

"Thanks. Any idea what this is?"

"Looks like a gold box to me? Sure is a pretty one. Maybe Mayan."

Could there be a connection to the lifetime with my dad and the Conquistadors, I wondered. "I want to know what's inside."

"Why? It feels empty. What you want is probably on the outside. The patterns of the inlays are the message."

"Do you know what it says?"

"No, the message is for you. You must discover it."

"What about this?" Kyle threw the carved piece to him.

He gave it a quick look. "This one's easy." He tossed it in the fire.

"Hey! What the hell are you doing?" I tried to pull it out but it was too late.

"Let it show you," he said calmly.

We watched the wood burn away. The ends melted like a hard brown wax, and there in the fire a shiny silver key emerged from the burnt wood. I quickly fished it out with two sticks and let it rest on the ground to cool. It was no ordinary house key, but old, like three keys pressed together.

"What's it go to?" Kyle asked.

"How should I know? It's not *my* key," Old Man answered.

"How did you know it was in there?" I asked.

"The outside carvings revealed that what you're looking for is inside."

"It just looked like a bunch of leaves and symbols to me."

"Languages aren't always words," he said, walking toward the trees. "Sometimes what you think you need to go after isn't always what you really need to be going after." He disappeared into the underbrush but yelled back, "Strategy, remember?"

It wouldn't be long before I learned what the strange key unlocked, and it would turn out to provide my best chance for survival.

*M*onday, *September 29*

The rising sun warming the tent woke me. I vaguely remembered Kyle leaving hours earlier while it was still dark. By now he'd be at school, having driven more than two hours to make the morning bell. Finding a soda in the cooler, I decided on a breakfast burrito and managed to heat it on the propane stove.

I hiked around the lake in search of the Old Man. Every so often I tried to get a signal for my cell phone to call my mother and Amber, but there was no reliable service.

Soon it was obvious I was being followed. There was no heat so it probably wasn't someone dangerous, but there was no reason to take chances. I broke into a run. After a quarter-mile sprint, it seemed safe to look back. I turned, crashed into the Old Man, and fell back on the ground.

"Blast! What's the matter with you? First you haul off and run away from me like a scared rabbit, and then you knock into me and fall on your ass. Are all teenagers this dang foolish?"

"Why'd you sneak up on me?"

"I don't sneak. This is my place." He swept his arms in a grand gesture.

"That's why I'm here."

"You're late."

"Why are you so grouchy?"

"Why are you so ornery?"

"I'm reacting to your mood."

"That's foolish. Why don't you learn to control yourself instead of letting others determine how you feel?"

"Okay fine, I'm in charge. I'm not looking for lessons right now. I need help rescuing my brother. Can you do that?"

"Every word I utter in your presence will help you get your brother because it will help you grow into someone who can do such things. Are you going to listen, boy?"

"You seem so angry."

"I'm the Old Man of the Lake, remember? I'm just a reflection. A reflection of you."

I took a deep breath and thought of Thich Nhat Hanh. He said, "Just because anger or hate is present does not mean that the capacity to love and accept is not there; love is always with you." Maybe the Old Man was right and he was a reflection of me. I was definitely angry, and it had been building for years: my dad's death, Dustin's imprisonment, Mom's disconnect—my family had left me all alone. And in the last few weeks everything had accelerated with my finding out about Dad's murder, Aunt Rose's kidnapping, Mom's accident, the attempts on my friends. Why? I'd done nothing wrong, committed no crime, and yet I was being hunted and those close to me hurt. I wanted my life back, wanted my dad back. Damn right I was angry. The Old Man was pulling it out of me, showing it to me. I screamed, a loud visceral sound.

"Good boy. Get it out! Better than taking it out on me."

"Why?" I screamed again, sinking onto a log and burying my face in my hands.

"Are you going to cry now?"

"No."

"Good. By now you've figured out you're no ordinary boy, so all that's left for me to do is guide you to some answers for questions you ain't thought of yet."

"My brother?"

"We're not going to start that again, are we?"

"Patience?"

"Yeah, patience. Good to see there is a brain in there some-where." He lightly knocked on my forehead. "Can you walk?"

"Of course I can walk. I'm emotionally damaged, not physically damaged."

He winked and led me down a very steep cliff, impossible without Skyclimbing. At the bottom he moved between two evergreens to a small sheltered cove in the cliff, about twenty feet above the water. "Sit," he said, pointing to a slab. "This lake is the center of the universe." He began lecturing like a professor. "Not actually, but it is as far as you're concerned. You have much ahead of you and I'm far from convinced you'll last, but it'll be fun to watch you take a shot. You're brave to try, I'll give you that, boy."

"I don't remember deciding to try. It was sort of thrust upon me."

"Circumstances define the man. No one wakes up and decides to be great. It's the events he's thrown into that determine if he is truly great. Survive or not is to be great or not."

"I'm not doing anything until I get my brother and aunt back. How is what you're saying going to help me get them?"

He ignored my question. "It's begun, boy. Too late to turn back now, as it's already begun." He squinted at me and paced for a couple of minutes. "You'll encounter fifteen mystics."

"Why so many?"

"If you stop and think how much there is to learn, you might ask why so few."

"Maybe you could explain exactly what a mystic is."

"It's someone who pursues awareness by searching for ultimate reality, the soul. This quest for spiritual truth is from within as he seeks experiences through instinct, intuition, and insight. A mystic grows closer to its soul by sharing knowledge with others on the path." He stopped speaking, I assumed, to allow me to absorb his words.

"You're a mystic, aren't you?"

"Isn't it obvious? I'm the first one you found. And you were more than early. I'm not talking about a week early.

Originally, you weren't due here for fourteen more years. But some series of unknown calamities in the world forced this premature debut."

"How many have I met so far?"

"You tell me."

"Spencer, Gibi, Amparo, Crowd, and you make five. So ten more to go?"

"Correct, they'll come five at a time. There are three periods until you complete your journey. You're in the first one now. After you encounter the fifteenth, you'll be a mystic yourself. But your journey is long."

"Really? I'll be a mystic?"

"Probably the youngest one in modern times—in human terms, anyway. It's not like you'll get a plaque or anything, boy. You keep seeking by sharing your knowledge. The more you share, the more you'll find."

"So where are the remaining mystics?"

"They'll appear when you're ready. Could be fifty years from now the way you act sometimes."

"If you're so enlightened, why are you so negative?"

"Just reflecting that aspect of you, Nayyy-thonn. Suppose your friend Linh was here and I was helping her. You might wonder if I was some saint of sweetness and light. It all depends on the student. Think of me as a mirror."

"I'm not like you."

He laughed hard and loud, calming just long enough to say, "Well, you shouldn't be, boy, that's for sure." Then he laughed some more.

What did he mean? I didn't act like him. I didn't talk to people like he did—well, maybe to my mother, but that was complicated. If my anger came out like his, why did I have such good friends?

He stared into my eyes, "When you're ready, I'll show you the entrance."

"The entrance?"

"Come back here in an hour, and I'll take you there."

I went back to the tent, filled my water bottle, ate, and tried the cell phone again in a few new spots. At the far end of the campground, I found that by standing on a picnic table and leaning a certain way there was just enough coverage for a call; the phone at the hospital rang. I waited, hoping the call wouldn't drop, while they connected me to Mom's room.

"Nate, I've been so worried. The doctor plans on releasing me tomorrow sometime."

"That's great news. Hey, have you heard anything from Tanya?"

"She came by to see me a little while ago. They let her go home. Have you seen Dustin?"

"He's okay. We're getting him tomorrow."

"How? Do you have help? I don't want you doing anything crazy."

I shouldn't have told her, but I knew she wasn't going to wait much longer before going to the police or the press. "I have more help than you can believe, Mom. He'll be free tomorrow. Trust me."

"I do, Sweetie. Just be careful. I just spoke with Sam. He called the restaurant when you didn't show up for the conference call with his sister this morning, and they told him I was here. Even if you get Dustin, we still need an attorney to sort this out and locate Rose. His sister sounds perfect."

"There was no way to make the meeting, and phone coverage here is no good. I'll call him tomorrow when I'm back in Ashland to set up another one."

"Okay. When there's news, you can get me at Josh's. I lost my phone in the accident. He's picking me up tomorrow, and I'm going to stay with him for a day so I'm not alone."

48

The Old Man was waiting at the cove.

"Where would you put a portal to a crossroads of multi-dimensional fields?" he asked.

"Wizard Island?"

"See, boy, you're much smarter than you look."

"How are we going to get out there?"

"Can't you swim?"

"Sure, but not in that cold water."

"Follow me." We took a trail to the shore where he knelt down and said, "Get on my shoulders."

He pointed to his shoulders and had a don't-argue-boy, look. Once I was on, he pushed out into the water. Instantly, I was standing on top of the tree trunk moving swiftly toward the island. I knew he was the floating tree! I couldn't wait to tell Kyle. The top of the trunk was wide enough to be very comfortable and, other than the bobbing, it was a smooth ride. Being on the Old Man of the Lake floating across the ancient volcanic crater made me feel as if I was at the center of the universe.

I gazed down at our reflection in the water, almost a perfect dark mirror. The Old Man was right; he was a reflection of me. The cliffs rose dramatically from the blue liquid, which couldn't possibly be water. Trees, oversaturated green from a dream, all looked like something Gibi had invented for my mind alone.

We came ashore on Wizard Island and once again I was on his shoulders, unsure how it happened. He sat on a boulder, which made it easy for me to climb off; I wasn't the least bit wet.

"You really are the king of shapeshifters," I said with a smile.

"I'm not the king of anything except maybe this lake. If you live long enough, I may teach you how one day."

"I'll remind you."

"You do that." He laughed.

"Why aren't there any people here?"

"No boats running this afternoon," he said with a wink. "Mechanical failure."

The three-hundred-acre island was formed out of the eruption, leaving a cinder cone that rose more than 750 feet out of the water. We followed a trail and a series of switchbacks that wound around to the top.

"Where's the vortex?"

"The whole lake is the vortex. Can't you feel it?"

"So, that's the portal?" I asked, staring down into the crater. It was about five hundred feet across and called the "Witches Cauldron." I could imagine Kyle rolling his eyes at the name. I gazed down a hundred feet or so to the bottom. It took a minute for my eyes to adjust enough to see the shimmers. It was similar to the portal in the redwoods, but this one was bigger, and because it was inside a crater rather than floating in thin air, it had a whole different appearance—dark and dense, rather than light and airy.

"Where does it go?"

"Through it you can travel wherever you want. But it's not like astral traveling. You'll arrive in your physical body, and you can stay."

"So I could just hop over to London right now?"

"Yes, you could. But you'd need to return on one of those fancy airplane things because you don't know where another portal is over there."

"Why couldn't I come back through the same portal?"

"Because as soon as you step out, it closes. It's a one-way road unless you stay inside."

"And how does it know where I want to go?"

"That's more of a quantum physics kind of question. Ask that smart friend of yours, Kyle; he might be able to explain it to you. I'm only an old fisherman. But I can tell you this: portals are a concentration of energy—a gargantuan concentration but still just a concentration— and the time and distances are only about perception. Everything is now, so... oh hell, you ain't gonna understand this anyway, even if I do figure out how to explain it."

"Okay, but what if I go somewhere through the portal and stay inside it. Can I reach out and pull something or someone back into it and then travel back through it to here?"

"I believe you could, but if you're thinking of rescuing your brother, I have to tell you that plenty can go wrong. Portals aren't child's play... boy."

Obviously, that's what I was thinking. I'd thought about it in Lost Monarch after coming out of the redwoods portal, but Gibi had explained that that portal was random, meaning I couldn't direct my travels. Through it, I would arrive where I needed to be, like seeing the destruction of trees and its deep connection to our suffering. But this was another thing altogether.

"How many are there like this?"

"Hard to say. Most portals have specific destinations. Some are random, but this is the only one I know of that lets you decide. There are probably others I don't know about. Like I said, I don't get out much. Course, there's Calyndra, south of here, but it's a tough one to find... and the past is better left alone."

"Do I jump?"

"If you're ready."

I climbed up to the rim and dove without a second thought. It went completely dark and I almost panicked, but then brightness overtook everything. I was inside the light. The same whirl of stars and the white sound of wind and ocean from the redwoods portal told me I was about there. I looked out at Rock Creek Cemetery in Washington, D.C., and was right in front of the antique door to the Hibbs family mausoleum. I pulled the key from my pocket and slid it into the lock. It turned. I smiled, then locked it again. A second later, I was back on Wizard Island.

All I had done once inside the portal was think, "What does this key go to?" and instantly and physically I was there. Now I knew where the key went but not why my dad had so carefully hidden it. My intuition told me that among the bodies buried in that tomb something else was concealed, something I needed.

49

Back at my picnic table with cell phone reception, I called Kyle and told him not to return for me yet. Instead, I asked him to meet me in another location Tuesday right after school.

"Nate, think everything through. Meditate on it, meditate for hours."

On my next call Amber answered, almost before it rang. "Kyle wouldn't tell me anything, just that you guys didn't stay in Brookings. Where are you? Is everything okay?"

"I'm at Crater Lake."

"Why?"

"It's safe."

"How long can you stay there? What are we going to do?"

"The longer I run, the stronger I get."

"What's that mean?"

"I know it sounds silly, but I feel like I'm in training."

"For what? Do you think you can get Dustin and Rose back by yourself?"

"I'm not alone—." The signal went, and I couldn't get it back.

Old Man came by with more wood and we talked for a while. "Did you find out where your key goes?" he asked.

"Yes, but not why I have it."

"A key like that keeps secrets buried. Are there secrets you need to know?"

"I don't know."

"We have a place deep in the woods, high in the mountains. It's a vault built into the earth and surrounded by stones where we keep what is most precious to my people."

"What is it?"

"Seeds."

"Sounds like a lot of trouble for something you can pick up at any hardware store."

"These are original seeds, sown by the ancestors, passed down, maintained, and protected. Your people are changing seeds, putting patents on them, genetically modifying them, angering Mother Earth, risking the very survival of food, of man..."

"I didn't know."

"Now you do. And now that you do, you shall do."

"Do what?"

"You'll think of something."

I finished dinner and was nagged by a strong feeling to check on Dustin. In less than a minute I was on the astral and horrified by what awaited me in his room.

"Can you see this, Nathan?" Fitts asked in a twisted voice as he hit Dustin's body with an aluminum bat and then repeatedly punched his face.

"Stop," I screamed. My presence brought a flash of recognition to Dustin. His eyes opened momentarily, filled with agony. It must have been going on for a while because his face was bloody, his screams hoarse and weak.

"I know you can see me, Nathan. You messed up my vocal cords with your cowardly kicks at the river. Now I'm going to make it so your brother can't talk. Enjoy the show while I kill him. And as soon as I'm done here, I'm coming to find you and end this once and for all."

I couldn't see Fitts' face, but I could almost hear his sinister smile as he delighted in the beating. Blood sprayed from Dustin's mouth. I was powerless to stop him, and Dustin seemed to know this as no fight remained in him. My screams were constant. "No, no, no! Stop please! I'll come, you can have me!"

Fitts couldn't hear me, but Dustin did. He shook his head slightly. He didn't want me to save him. It was too late.

Then I remembered the portal. I could get to him. But how long would it take me to get to Wizard Island without the Old Man? Once I was there, I could be in his room in an instant. I could shove a Lusan down Fitts' throat and then use one to heal Dustin. But how long would that take? I'd have to leave the astral while I tried to get to the island, which meant not seeing what was going on. There was no point in watching him die. I ran toward the cove. "How does he know I can see him? How does he know where I am?" I asked myself as I rushed through the trees.

I kept hoping to see the Old Man. It was dark, but my night vision easily showed a hundred feet ahead. I Skyclimbed down to the cove, and miraculously he was there. He'll take me to the island. I'll be with Dustin in minutes.

"Old Man!" I shouted.

The figure turned. It wasn't the Old Man, and as I saw his face, I knew I wasn't going to save Dustin.

50

Spencer's look was at once pleading, compassionate and forceful.

"Help me Spencer!" I cried. "He's killing Dustin! There's no time!"

He shook his head and came close to hug me.

"No!" I pushed him away. "We have to go now." I scoured the area for the Old Man, a boat, anything that could get me to the island. "Help me, Spencer. You have to help me."

"Nate, no. It isn't time."

"There *is* no time. You didn't see what they're doing to him."

"I have seen. I'm seeing it right now."

"You can see Dustin? Is he still alive? Is Fitts still beating him?"

"He's alive at the moment."

I collapsed to the ground.

"Fitts has left the room."

I tried to see for myself, but calm and focus were required to access the astral, neither of which I had at the moment. Spencer helped me up. I shoved him again. "This is your fault. If you had let me go when I wanted to, he'd be here now and not dying alone in some room."

"Nate," his voice gentle and soft.

"No! If he dies, I'm not playing anymore. I'll renounce all my abilities just like my dad did. You can find yourself another boy wonder."

"They won't let him die."

"You don't know that. You're just seeing how it looks now. And you saw him. Fitts beat him to a pulp. Will he be brain-damaged, crippled? He could be bleeding to death. Where in hell have you been, anyway?"

His empathetic eyes never left me.

"You're trying to calm me like I did the seagull. You're in my mind. Stop, I don't like that." No wonder Kyle got mad at me; it's not fun having someone mess with your head for real. "Why are you doing this?"

"Because you have to be sedated."

"I'm not staying here. I'll find a way to—"

Tuesday, September 30

It was still dark when I woke in the cove; a campfire burned. Although Spencer was no longer sending me calming suggestions, I was relaxed and rested. He must have known I was awake but kept staring into the darkness toward the lake. My cell phone indicated it was just before five a.m. I'd slept all night.

Getting on the astral was easy. Dustin was crumpled on the floor next to the bed, bloodied and not moving. I couldn't be sure he was breathing and tried speaking to him, telling him I'd be there soon. No response. Even if he heard, he wouldn't believe me anymore.

"I should have gone yesterday," I said quietly.

"You and Dustin would be dead. I have no doubt. Today's the only day there's a chance."

"You think he's still alive?"

Spencer nodded.

"So you'll help?"

"Tell me your plan."

I explained my ideas to use some of my powers.

"Sounds like you're counting on a lot of luck. You're too new to Solteer, and you shouldn't even know how to plant thoughts yet. Making people see things takes control that you won't have in this type of confrontation. Gibi was premature in showing you."

"You know Gibi? She said she never heard of you."

"Gibi knows me by another name."

"What name? Cope?"

"No. It's not a word. Let's get back to your plan."

"The only way I can get rid of the guards is with Lusans."

"It's not a weapon," he said firmly.

"I know, but it's all I've got. What if I could get a gun?"

"Do you know how to shoot a gun?"

"No, but I've seen a lot of movies."

"Let's leave the guns to experts." He stared at me sternly. "What if Fitts is there, too?"

"That would be a nightmare. Spencer, can you come with me?"

"No."

"Why? Don't tell me it's complicated," I said with a glare. "Am I going to be able to do this?"

"Today's the first day you've had any chance. It's still iffy, but if you don't get him today, Dustin will be dead tomorrow. There is no question."

"You don't think I should go, do you?"

"I know you have to."

"You didn't answer."

"No, I didn't. Only you can decide. If you go, you and Dustin both may die today. If you don't, Dustin will be dead tomorrow and you'll never forgive yourself. If he dies like this, part of you will die, too, the best part. So, it doesn't matter what I think."

Neither of us spoke for a while.

"Can't you teach me some other power I can use?"

"Nate, you need time to absorb what you've already remembered. None of what you've been doing is strong enough because you're too scattered. Anything more and your strength will dilute beyond usefulness."

"Throw me into a slaughter then. I don't want to talk about the plan anymore. I'm going today, and I'll figure it out when I get there." I tossed a branch into the fire. The sky was showing the first signs of light. "Why isn't Rose being held with Dustin?"

He didn't say anything.

"Do you know where they have her?" I demanded.

"I can't say."

"You mean you won't say. Tell me."

"It would be interfering."

"Interfering? What does that mean? Are you worried I'll alter some cosmic plan? Afraid if I know where my Aunt Rose is before it's time, I'll end up missing an appointment with a mystic? Maybe they'll tell me something I'm not supposed to know yet. I can't believe you."

I pushed the rocks nearest me into the fire.

"Who made you God?"

I left him there.

51

I walked back to my tent. The Old Man was sitting on a log nearby. "About time!"

I wasn't in the mood for another mystic, but needed to get to Wizard Island. "Looking for me?"

"I'm not sitting here waiting for a train."

I should just call Fitts and offer to trade myself for Dustin. I wasn't one of the seven. Someone made a big mistake. I wasn't cut out for any of this.

"Can you take me to Wizard Island later?"

"That's why I'm here. Come get me when you're ready."

"Thank you."

He nodded once, then started walking away.

"How will I find you?"

"Come to the shore, anywhere, I'll be there."

My cell phone found a signal on the picnic table, but Kyle's phone went to voicemail; I left a message changing the meeting time to ten-thirty. He'd have to cut a few classes, but his perfect grades could handle it. Dustin couldn't afford any more hours. The bigger question was would he hold together if we were chased. Mom would probably love to hear from me and a call was important just in case I didn't make it back, but I couldn't bring myself to do it.

Amber's friendly voice would have been nice, but it was too coincidental how Lightyear kept locating me. Kyle was right; Amber was the only one who knew where I was every time they attacked. I didn't want to believe it but couldn't take any chances two hours before taking the battle to Lightyear. Spencer said the Lightyear psychics couldn't track me yet. He tried to explain all the reasons, but my head started hurting again. I took his word for it.

I meditated for an hour then watched Dustin on the astral. He was still lying there not moving, possibly dead. I studied the guards, the layout of the house and property again. It was time. At the cove, Spencer was gone; the Old Man came out of the trees.

"Ready?"

"No, but I'm going anyway. I mean, yes, I think I'm ready."

"Take in the calm of the water while we go across. Let it fill you with its energy. The vortex can make you see what is normally blind to you."

There was a quiet peace once we were on the island. The lake recharged me and stripped away any doubts, including all other remaining options; it focused my energy on the most important priority, rescuing my brother.

"Spencer said to tell you, 'Fitts is on his way here to kill you.'"

"To the lake? How did he find me?"

"I don't know anything. That's all he said about that."

"That's great news. He won't be at the house. Maybe I have a chance."

No one was on the island. It wasn't clear if it was too early for tourists or if the Old Man fiddled with the boats again. We walked the trail to the top of the cone in silence. Looking down into the crater for a moment, the Old Man put his arm around my shoulders.

"Spencer said to tell you one last thing. 'Trust the universe.'" He looked at me and smiled. "There's power in you, boy. You can do this."

I threw myself into the crater and seconds later Dustin was in front of me, heaped on the floor just where I'd last seen him. Fate was on my side, as I could reach him without stepping out of the portal. Being this close, I realized he was even worse than I thought and could die any moment. He was heavy, but my strength had increased because of the vortex at the lake and the power of the portal. Unfortunately, the door to his room was ajar.

Dustin cried out when I moved him. A shocked guard entered—only my upper body was visible outside the portal—and he came at us. I'm not sure what happened, but there was a struggle. Somehow I pulled Dustin into the portal, but the guard wrestled me out. As the portal closed, enveloping Dustin, I managed, in my mind, to order him transported home but had no idea if it would work. He might wind up on Wizard Island or even in some other time or dimension. I'd have to worry about that later. He was out of the clutches of Lightyear and Fitts at last.

The guard pinned me, but I used Gogen to send one of Dustin's discarded shoes flying into his head. It wasn't enough to hurt, but I broke free when he turned to see who threw it. Instead of psychic skills, it was the power of my kicking his head with all my strength that sent him reeling backward, dazed. It was a perfect hit. I grabbed the gun from his shoulder holster and, just before he yelled for help, brought it crashing across his face just like I'd seen Ray Liota do in *Goodfellas*. There was blood everywhere, and I think he was actually crying. I thought of Fitts beating Dustin and I hit him again, knocking him out.

The outside guards hadn't shown, presumably still stationed on the wrap-around deck. I caught my breath and went on the astral to see where they were; one was on the east side, the other on the north. I was in the bedroom on the south side. The east guard would be there soon, so I had to move fast. Attack or run?

I quickly made two Lusans and cradled them in my left arm while holding the gun in my right hand. I wanted to flee, but if my timing was wrong, I'd be caught, or worse. Attack or run? Time to decide. Just as I was running toward the door, the east guard spotted me through a window. He called the other guard. I fired a shot at the window. The force of it surprised me, and the gun flew from my hand.

I ran downstairs, two at a time. The basement had a few windows and a door leading outside. It was secured from the inside with a two-by-four screwed across it. I scanned for tools, nothing. They were coming down the steps now, knowing I'd be trapped. I moved back across to the other side of the room. When the first one emerged from the stairway, I threw a Lusan. It wasn't possible to see what happened, but the men screamed as wood and drywall shattered.

Sending the other Lusan through a window, I followed it out, slicing my arm on a piece of glass, and raced down an old deer trail. The first shot whistled passed, so I tumbled into the thick brush and clawed my way through until I reached a small clearing. Apparently, at least one guard survived the Lusan attack.

Trees obscured the house, so I couldn't see where they were, but I knew from my astral observations that the long gravel driveway came from the road then made a sweeping half-mile circle around the house. The property was criss-crossed with fences, old tractor roads, and trails. Farms, orchards, and a vineyard surrounded the whole place. My escape route would not be simple. Getting my bearings, it seemed easiest to go back up the driveway, past the house, then down a sloping field to my rendezvous point with Kyle— if he'd gotten the message. I figured the one or two surviving guards would follow me into the trees and never guess I'd head back to the house. No better alternative surfaced in the seconds available to decide.

After navigating through more brambles, the barbed wire fence bordering the gravel driveway was in front of me. I got over it quickly, ran along the opposite fence line, around a curve and up the small hill until I could see the house again. No guards in sight. I jogged off a side trail parallel to the drive-way. A grove of young trees shielded me from the house.

"Freeze!" shouted a guard from behind.

Did he still have orders to take me alive? Fitts said he was coming to kill me, so it was unlikely. I turned slowly. Ten feet away, he leveled his gun.

"Don't move, kid," he held my stare as he slowly approached.

I was about to be taken into custody and then likely tortured at the hands of Fitts and probable death. I summoned all that I had learned, called upon every mystic I'd met, and prayed to every god I'd ever heard of in my life. It was for this moment that Spencer had asked me to make the seagull sleep. The guard was very close now, our eyes still locked.

"Now listen, you punk, raise your hands slowly."

I did as ordered.

"That's it. Good, good. Now turn around and start marching to the house."

I just stared.

"Turn around, or I'll shoot you right here. I'm not going to ask again."

It was working.

"Hey! What the hell? You're doing some kind of voodoo on me—"

He dropped at my feet. His gun was under his body, and I didn't know how long he would be out, maybe just seconds. I turned and ran.

Crossing back onto the driveway, I headed in the direction of the road. It was very likely that the Lusan at the house had left the other guard out of commission because he hadn't appeared again. I'd taken out three federal agents; my adrenaline was pumping. I was going to make it.

The roar of a car engine caused me to turn. A cloud of dust and small rocks spewed as the car barreled toward me. I froze. If only I'd taken that gun. Panic. Could I make a Lusan? At the very last second, I dove from its path. Untangling from a rose bush and stumbling to my feet, I gripped dirt and grass trying to get up a steep slope. The car skidded on the gravel and stopped thirty feet away. Breathlessly clawing my way up, I heard a wounded agent yelled from the house, "Fitts, he's getting away. There, up the hill!"

Fitts? I thought he was at the lake looking for me. Why was he back here? I started trembling. Desperately fighting the hill, weed, and sticks slicing my hands, I climbed. Fitts' first shot was nowhere near me. The second grazed the ground as I got to my feet and pushed myself into a run. It was his third shot that knocked me back down, my left shoulder hit. Blood covered me too fast, and pain took control of my thoughts.

There was no time to recover. I scurried through leaves, got behind a tree, then struggled to stand. Fitts had stopped to aim and was only now starting after me. My lead was still considerable, but I was choking for air and shaking. Somehow, with the crest of the hill behind me and temporarily out of his sight, I kept climbing higher. Thick underbrush, cedars, and pines slowed my progress, but eventually I reached another fence line on a small ridge. The hill, covered with dense trees, fell steeply toward a barn just beyond the road. I hoped it would take me to Kyle, so I kept moving.

My shoulder was on fire, my arm numb, and my bleeding increased. I leaned against a large ponderosa and started making a Lusan. A figure, most likely Fitts, cut across the hill. He hadn't seen me yet. I quickly Skyclimbed the other side of the tree, but halfway up I nearly fell. Clutching a bulky branch, I fought my way in toward the trunk. The loss of blood was robbing my strength. More than thirty feet off the ground and safe for the moment, I woozily pushed my back into the trunk to steady myself. I finished the Lusan, balanced precariously on three narrow limbs. The bullet had passed through—I knew from movies that this was a good thing. The healing orb pressed against my wound helped me slow my breathing.

A crowded stand of mature trees protected me. A few minutes later, someone passed close to my hiding place but kept going. "Thank you," I whispered. His DHS ball cap and familiar blue parka were visible through the branches about fifty yards away. For all he knew I'd escaped. Moving the Lusan back and forth between the entry and exit holes in my shoulder eased the pain, and after about ten minutes, the bleeding stopped completely. Ten more minutes passed before the crunch of footsteps passed again, very near, as Fitts headed back to the house.

Seven minutes more and the healing was good enough—two indentations, thick scabs, and my very red and swollen shoulder was battle-ready. I Skyclimbed to the top of the tree and caught a quick blur of the guard, who I'd dropped into sleep, talking with Fitts on the driveway. This was my chance, if my strength held. I Skyclimbed from tree to tree, heading down the hill, away from them and toward the road.

The cover of trees gave way to a pasture dotted with blackberry and wild rose bushes. I came down hard, my strength slipping, and cut a leg vaulting over a barbed wire fence. I had clear, open field now, making an easy target. One last barrier and then the road. I tried to vault the fence, took a jolt, and burned myself as the top wire was electrified. I ran full speed up the narrow country road, crested a rise, and spotted the Subaru. Kyle saw me too; he started his car and raced toward me. He must have been waiting there for more than an hour. I jumped into the car.

"Go!"

"Where's Dustin?" Kyle was sweating and shaking.

"Get me out of here! We can't go that way."

He screeched a U-turn and misjudged; the car strained to escape the ditch. His hands were trembling on the steering wheel.

"Are you all right?" he asked, while watching and speeding down the narrow road.

"Turn here fast, and head back to town!"

"Where's Dustin?" he repeated, his face dripping sweat.

"I don't know. Whirling through time somewhere."

"He's dead?"

"I don't know. I'm hoping he's at my house."

"How? Why would he be there?

"I put him in a portal—like a wormhole—and sent him to my house."

"Seriously? That's incredible... Oh man, whose blood is that all over you?"

"Mine."

It wouldn't be long before they were searching the area.

"What happened back there? Are you okay?"

"Yeah." But I wasn't feeling well at all.

"We're going to your house, right?

"Uh-huh."

"What if he's not there?"

"We head back to the lake. Stop the car, quick, I'm going to be sick." I got the car door open before he stopped and threw up. I was sweating and very cold.

"Man, you look terrible."

"I'll be okay." I closed my eyes, and when I opened them again we were in my driveway. Kyle was standing outside my door.

"We're here. Are you gonna make it?"

"Yeah, yeah. How long was I out?"

"Ten minutes."

"I think that helped. I'm really feeling better."

"How long do you think we have before Fitts shows up here?"

"I don't know. I wish there'd been time to think of someplace else to send him. All we can do is hope Fitts wouldn't dream I'd be dumb enough to come to my house. And if Dustin's not here, we'll be gone in a few minutes," I said.

"But if he is, we may not be able to move him for a while," Kyle said, worried.

52

I hadn't been home in two weeks. It felt foreign, as if I were wandering through an old dream. After checking the ground floor, we moved upstairs. The steps left me winded, and my shoulder was bleeding again. We found Dustin slumped in the doorway to his old bedroom, his eyes open. Kyle was utterly amazed.

"Wormholes are just a fringe theory, and you just proved—"

"Okay, we'll publish in a science journal later, but right now, help me get him into bed."

"Dustin, can you walk?" I asked. He looked a little better than when I found him earlier. Maybe the portal helped. "Dustin?"

He didn't move.

I got right in front of his face. "Dustin, are you in there?"

He blinked.

"Was that an answer?"

His lips moved, but no sound.

We carried him to his bed. I glanced out the window as we laid him down. Crowd, the mystic who burned the money, was standing on the sidewalk looking up at me. Our eyes met.

"Kyle, we've got to go! We've got to go now!"

"What?"

"Fitts is on his way."

"When?"

"Any minute." I ran to my room and scooped up a comforter and some clothes. Kyle had Dustin back in the hall by the time I got back. Dustin cried out several times as we negotiated him down the stairs and burst out the front door. Crowd was gone. I held Dustin up while Kyle opened the hatchback, folded down the backseats, and spread out the comforter. Then we painfully laid Dustin inside. We made it to Main Street without seeing Fitts.

"I think you both need to be in a hospital."

"No!" I was fading again.

The next thing I remember was Linh's face. I was on a bed, and she was holding a cold wet washcloth to my forehead. "Where?" I pulled myself up and pushed her out of the way. "Dustin?"

"It's okay," Linh gently grabbed me. "Dustin is right here." She pointed to the next bed. Bà was tending him. We were in a motel room somewhere. I only had boxers on. She eased me back down.

"Kyle?"

"Kyle insists on watching the parking lot. He's out there sitting in his car but asked me to get him when you woke." She walked to the window and stuck her hand between the curtains.

"How long?"

"We got here three hours ago. I'm not sure when you did. It's around six now."

"How's Dustin?" I closed my eyes.

"Not great. Bà's been getting some herbs into him, but he has cracked ribs and deep bruises everywhere, a broken leg and an arm already setting wrong. What happened to you guys?" She touched my gunshot wound softly.

"I need to make a Lusan." I tried to sit up.

Linh pushed me back down. "You can't do anything right now."

Bà dripped some kind of tea or potion into Dustin's swollen mouth with an eyedropper. His face was a mess.

Spencer had been right; they hadn't wanted to kill him, just make me go there.

"I shouldn't be here. Lightyear always finds me."

Kyle came in while I was talking. "The only people who know we're here are in this room right now. Lightyear isn't going to find us because Amber doesn't know where you are."

"What are you talking about Kyle?" Linh asked.

"Every time Lightyear has found Nate, Amber has always known where he was."

"So you think Amber has been helping them? Why? Why would she do that, Kyle?"

"I don't know."

"You don't know because there is no reason. She wouldn't," Linh said. "She called again today. I told her you and Dustin were safe, but we couldn't trust the phones. She was so happy to hear you guys were all right. She didn't press for details or anything. Lightyear must have a million ways to track and find Nate. They don't need her."

"That's why I have to leave. Kyle, take me away from here. Everyone is in danger as long as I'm here."

"If you take him anywhere, it should be a hospital," Linh said.

"I didn't risk my life getting Dustin so they could just come here and finish him off. And Linh, you know they would do the same to you and Bà just for being here."

"I'll take you," Kyle said.

She ignored me and started assisting Bà.

Kyle went to get me some clothes while I tried to make a Lusan. It took a while, and it was only the size of a golf ball, but it was something. Bà acted as if she'd seen hundreds of them. After explaining how it works, Linh made slow passes over Dustin's body, concentrating on his torso and face. She pulled off the sheet, which showed bruises every shade of awful. It was agony just looking at the injuries. I kissed his forehead and whispered, "I love you."

Between making the Lusan and getting dressed, I needed to rest again. Bà made me drink some awful tasting liquid. She had a two-burner hot plate going and a couple of old leather suitcases open on the dresser filled with glass medicine bottles, pouches, and even fresh leaves, which made the room smell like a combination of the forest, old laundry, and manure.

"Take care of him," Linh told Kyle.

"And you take care of *him*," I said, motioning toward Dustin.

Kyle parked behind an old fruit stand just outside of town. There were four exits routes to three different roads. It made him feel better, but if Lightyear found us, we weren't going to win a car chase no matter how many movies we'd seen. Kyle was fighting his phobias mightily.

He took a worn unused cigarette from his mouth and replaced it with another, then he told me to meditate. I'm sure he knew in my condition it would make me sleep almost immediately, and it did. When I awoke, it was dark outside and we were somewhere else. There was a cold Coke and a warm twelve-inch sub. I only made it halfway through both but felt like a living person again. I dialed Josh's number.

"Hey Josh, is my mom there?"

"Sure. You okay, buddy? We've been worried."

"I'm good. How's Mom?"

"Much better. Here she is."

"Nate, that's a long time between calls. Our deal was—"

"We've got Dustin."

"Oh, Nate! Oh, Nate, is he all right?"

"He's pretty beat up."

"Where is he?"

"I don't want to say anything more over the phones."

"We have to go to the FBI. Tonight. I can call from here."

"No! Nothing has changed. They can't protect us. And we still have to find Rose."

"But—"

"Promise me. I told you we'd get Dustin back and we have him. Now keep trusting me."

"You're too young to fight all this."

"I'll talk to Sam again. His sister will help. But if you go to the authorities or the media, you'll get me killed."

"Don't say that."

"You don't believe me? Ask Dad."

Silence. "I want to see Dustin."

"It's too dangerous right now. You can talk to him tomorrow."

"Okay, Nate. I love you."

"I'll call tomorrow." I leaned back in the seat. "Geez, that was fun. Why doesn't she get it? She keeps wanting to call the cops."

"Nate, I've been in this from the beginning and seen lots of crazy stuff with you, and I don't get it either. Everyone thinks when you're in trouble you call the police."

"Tell that to Lee Duncan."

It was after ten p.m. when I woke next.

"I need to take Linh home," Kyle said. "I told my uncle enough to get Bà to help but not enough for Linh and I to stay out all night on a school night. I've got the keys to the Shakespeare Theatre ..."

"Perfect." I'd thought of crashing at Sam's, but it was too risky to go near my street.

As we were driving, Kyle asked the question I'd been struggling with. "Where's Rose? Why weren't they holding her at the same place?"

"I know. I keep thinking they want to force me to come get her, too, so they'll have two shots at me. But then, why can't I find her on the astral?"

"Maybe, they're holding her somewhere surrounded by water," Kyle said. "Remember when we first met Spencer, he said the remote viewers had a problem seeing around water."

"Yeah, you're right. They must know I'm searching the astral. They used Dustin as bait. They'll do the same thing with Rose and move her somewhere so I can find her. They'll want another chance to get me. Why didn't I think of that? I feel better."

"You feel better because you may have to go on another suicide rescue mission? Do you know how lucky you are to still be alive? Do you know how crazy you sound?"

"Of course I don't *want* to do it again, but I'll have to. No one else is going to save Rose—they have her listed as a fugitive. The police won't help us. I have to face Fitts again."

"Why does he want to destroy your family? He killed your dad and tried to kill your mom, your brother, and you, and he's holding your aunt hostage. This guy seriously hates Ryders."

"Yeah, well, I'm no fan of him either. I have to find a way to expose him, or my family will never be safe."

"It might be easier to kill him," Kyle said.

"I thought you were a committed pacifist."

"Sometimes we either defend ourselves or die. I don't want you to die."

He pulled up to the theater and I grabbed the other half of the sandwich.

"What about karma?" I asked.

"Occasionally unavoidable... unless you want to die a martyr."

53

W*ednesday, October 1*
After a deep sleep in the theater, my shoulder pain eased. As usual, Kyle was on time, and he and Linh brought doughnuts. I wasn't sure I deserved such good friends but stopped worrying about it to concentrate on eating a second frosted coconut-sprinkled pastry.

"Bà said Dustin had a good night," Linh said, but she looked as if she'd been crying.

"What's wrong?"

We were at a stop sign. Linh got out of the car and then climbed in the back with me.

"Linh, what's going on? Is Dustin all right?"

"Oh, Nate," she collapsed on me, crying. "It's not Dustin."

"Kyle?" I pleaded to him for an answer. He looked at me in the rearview mirror.

Linh wiped her eyes and sniffled. "It's Rose. She's dead."

A lump formed in my throat. "How do you know?"

"She came to me in a dream. But it wasn't like a dream. She spoke to me, and said Fitts had killed her with some kind of injection the night they took her." Linh fought her tears for a moment. "They questioned her about you, what you knew about Lightyear, where you were, what powers you had."

"She didn't tell them a thing, did she?" I asked.

"No."

"They would have killed her even if she'd told them everything."

Somebody else might have doubted the accuracy of the news coming from a dream, but not me. I wanted memories of Aunt Rose but all I could think of was Fitts and shooting that evil man.

Lightyear wanted me dead to stop any information I *may* have from getting out and this was just a means to that end. Fitts didn't need to murder her or kill the eleven people named Montgomery Ryder. They did it because they could. The bastards at Lightyear were so sure of their power that being careful was an unknown concept to them.

Rose was gone. Still, I knew she was only dead in our limited human definition of that scary word. I knew her soul was free. Rose would find me soon, of that I was sure. Fitts couldn't take her from me, just like he hadn't been able to silence Lee Duncan or my dad. I would finish their work; none of them had died in vain if I could expose Lightyear.

I thought of Tanya. She would be devastated. After reading Tanya's life, it was obvious no one was more important to her than Rose. I couldn't give this news on the phone; I needed to return to Merlin and tell her in person.

We did the normal backtracking to make sure we weren't being followed, so it was almost six-twenty when we reached the motel. Dustin was peacefully asleep and looked better. Soon he opened his eyes.

"Nate?" his voice still weak and hoarse.

"Right here," I took his hand.

"Thank you." He stared for a moment and then his eyes closed again.

"You would have done the same for me."

"I might have gotten you out a day sooner." He coughed a laugh out before the pain in his ribs stopped it.

Lifting the blanket to inspect his bruises, I saw the small Lusan next to the worst one. I picked the Lusan up and was soon able to grow it to the normal size. Then I rubbed it over his injuries.

He looked at me. "Where'd you get that handy little item?"

"Made it."

"You're gonna have to teach me that trick."

"As soon as you're up to it."

"When are we going to Shasta?"

"Same answer."

He fell asleep again.

Bà nudged me out of the way and went back to her patient. After she was satisfied I hadn't messed up any of her work, she turned to me.

"He is better. He will be good."

"Bà, you saved his life." I hugged her. "You're our grandmother now, too."

"You healer, too," she said, pointing to the Lusan. "We worked together, Nathan." She smiled.

We decided to move Dustin to a different motel. They would do it during lunch; I'd be in Merlin by then. I gave to Kyle Mom's other hundred dollars and promised more once I got my savings out of the bank.

"Will you run me to Amber's?"

"Don't tell her where Dustin is," Kyle cautioned.

"We can trust her," Linh said.

"I'm not even going to tell my mother where he is. Until we figure out how they're finding me, I'm not taking any chances. But Linh's right—Amber wouldn't hurt me."

"You better be right," Kyle said.

Dustin awoke as we were getting ready to go. Bà took the opportunity to get more of the greenish-black stinky syrup into him. He drank it like it was fruit juice. I wondered if he really liked it, or if he'd lost an argument with Bà about it last night.

"Hey, little brother, who else helped you get me out?"

"I went in alone, but Kyle drove the getaway car and these two women nursed you back from the dead."

"I'm in love with them both."

"They're going to upgrade your room later today, and I'll be back for visiting hours tomorrow morning. I need you to call Mom soon. Linh will fix you up with a phone."

"What's your plan after you see Tanya?" Kyle asked, on the way to Amber's.

"All I've been focused on was getting Dustin and finding Rose. Now I need to shift to stopping Fitts from coming after us, all of us."

"You're in the most danger, but as they've shown with Dustin and your mom, everyone who helps you puts their life at risk," Kyle said.

"I know I got Rose killed. You guys or anyone I love could be next. I'm so sorry."

"You didn't start this, Nate. We've all just gotten caught up in it. It's not your fault," Linh reminded me.

"Then why does it feel like my fault?"

"Because, if you were dead, they'd leave the rest of us alone." Kyle said. "I'm not suggesting you go shoot yourself or anything, but it's a fact, and in that truth is the seed to our solution."

"Which is?" I asked.

"We have to look at it from that angle because we can't all become fugitives hiding in the woods."

"What if I faked my death?"

"That's the way we need to be thinking," Kyle said. "We can't win a war with them, and we can't keep hiding you. And how soon until they pick the rest of us up on terrorist charges or my whole family dies in a mysterious house fire?"

"What about negotiating with Fitts?" Linh asked.

"This is how he negotiates," I pulled my T-shirt down off my shoulder.

"Don't rule it out completely," Kyle said. "There may be some way to do it—something he wants, or better yet, something he needs."

"I didn't think we needed Sam's sister anymore, with Dustin safe and Rose gone, but maybe she could get us to the right law enforcement agency or negotiate something with Lightyear. But what?"

"Talk to her. She's the expert," Linh said.

Kyle pushed the intercom button on the gate at the end of Amber's driveway. We couldn't see the house from here.

It took a couple of minutes before she answered, "It's about time!" Amber was on the porch and started to run down when she saw us.

"Don't forget you said you'd ask her about Lightyear," Kyle said.

"Ask her about what?" Linh asked.

"I told Kyle I'd talk to Amber about how Fitts only seems to find me when she knows where I am."

"Oh Nate, don't do it. You'll break her heart," Linh said.

"I just want to get it out in the open. We need to know."

"Boys are so dumb. She's not working for Fitts," Linh said.

"I don't think so either, but how do you know that?"

"The same way you do. I just know."

"Will you call me once Dustin's moved and after he's talked to my mom?"

"Of course," Linh said handing me a poem. "It's for Rose."

Amber came over and greeted us. I don't think she noticed Kyle being aloof because Linh was as friendly as ever. When they were gone, Amber said, "I feel like we haven't seen each other in a month. You look so much older. What's happened? Tell me everything."

"Will you blow off school today and drive me to Merlin?"

"Rose is back?" she asked excitedly.

I shook my head. "No, I need to see Tanya."

54

Once in the house, I grabbed a quick shower. Alone in the bathroom, I read Linh's poem.

> She sang so sweet
> and flowed like light
> her essence as a perfumed candle
> too strong, and overdone, yet
> rooted and flighty, like a tree
>
> that shimmered and shone
> like tinsel, her mantra a smile
> and eyes were stones
> She held a universe, so close, so clear
> it tipped and turned like a globe
> whose edges dropped into forever
> but then, caught, a mirror
> came back at me
>
> She gave me hope, and fear inside
> contained and coiled of power
> her hands were bony, shaped like knives
> they cut the air before tears were known
> that gentle stare and severe honesty
> whose loose skin were barely contained

a child at play, her scarves and colors
danced around pastel flowered rooms
crystals and balls, and flying mats
her wizardry sloppy and sure

oh Rose, a bowlful of memory
agitated, a sigh, could never compare
to that of a beautiful scene
whose mockery and flight
are seconds away
she would motion, go over there

and in my dream, I can touch and see
this distilled and ancient image
of a woman, a seer, a crone, a jewel
not dead, but flying wild

She is free, yes, free, compelling and true,
she has leashed the heavens
and juiced the stars
in her hands, filled with light, and luminous things,
she offers, to us, a taste.

My eyes stung with tears. Why was death following me through life? Why were people going about their lives, watching TV, shopping, going to football games as if nothing was wrong, as if our identities hadn't been stolen? I was so angry. Kyle's words found their way into my rage. "Breathe, get calm, keep it together," I told myself. So I did, but only after resolving to find a way to contact Rose on the other side.

I was nervous being in one place too long. So less than fifteen minutes after we had arrived, we were on the road again, munching a breakfast burrito Amber miraculously had produced. I took her through most of the major events since we'd last spoken a few days earlier. I left out the part about me getting shot and Rose being dead—I wasn't ready for that. Amber was a little hurt that I hadn't called her as soon as

Dustin and I were safe, but she let it go. Instead, she pushed for more details on Gibi, Skyclimbing and the portals. After telling her about the lost Calyndra Portal and its potential to transport me to another time, she asked, "When are we going to Big Basin Redwoods State Park?"

"Do you really want to? Because I've been thinking if I could find the portal and return to Ashland *before* Lee Duncan and my dad got killed, then maybe I could prevent all this."

"I thought things couldn't be changed with time travel."

"That's just in the movies because it complicates the script too much if everything could change but no one knows. And even if that did turn out to be true, I could still find out a lot of stuff that might make the future easier, might save my life. If nothing else, the portal would literally buy me time. I could go to different times and places until I figure out what to do. We know if they find me they will kill me. A portal may be the only safe place to hide."

"It's hard to believe something like that really exists."

"For me, too, until I was in one. That changes *everything*."

"If I drive you there and if we find it, could I go inside Calyndra with you?"

"Of course! It's about an hour south of San Francisco, maybe a six-hour drive. Let's leave Friday night. Oh my God, can you imagine?"

"We have to find it. Do you get how much you mean to me? I'll drop out of school and go into hiding with you. You're the most important person in my world!"

"I am?"

"Yes! I don't want to have sex or anything like that, but I'm definitely in love with you. You must know that, right?"

"Uh?"

Amber laughed and pulled onto the shoulder. "Maybe we should have sex if that would make it easier for you."

"Amber? Uh?"

"You're so funny when you're all nervous and shy." She leaned over and kissed me, a real kiss, on the lip—a movie star kiss that I didn't want to end, that I didn't want anything else in the universe to interrupt, ever. When she stopped, I really couldn't speak. In fact I was barely breathing.

"Your first kiss?" Amber smiled.

"Yeah," I said, recovering. "If you don't count Suzy Stover in the sixth grade."

"Sixth-grade kisses definitely don't count… well, after sixth grade anyway. I like it that I'm your first kiss. You'll remember me forever now."

"That was never really in doubt."

We were driving again. How was I going to bring up Kyle's concerns after that? Was there any way that this bubbly and beautiful girl next to me could be aiding the enemy? Not knowingly. Maybe Fitts got her prepaid cell phone bugged or her whole house wired, maybe even this car.

"So why are we going to Tanya's?" she asked.

I hesitated. "Rose is dead. Fitts killed her the night she disappeared."

"My God! I'm so sorry. Tanya doesn't know yet? They were close, right?"

"Very."

"I wish I'd met Rose."

"You two would have been best friends."

I changed the subject and told her of the three betrayals of Amparo. She listened so intently that by the time I told her about Rachel and Erich in the concentration camp she had to pull over.

"That's the most tragic story I've ever heard."

"Amparo opened a connection between the current me and the me from those past lives as if it's all been one long life. And I suppose, for my soul, it has been. I can remember being at Dachau just the same as I remember being at Crater Lake. It's that fresh; it's all part of me."

"That's why you look so different."

"That and getting shot."

"When?" Her face lost color.

"Fitts. While I was trying to escape after getting Dustin."

"Where? Show me."

I lifted my shirt, and she touched both wounds, so soft and tenderly that it made me shiver. She stared long into my eyes like she was looking for Erich or maybe the lifetime when we were sisters. I thought she was going to kiss me again, but the moment was so intense I wouldn't trade it. Two of her fingers traced my cheekbone to my chin before she turned away.

"We've gotta keep you alive," she said, pulling back onto the interstate.

55

The last time at Tanya's I was fleeing from Fitts.

"Hey, what are you guys doing here?" Tanya said, standing at the doorway.

"Can we come in?"

"Sure."

"How's the leg?" Amber asked.

"It'll heal."

"Tanya, you should sit down."

"No, I'm good."

"I've got some bad news... I'm sorry... Rose is dead."

"What do you mean?"

"Fitts killed her."

"I don't think so."

"I know it's hard but—"

"I talked to Agent Fitts this morning."

"You what?" I frantically looked around. Was he in the next room?

"He came to visit me in the hospital and explained everything."

"Jesus!" Amber said.

"How could he justify trying to kill my entire family?"

"He's a *federal* agent! This isn't a Bourne movie. He told me he released Dustin—"

"Released? That's a lie. I rescued him. Fitts shot me. You can't believe this guy, Tanya. He took Rose."

"He arrested Rose because she was aiding a known terrorist."

"What terrorist?"

"You."

"*Me?*"

"That's right. They're trying to apprehend you, and he told me this morning that you've assaulted six federal agents in the past few days."

"This morning? Tanya. You weren't in the hospital this morning."

"He checks in with me. I have his cell phone number. He said to call if I heard from you."

"I can't believe this."

"Nate's not a terrorist," Amber said.

"Then why are they trying to arrest him?"

"Because they're corrupt."

"You're his girlfriend, and you have to believe him. I don't. If Nate's worried about corruption in the CIA, then turn yourself in to my friend—he's a cop—or the FBI, the state police, the Coast Guard, mall security. Or are they all in on the conspiracy?" She glared at me.

"Tanya?"

"Come on, Nate. You're not safe here," Amber said.

"*Is* Amber right, Tanya? Is Fitts listening to us now? Is he on his way?"

"He's waiting for my call."

"Tanya, Rose is dead. Fitts killed her."

"That's not true. Have you seen her body?"

"No, but—."

"Then how do you know?" she demanded.

"How did I know about your childhood, the beatings, about your mother's suicide?"

"What?" she stared, disbelieving. "My mother didn't kill herself!"

"I didn't mean to say that, Tanya. It slipped. I'm sorry you never knew."

"It wasn't suicide." Her voice cracked. She shook her head. "Get out of here, Nate. You don't know what you're talking about. My mother's alive. I mean, Rose is alive, and I don't want you here. You're going to get everyone killed. Turn yourself in."

"Come on, Nate!" Amber grabbed my arm.

Tanya held up her cell phone. "I'm calling Agent Fitts right now. You'll see this is all in your imagination. You're better off in custody. Rose can come home."

"Tanya!"

She was dialing.

Amber was pulling me to the door.

I followed. "How did he convince her I'm the bad guy?" I asked, once we were outside.

"Get in. Let's go," Amber said.

56

Amber peeled away and hit the highway doing seventy. "How did you find out about Rose anyway?" she asked.

"Rose came to Linh in a dream."

"So she really could be alive?"

"If she was alive I would have seen her on the astral."

"Are you sure?"

"I don't know. It's not easy being sure of anything anymore."

"Let's go to Rose's house," Amber suggested.

"Not a good idea."

"You don't want to?"

"Yeah, let's go." If Amber's car was bugged, I thought, they would have been waiting for us at Tanya's, especially because she's cooperating with Fitts. "But let's make it quick."

"Maybe we can find something at Rose's that'll help us know for sure if she's alive or not," Amber said.

"Is it true about Tanya's mom?" she asked.

"Yeah."

"How did you know?"

"I read her. It's a power Spencer showed me. If while I embrace someone I consciously search and connect with them, I can see their entire life."

"That's wild! I'll be careful next time we hug," she said with a laugh.

Being back at Rose's house was distressing, and in the reading room, I was certain she was dead. There was a deep emptiness, as if a vacuum had sucked every trace of her energy out of the place. I pulled down a colorful scarf for Linh and picked up a pretty stone for me. In another room, Amber was admiring Rose's collection of books on tarot, astrology, numerology, colors, dreams, reincarnation, the mind—every new age topic. "Look at this," she said, handing me a leather-bound volume.

"It's Rose's handwriting. It looks like her journal."

"You should take it, Nate."

"It doesn't seem right to take something so personal."

"Don't leave it for Lightyear." I took it.

I closed up the house and fought my anger, sure I'd never see Rose alive again. We found an empty pull-off overlooking the Rogue River. Amber took sandwiches out of a bag and handed me a soda as we sat at a picnic table.

"Kyle thinks someone close to me is getting information to Lightyear."

"Yeah, Tanya."

"No, that's only been for a few days, since the hospital. From the beginning, someone has helped Fitts find me."

"Who? How many people have known where you were?"

"Kyle thinks you're the only one."

"Are you serious?"

"I don't think so, and Linh doesn't either—"

"You all have actually had a conversation about me helping Fitts find you? I don't believe this… Why would—"

"Amber, sit down. I've never once considered the possibility that it could be you. Neither has Linh."

"But your best friend thinks I'm trying to get you killed. Nate, I love you. Do you get that? You've completely taken over my life." She wiped tears. "Read me, Nate. You can see everything, all my secrets, all my fears. I want you to know me completely. You'll see nothing but love for you, you jerk." Her arms held wide, waiting for me.

"No."

"Read me, damn it!" she yelled.

"I'd rather get to know you little by little."

"Why?"

"Because it feels more real. I want to know you as a person, like our souls already do."

"I don't want you to have any doubts."

"I never have."

We stared at each other.

"You're still a jerk."

"Why?"

"For not telling Kyle he doesn't know what the hell he's talking about," she cried.

"I did. Both Linh and I told him he was wrong. He's just trying to protect me. When Lightyear first came after us at your house, then at Tanya's and your beach house, you were the only one who knew where I was. You also knew my mom and I were going to pick up Dustin at Mountain View, that Aunt Rose was helping me, and that my mom was coming to see us at Tanya's."

"Wait a minute. Kyle, Linh, and your mother knew all those things, too."

"Actually, my mom didn't know I was with you that night or at your beach house."

"But both those times you didn't ever see anyone stalking you. It was just your heat sensor thing."

"They were there."

"Okay, I'm just saying."

"I was thinking maybe they got to your phone or bugged your house."

"I bought that phone randomly when I got the others. I don't think it's been out of my sight since. In fact, most nights I fall asleep with it talking to my sister."

"You talk to Bridgette *every* day? I didn't know you two were *that* close."

"We're very close. And she's helped me keep all this in perspective-"

"You've been telling her about what's been going on?"

"Yeah, she's my sister. Bridge isn't telling anyone. She's buried at that art college. My sister isn't repeating our conversations."

"What if Fitts tapped her phone?" I asked.

"What if he tapped the phones of everyone we know? That's a lot of phones."

"It's the United States government; it can do anything. Call Bridgette, and say we rescued Dustin."

"She thinks he's nuts. What's that going to prove?"

"You tell her I'm going to stay at your parents' beach house for a few days to mend. Tell her I got shot trying to get away. I'll go on the astral and watch the call and what she does afterward. If I can't hide, I'll be dead soon. They have a way to find out where I am, and it's only a matter of time before they corner me. I need to know how they're doing it."

I sat in the grass close to the river so I wouldn't hear Amber. A minute later I saw Bridgette inside an old building in downtown San Francisco. Amber's number displayed on her phone, and she stepped out of a lecture to take the call. It only lasted about four minutes. Amber asked her if she thought either of their parents would be going to the beach house for the next few days. It was a good reason to call her in the middle of the day. After they hung up, instead of returning to class, Bridgette left the building.

I watched her walk down the street until she found a quiet doorway. She pushed a number on her cell phone and was connected to a desk in Langley, Virginia—CIA headquarters. The woman on the other end of the line asked her a few questions and said they would contact her if the field agent needed any further clarification. Amber's sister closed her phone and walked back to class. I had not expected this. Watching her on the astral was a long shot. I'd thought maybe it would clear her sister, but this was brutal. I wondered if one of Amparo's current incarnations was Bridgette Mayes. How was I going to tell Amber? When I opened my eyes, she was next to me.

"Well?"

"It's her. As soon as your call ended, she phoned the CIA and reported your whole conversation."

"She wouldn't even know how to call the CIA. I got my dad's brains. Bridge got Mom's."

"There's a CIA number programmed on her cell, and she acted like this was part of her daily routine."

"Why?"

"Money?"

"Please. Our parents compete to see which of them can give us the biggest allowance."

"Maybe she doesn't want you hanging out with another Ryder nut-job."

"She's definitely not convinced you're sane. Her time with Dustin really messed her up. She thinks the danger is all in your mind. But, if they turned Tanya and Bridge, maybe you should think about who else might be helping them."

"How much have you told Bridgette?"

She looked at me pleadingly. "I'm so sorry, Nate."

"I trust Dustin that way, too. It's not your fault."

"It is. I shouldn't have told anyone. I have to call her back to find out why she did this."

"No! I don't want Fitts knowing anything else, especially that we know about her."

"Then we have to go there. Nate, I have to talk to her. She may be in trouble. It's not just you. My sister has betrayed me, and I need to know why."

"You want to go to San Francisco?"

"I want *us* to. Right now."

"I don't want you to get in this any deeper."

"My sister is relaying my private conversations to the CIA, which may get the guy I love killed. How much deeper in can I get?"

"They can kill you."

"They can't do it any easier if I'm in San Francisco or Grants Pass. Come with me. We'll confront Bridge and then go on to the Calyndra Portal. We were going in two days anyway, so what's the difference?"

"You have school."

"I don't care about that right now. I'm going to San Francisco with or without you, but I'm going. I need to look Bridge in the eye when she explains why she has done this."

Where else was I going to go? Everywhere I went in Oregon, Fitts seemed to find me. If I left the state, it might buy a little time. And if I could really discover the Calyndra Portal, then everything could change. "Let's go!"

57

Linh called when we were just outside Ashland and said Dustin was safely in a new location. "I don't need to know where. How is he?"

"Better. He called your mom, and I think that went okay."

"Good. And Bà's all right staying with him another night?"

"He's charmed her so much that I think she wants him to move into our house."

"That sounds like him. Hey, I'm going to be out of range for a while, so I'll check in with you in the morning, but call if anything comes up."

We hung up, and I immediately phoned Mom. "I hear you talked to Dustin?"

"I did. I can't believe it. You saved him, Nate. I'm so proud of you."

"So you're happy now?"

"I asked him if he'd ever be able to forgive me."

"Mom, I haven't even forgiven you yet."

"I'm just so... he said he didn't think he could have that conversation right now."

"Of course not."

"Is it true about Rose? Is she dead?"

"Who told you?"

"Dustin."

"Dustin? Who told him?"

"He said you did. Not in words, but he could see it on you this morning. Is she gone?"

"Yes."

"Oh, no!"

There was silence.

"She was in the custody of federal agents, the same ones who arrested Dustin and almost killed him. You need to be careful, Mom. I still think Fitts was behind your accident. Do me a favor and stay with Josh a few more days."

"We need help with this."

"I know. We need Sam's sister to make contact with them. Can you get ahold of him and see if he can arrange another conference call with his sister for tomorrow or Friday morning? Tell him to give her all the details about what happened with Dustin and Rose and about them trying to arrest me at Tanya's. We need someone working on this."

After I ended the call, Amber said, "That didn't sound fun."

"I want to do drugs. Or at least have a candy bar." It wasn't long before we were in California. "Do you mind if I crash for a few minutes?" I asked.

"Sure. Tanya and Bridgette in one day, it's a lot to handle, isn't it?"

Half the trip was gone before I surfaced again.

58

"I don't want it to be true about Bridgette. Our parents were so into themselves. Bridge and I were like trophies for them to argue about. So, we were all each of us had, you know, much more than sisters. I'm just sick. It's impossible! I can't believe she's helping them." The rest of the drive—at the end of rush-hour traffic—was more stressful as we played out the best way to get the truth from Bridgette.

We stopped for a quick dinner at a mall so Amber could get a change of clothes. "You could use something else to wear yourself." She waved a credit card at me. "It's Mom's!" The mall trip made me feel almost normal again, as if we were just a couple of teenagers shopping for clothes. Mom phoned and said the call with the attorney and Sam was set for noon tomorrow, and that if it went well, his sister would fly in to meet us over the weekend. She has reliable sources within the media and Homeland Security, and she even has a contact on the Senate Select Committee on Intelligence, which oversees the CIA. Sam talked her into taking our case for a very reduced fee. Finally some good news. Things were looking up.

The Academy of Art University occupied several buildings in downtown San Francisco. I was surprised there were more than 17,000 students and wondered where they kept them all. Amber had been there before and easily found the right building, although we had to park a few blocks away. Standing in the hall outside Bridgette's dorm room, I asked if she was ready.

"No." She knocked.

Rod, Bridgette's boyfriend, opened the door and was visibly shocked to see us.

"Bridge, uh… Amber's here with, uh… Nate."

"What?" Bridgette appeared behind him. "Amber, what are you doing here? I thought… Wasn't Nate going to the beach house?"

"Bridge, can we go for a walk?"

"Yeah. Sure. What's going on?"

Rod and I followed uncomfortably as the girls went down the stairs. By the time we were out on the street, they had erupted into an argument.

"I am not helping the government!"

"You're lying. We came all the way here to get the truth."

"This whole thing with Nate is crazy. I mean his whole family is *crazy!*"

"Bridgette, has the field agent called you for further clarification of the data?" I shouted.

She turned to me stunned.

"We haven't done anything wrong—" Rod started to say.

Bridgette held up her hand.

"Bridge, Nate's not crazy; he's psychic."

"Oh yeah, then what am I thinking right now?"

"It doesn't work that way."

"I'll bet it doesn't."

"Hey, you're the one who betrayed us."

"Us? What, are you two married now?"

"Shut up Bridge. Just admit it."

"Don't admit anything Bridge. They don't know anything," Rod said.

People were staring. Amber led us to a bench on the corner in one of those micro parks.

"What don't we know?" Amber yelled at Bridgette.

"Nothing."

"Let me see your phone. There's a 703 area code on there from this morning, I can tell you the whole number if you want," I said, reaching for her phone.

Rod shoved me.

"Let me see your phone," Amber said calmly. "If there's no 703 number on there, I'll believe you."

"No."

"We didn't do anything wrong," Rod repeated.

"Why'd you do it?" Amber asked softly.

"It's all so intense—"

"Don't!" Rod snapped.

"Rod got into this big mess," she said. "He needed money for tuition. His mom died, and he had this job waiting tables."

Rod sat on the bench with his head in his hands.

"At first he just double-charged customers' credit cards, but soon he started selling the numbers. Then he got a couple more people involved, and it just got out of hand. I only helped a little near the end. Then, we got busted. And it turned into a federal crime because of some interstate commerce thing, and soon the FBI was talking to us. We were going to get indicted when suddenly they offered us a deal."

"What kind of deal?" Amber asked.

"Full immunity for Rod and me if I just told them everything you said about Nate."

"So, you didn't care about what I was going through. You just needed to fulfill your contract."

"No, I care about you more than anything, Amber."

"So you turned on us?"

"If I got arrested… you think the media is having a field day with Mom about the divorce? They'd destroy her over this."

"So, get Nate and maybe me killed so Mom doesn't get on the cover of the Enquirer again this month?"

"They aren't going to kill anyone. You guys are a couple of minors. I doubt they could even get any charges to stick. Amber, they don't even have anything on you."

"You're incredibly stupid sometimes."

"I'm not the one running around with a fugitive psycho."

"Yeah, congratulations. You're running around with Mr. Credit Card Fraud over there."

Rod looked up but didn't say anything.

"I love him, Amber. He's not a horrible person—he just made a mistake. We've all done things we'd like to take back."

"What's going to happen now?" Amber asked. "I mean, I'm not going to tell you another syllable about my life. What happens to your deal when you have no more information for them?"

"I don't know."

"Did you even talk to an attorney?" Amber asked.

"No."

"Who cares if she talked to an attorney?" I said. "She almost got me killed. I'm lucky to be here. Because of her, Fitts got to Dustin before we did. And Rose is dead as a direct result of Bridgette talking to them," I screamed at Bridgette, stopping just short of pushing her down. "You're a stupid, self-absorbed airhead!"

"It's true Bridge, it's really true."

"They told us Nate and Dustin were involved in some domestic terrorism plot," Rod said.

"Do I look like a terrorist?" I asked. "Bridgette, you may think Dustin's a loon, but you know he's been locked away in an institution for two years and I'm like a goody-two-shoes. Terrorists? That's what they say now to get around all the rules and throw out the Constitution." I wanted to shake them both. "Every government in the history of the world has eventually betrayed its people. And it's not like the whole government is after me. They're just a small part, but the bureaucracy is so massive that even a corrupt few can wield incredible power against anyone who gets in their way.

"Power corrupts and absolute power corrupts absolutely," I continued. "They have the power. Any suspicion at all, real or imagined, and they can throw you in a military prison indefinitely. No evidence, no formal charge, no jury, no trial, just jail for as long as they want. It's like the Inquisition all over again."

"Why are they after you?" Bridgette asked.

"Come on, Amber's told you enough. They killed my dad, and they know I know it. They think I have proof of that and of many other murders, including my aunt's."

"Do you?" Rod asked.

"I'm not telling you two anything."

"What can we do?" Bridgette asked.

"I think you better find a good attorney and get them to look at your deal," Amber said.

"They didn't give us anything in writing," Rod said.

"Of course they didn't." I shook my head.

"Amber, we really should go. If they've bugged her room, then they know we're here."

"My room may be bugged?"

We didn't talk until we were half a block away. "Poor Bridge," Amber said.

"I wouldn't want her karma."

"Maybe we can still help her clear it."

"I'm only trying to figure out the ramifications of what she's done."

59

After a call with her mother, Amber hung up, smiling. "We've got a room."

It was only a couple of blocks away. Halfway there, a bum holding a cardboard sign that read, "The end is near," caught my eye.

"If it isn't the young wizard. Nathan, quick, don't look now, but I think there's a beautiful girl following you."

"Crowd, what are you doing *here?*"

"You two know each other?" Amber scrunched her face.

"Oh, my pretty, he has lots of dirty friends. We party in the sewers, eat in dumpsters, shop at the landfill and sometimes we take little girls like you into our secret leper colonies and do things I hesitate to mention here on a public street."

Amber started laughing.

"A sense of humor? I should have known you'd pick a girl who knows how to laugh." He motioned back to Amber. "Excuse me, sweetheart, I really need to urinate, could you give me a hand."

"You're disgusting."

"I could say the same about you, Amber." He smiled.

"How do you know my name?"

"Amber, meet Crowd, he's a mystic."

"*He's* a mystic?"

"Not what you pictured, huh Missy?"

"Not even close." She studied him, trying to find the wise man under the filth.

He was dirtier and smellier than when I first met him.

"That's okay, you and Nate don't look like who you really are either."

"Why are you here?" I asked.

"A warning, my young brother. This city is crossed by faults in the earth. It's a shaky place."

"Should I leave?"

"Why leave? What difference would it make? Wherever you go, there you are."

"If you're here to warn me, then I need something a little more specific."

"Then remember these words, when the wind is at your back, don't trust a dying man."

I couldn't make sense of anything he was saying.

"Now, get out of here. Isn't it past your bedtime?"

"Do you need any money?" Amber asked.

He winked at me.

"Crowd, we've got a room nearby. You want to come and take a shower, clean up a bit? Sleep inside?"

"No, you kids go have fun. But Nate," he added, looking me in the eyes, "thank you for the offer."

We continued on toward the hotel, and I told Amber about Crowd burning the five-dollar bills.

"Where did he get all the money?"

"I never found out for sure, but I believe he conjured it out of air."

"Why live on the streets then?"

"He says possessions, of any kind, block us from reaching the power of our soul."

"But you have stuff, don't you?"

"Yeah, but during the past few weeks, I haven't been able to hold onto any of it."

"You think it's connected?"

"I think everything's connected."

60

To avoid any trouble checking in, Amber went to the front desk alone. Our room was on the forty-fifth floor.

"The concierge made the connection with my mother, and went on and on, saying 'I've known Ivy Mayes for years. She always stays here whenever she's in town and if she needs this or that, I always get it for her.' I told him that she said if I needed any help to just call Seth, and he beamed."

"What would your mother do if she knew we were staying together?"

Amber shrugged.

"What do you think this cost?" I asked as we walked into the posh room.

"Four hundred give or take?"

"Seriously? Your mom's crazy."

"Yeah she's definitely out of touch, but you gotta love that view."

It was a postcard. We could see the whole city skyline lit up. The Bay reflected lights along the shore, the Golden Gate Bridge, and the Transamerica Pyramid, and Amber pointed out Alcatraz. It was so stunning, looking out, standing there with Amber. I was buzzing.

"Look, bubble bath. I love hot baths. I'm going to take one, okay?"

"Yeah, go for it."

A few minutes later she called, "Come in and look at this bathroom."

There she was, a scene from a movie I wasn't old enough to watch. She reclined in the round tub surrounded by bubbles that covered all the right places. Amber somehow conveyed innocence while glowing seductively.

"Do you want to get in?"

"Yes."

"You can."

We stared at each other until she laughed.

"Nothing will happen." She smiled.

"What if I wanted it to?"

"Then it could."

We stared again; this time there was no laugh.

"I already got your first kiss. You should save your first time for your real girlfriend."

"Who's my real girlfriend?"

"Linh."

"Linh?" I scoffed. "We're just friends."

"Maybe, but she *wants* to be your girlfriend."

"How do you know?"

"How do you *not* know?"

I walked into the other room, puzzled.

Room service arrived just as she was finishing up. I wrote in a good tip on the bill and signed "A. Mayes." After the door closed, Amber came out in a white, fluffy, terry-cloth bathrobe with the hotel logo on the pocket.

"You okay?"

"Yeah, I'm just not okay with the teasing."

She took my hand and met my eyes, "I'm not teasing. I would never do that to you."

"I'm confused about us."

"Me too, sometimes."

"What should we do?"

"Right now I think we should eat. Your fries are hot, and the night is young."

It was nice to have a fancy hot meal after weeks of cold

sandwiches and road food. We tried to keep the conversation light, Amber telling me all the fun things we should do in San Francisco, pretending we were tourists rather than "terrorists."

"I'm going to grab a shower… a cold one." I smiled.

"Stop it. Now who's teasing?"

Actually, I took a long hot shower, thinking about Linh, Amber, even Gibi, Tanya, and Bridgette. A month ago the only one involved in my life was Linh. I'd thought of her as a sister, best friend, and, I must admit, a few times as more. Was it really possible she wanted more from me? And what about every guy's fantasy in the next room? I didn't know what to do with her. No question my hormones were lobbying for action, but what I'd suspected that first day with Amber was true. She, more than anyone, was holding me together with a combination of soul talk, teasing, and an inspiring energy. And I couldn't deny that, in her arms, there was more than excitement; there was serenity.

Amber changed into a light tank top and cotton shorts. I slipped on boxers and we fell asleep tangled together.

I woke in oppressive humidity; it was an Outview. The date 1904 was on a smeared document in my dirty fist. Through tangled trees stood the Pyramid of Kukulkan at Chichen Itza, bleached and glistening in the sun. I was American, probably close to age thirty. With another man, we hurried along a thin trail into the jungle toward massive etched columns.

Just before passing through a small stone structure, I saw his eyes. My dad from this life! Our second lifetime together was in Mayan lands. He pulled out a chisel and hammer and soon dislodged a slab of rock from an upper wall. Behind it was, incredibly, the gold box from his desk that I had found in this lifetime.

"What is it?" I, as the young man, asked.

"It is the most important object in existence," my friend said. "Almost four hundred years ago, you died protecting it. Nine took the oath, but a traitor was among us. The conquistadors pushed you in the cenote. Once they were gone, I dove in, freed this from your body and hid it here. I've tried during many lifetimes to get back to retrieve it, hoping to beat the traitor."

Suddenly a man burst in behind us, slit my throat, and without hesitation, my friend killed the attacker. The Outview ended. I sat on the bed wondering who had killed me. What made the gold box so important, and how—during the intervening hundred-plus years—had it wound up in my dad's desk? Unbelievable! I stared into the darkness, and exhaustion soon took me back to sleep where no answers were to be found.

61

Thursday, October 2

I woke up before Amber and softly kissed her lips. She came awake just as her phone rang. "It's my sister."

"You better take it," I said reluctantly.

They talked for a while. After the call, Amber sat on the edge of the bed; she looked small, sad, even innocent. Bridge was so sorry; Rod wasn't a bad guy; they never dreamed of the trouble they could cause; If they had any part of getting someone killed, they couldn't live with it; they wanted to help; blah, blah, blah. We quickly dressed and ordered breakfast. The tension washed over us as we plowed through our food.

"Fitts is still after you," Amber said. "We can't pretend that's not happening."

"Hopefully he thinks we're at your beach house. But getting out of Oregon was smart. And if we find Calyndra, no one will know where we are. We should get out of here soon, and do the call with Sam's sister from the road."

The phone rang again but this time it was the room phone. We both looked at it, unsure what to do, like it was some foreign object we'd never seen before. Who could possibly be calling? No one but her mother knew we were here. Amber answered.

"Mom? No, uh. Oh God, no! Hold on." She covered the phone. "Turn on the TV," she whispered. "Bridgette and Rod have been arrested!"

I got the TV on, quickly found the twenty-four-hour entertainment channel, and there they were. They were being put into an unmarked van by men and women wearing windbreakers with the large letters "FBI" on their backs. Background video of Amber's mother came next. The media had obviously been tipped off in advance.

"My mom was pretty upset and yelling, 'I don't know what's going on down there, but I want you up here now. I have you booked on a two o'clock flight to Portland.' I tried to argue, but it was pointless. Oh, God, Bridge was arrested!"

"Fitts must know she isn't going to be of any use now."

"How did he know that already?"

"Either because we didn't show at the beach house, or her room really is bugged."

Just then the phone rang again. We were sure Amber's mom had more to say. Instead it was the concierge from last night. Amber's face registered total fear. She slammed the phone.

"Agents are at the front desk asking for our room number. They'll be here any minute!"

We grabbed some things, raced for the stairs, and were down thirty-three flights before they barged into the stairwell above us. We dashed through the lobby and almost ran into a black SUV parked in front. Sprinting toward Amber's car, my heart was pounding.

"Where to? Where to?" Amber's voice panicked.

"Just drive! I don't know!"

We had only driven a few blocks when my phone rang. "It's Tanya."

"Answer it."

"Hello."

"Hello, Nathan, this is Agent Fitts." His voice was raspy.

My eyes widened. "Fitts," I whispered to Amber.

"What do you want?"

"What do I want? That's most amusing isn't it? We both know what I want. I'm sorry I missed you at the hotel."

I hung up.

"What did he say?"

"He said it was him at the hotel."

"God, what do we do? Where should we go?"

"Just head out of town."

The phone rang again.

"Don't answer."

"I have an idea." I let it ring again, then answered. "How did you get Tanya's phone?"

"She was good enough to lend it to me," Fitts said.

"What if I agree to meet with you? Will you arrest me?"

"That *is* my plan. It's what I do."

I resisted the urge to say I thought what he did was kill innocent people.

"I'll meet with you in a public place if you give me your word you won't arrest me."

"Why would I do that? You'll be in custody within the hour anyway."

"Maybe, but you don't know for sure what I can do and who's helping me. I may get away. I have before."

"Yes, you have. What would this meeting be about?"

"I'll tell you things you don't know, and we could make a deal."

"What do you have to deal with?"

"That's what we need to discuss. You might be surprised."

"You've piqued my interest. Do you have a place in mind? Back at the hotel perhaps?"

"No. In front of the Transamerica building at eleven."

"Are you trying to make me laugh? Not eleven. Right now."

"Okay."

"And Nathan, if you aren't there by nine-thirty, I'll bring the whole city down on you."

"I'll be there." I hung up.

"We're going to meet that cobra?"

"Not a chance. I'm just trying to buy time. Drive south, we'll try to make it to Calyndra."

"He'll just put out an APB or whatever on us, and we'll be picked up in minutes."

"I don't know what else to do except run."

For the next ten minutes we debated all possible options, including Amber just dropping me off somewhere and heading to the airport for her flight to Portland. I thought it was the best idea, but not surprisingly, Amber didn't agree. We made a wrong turn and found ourselves heading onto the Golden Gate Bridge.

"Come with me to Portland. I'll get you another ticket."

"They'll be waiting for me when I get off the plane."

"Someone has to be able to help us... "

"You have to let me get out somewhere."

"No."

The phone rang again.

"Don't."

"I have to. He's probably wondering why we're not there yet. I'll stall some more."

I answered.

"Nathan, you disappoint me. You're never where you're supposed to be," Fitts said.

"What? We're on our way. I'll be there in two minutes."

"Not unless you head in the other direction."

"Oh my God, I think they're behind us," Amber screamed.

"Yes, we are. Why don't you be a good boy and tell that little girl to pull over as soon as we get off the bridge."

I turned and saw a black SUV following close. I threw my phone at it.

"What are we going to do?"

"Don't panic. Get me to trees. It's the only chance. My powers are strongest in nature. Gibi said the trees will always protect me."

"Spencer said people will always help you, and I don't see anyone."

"It's not over yet."

"What if they start shooting?"

"On the middle of the Golden Gate Bridge? Firing shots at the daughter of Ivy Mayes? No, they have us now. We're not going to out run them in a 1969 Bug. They'll just follow us until we run out of gas."

"Where am I supposed to find trees?"

"Just keep driving. They aren't going to force us off the road."

"Tell that to *your mom*."

"You could pull over and let me out. They won't follow you."

"And just let them have you?"

"No, I'll jump off the bridge. I read once that a few people have lived. I might even be able to Skyclimb a little."

"No, that's crazy."

"I don't want you to get hurt."

"Likewise."

Soon we were off the bridge, and it was less claustrophobic. The land opened to hills and trees on either side. Amber swerved the car at the last minute onto an exit and followed it into the Golden Gate National Recreation Area; they made it, too. We worked to get enough of a lead to pull into the trees. After a minute, there was a dead end barrier ahead at the beach.

"Now what?" Amber shouted.

"We're gonna have to run?"

"I'll try a U-turn."

We were going too fast, the turn radius wasn't there and we crashed into a brick buttress, with the engine in the rear, the whole front of the car caved in.

"Are you okay?"

"Yes, I think." We were both unharmed.

They screeched to a halt behind us.

"Run!" I yelled.

"Nate!" Amber screamed.

"Run!" I repeated. We were forced in opposite directions.

62

"You get her. He's mine!" Fitts yelled, as he took off chasing me. "Call Tipton and Michaels with our location."

He fired two shots as he ran, both missed.

Several park visitors screamed and hit the ground, while others dove into the trees. I did the same.

"I believe the fourth bullet found you last time," he shouted, firing two more. Both hit a boulder, fragments of rock stung me. The ground continued to climb and my younger legs were able to put more distance between us. His next shot also missed.

"Where's my help?" I yelled to the trees. "Guides, Mystics, Dad?"

I came out of the woods suddenly on top of a high cliff overlooking the bay. I hesitated, not sure where to go. It cost precious seconds. He was right behind me. I turned and started to Skyclimb up a tree. He fired again, my leg seemed cut in half with a glowing fireplace poker. I crashed down to the ground landing with a thud.

Fitts was on me and expertly secured my hands behind my back with zip-tie cuffs. He rolled me over and the shock gutted and choked me.

It was Sam!

"Hello, Nate. You see, I was hoping to avoid this whole scene," he said.

"Sam what are you doing?" I screamed.

He caught his breath. It was painful as he straddled me.

"I think it'll be easier in these final moments if you address me as Agent Fitts."

"I don't believe it!" I realized I'd never gotten a good look at Fitts' face before. But this was incredible! "Why are you Fitts?"

He fumbled with a mini-syringe.

"Look, I don't want a long thing here. I really liked you, Nate, and I'm truly sorry it turned out to be you."

I was unable to speak.

"Once we discovered Lee Duncan had gotten evidence to someone named Montgomery Ryder, we completely eliminated that threat, but then there were the families. They needed to be watched and monitored. We thought it might take months; instead four years choked by before you made the mistake that told us your father was the right Montgomery Ryder. I've kept tabs on five families all these miserable years."

His words were unbelievable. But the pain of my leg and my bound arms under me kept me focused. "Why didn't you kill me that first day?"

"We wanted you to lead us to the evidence and to anyone else. After we gave up on that, I made up the stuff about helping you with a lawyer so we could trap you." He laughed. "I don't even have a damn sister! But enough reminiscing."

He caught me looking at the syringe.

"This is the same substance I used on your father. Don't worry, it's just going to be a quick pinprick, and then your heart will stop in about six to eight minutes."

"You think anyone is going to believe a healthy sixteen-year-old kid died of a heart attack?" I could barely breathe but needed to keep us both talking.

"Once the autopsy shows you had a pre-existing *hereditary* condition, and all the exertion of running from federal agents, you know, it was just too much for you." He had the syringe ready. "And most people will think that another terrorist got what he deserved. They'll come up with a nice nickname for you, 'Bridge Bomber' or some such thing, and then they won't think about it much at all."

"Not everyone believes everything the government tells them."

"You'd be surprised." He positioned the syringe in his fingers.

"No. There are people out there who know what's really going on."

"Sure, there are some on the fringe, and they'd end up turning you into some kind of cult leader. Make a religion around you or something. What a freak show! I'm actually doing you a favor by killing you."

He was about to stick me with it when Amber shrieked my name. He turned to look, and it gave me just enough of an opening to use his turning momentum into a push so I could spin out from under him. I stepped on his back to half leap, half Skyclimb toward the rocks where I landed hard, my leg refusing to walk. I saw Amber with her arms behind her back being held by the other agent about eighty feet away. He started advancing, but as Fitts got to his feet the agent paused. I could hear the waves crashing below. The cliff was behind me and a steep rock was to my left. Sam/Fitts in front not more than five feet away; I couldn't back up another inch. The agent with Amber was to the right. I was pinned in. Then I saw Fitts pull the syringe out of his stomach.

He saw me looking and shook his head. "Even if I could get to the hospital in two minutes, they couldn't save me. The chemists at the agency have perfected this foolproof little cocktail," he shouted over the gusts. The other agent didn't know Fitts was dying, and Fitts knew it didn't matter.

I didn't say anything.

"Your father never saw it coming. Your aunt, on the other hand, knew what I was about to do. She seemed to almost welcome death, saying something about lots of old friends to see on the other side. Never imagined I'd check out the same way. I guess it's kind of ironic."

"Kind of karmic, if you ask me."

"I didn't ask you," he gritted angrily.

"Where's Rose's body, Sam?" Blood was running out of the wound on my leg. My hands still cuffed behind me, I scanned for some chance to get away.

"No one will ever find that body. Maybe your pal Spencer Copeland—or whatever he's calling himself these days—could locate her." He looked up at the sky. "We've been after that troublemaker for years. But you can tell him that you've helped us get much closer. They'll have him soon."

Amber and the agent were both just staring at us but hadn't moved. Fitts would be dead in a few minutes. I needed to stall for time. "I have proof about what's going on at Lightyear and about all the murders."

"I doubt you have proof of *all* the murders, but if you've got Duncan's stuff, then you have more trouble than you can handle."

Sirens filled the air. Shots fired in a national park—lots of police were on their way. I wasn't sure if it was good or bad for me, but right now I was leaning toward good.

"Sam, I want you to know before you cross over that I forgive you for everything you've done to me and my family."

"Oh, thank you very much, *Jesus*. How dare you pass judgment on me, Nate."

"I'm serious. I forgive you." And I meant it.

He squeezed his left arm and winced.

"Do you know you killed me in a past life?"

"Do you forgive me for that, too?" he asked sarcastically, his voice straining.

"Yes."

"Well then, I guess I'll have to kill you again." His words hadn't even registered when I realized he was lunging toward me. His body hit mine with incredible force and I went sailing backward over the cliff.

The last thing I heard was an awful, agonized scream; it was Amber. Then everything went black.

63

Saturday, October 4

I regained some form of consciousness and, after remembering my name was Nate Ryder, opened my eyes or at least tried. There was nothing but blackness. It made me nervous. I tried to recall what had happened, but my mind shut down.

There is no way to know how much time passed before I regained consciousness. Now, I realized my arms couldn't move. Could I move anything? With great effort my heavy head could do a full range of motions. It seemed like I was lying down, but the lack of light left me so disorientated it was impossible to know. My feet could both do whatever they were told except walk. What was keeping me from getting up and walking around? Where was I? What happened?

I must have passed out again because there was a long pause in my thoughts. I was still floating in blackness. Panic took over. I must be dead. Why didn't I realize it before? Then I remembered Fitts shooting me. Why didn't my leg hurt? He had shoved me off a cliff. I couldn't have lived.

"Amber!" I yelled out. What happened to her? She was in custody. I remembered her scream. Would they kill her like Rose? Would she be treated as a terrorist and thrown in prison?

"Welcome, Nate."

"Who said that?"

"I did. My name is Trevor."

"Welcome where?"

"You're on a boat somewhere drifting in the sun."

"Is that a metaphor for heaven or something?"

"No." He laughed.

"If we're drifting in the sun, why can't I see?" I braced myself.

"Your blindness should only be temporary."

"Am I dead?"

"No." He laughed again. "I'm sorry. You're bound to be fuzzy after everything. Let me tell you what's happened, at least what I understand."

"First tell me, is Amber okay?"

"I was told you would ask, and I'm to tell you she's fine."

"Is she free? Because you sound a little scripted. Am I a prisoner?"

"Nate, take a deep breath. You're safe. Sometime on Thursday, Crowd brought you here. You're on the *Ninth Wave*, my boat."

"That explains the floating sensation," I said relieved.

"Yes, it's a bit choppy today. Anyway, Crowd asked me to keep you out at sea until you healed enough. You've come a long way since you arrived. I thought you were dead, and I guess you were very close but Spencer—"

"Spencer's been here?"

"Many times. I'm sure you wouldn't have survived without his healings."

"What day is it?"

"Time's a funny thing."

"How long have I been on your boat?"

"Well, those are two different questions, aren't they?"

"Not normally."

"It's Saturday."

"You said I've been here since Thursday? So, two days?"

"Yes, but Spencer did something because he's been here once a day every day."

"So."

"He's been here sixteen times."

"You're the sixth mystic, aren't you?"

"No, I'm not even the first mystic. Listen, you had a severe head injury that affected your vision. Spencer did a lot of stuff and said we could take the bandages off once you woke up."

"What are we waiting for? Why can't I move my arms?"

"They were both badly broken. Crowd said they were tied behind your back and you landed on them... falling off a cliff."

"Yeah, I remember."

"Spencer did healings on them too, but he wanted both arms to remain immobile for at least forty-eight hours, which by my clock is up. By his time, it's been a couple of weeks."

He untied the straps, and although my arms felt like gliding through jello, they functioned.

"Spencer worked on your leg, too. Want the bullet? It took him a while to get it out."

"He did surgery?"

"Well, not with any instruments."

"No, of course not."

"Let's do your eyes now." He slowly unwrapped the cloth from around my head and then pulled the tape from the pads over my eyes. I opened them cautiously then blinked several times to shake the blurriness. It sounded as if Trevor gasped.

"It's like I'm wearing someone's prescription glasses."

"You'll be fine. Give it a little time. I need to run topside for a few minutes. Next room over is the galley. There're fresh clothes on the chair; they should fit."

After he left, I climbed off the bed and tested my leg. It wasn't even sore. I wondered where Amber was while putting on the new clothes. Sam was Fitts. He killed my dad and Rose. They were unbearable thoughts. Stacked nearby were the precious gold box, blue stone, mausoleum key, and my wallet. I put them in my pockets. Soon my eyes were good enough to find the galley. A well-stocked fridge tempted me with fruit juices and my favorite sodas. I grabbed a Coke. Trevor hadn't returned, so I wandered into the next room.

We were on a small yacht. One of the bedrooms was an art studio with spectacular paintings lining the floor, hanging on the wall, on easels, even suspended from the ceiling. Trevor had signed them. They all depicted water scenes—islands, coastal shores, and seascapes.

"You found my work. I want you to have one."

"Really? Thanks. And not just for the painting," I turned to look at him. "My God, you're Rachel!" The concentration camp's reeking stench suffocated the tiny room.

"And you're Erich."

"When did you know?" I asked, recovering.

"As soon as the bandages came off, I saw it in your eyes." He didn't hide his tears. "I discovered my life as Rachel twelve years ago. My parents were killed by a drunk driver coming across the median when I was in grad school."

"Oh man, I'm so sorry."

He nodded. "It really roughed me up. A friend suggested a psychic. My parents came through and told me to forget about the law degree and follow my heart. After a few more sessions, the psychic suggested regression. And boom, there I was trapped in Dachau with you. This is my first incarnation since Rachel."

I searched his eyes. "So, why a boat?"

"I was never comfortable around people but didn't know why until I saw that past life. I needed freedom to move all the time. An RV is too much like a railcar to me."

I nodded, remembering Erich and Rachel's last train ride.

"After getting on the water, I never wanted to go back on land permanently. I took most of the money my folks left, bought this boat, and took up painting. A gallery down in La Jolla does pretty well with them. That's where I first met Crowd. He approached me about eight months ago and told me something about my mother only I knew, then he asked me to meet with Spencer at Brookings Harbor."

"Sounds familiar."

"A couple of weeks later I went. Spencer told me about someone who could bring positive changes to the world. He explained that much of the inequality and suffering we face on this planet is due to human inventions such as greed, judgment, fear, corruption, war. I didn't need convincing. He said this person was our best hope and that in about eight months he would need my help. The person he was talking about, of course, is you."

"I didn't even know Spencer until a few weeks ago."

"Time's a funny thing."

"Spencer makes me sound too important. I'm just Nate."

"He said people wouldn't be following you as much as your story. A lot of people know something's wrong, that we're missing part of ourselves. All you're going to do is show us how to find that."

"Oh, is that all," I said sarcastically. "Spencer thinks I can save the world."

"If you could have seen the torment in his face when he first saw you—he was destroyed. The tortured look didn't leave his eyes until the fifth visit. We weren't sure you would make it."

"Yeah, but was it Nate he was saving or the savior?"

"Just because you're a teenager doesn't mean you have to act like one. Get that chip off your shoulder. Grow up."

"I've grown up a lot in the last three weeks."

"Then I'm glad we didn't meet until now."

"Why are you so touchy all of a sudden?"

"Because you're not Erich."

"No. The Nazis murdered Erich."

"Part of him is alive in your soul, Nate. Find that part. Erich would have taken Spencer's challenge and never looked back."

"I know he would have. I *was* Erich. But Nate's not as brave."

"So you're afraid? That's why the reluctance?"

"I'm terrified."

"Of them killing you?"

"No, of succeeding. Changing the world sounds like a bumper sticker, but look through history at the times people have truly changed things. Even the small ones were painful. Imagine what this would be."

"Yes, *imagine*."

We were quiet.

"So, you want to tell me which painting you want?"

"I'm sort of on the run. I'd have no place to hang it."

"I'll keep it for you. Choose."

I studied them and was drawn to one of a stormy sky over rough seas with a cluster of rocks sticking out of the water.

"Why that one?"

"I don't know. It just pulled me in."

He smiled. "It's called 'Endure,' and it's for you."

64

U p on deck we were still far enough off the coast that everything looked undisturbed, a thick line of green trees and rocky cliffs on the horizon.

"No one knows I'm alive? My mom's probably called the FBI by now."

"I believe Crowd was going to get word to your mother. Here," he handed me a pair of dark wrap-around sunglasses. "You still need to take it easy on your eyes."

"Why do you call your boat *Ninth Wave?*"

"It's after an 1850s painting by Aivazovsky, depicting a violent storm during a night when a ship sank leaving seven survivors clinging to a piece of wreckage. The sea remained very rough, but a rising sun promised the slightest wisp of hope. Still, they had to deal with the ninth wave, which threatened to engulf them. You know, waves are in series, growing until they peak at the ninth. It's been called one of the most glorious seascapes ever painted, but for me it is more. It's where we are, the human race—we're facing the ninth wave."

"I can see why you defend Spencer."

He smiled.

"I should contact my brother and friends now."

"No way from here."

"I can do it over the astral."

"Incredible."

I readied myself and then was looking at Dustin.

"I heard a rumor you might be alive," Dustin said with a smile. "You are alive, aren't you?"

"Yeah, and you're looking better than me for a change."

"It's Bà's black liquid. I'll get you a bottle."

"Maybe a case.

"Mom, as usual, is worried. Everyone has been. Now, hopefully, you'll get patched up and come back here because you're taking all the attention away from me." He laughed. "Hey, can you see my TV?"

"Sure."

He switched a few channels. "Here you go. It's been on a lot."

I shuttered as the screen showed a photo of Sam, even though the caption said "DHS Agent Sanford Fitts." The anchor said Fitts was working on a national security threat in San Francisco when he was strangled by the alleged terrorist. They cut to an exterior shot of the White House and announced the president had issued a statement calling Fitts a hero. The president had promised to apprehend the suspect whose name was not being released so as not to jeopardize an ongoing investigation. A spokesman assured viewers that Fitts had foiled any planned attacks, and there was no longer a danger. They kept showing images of the Golden Gate, which seemed to imply the bridge was somehow a "target."

"Don't believe anything you see on TV," I said.

"But, that's Sam! That explains why the guards never let me see him. Even the beating was started by one of the others. Was Sam always Fitts? I mean, always an agent?"

"I'll tell you everything in person."

"When are you coming home?"

"I don't know what home is anymore, but I'll be in Ashland tomorrow."

Afterward, my plans to contact Amber and Kyle on the astral were forgotten, as I was completely exhausted. I stumbled back to bed and collapsed.

When he woke me, we were docked in Brookings Harbor. Fourteen hours had elapsed. It was just before dawn on Sunday.

"Your ride is out there. It's a friend of Amparo's."

"You know Amparo?"

"She betrayed me too, remember? She hunted me down a few years ago and begged forgiveness."

"Did you?"

"How could I not? The feeling was so empowering that I forgave everyone for anything. I've been regressed many times just to look for people from past lives to forgive, even the drunk driver who took my folks."

"How'd you know my clothes size, the sodas I like, even breakfast wraps?"

"Spencer gave me specific instructions... eight months ago. Kind of spooky. But he also told me you might not come. Your survival was never written in stone."

That revelation stopped me. I should have been dead. If not for Spencer, Lightyear would have gotten me weeks ago, and going over the cliff certainly would have ended differently. Trevor was right; I may have grown up a lot but not enough yet. I hugged Trevor *and Rachel*.

I slept most of the three-hour drive to Ashland, waking a few times after nightmares where Fitts was still alive and holding Amber.

Sunday, October 5
Bà answered the door at Kyle and Linh's house and studied me with concern. "You need wolfberry and horsetail. I bring to you. They be so happy to see you. Upstairs."

Amber's kiss was quick, but her arms lingered around me and her tears wet my face. "I wasn't sure I'd be able to do this again," she said softly.

I opened my eyes and saw Kyle beaming; Linh was smiling, too, but already wiping her own tears. During a hug, I kissed her cheek. "I didn't want to cry," she said.

"I might not have recognized you if you didn't," I teased. It made her laugh.

We sat down in our regular positions, facing each other across the triangular table; the only difference was Amber next to me.

"Your mom let us know you were alive. But we didn't know anything else. Amber told us what happened on the cliff," Linh said. "How did you survive?"

"I need to hear Amber's story first. It's the only way I can clear the fog." I stared at Amber. "How did *you* escape?"

"As soon as Fitts pushed you over the cliff, I was sure you were dead."

"Is Fitts *really* dead?"

"I never saw him move. Two more agents showed up.

They saw you down on the rocks, presumably dead, and said, 'Let SFPD clean this up.' The police sirens were so close."

"But Fitts was Sam or vice versa," Kyle snapped.

"Yeah. He killed my dad and the others, then he watched a bunch of Ryder families for four years until we discovered the conspiracy. That's why he was out of town so much. He was never a geologist—he just had other families to watch."

"What are they afraid of?" Kyle asked. "Spencer wasn't kidding. This is huge!"

I didn't want to think about what Kyle was saying. "Amber, what happened?"

"They didn't have time, and no one seemed in charge with Fitts gone. One said, 'Let's go now,' and another answered, 'What about the girl?' I thought they were going to shoot me. 'Leave her. The boy's dead; she's no use to us now. And we don't need any more publicity. Her family's already all over the news.' Another agreed, saying, 'I'd rather have The New York Times dogging us than the tabloids.' They cut my cuffs off and left."

"How'd you avoid the cops?"

"Even before they were out of sight I was at the cliff trying to get down to you, but there was no way. You looked mangled, a pool of blood at your head and another by your leg, and your arms weren't even visible."

Linh started to cry. Amber was trembling as she spoke. "Suddenly, Crowd was there. He said we had to go. I told him we couldn't leave you like that. He promised you'd be taken care of and said, 'you have a plane to catch.' I had like ten seconds to grab a few things from my car on the way out. Crowd repeated he would get you. I assumed he meant just your body."

Linh reached across the table and gently unclenched my fists.

"I'm not sure how we got out of there," Amber continued. "It was weird. He moved me into the trees, and remember, I was in shock—the crash, getting captured, watching you thrown off a cliff. The next thing I knew, I was in a cab going back across the Golden Gate Bridge, heading toward the airport. The flight was a blur, and then mom was there in Portland."

"Have you seen the coverage of Fitts' death?" Kyle asked. "Why haven't they identified you as the most wanted guy in the world?"

"Because he's done nothing wrong. What can they do?" Linh asked.

"Throw me in a military prison."

"They've already shown their plan: kill you during an arrest and say you were trying to escape," Kyle said. "Don't stay in one place too long."

"Nate, what happened? How did you live through that?" Linh exclaimed.

"At the same time Crowd was leading Amber out of the park, he somehow got me off the cliff and onto a boat. That's where I've been healing for the past few days. But I was actually out there for more than two weeks. Spencer manipulated time so he could heal me and still get me back here *today*. Why? I don't know."

"Explain how Spencer changed time and how Crowd was in two places at once." Amber said.

"I can't. I've tried finding Spencer. There's never a trace. He's always around water. But Fitts told me Lightyear had been chasing Spencer for years and was getting closer. The mystics can do all kinds of amazing things; Lightyear is probably after them all. The Old Man of the Lake said when I find ten more, I'll become one. It's part of my quest now. If I had the power and understanding that they possess... "

"Are you reading all those right now?" Linh asked, pointing to the stacks of books I'd been passing through my hands without even thinking about it.

"I guess so."

Bà brought up some herbal potion and waited while I drank it. It tasted slightly sweet, but even if it had been flavored with skunk oil, I would have downed it. I revered that woman, as if she were a mystic herself. Amber took advantage of the interruption and handed me my pack she'd grabbed before fleeing with Crowd. Inside among some clothes were Rose's journal, rock, and scarf. I gave the scarf to Linh, and we talked about Rose.

Kyle took me to the other end of the loft where he had a stack of maps of all the national forests in the area. Highlighted were the most remote areas to camp, but areas that were still close enough to roads for escape. "Don't worry, I did all my research on computers at the library."

While Kyle and I were talking, I could overhear Amber and Linh whispering, as if they were speaking directly into my ear. It didn't seem right using this new power to spy on my friends, but I couldn't turn it off.

"Linh, it's not like that with Nate and me," Amber said. "I love him completely."

Linh shifted uncomfortably.

"It's not how it sounds," Amber continued. "I don't want to be his girlfriend; it's deeper than that. I just want to know him, experience parts of our lives together, but not share his life. Look, what I'm trying to say is nothing physical happened between us." I guess Amber decided that the two interruptions at the hotel were a sign. She was into signs. I was, too, but thought maybe it should be three strikes and then you're out. Amber and I would have to talk about that sometime. I didn't know it then, but it would be months before we got the chance.

As I was leaving, Amber whispered to me, "What about Calyndra?"

"I've got to do something with Dustin first. Then I'll think about Calyndra."

I could see her disappointment, but she gave me a tight hug. "You know where to find me. I'll wait for you."

Linh kissed me, too. I looked back as we backed out of the driveway; she was at the door waving, sad.

Kyle drove to the motel. "We've moved Dustin two more times. He's been staying alone, but Bà goes to check on him a few times a day."

"I don't think I can ever repay you for everything you've done."

"We're friends, Nate. You don't owe me anything. But if you seriously want to do something, find a way to stay away from trouble."

"I'm trying, but karma is hard to avoid."

"When will we meet again?"

"I don't know, but I'll find you on the astral."

66

I used Kyle's key to enter. "Nice to see you up and around," I said to Dustin.

"It's a relief seeing you in the flesh. Your voice floating around my head is kind of cool, but the novelty wears off."

"You look good." I pulled him into a hug.

"I owe you my life, Nate."

"We're brothers, Dustin. You don't owe me anything." I echoed Kyle's words.

"Are you up for traveling? Mount Shasta."

"I had a feeling you'd say that. Let's leave in the morning."

The door opened, terrifying me for a moment. Then, my mom grabbed and held me so tight I thought I might need to make a Lusan. Kisses and tears were all she could manage for a couple of minutes. "My boys are safe." She'd brought glorious food.

"Somehow the three of us are still alive: the three remaining Ryders," I said.

After the initial glow, our reunion dimmed. She was devastated with our plans to leave. Although to her we would always be her little boys—and I was still relatively young by the Roman calendar—she knew we'd outgrown her control. I gave them a rundown of what had happened, starting with my first trip to Crater Lake and ending on the boat. Mom could hardly speak Sam's name, saying it was the greatest betrayal she'd ever known. "Sam was an Amparo-esque betrayal," Dustin said, after he'd heard that part of my story.

It took almost three hours to answer all of their questions. Telling it like that, for the first time from beginning to end, was extremely illuminating. I saw how incredible it all was, the magic and synchronicity of it. My mother was moved. There were tears in her eyes, and a look of love, but she knew I had to go. Dustin stood up and walked to the window, then turned to Mom.

"I'm not crazy. I was never crazy. It wasn't the drugs." He was shaking. "It was your fear and close-mindedness that took two years of my life." He pointed at her. "They gave me meds that probably aren't even approved for the normal population. I lived for two chemical years, hidden from the truth—my truth. If it weren't for Rose, I'd probably be a vegetable by now. And she's dead." He glared at her. "Forgiveness? I guess if Nate can forgive the Nazis or whatever, then I can forgive you *eventually*. But the real question, Mom, is how are you ever going to live with yourself?"

67

Monday, October 6

We were ready to go at sunrise. Mom brought a cooler filled with Station sandwiches, desserts, and sodas. She also handed us each a handful of cash and two "clean" phones. She and Josh brought over Dustin's truck. "We had it tuned up. It should do well for you." Josh handed Dustin the keys. "Remember how to drive?" he joked.

"I'll figure it out. Nice shirt, Josh."

He smiled, proud of his neon purple tee.

We had mostly said goodbye to Mom the night before. Although it was still tense between her and Dustin, we kept it cordial and were very relieved to be on the road.

"I can't even tell that you haven't driven for two years," I said, while heading up the Siskiyou Pass.

"Only because I haven't opened my eyes yet."

"So, are you going to tell me what's at Shasta? I don't like surprises."

"You'll like this one."

"We're not going to try to take a long nap above snowline are we?" I said with a smile.

"You do know Mom got that mixed up. I was never trying to kill myself, just trying to get back to what I want to show you. I'd have come home... alive."

"Two years in Mountain View over a misunderstanding..."

"It was a complicated time. I was pretty confused. You'll see."

"Mom regrets it now, I think."

"You know, every time Mom visited she brought me sandwiches and desserts from the Station. It may not seem like much, but it was a connection to home, to the real world... I looked forward more to the food than seeing her."

Heading down the other side of the pass, a flagman waved us to a stop. Vehicles lined up. The flagman was staring at us. He stepped toward our truck and motioned Dustin to roll down the window.

He broke into a big smile, "Dusty, Dude, where you been?"

"Crowd, I don't believe it!" Dustin shouted.

It took me a moment. He had much shorter hair under his hardhat and a blaze orange safety vest worn over *clean* clothes, but it was definitely Crowd. I couldn't believe it either.

"Nate, I forgot how much you two favor each other. You guys headin' up today?"

"Yeah," Dustin said, "And I thought I'd have to find it myself. Can you remind me of the second and third signs?"

"Sure. You know when to leave the trail?"

"I think so."

"Yeah, you do. You'll remember. Then there'll be a hawk perched on a naked tree, the first sign."

Dustin nodded.

"Good. Then after some time you'll come to a rock outcropping, the second sign. It's hard to say how far until you reach it because it moves, but you'll recognize it. Finally, you'll find the third sign, a spring, and from there you'll have to feel it."

The instant he finished speaking, a call came over his radio and he waved us on. "See you," Dustin shouted.

"I'm stunned you know Crowd. Where did you meet him?" I asked.

"I couldn't tell you."

"Why not?"

"I don't remember."

"Wow, you really were doing some powerful drugs back then."

"True, but that's not why I don't remember him. You should have a sense of what I'm talking about, from when you thought you were going crazy, too. But for me, it was a bit messier because as soon as I started hearing voices and seeing colors and all that stuff, I started drinking more and experimenting with drugs. Part of me wanted it all to stop, and another part wanted to go and see what I could see, get all Alice-In-Wonderlanded out."

"Take a long strange trip?"

"Yeah, I mean I didn't know it was all connected to the soul at that point. I didn't know what was happening, and then it started really getting weird. Yesterday would happen in the middle of my English class, with bits of tomorrow and today all mixed up."

"Time's a funny thing..."

"There wasn't anything funny about it to me. I was losing it, didn't know what was real or when was when. Then I met a few interesting characters who seemed just as lost as I was. And one of them was Crowd. But I can't sift through the psychedelic stupor of those months and the haze of Mountain View to figure it all out."

"But you remember going to Shasta with him?"

"Well, parts of it, anyway. He wasn't with me that final night. We did go together the first time. But, Nate, it was so fantastic that until I saw Crowd just now, I wasn't sure it was real. That's part of why I didn't want to tell you anything about it because we might get there and it would all just be trees on a mountain."

We were flagged to a stop again just outside the town of Yreka. There was some minor work being done ahead. Amazingly, it was Crowd again.

"Yo, Ryders Deux," he greeted us.

"You're gonna get me sent back to the psych ward if you keep doing stuff like this Crowd."

"Well, we didn't get to finish our talk so I... you know they needed some work down here, too."

"Hey, Crowd," I began. "How do I thank you for San Francisco?"

"No need, just doing my job." He smiled wide, but his eyes shone something else—sadness?

"Crowd, what's up? Nate tells me you're a mystic. How come I never knew?" Dustin asked.

"Just depends where you are on the road, know what I mean?"

Dustin shook his head.

"It's good to see you finally decided to get a job," I joked.

He laughed hard. "Gonna save up for that house above the boulevard, don't you know?"

"So, since we're seeing you again, you must have more things to teach us?" I asked.

"Yeah, first we'll start with fly fishing and then rope climbing and then... "

I gave him a look.

He started laughing. "Ain't it obvious" I'm *the* guide."

"I thought all the mystics were guides."

"A common misconception. No, they're just ordinary mystics. I'm not only a mystic—and quite extraordinary, I must say—but in addition, I'm *your* guide."

"I only have one guide?"

"My goodness, you're not getting this are you? You have many guides, but they're either not currently in the earthly realm or if they are, you'll have only fleeting encounters with them. I, on the other hand, am quite available on an ongoing basis."

"Is there a fee for this?"

He laughed hard. "A fee? You're almost as funny as Dusty, and you're not even *on* anything, are you?"

"I'm not either," Dustin broke in. "Unfortunately."

"So, are you a guide for both of us?"

"Sure am, I get a two-for. I'm very efficient that way."

"Can you *guide* me to other mystics?"

"Well, not specifically, but my job is to help keep you on your path, so if meeting them is on your path, then yes."

"Want a sandwich?" Dustin offered.

"Hey, is that a Pink Floyd? I love Pink Floyds. Did you get it with extra pickles and extra lettuce?"

"You eat at the Station?"

"Well, their dumpster mostly." He smiled, shyly.

A state trooper came from the opposite direction and slowed to look at us. I thought it was over, but he kept moving.

"You boys need to get to the mountain."

"When can we talk?" I asked, as we started rolling. "I need to know about finding other mystics."

"Depends on traffic." He laughed, waving the flags dramatically like he was guiding a landing plane. "Maybe tomorrow. But Nate, remember, time's a funny thing."

Mount Shasta is a stunning peak more than 14,000 feet above sea level, and although it's part of the Cascade Range, it isn't connected to any other mountains. Instead, it rises dramatically 10,000 feet above the surrounding terrain and appears a majestic spirit. Every time it came into view, I remembered what the naturalist John Muir said: "When I first caught sight of it over the braided folds of the Sacramento Valley, I was fifty miles away and afoot, alone and weary. Yet all my blood turned to wine, and I have not been weary since." I had more than two hundred photos of Shasta taken over the years, always a favorite subject.

The peak is actually composed of four volcanic cones, home to several glaciers, snowcapped year-round, and shrouded in mystery. The Old Man had told me there is a powerful portal on the summit, but Dustin and I weren't planning on that kind of trek. I knew the stories: the region's Native Americans believed the Great Spirit lived in Shasta, while other tribes have talked of "little people" who dwell in the forest on Shasta; more than a century ago, tales surfaced about descendants of survivors from the lost continent of Lemuria, some even claimed proof it's a landing base for starships; there are books describing the higher-dimensional city of Telos, located inside the dormant volcano; some give first-hand accounts of meeting its inhabitants either within or on the mountain; and even more spoke of Ascended Masters, subterranean tunnels, and even encounters with Bigfoot. Mount Shasta is one of the most mythical places in the Western Hemisphere, and for that reason, it attracts seekers, sages, and quacks.

We followed a trail for twenty or thirty minutes before Dustin decided it was the right place to cut into the woods. About ten minutes later, we found the naked tree and sure enough there was a hawk perched on a branch about two thirds of the way up. It flew away as soon as we approached. It was a long time before we came to the outcropping, and I was worried we had gone too far until I saw Spencer sitting on the biggest stone.

68

"Last time I saw you, you weren't looking so good." Spencer smiled.

"Last time I saw you, I was angry. I'm sorry about that."

"It's forgotten. I know this has been tough on you."

"Not the part where the prettiest girl in school falls for him," Dustin added.

"Dustin, this is one of Dad's oldest friends and a mystic, Spencer Copeland."

"I remember you from Dad's funeral. You told me that the world may have lost a great man, but Dad was not really gone. His spirit was still with us."

Spencer nodded.

"I think you started me on the road to insanity."

"I didn't know you were at the funeral," I said.

"Oh yes, I wouldn't have missed it."

"But Fitts was there, too. How did you avoid him?"

"He didn't know what I looked like."

"Really? He's been after you for years. How could he not know what you looked like?"

"Simple. We've never met."

"Fitts *is* dead, right?"

"Yes, in human terms, anyway."

"Great," I said with a sigh. Would there ever be closure?

"How come you didn't know Fitts was actually my neighbor?"

"I'm sorry to say I don't know everything. I did pick up that Fitts was watching your house, on and off over the last few weeks, but I had no idea he was living there, too."

"When did you discover that?"

"Not until I was healing you on Trevor's boat. I read it in you."

"How'd Crowd get Amber and me out at the same time?"

"It's called bilocating. He was in two places at the same time."

"Cool," Dustin said.

"Where are the other mystics I'm supposed to meet?"

"There are far more mystics than you think. People walk among mystics during their normal lives and never know it. You've met dozens, and they help you, but it's not the same as actually being instructed by them."

"More to learn?"

"Unimaginable things. Even more remarkable powers await you. Both of you can move toward your soul and—"

"Is it really possible to reach it and be just that—no more human clutter?" Dustin interrupted.

"No one knows for sure, but I believe it completely. And the closer you get, the more you'll believe it, and the journey is so... I don't think a word exists that can adequately describe what it's like. It's pure life; it's everything. If you continue to look for the answers to the great questions—why are we here, where did we come from, what is the universe, how powerful is love—you will find things that even now you couldn't begin to dream of. Doesn't that excite you?"

"It does, and as you once told me, I don't have a choice anyway."

"I want to see it all," Dustin added.

Spencer smiled. "Once you're done here, meet me at an island called Cervantes, and I'll explain what's next."

"Where is it? How will we find it?"

"You'll figure it out."

"Do you live there?"

"No, I prefer more modest lodgings."

"Then how will you know we're there?"

He smiled modestly and cocked his head as if it should be obvious by now.

"Thanks, Spencer."

He extended his arm. We shook hands, and our eyes spoke for a moment.

"It's I who should thank you, Nate."

"No."

"I'll see you another time." He walked away and, once the trees blocked our view, he did not reappear.

Crowd was gone. Spencer was gone. It was just Dustin and me. All the hikes we'd done growing up together—with and without our dad—came back, as our bond was like no other. And being among the trees always left me at ease with a sense of peace.

"Do you hear that?" I asked.

"What?"

"It sounds like a helicopter."

"I don't hear anything."

We weren't far from a clearing; I moved toward it, Dustin followed. "I hear it now," he said. "Definitely a helicopter."

We stayed in the trees and looked through the opening toward the sky. A minute later there was a black military chopper flying just above the treetops. It made several passes, but we were convinced they couldn't see us.

"Maybe we should bail?" I said to Dustin.

"And go where?"

Minutes later, it was hovering a few thousand feet behind us.

"They're looking for us," I yelled to Dustin.

"We're almost there."

"Here!" I shouted, as I saw the lush patch of greenery surrounding the tiny spring.

"Okay, we're close."

The chopper was loud and my temperature was rising. Six soldiers slid down ropes into the woods.

"Dustin, look!" I was terrified.

He glanced back, only for a second.

"They're here for us. We've gotta run," I screamed.

Dustin was too busy searching for whatever he was looking for to run. Although we were moving away from them and still seemed hidden, if we didn't increase our pace, the soldiers would have us in minutes. They obviously had some way to track me because they knew we were on the mountain and had narrowed their search from the 2.2 million acres of wilderness to a half-mile radius. I thought with Fitts gone, Lightyear would disappear. Was running going to be my life?

"Dustin, we have to hide somewhere." They now blamed me for the death of an agent, and that was added to the long list of other reasons to eliminate me. Kyle was right. They would never run out of agents. There weren't enough places to hide. How long could I run? I needed a plan. Strategy, Old Man would call it.

Soldiers were getting closer. The heat was suffocating.

Was there any way I could beat Lightyear? If I didn't find a way, I would die, probably soon. Then, I remembered something someone said: to defeat darkness you must expose it to the light. I would have to find a way to expose Lightyear.

"This is it! Are you ready?" Dustin suddenly yelled.

"This is where you've been wanting to get back to? This is what you almost died trying to reach that night? You got locked in an asylum to get to this spot in the woods?" I screamed.

"It's not just a spot in the woods." I could barely hear his words.

"That's what it looks like to me." I gazed around. It was like the rest of the forest, pretty but nothing extraordinary. A second chopper approached. "We're dead."

"Are you ready?" he repeated. Something in his look made me feel as if we were about to do something remarkable, like ancient explorers sailing into the unknown, off the edge of the world, Yuri Gagarin hurtling into space in 1961. But we were just two teenagers in the middle of a pine forest on Mount Shasta.

I could see soldiers through the trees; they hadn't spotted us but were within a few hundred feet now. The helicopters were thunderous, leaves whipped from the giant blades.

"Yes. I'm ready," I shouted.

He reached his arms high above his head. For a moment, his hands appeared to be grasping for something, almost swimming in slow motion through the air. There was nothing I could see. Then he smiled. His arms moved apart and with them the air separated like a curtain. He held the invisible veil open, and inside I saw an entirely different scene than the trees and shrubs surrounding us. Through that seam was not an ordinary portal like the other two I'd been in, which were merely passages. This was another place all its own, some undiscovered realm, a channel into a secret world. I looked at Dustin questioningly.

"Are you ready?" he yelled again.

We stepped inside.

END OF BOOK ONE

Acknowledgements

Writing is the hardest work I've ever done and also the most exciting. Many writers helped me along the way: my mother, Barbara Blair, who encouraged me in everything I've done and is now happily writing her own stories; my late father, Bill Legg, whose zest for life taught me to live; Lee Davis, the first to show me the meaning of "show, don't tell;" my grandfather, Wilbur Blair, who questioned logic in each line I wrote; Gene Legg, for showing up during the hardest time in my own story; and my four very different brothers (Blair, Bryce, Baughan and Brae) for four very different reasons; Mollie Gregory for her brutal wisdom, caring critique and important suggestions; Mike Sager for the nuggets of writing wisdom he has generously given through the years; Harriet Greene for following the threads; Marty Goldman for redirecting several scenes; mostly to Roanne Lewis, whose poetry of such beauty and deep meaning inspires me; and finally Teakki, who patiently waited while I wrote, instead of playing cars and trucks.

About the Author

Brandt Legg was a child prodigy who, after the tragic loss of his father and crippling migraine headaches, turned an interest in stamp collecting into a multi-million dollar business empire. By eighteen, the high-flying Legg, known to the media as the "Teen Tycoon," became ensnarled in the financial whirlwind of the junk bond eighties, lost his entire fortune... and ended up serving time in federal prison for financial improprieties. Legg emerged, chastened and wiser, one year later and began anew in retail and real estate. From there his life adventures have led him through magazine publishing, newspaper writing, FM radio (behind the mic and in the business office), and music production, including CDs and concerts. Outview is the first book of his Inner Movement trilogy. For more information, please see www.BrandtLegg.com.